£1.25

Hilda McKenzie was born and brought up in Cardiff. She left school at fourteen to become an apprentice at a drapery store, left there to learn book binding at a local printers, was an assistant and a cashier for a grocery firm and later became a telephonist at a turf accountant's office. She was fifteen when her first short story was published and she has written three previous novels, *Rosie Edwards*, *Bronwen* and *The Sisters*. She has a grown-up son and daughter, and still lives in Cardiff with her husband.

D1339233

Also by Hilda McKenzie

Rosie Edwards
Bronwen
The Sisters

A Ray of Sunshine

Hilda McKenzie

HEADLINE

Copyright © 1995 Hilda McKenzie

The right of Hilda McKenzie to be identified as the Author of
the Work has been asserted by her in accordance with the
Copyright, Designs and Patents Act 1988.

First published in 1995
by HEADLINE BOOK PUBLISHING

First published in paperback in 1996
by HEADLINE BOOK PUBLISHING

10 9 8 7 6 5 4 3 2 1

All rights reserved. No part of this publication may be
reproduced, stored in a retrieval system, or transmitted,
in any form or by any means without the prior written
permission of the publisher, nor be otherwise circulated
in any form of binding or cover other than that in which
it is published and without a similar condition being
imposed on the subsequent purchaser.

All characters in this publication are fictitious
and any resemblance to real persons, living or dead,
is purely coincidental.

ISBN 0 7472 4917 2

Typeset by CBS, Felixstowe, Suffolk

Printed and bound in Great Britain by
Cox & Wyman Ltd, Reading, Berks

HEADLINE BOOK PUBLISHING
A division of Hodder Headline PLC
338 Euston Road
London NW1 3BH

For Lynn Curtis.
Many thanks for steering me in the right direction

ACKNOWLEDGEMENTS

My grateful thanks to the following:

The ever helpful staff of Cardiff Central Library, especially Local Studies and the Information Desk. Also the staff of Trowbridge and St Mellons Library. What would I do without them?

And my editor, Clare Going, to whom I'm indebted for the title of this book and much more.

Chapter One

Emma Meredith huddled into the lumpy cushions of the armchair drawn up to the side of the kitchen range. The funeral had been over by early-afternoon, and her three aunts, their faces sombre with grief, were about to divide up Nana's possessions amongst themselves for the rent of the house had been paid only until the end of the week. They had just closed the kitchen door behind them and their voices, muffled now, had come to her from the passage. What she heard caused the tears to spurt from her eyes once more.

'Too much for Mam it was, having to look after Emma from the time she was born,' said Aunt Mattie.

'Rest is what she needed at her age,' Aunt Clara agreed. 'Eleven years she's looked after . . .' But Aunt Mabel's voice burst in with, 'Talking nonsense you are, both of you. Lonely and unhappy Mam was when our Jack died so young. Only too pleased she was to look after his baby when poor Miriam went just after Emma was born.'

When she heard the front room door shut behind them, the girl closed her eyes in a vain attempt to stop the hot tears rolling down her cheeks. What was to become of her? She'd thought one of her aunts might take her home but that didn't seem likely now, did it? Not after what she'd overheard. She was eleven years old and she'd never felt so alone in her life. Would she have to go into the workhouse like one of the girls at school had suggested? The tears fell fast at the thought. Did they still put children in the workhouse now in 1905, or would she be sent to an orphanage? Only she didn't want to go to one of those either. For a bleak moment she saw herself walking in the long crocodile of subdued-looking children she sometimes saw on their way to church or school.

Emma looked wistfully around the comfortable kitchen. She'd always felt so loved and wanted living here with her nan. They'd done everything together: the washing, cleaning, shopping. The cheerful glow from the fire was reflected warmly in the china and glasses on the dresser, and twinkled amongst the brass ornaments on the shelf above. Less than a week ago she and Nan had polished the brasses together; not just the ones on the shelf but the twisted candlesticks and prancing horses either side of the marble clock on the mantelpiece, and the rose bowl that stood in the middle of the dark red chenille cloth on the table.

An elderly Queen Victoria looked solemnly down on her from the opposite wall. Nan had told her that the Queen looked sad because her husband, Prince Albert, had died many years before. She'd be happy now though, wouldn't she, for the Queen herself had passed away early in 1901 so they'd be together in Heaven. Would Nan meet the Queen up there? Emma wondered.

She looked down proudly at the black serge dress with the braided sailor collar that Aunt Clara had bought her, the dark colour emphasising the creamy pallor of her sensitive young face and the pale gold of her hair. If only they'd come and tell her what was going to happen.

If after all she was to live with one of her aunts, which one would it be? Maybe Aunt Mattie and her husband, Uncle Fred who lived only a short distance away in Wilfred Street? But they themselves were only in rooms with Uncle Fred's mam, and Emma had heard enough talk to know that the two women didn't get on. Besides there was only one small spare bedroom and her little cousin David would be needing a room of his own very soon.

Mattie was the eldest of the three sisters: a big woman though not really fat, with a rosy complexion and dark brown eyes. Whenever they'd gone to visit she'd been washing or polishing, bath-bricking the step or scrubbing the arm's-reach patch outside the front door. Her window-sill, her step and patch were easily the whitest in the street, as were the stiff lace curtains at the parlour window. Nan had told Emma all this was to try and please her mother-in-law, but it hadn't worked for they always seemed to be at each other's throats.

Perhaps Emma would live with Aunt Mabel? She was kind and easy to get on with but definitely not houseproud like Aunt Mattie. 'Slovenly' Nan had called her one day, but she'd told Emma afterwards that it wasn't really Mabel's fault; her husband had left her years before, and living alone with Ellie didn't give her much heart. Cousin Ellie was nearly two years older than Emma herself but didn't act anything like her age for poor Ellie would never grow up. She was short and plump with long straight brown hair. Her face was round and would have been quite pretty except for her slack lips and babyish expression. Ellie would slobber all over you, giving you great wet kisses, and the weight of her body as she flung her arms about you would almost knock you down. If Aunt Mabel was around you just had to endure it for fear of hurting her maternal feelings.

3

Aunt Clara was the youngest sister and had married into trade. Nana had said she'd done very well for herself. She and Uncle Lionel, whom Emma had heard was younger than his wife, lived in the spacious rooms above his drapery shop in Duke Street. Aunt Clara wore beautiful clothes. The only aprons Emma had ever seen her wear were frilly ones for they had someone in to do the rough work.

Emma had liked going to visit them because of the dainty little sandwiches with the crusts cut off, the Welsh cakes with cherries in them, the cocoa always frothy and delicious, made with boiled milk. But on every occasion she'd be a bundle of nerves for you had to be careful not to stain the white damask cloth and Emma would soon wish she was eating at the scrubbed table in the kitchen at home, with the chenille cloth taken off.

When she heard the door open and her aunts coming towards the kitchen Emma grew tense, gripping her hands until the finger nails dug into her palms. It was Mabel who stepped down into the kitchen first, her face flushed, plump arms wobbling like a jelly. Taking Emma's hands in hers, she cried, 'Going to live with each one of us in turn you are, love, four months at a time. You'll like that, won't you?'

Relief flooded through Emma as visions of being taken to the workhouse vanished into thin air, together with the crocodile of orphans on their way to school.

'Well, love?' Aunt Mabel was smiling at her expectantly.

'Oh, ta, all of you.' Then, seeing Aunt Clara's look of disapproval Emma added quickly, 'Thank you. Thanks very much,' and kissed each of them warmly on the cheek.

'Coming home with me first you are, Emma,' Aunt Mattie told her. 'I'll have to go now to get Uncle Fred's tea. You go and put some things together, just what you need for tonight. I expect you'll want to say goodbye to Mrs Davies? You can let yourself in with the string.'

Mrs Davies had been Nana's best friend and had lived in the middle room as a lodger ever since Emma could remember. She had been at the service held in the parlour, a hankie to her eyes as she'd sung the hymns, but after helping with the sandwiches and tea, she'd gone back to her own room, leaving Emma's aunts to decide what best to do.

They were putting their coats on now, all of them sombre black. Mattie's was of a serviceable woollen cloth, almost covering her long black skirt. Clara's was a costume coat, its collar trimmed with fur. It hugged her tiny waist before flaring almost to the hips of her elegant matching gaberdine skirt with its dust fringe sweeping the floor, and the hat she put on now at the mirror set in the hall-stand dipped becomingly over one eye, adorned with a bunch of black satin rosebuds. The coat Mabel had borrowed for the funeral was far too small for her ample figure. Emma couldn't remember seeing her in anything but a shawl before, a heavy black one in winter, and a light one for summer evenings.

When they'd gone she put together the few things she'd need and brought down Esmeralda, the lovely china-headed doll her own mother had been given one day by the mistress of the house where she was in service when a room was being cleared for redecoration. Esmeralda wore a faded blue silk dress on top of several petticoats. She wore short boots buttoned at the side and had long dark brown ringlets and big brown eyes that stared unblinkingly back into Emma's own.

It was her mam who'd given the doll the name 'Esmeralda' long before Emma was born. It was the only thing she had that had belonged to her mam, and although at eleven she felt she was too old to play with dolls, she cwtched the soft kid body close to her own and vowed she'd never part with it.

Now it was time to say goodbye to Mrs Davies. She tapped on the door and, as though she'd been waiting for the knock, the old lady opened it at once and drew Emma gently inside, saying, 'Going to miss you, cariad, I am, and that's a fact. But tell me, which of youer aunties are you going to live with?'

'Aunt Mattie first, then I'm going to stay with each of them in turn.'

'You won't have very far to go tonight then, will you, love?'

Emma pressed her cheek against the plump rosy one and hugged her warmly. She knew that Nana's friend had come to live in Cardiff when her husband's chest became too bad to go on working in the pit. Her voice still had the friendly lilt of the valleys. She lived alone now, her married children scattered in the streets around. Nana herself had come from Somerset as a young child, with her mother and a father hungry for work. She too had married a man from the valleys, though Emma had never known her grandad.

'I'm going to miss you, Mrs Davies, and I'm going to miss this house, and – and – my nan.' As Emma's voice broke, the old lady cwtched her close, saying, 'Come round any time you like, cariad. Any time, mind.'

One thing was certain, she thought as she watched Emma carrying the precious doll and her bundle of clothing up the street, she'd be right about missing her nan. Was that the best the family could do for her, dragging her around from pillar to post? Closing the door behind her, she spoke her thoughts aloud, voice filled with disgust. 'Dragged from pillar to post, that's what she's going to be. Pooer little soul!'

Chapter Two

As Emma approached the front door and fumbled through the letter-box for the key, she was disturbed to hear angry voices coming from the house. But it wasn't until she stood in the narrow passage that she realised, with a sinking heart, that she was the cause of the dissent.

'. . . took too much for granted you did. Landed you in the soup, hasn't it, my girl?' Old Mrs Thomas's voice sounded triumphant.

'But you said we could have the room for our David whenever we needed it.'

'For David, yes, I don't mind clearin' the room out for him, he's my grandson. If that girl's given the room, he'll 'ave to stay put where he is though, won't he?'

As the voices rose and became more bitter Emma stood as though frozen to the spot. She didn't hear the door open quietly behind her, and when Uncle Fred's hand landed gently on her shoulder, turned a startled face to him. He said, 'At it again they are. Come on in, love, and sit youerself by the fire.' As he pushed her gently towards the middle room, he added, 'I wonder what it's about this time?'

Before she could even begin to explain that her aunt had invited her to stay with them, Mattie herself came into the room, her jaw mutinous, brown eyes blazing, crying angrily: 'I'll swing for your mother one of these days, Fred. I will, God help me!'

'What's it about this time then?' he asked wearily. When she told him about Emma coming to stay with them, he said, 'You should have asked her first. You know she likes to be asked.'

'What am I thinking of?' Mattie jumped up suddenly and put the kettle over the coals, saying, 'With all the rumpus, I haven't even started the tea.'

'Where's David?'

'Out there with her, of course. It's no good for him, is it, all this rowing? I'll bet she'll give him something to eat now to spoil his tea.'

'She means well, Mattie. Dotes on that boy she does.'

Mattie went into the passage, yelling: 'David! David! Your tea's ready.'

When, after calling again, he still didn't come, she was about to thrust the door open when her son appeared with Mrs Thomas still scrubbing with a hankie at the chocolate on his mouth. Giving one look at his mother's angry face, he ran before her into the middle room and jumped on to his father's knee.

'Hello, David,' Emma greeted her cousin.

''lo.'

'I'll tell you a story after tea if you like?'

'The one about the rocking horse that galloped away to the forest?'

'Yes, that one. But come and eat your toast and egg first.'

When the meal was over Emma, anxious to please, fetched the tin bowl from the cupboard by the side of the fire, and opening the door that led to the yard, went to the wash-house to fetch some cold water, as she'd often done when helping

Aunt Mattie, thankful that she didn't have to go through the kitchen to reach the tap. Setting the bowl on the table once more, she poured hot water from the kettle into the cold, shaking some Hudson's washing up powder into the water and swishing the cloth around to make bubbles as she began to wash up. This done, it was time to fetch another bowl for Aunt Mattie to wash David ready for bed, after which he cwtched into Emma on the couch while she told him a story. He was warm and smelt of lavender soap, and for the first time since she'd arrived, with her arm about her little cousin, and his curly head against her chin, she began to relax.

When David was in bed and Uncle Fred had put his coat on to go for the nightly pint he enjoyed with his mates, Aunt Mattie took the darning basket and started on the threadbare heel of a sock. Emma sat on the sofa and took Esmeralda in her arms. Without a bedroom to sleep in, how was she to keep the doll safe? Licking her lips, she ventured to ask, 'Where will I go to bed then, Aunt Mattie?'

Looking troubled, her aunt put the sock aside, saying, 'I suppose you'll have to sleep on the couch, love. I'll bring down some sheets and blankets as soon as our David goes off.' Then she added, her tone bitter: 'That old witch won't let me put you in the spare room.'

'I don't mind, Aunt Mattie,' Emma assured her. The dark red plush upholstery looked inviting enough to her tired eyes. But where was she to put her clothes and things?

When her aunt had finished the darning Emma helped to bring down the bedding, and when the couch was made up she looked longingly at it, knowing full well that as she was to sleep in the living room it would be some time before she could undress and settle down. It was in fact another couple of hours before Uncle Fred had returned and had his supper of bread and cheese and pickled onions and Aunt Mattie had squeezed the tea-pot dry. Then the dishes had to be washed and the fire banked down for the night.

As Uncle Fred climbed the stairs, Aunt Mattie said, 'You get yourself undressed, Emma. I'll be down in a few minutes to turn off the lamp.'

She undressed quickly, leaving her clothes in a neat pile at the foot of the couch, scrambling into her long flannel nightgown and slipping thankfully between the sheets.

When Aunt Mattie returned Emma was almost asleep. Her aunt sat down beside her. Bending over, her rag curlers pressing against Emma's cheek, she said, 'You know, love, I've always wanted a daughter, and that's just what you're going to be to me.' Then she got up and, turning off the oil lamp, closed the door quietly behind her.

In the sudden darkness, relieved only by the dim glow from the banked down fire, Emma swallowed hard, thinking longingly of the small back bedroom at Nana's house that had been her very own. Esmeralda had been safe there, nestling amongst the cushions of the wicker armchair. Her favourite books had stood on the shelf that Uncle Fred had put up for her and Nan had given her a pair of china Pekinese dogs to use as book-ends. What was she to do with all these things now she had no place of her own?

The clock on the mantelpiece ticked ponderously, each tick seeming to drag on to the next. Turning carefully, for the couch was much narrower than her bed, she sank her head into the feather pillow, but tired as she was, sleep wouldn't come. She lay wide-eyed, listening to the sounds of coals sinking in the grate, an occasional creak from the furniture, the long drawn out ticking of the clock. Suddenly there was a new sound, a quick pattering as something scampered across the oil-cloth, and Emma lay rigid with fright for the scampering was almost certainly that of a mouse.

In the bedroom above Mattie Thomas also lay awake, calling herself all kinds of a fool for letting her heart rule her head like she had. She'd really put her foot in it this time, offering Emma a home when she knew she had nowhere for her to sleep, even if it was for only four months of the year. Had she really imagined that her mother-in-law would give in over the bedroom? And wasn't the old lady right when she said that if Emma had the back bedroom then it would be awkward later on when young David needed a place of his own? It was awkward sometimes even now when he woke up with tummy- or tooth-ache just as Fred was getting going.

There was no doubting the old lady's love for her grandson; spoilt him rotten she did. Look at all the fuss she had made last summer when Mattie had decided it was time to have David's curls cut short and to put him into breeches. Cried the old lady had, genuine tears, saying that in her day he wouldn't have been breeched for at least another year. Mattie herself had wept in secret after he was shorn. Wearing frocks, David had looked like a little angel with his blue eyes and fair curls. He looked like a real boy now, though, and Mattie was glad that it was done.

Now there was Emma to complicate matters. Very soon she would be a young woman. Things weren't going to get any easier, were they? Mrs Davies had enquired if she intended to ask for the tenancy of her mother's house, otherwise one of her own daughters was thinking of doing so. Mam and Mrs Davies had been on friendly terms with the landlord and he'd always had a cup of tea and a chat with them on rent days.

When Mattie had told Fred he'd said bluntly that she'd go on her own if she did. He'd refused to discuss it with her, saying, 'You wouldn't be any better off for room than you are here, Mattie, with Mrs Davies still having the two middle rooms. You know Mam will give you the room for ouer David when he needs it.'

But they'd have had the parlour as well as the kitchen, wouldn't they? Houseproud as she was, Mattie wouldn't really have liked the parlour being used as a bedroom for Emma, but it would have made things easier for the time being, wouldn't it? And Mrs Davies was such a friendly soul . . .

'I couldn't leave my mam in the lurch like that. What sort of son do you think I am?' Fred had asked her angrily.

She should have known, shouldn't she? An only child brought up by his widowed mother. It might have been easier if he'd had a brother or sister, but she'd been head over heels in love, and knew how much Fred cared for her too.

It was half-past five in the morning and still pitch black beyond the glass panels of the door that led into the yard when Emma realised what being a daughter to Aunt Mattie really meant. She was startled out of a deep sleep by a none too gentle shaking and her aunt's voice urgently beseeching her to get up.

'Come on, Emma, your Uncle Fred has to leave for work by half-past six. Get dressed as quick as you can, there's an awful lot to be done.'

When Aunt Mattie had lit the oil lamp and pulled the curtain for privacy, Emma scrambled into her clothes then went to sluice her face under the cold tap in the wash-house, shivering as she dried herself as best she could on the rough roller towel behind the door.

Aunt Mattie passed her on her way to fill the big iron kettle, saying, 'See if you can get the fire going. Put a bit of blacklead on the grate first. I'll get up half-an-hour earlier tomorrow to give it a good do. I'd better call your uncle now, then I can start the porridge as soon as the fire's going.'

The porridge was lumpy, and Uncle Fred was late leaving for work, and Aunt Mattie blamed it all on getting up late. If she'd got up any earlier, Emma thought, it would have been a waste of time going to bed at all. After Uncle Fred left, they didn't stop. First the dishes had to be washed, then the fire had to be topped up with coal which meant another journey into the yard in the freezing February dawn. She'd no sooner washed her hands and was thankfully about to close the door and warm herself at the fire when her aunt said: 'Fill that kettle again, Emma, I'll have to give our David a good wash, I only gave him a lick and a promise last night.'

It was a quarter-to-nine when she came back in with the kettle and Emma knew if she didn't leave very soon she was going to be late for school. Aunt Mattie stood by the door to watch her go, but as soon as she'd turned the corner into Broadway Emma lifted her skirts and began to run. When she paused at last for breath she thought longingly of the peaceful breakfasts she'd enjoyed at Nana's house with plenty of time for a second cup of tea, and even a chance to sit by the fire before she went to school.

Chapter Three

It was almost a week later when, coming home from school at midday, thankful to close the door on the biting wind, Emma heard old Mrs Thomas calling from the kitchen: 'Girl! Girl!' And for the first time since she'd arrived at the house she went along the narrow little passage by the side of the stairs and down the three stone steps that led to Mrs Thomas's favourite haunt.

'Want you to go a couple of errands for me I do.' The round, almost black eyes, were watching her not unkindly as she continued: 'There's some embroidery silks I want from Peacock's. Put some scraps in with the note I have so's they can match them up. Then I want you to go to the fishmonger's to get a pair of kippers.'

'I'll just tell Aunt Mattie where I'm going,' Emma told her, heart sinking at the thought of going out into the bitter cold again without having her dinner, for breakfast had been at six o'clock. But the old lady brushed her words aside with, 'Gone over the road she is. You won't be long anyway with youer young legs.'

It was funny, Emma thought, though all the neighbours spoke with a Welsh accent, those who'd been brought up in the valleys like Mrs Thomas, Uncle Fred and Mrs Davies, sounded quite different to her nan and aunties whose family was originally from the West Country. Even those who were truly Welsh didn't all speak the same. She sat by a girl in school who had moved here last year from Caerphilly and she always said 'goying' instead of going, pronouncing the 'y' as in yellow, much to Miss Williams' annoyance.

'Well, get along with you, girl.' Mrs Thomas was ushering her towards the door. Emma wound her long woollen scarf about her neck once more, and jammed her tam down firmly over her ears. It was a squally day of wind and showers, the sky dark with clouds, as she turned into Broadway where the shop blinds, heavy with water, groaned on their hinges as they rose and fell with the force of the wind, showering her more than once as she walked beneath.

At the drapers the only assistant on the haberdashery counter, a tall thin lady wearing a long black skirt and black blouse with a high whale-boned collar trimmed with braid, was staring despondently at the counter where it seemed the whole stock of lace trimming was out on display. A plump well-dressed woman, her wide-brimmed hat anchored to her head by several lethal-looking hat-pins, was fingering each block of lace in turn, obviously unable to make up her mind.

Wondering what time it was, Emma shifted uneasily from one foot to the other as the assistant at last tried to help the woman decide, but she wasn't to be hurried. The fishmonger would be closing at one o'clock. Just as Emma made up her mind to leave the embroidery silks and go there first, the woman finally made her choice.

Emma reached the fishmonger's as he was about to bolt the door and he was none too pleased to let her in.

The force of the wind seemed to increase as she hurried

homewards, crossing the busy road in Clifton Street once more, dodging the horses that drew a coal-cart and bread-van, and almost bumping into a ragged boy pushing a hand-cart. Back in Wilfred Street she opened the front door and made for the kitchen but as she was passing the middle room the door flew open and Aunt Mattie, her face red with anger, cried, 'Where've you been? Your dinner's spoilt but you'll have to eat it 'cos there's nothing else.'

'I went a message for Mrs Thomas.'

As Aunt Mattie cried, 'You did what?' the kitchen door opened and the old lady took the parcels from Emma, pressing a half-penny into her hand.

'Oh! No, thank you. I don't want . . .' Emma began. But Mrs Thomas said, 'Nonsense, girl, you've earned it,' and closed the door.

Following her aunt to the middle room, Emma watched her take a cloth and lift a dried up plate of egg, bacon and potato from the oven. Slamming it down on the scrubbed wooden table, she cried, 'Left a note I did telling you where your dinner was. Why didn't you have it before you went?'

'I didn't come into the room, Aunt Mattie. She told me you were over the road.'

Lifting her knife and fork, Emma looked down at the food. The bacon was burnt and the egg stuck hard to the plate. As she tried to prise it away, her aunt said bitterly, 'I might have known she'd mess things up!' Then she picked up the kettle and, her hand on the doorknob, murmured as though to herself, 'I might just as well have had that egg myself the other night for all the good it's doing now.' Emma paused, her fork in mid-air, as she remembered tea-time the night before last and Aunt Mattie insisting that she didn't want a boiled egg herself and

19

sitting down to bread and jam. Uncle Fred had seemed surprised, saying, 'But boiled eggs are youer favourites, Mattie,' and she'd replied, 'I know, Fred, but I won't have one tonight.' Aunt Mattie must have done without for Emma to have one with her dinner today. She could understand why her aunt had been so angry.

A lump in her throat made it impossible to swallow the food. The tears rolled silently down her cheeks and fell on to her plate, but when through the glass panel of the door she saw her aunt returning, she scrubbed frantically at her wet face with her handkerchief, telling herself that since Nana had died she'd only been sorry for herself and all she'd lost, she hadn't really thought about how her aunts would be feeling at losing their mother. Now she remembered their tears at the funeral.

Her coming to live here had caused a lot of problems for Aunt Mattie, she'd have to be blind not to know that. Would it be the same when she went to the others? At least Aunt Clara had plenty of room and money . . .

Her aunt was bending over her, saying in a normal voice now, 'You can't eat that, Emma, I'll get you some bread and cheese.' The kindness was too much for Emma who burst into floods of tears. As Aunt Mattie's arms came about her, she whispered, 'I'm sorry.' But her aunt cwtched her closer, saying, 'It's me who should be sorry, love. Makes me see red she does. Our David's out there now being spoilt. Keeps a bag of sweets in she does, just for him.'

I'll make it up to Aunt Mattie, Emma thought as she dried her eyes and got ready to go to school. I'll keep David amused and perhaps he won't spend so much time in the kitchen, and I'll tell her before I go any errand for Mrs Thomas again.

That afternoon she found it difficult to concentrate on her

lessons. What would it be like when she went to Aunt Mabel's? She wasn't well off either. Would things be any easier there?

As Emma read a book at the table that evening, Fred Thomas sucked on his pipe and stared into the fire. Mattie had just gone to bed and he would have to go up soon for it was already half-past-ten and well past Emma's bedtime, but he'd always loved this time of night when he could sit back and relax and puff on his pipe.

His brown eyes grew sad as he thought what a pity it was that the two women he loved so much didn't get on. He knew how much Mattie would like to get away from this house but his mother depended on him too, didn't she? He'd never really known his dad for he'd died while his small son was still in petticoats, but his mam had been his world, and she had been determined her son was not going to suffer. His dad hadn't been dead a month before she began taking in washing and ironing, and as soon as he'd been old enough to go to school she'd gone out scrubbing several mornings a week at a big house in Newport Road.

He well remembered the middle room being turned into a drying room for the endless washing, and it was here his mam worked at the mounds of ironing that never seemed to decrease. The smell of soap suds and washing soda pervaded the house, but he'd never gone ragged or hungry, nor had he ever had to stay away from school for lack of a pair of boots. Everything had been fine until he'd got himself a young lady. There'd been three before Mattie and his mother had frightened them all away. But he'd no regrets now, and thank goodness Mattie had been made of sterner stuff than her predecessors.

He gazed around the comfortable room, thinking how

different it looked now. The two brown leather armchairs had been picked up for a song when someone was selling up, and his mam had given them the couch for although she was often prickly with Mattie she could be generous too. One thing the two women had in common was that they were both fanatically houseproud; his mother couldn't fault Mattie there.

Stroking his silky moustache, Fred thought of the conversation with Mattie in bed last night. It was the only place they could discuss anything now that Emma was always there. He'd known that Mattie was worrying about being short of money, but it was her own fault and he'd tackled her about it, saying: 'You shouldn't have bought those new clothes for the funeral. Youer mam would be the last one to want you to put youerself in queer street, you know that.'

'And you know very well, Fred, that I did it out of respect. I owed Mam that much, didn't I?'

'And you'll be paying that old crone around the corner for twenty weeks – twenty-one, counting the interest. How are you going to pay that money club? You'll need extra money not less now Emma's staying with us.'

'We'll manage,' she told him, but he knew that she was worried.

The coals shifting in the grate brought his thoughts back to the present and he looked over to where Emma sat reading at the table, the glow from the ruby glass shade of the lamp turning her fair hair to red-gold. When she yawned widely he reluctantly got up and knocked the ash from his pipe, saying, 'Better get ready for bed now, Emma.' Lifting the tin candle-dish and matches from the shelf, he added, 'Go and get washed then I can bolt the door.'

Emma lit the candle and dropped the box of matches into

the pocket of her dress. Then putting a shawl about her shoulders, and shielding the flame with her hand, she stepped into the yard past the kitchen and wash-house and around the corner to the WC. As she reached the door the flame flickered and died so she set the candle-dish down on the broad wooden seat and struck a match, jumping back quickly until the last of the cockroaches had scuttled away, knowing that tonight she wouldn't linger as she sometimes did in the daytime to read the scraps of newspaper that were strung up on the nail, growing frustrated when she couldn't find another piece that continued the story she was reading.

A few minutes later she was in the wash-house, carbolic soap stinging her eyes as she sluiced her face with ice cold water, thinking longingly of Aunt Clara's newly installed bathroom and water closet. Emma sighed, knowing that it would be the end of summer before it was Aunt Clara's turn to have her and by then the cold dark nights of winter would have passed.

Chapter Four

On a day late in March Emma came home from school at midday to find David being cwtched in his grandmother's arms and Aunt Mattie pouring cough medicine into a spoon. When another fit of coughing left her little cousin red-faced and struggling for breath, Mrs Thomas cried, her voice sharp with anxiety: 'It's under the doctor this child should be, Mattie! Send Emma for Doctor Powell. Go half with you I will, whatever it costs.'

Emma flew up the street and along Broadway, stopping only when, with a stitch in her side and out of breath, she had to wait to cross the busy Newport Road. The doctor was out on his rounds but as she closed the door of the surgery, behind her having left a message, she was relieved to see his gig coming out of Broadway.

By the time she arrived home from school in the afternoon a bed had been made up for David on the couch and he was asleep, face flushed, curls clinging damply to his forehead.

'Have to stay downstairs he will, Emma,' Aunt Mattie explained. 'Going back upstairs in the cold would only start him coughing again. Put your bedclothes in the spare room I have – Fred's mam said it would be all right. It's in a real muddle up there though, hasn't been cleared out for years. I've put you a clean tick for the feather mattress and I'll get an extra blanket from the chest.'

'Shall I go and tidy the room now?' Emma asked, but her aunt was closing the door. Coming back, she opened her mouth to speak but at first no words came. Swallowing hard, she bent down to whisper,

'There's something I want you to do for me, love, only don't let on to her.' She nodded in the direction of the kitchen. When Emma herself had nodded her aunt went on, 'The truth of it is that paying my share of the half-a-crown for the doctor has left me short for the week. I don't want Fred's mam to know how things are with us so I want you to take those things on the table to the pawnbroker's for me. I don't suppose you've ever been sent there before but you must know where it is, and what you get will tide us over until your Uncle Fred gets paid.'

With a sinking heart Emma stared at the bundle of clothes on the table, watching apprehensively as her aunt put them into a rush basket, folding the new black dress she'd bought for Nana's funeral carefully on top.

As she hurried along Broadway the icy wind made Emma pull her scarf tightly about her throat. Passing the fried fish shop, she sniffed appreciatively. Nan had sometimes sent her here when she hadn't had time to cook. Emma could remember hurrying home with the savoury parcel, her mouth watering in anticipation of the meal to come.

As she neared the shop with the three brass balls hanging above it her steps slowed and she looked around anxiously. Even the pangs of hunger the fried fish shop had evoked were forgotten as she licked dry lips and opened the door, causing a bell to clang loudly. Emma stepped into the dimly lit shop, walking nervously towards a dark wood counter where a thin man with curly waxed moustaches was writing in a ledger.

As he shook out and carefully inspected the contents of her basket, Emma looked past him to the room beyond, the walls of which were hung chock-a-block with garments of every description, though one wall seemed to be reserved for musical instruments. Violins, brass trumpets and concertinas among others covered every available inch of space.

When suddenly the bell clanged once more Emma turned nervously, her blood freezing in her veins as she recognised one of her classmates. But she relaxed with relief when she saw that Lizzie too was clasping a large bundle and must be on the same errand as herself.

As they smiled at each other in sympathy the man spoke for the first time, saying disparagingly, 'Can't give you much for this lot. Nothin' new except that dress.'

Folding the garments carefully, he sorted them on to the shelves at the side of the counter and handed her the pledge ticket together with some coins, then pulled Lizzie's bundle towards him.

'Will you wait for me, Emma? I want to ask you something.' The girl's expression was pleading.

Hoping Lizzie wouldn't be long, Emma stared into a glass-fronted cabinet at rings, necklaces, bracelets and fob watches ticketed and arrayed on plate glass shelves. As they were leaving the shop Lizzie said anxiously. 'Swear you won't tell no one you saw me in the pawn shop?'

''Course I won't. Will you swear you won't tell anyone about me?'

'Cross my heart and hope to die,' Lizzie told her solemnly, making a quick cross with her fingers over that part of her anatomy. 'Our Albie didn't 'ave no boots to go to school,' she confided. 'Dada was always mending them with bits of old rubber tyres but now they're too small. Why did you 'ave to take things to the pawn shop, Emma?'

She didn't answer the question right away for Lizzie's words were causing her to wonder anxiously just who would provide *her* with new boots and other clothes when her own became too small.

'Don't you know?' Lizzie prompted.

'It was because our David got ill and had to have the doctor.'

Giggling with relief after their mutual confidences and promising to see each other at school next day, they parted at the corner of Lizzie's street, then Emma ran the rest of the way home. Flushed with running and happy at her new friendship, she put the money and pawn ticket on to the table, the feeling of euphoria leaving her as she saw her aunt's expression change rapidly from disbelief to anger as she cried, 'Is that all he gave you?'

Emma nodded dumbly.

'But there were half a dozen things in that bundle!'

'He said your dress was the only thing of any value.'

'The cheeky sod!' Mattie's plump cheeks were red with fury. 'Like to give him a piece of my mind I would.'

Scooping up the coins and pledge ticket she put them into her purse, saying, 'Not a word about this to anyone, mind. All right?'

As soon as the dishes were washed Emma was sent upstairs to try to tidy the back bedroom where she was to sleep until her little cousin was well again. Packed from floor to ceiling with old-fashioned furniture, rolled up rugs threadbare even from the back, pictures, ornaments and leftover pieces of oil-cloth too small to be of any use, it was a hopeless task.

With a great effort Emma managed to move a tea-chest full of things wrapped in newspaper so she could reach the brass bedstead, then taking the clean tick cover she endeavoured to persuade the lumpy feather mattress inside, falling on to the bed at last with exhaustion. But it was no use, and every movement caused the rusty springs to moan and groan. Perspiring with the effort in the airless room, Emma looked longingly towards the window. Why not open it? she thought. The room could do with some fresh air. Climbing over the tea-chest, she knelt on the blanket box under the window and released the catch. She lifted with all her might, surprised when the window rose easily.

As she took her hands from the frame she sprang back in fright, almost losing her balance as the bottom frame of the window fell with an almighty crash, showering the room with splinters of glass which fell also on to the sloping roof of the wash-house below. Frozen with horror, Emma heard shouting from the passage then footsteps running up the stairs. Shards of glass clung to her dark merino dress and blood was oozing from a gash in her arm but she couldn't move, even when the blood was trickling on to the lace cover of the blanket box. She saw the door burst open and Mrs Thomas's jaw drop before she cried, 'Why couldn't you 'ave left that window alone, you interfering little hussy?'

Aunt Mattie was climbing with difficulty over the obstacles to reach her, crying anxiously, 'You're bleeding Emma. Come on, girl, let's get you downstairs and bathe that arm.' She pulled a hankie from her pocket and held it out but Emma couldn't persuade her legs to move towards her. Only her mind was working telling her that she'd caused awful trouble for her aunt who'd always been so kind to her. Oh, if only she'd left the window alone!

'Get her out of here, Mattie, she's bleeding over everything.' It was Mrs Thomas's angry voice that made her move at last, then after wrapping the hankie as best she could about her arm, Aunt Mattie helped her over the bed and down the stairs.

'You know the landlord won't pay to repair that window now,' the angry voice shouted after them. 'Going to tell him about the broken sash I was as soon as we'd cleared the room for ouer David. They couldn't have got in to mend it before.'

Mattie took a few steps back up the stairs. 'You mean you knew all the time that that sash was broken?' she cried incredulously. 'You could have killed the girl, you fool!'

'Don't you call me a fool, Mattie. Glad enough of my help you were when you wanted money for the doctor.'

Aunt Mattie's lips were pressed tightly together, her bosom rising and falling rapidly as she rejoined Emma and helped her down the stairs. Old Mrs Thomas had come out to the landing, crying after them: ''ow about all this mess? Who's going to clear it up?'

'I'm awful sorry for all the trouble I've caused.' Emma sat shamefaced as her aunt bathed her arm and dressed it with some well-boiled sheeting.

Mattie managed a rueful smile, saying, 'Don't worry about it, love. Trouble is my middle name.'

Five minutes later, her face as white as lint, Emma leaned back in Uncle Fred's armchair, her brown eyes anxious as she heard footsteps in the passage and Mrs Thomas calling from the kitchen, 'Fred, is that you? Want a word with you I do before you go in there.'

Poor Uncle Fred. Poor Aunt Mattie, Emma thought as the

footsteps passed the middle room. There'd be even more trouble now. Since David had been poorly things had been so much better between them, and it was all her fault if they deteriorated now. None of this would have happened if she'd left that window alone.

Uncle Fred was soon flinging open the door, crying, 'Mattie, what was that you called my mam? Better watch youer tongue you had, girl. Waiting for an apology, she is.'

Emma's arm was throbbing painfully. Tears began to roll once more down her cheeks, a grey mist floated in front of her eyes, and the angry voices grew faint as she slumped against the cushions and the room receded into nothingness.

Chapter Five

That night Emma was to sleep in her uncle's armchair by the fire, for despite his staying upstairs all evening picking up splinters of glass by the light of an oil-lamp, and tacking stout cardboard over the window frame, he'd declared the room unfit for her to sleep in.

Uncle Fred had finally come down bleary-eyed and weary, and when Emma got up for him to sit down, he'd waved her back, saying, 'It's off to bed I am, cariad, soon as I've had a cup of tea.'

'I'll put a couple of pillows behind you before we go up,' her aunt told her kindly. 'Bring down some of your bedding I will. You can rest your legs on that chair.' Sighing deeply, she added, 'Have to think of somewhere else before tomorrow night we will.'

The clock had barely finished striking ten when Aunt Mattie put out the lamp and followed Uncle Fred to bed. Soon David's regular breathing told Emma that the medicine was working and he was fast asleep. With troubled eyes she watched the coals sinking slowly in the grate, jumping nervously when a tap came at the door. As it slowly opened her startled gaze came to rest on the apparition in the doorway, a candle held aloft casting sinister shadows over the long thin face, the grey hair

33

released from its pins forming a cloak about her shoulders, a voluminous flannel nightgown falling in folds about her feet.

When a bony finger rose from the folds to beckon her, a petrified Emma clutched the blankets tighter until a hoarse whisper bade her: 'Come on, girl, or you'll wake 'im up.'

Once in the passageway it was clear the old lady wished Emma to follow her up the stairs. In her bedroom Mrs Thomas put the candle-dish down on the chest of drawers, saying, 'You'll be more comfortable 'ere than in that chair. Get in, girl, or you'll freeze to death.'

Teeth chattering as much with fright as cold, Emma did as she was bid. As she sank deep into the feather mattress, the old lady went on: 'Worrying about you I was. Mattie will tell you my bark's much worse than my bite!' And she chuckled hoarsely.

Doubting her aunt would tell her any such thing, Emma murmured her thanks and closed her eyes, willing sleep to come quickly. She was just dozing off when the snoring began, and as the raucous sound increased in volume even the bed seemed to shake beneath her. Clapping her hands to her ears, Emma wished she had the courage to get out of bed and go downstairs to the sanctuary of the armchair by the fire. Presently, with a heave of the bedclothes the old lady turned over and the snoring stopped as suddenly as it had begun, but now Emma couldn't sleep but lay staring into the darkness, longing for the first signs of dawn to lick the curled edges of the paper blind.

The next thing she knew she was being shaken awake and Mrs Thomas was whispering urgently, 'Wake up! Wake up, girl. It's best Mattie doesn't know. Think I'm going soft she will.'

Still half asleep Emma got out of bed and, clutching the banisters, fumbled her way downstairs. She had just settled herself in the armchair again when she heard footsteps on the stairs. The door opened and Aunt Mattie set the flickering candle down on the table and lit the oil lamp before snuffing out the flame. Turning to Emma she said worriedly, 'Made up my mind I have, love, I'm going round to see our Mabel, see what can be arranged. You can't sleep in that chair again tonight.'

With breakfast over and Uncle Fred off to work, her aunt pinned on her hat, saying, 'See to David, Emma, I won't be very long.'

Would her Aunt Mabel want to have her, Emma wondered, or would she be upset at being asked to take her before her turn?

When Aunt Mattie returned she was smiling as she told Emma, 'Would you believe it, love? Our Mabel was coming round today to see if she could have you earlier, and Ellie was as happy as a dog with two tails.'

Even the thought of her cousin's sloppy kisses couldn't dampen Emma's joy. Aunt Mabel really wanted her to come.

'I'll bandage that arm again, Emma, then you can get ready.' Mattie seemed relieved, as though a burden had been lifted from her shoulders. But Emma wouldn't be a burden where she was going; she'd be able to help with Ellie and would make herself really useful.

Half-an-hour later, carrying the straw holdall, her free arm about Esmeralda, Emma was walking up the street. Passing the Llewellyns' house, she remembered when they'd kept a shop in the parlour. Nan would often go there on her way to visit Aunt Mattie and Mair and Gwen Llewellyn would be behind the counter, but Emma hardly knew them for although they'd gone to the same school as she they were much older, and Lucy the youngest daughter was just a baby then.

Soon she was approaching the street of small houses where Aunt Mabel and Ellie lived. Her aunt opened the door, giving her a welcoming smile, then she was being crushed in Ellie's plump arms while kisses rained down on her face. When Emma managed to extricate her doll and put it on to the table, her cousin broke away to pick it up and hug Esmeralda with the same fervour as she had Emma herself.

'Mind her hat, Ellie,' Emma wanted to warn, but aware of Aunt Mabel's contented smile as she watched her daughter, said nothing.

'You girls are going to get on like a house on fire.' Her aunt beamed at them warmly before lifting the tea-pot from the hob. While they sat munching biscuits and sipping tea, Emma tried hard not to look around the room. She didn't want anything to detract from the happiness of knowing that here she was really wanted, but she couldn't help noticing that it was a sorry sight. It must be because at Aunt Mattie's everything was spic and span, she thought. Out of the corner of her eye she could see the stuffing bulging from the stained velveteen of the old armchair, and the rug in front of the fire was badly stained too. Poor Aunt Mabel. Nana had said she had her work cut out looking after Ellie who either couldn't or wouldn't look after herself and was messy with her food.

Despite the appearance of the room, a warm glow of contentment at being so obviously wanted was still with her. Emma showed Ellie how to take off Esmeralda's boots and socks carefully and then put them back on again. Ellie had hardly put the doll down since she'd arrived with it and it was with relief that at last Emma heard her aunt saying, 'Better put that doll away safe before anything happens to it.' And despite her daughter's tears and protests she packed it into a cardboard box and took it upstairs to put it on top of the wardrobe.

They were washing up the dishes when her aunt said, 'I've got a job to go to on Saturday mornings, Emma. Rough cleaning the lady said, and I can do with the money, God knows. It was lucky you could come to me this week. Going to ask Mattie I was if you could come to look after Ellie while I was away.'

Emma felt suddenly sick as she struggled with tears. She'd thought her aunt had wanted her for herself. Then the thought struck her that she was really needed. Aunt Mabel couldn't have taken that job if she wasn't here to look after Ellie. She'd be helping to earn her keep, wouldn't she? And there were other ways she could make herself useful, like tidying up after Ellie and cleaning up the room. Better to be needed than just wanted, she told herself, putting on a brave smile.

Mabel Evans lay in bed staring up at a patch of light on the bedroom ceiling, wondering what it was she'd said to Emma to upset her like that. The girl had seemed so happy until she'd mentioned that she had a job to go to, then her lips had trembled and tears had come to her eyes. Emma had tried to brush them away but not before Mabel had seen them. Still, the girl had perked up afterwards. It couldn't be because she'd be expected to mind Ellie; she was always coming around asking to do that when Mam was alive. She hadn't been around much lately but that would be Mattie keeping her nose to the grindstone. Mattie wouldn't give anyone time to spit! Mabel had been houseproud herself until Ellie came along, but there didn't seem much point once Joe had gone and she was past crying over that now.

She didn't need to ask herself what went wrong with her marriage, Joe had always had an eye for a pretty girl, but she didn't think he'd have left her for Mary if it hadn't been for

Ellie being like she was. It had been a long birthing with complications and they'd thought the baby was dead. Once, in a temper, Joe had said it was a pity that she wasn't. He'd apologised afterwards but she'd wondered if that was how he really felt about his backward daughter? They'd been happy enough until they'd realised that something was wrong. Ellie had been so slow sitting up, crawling, learning to walk and talk. Placid most of the time, she could still fly into violent tempers if she didn't get her own way. If a meal was on the table she'd bang her fist down on to the plates, sending food flying in all directions.

Mabel sighed. She'd given up the battle to keep the house nice years ago, but she'd been upset when she'd seen Emma's obvious disapproval. But she was just a child, wasn't she? For all that Mabel was grateful to have her here; now she could take that job. She'd half expected Mattie to laugh when she'd told her that she was going out cleaning. But she'd seemed quite pleased for Mabel, told her it would do her good to get out of the house.

Mrs Grey, the woman she was to work for, had been left a big house in Newport Road by her elderly aunt.

'What I want you to do, Mrs Evans,' she'd told Mabel, 'is to help me sort everything out, do the heavy lifting and pack the stuff I don't need into boxes. I haven't decided what furniture I want to keep yet, but all the drawers can be gone through and we can clear the attic.' Then she'd turned round and said, 'I'll want someone to do the rough cleaning when I finally move in. We'll see how you get along, shall we?'

Coming home from the interview she'd been bubbling with excitement, and it was a very long time since she'd felt any of that. She'd been sure Mattie would let Emma come to look after things on Saturday mornings. Any job that got her out of the house would be wonderful, but the task of turning out an attic and sorting through drawers with Mrs Grey promised entertainment as well. She'd be able to buy Ellie some new clothes with the money: a pretty bonnet for Whitsun with flowers and ribbons on it – in a younger girl's style of course in the hope that people would think she was the child she behaved like instead of going on thirteen.

Mabel raised herself on one elbow to listen for any sound from the girls' bedroom. They must be asleep. Having Emma here was going to make a big difference. She'd been worried about taking Emma when it was her own turn because there was barely enough for the two of them. But her new job would make things easier, and she might even get round to taking an interest in her own place once more.

Chapter Six

When Saturday came Mabel was up early, her freshly washed hair braided and twisted into a neat bun. She'd put on a clean blouse but hesitated about wearing the rusty black skirt she wore every day. Still, Mrs Grey had told her they were to turn out the attics and that was bound to be a dusty job.

By the time she was ready to leave Emma had washed up the breakfast things. She was a good child and so reliable, Mabel was thankful she could leave Ellie in her care.

'See she goes to the lav when she needs to,' she told her niece, nodding towards her daughter who often put off going out into the cold until the last minute. 'Well, I'd better be on my way. There's a bowl of that stew from yesterday in the safe, Emma. You can put it on the hob about half-past-one.'

In more than twelve years she couldn't remember going past the street corner without Ellie. Make it up to the girls she would. Give them a copper each to spend in Clifton Street or Splott Road when Mrs Grey gave her the few shillings she'd earn for her morning's work.

When she'd arrived at the house and had taken her shawl off and was tying her black alpaca apron about her ample waist, she looked around the hall with interest. On the black and white diamond tiles stood four heavy majolica pots, two of which contained aspidistras and two ferns. A Turkey carpet runner stretched the length of the front hall and continued up the stairs, anchored by tarnished brass stair rods. Mrs Grey was waiting to take her through the narrower back hall to the kitchen where Mabel hung her shawl on a peg behind the door, telling herself that maybe she'd be able to buy a coat by next winter if, as she hoped, the job went on till then.

'Light a fire in the kitchen range, Mabel,' Mrs Grey was telling her. 'The sticks and coal are in the shed in the yard. Oh! And that grate could do with blackleading. Just give it a quick one today, we shall be needing hot water as soon as possible. I've put the blacklead and brushes on the bench in the scullery.'

Mabel was glad now that she'd worn her workaday skirt. She only had one other and that was old too, but it was respectable and she kept it for her rare visits to Mattie's or Clara's – rare because up till now she'd had to take Ellie with her. Both her sisters being houseproud, they watched Ellie like a hawk, especially when she was eating.

The first hurried brushing left little impression on the rusty grate, but soon orange flames were dancing around the coals as Mabel filled the big iron kettle and settled it on top.

'Come up here as soon as you've finished,' Mrs Grey was calling from the landing, and she hurriedly brushed up the hearth then wiped over the tiles with a soapy cloth. Taking off the sacking apron her employer had provided, she washed her hands and climbed the two flights of carpeted stairs, her legs already weary but her spirits soaring at this welcome change in her humdrum existence.

When, with some difficulty, she'd heaved herself up the flight of steep uncarpeted stairs that led to the attic she found Mrs

Grey sitting in an old rocking chair, unpacking books from a tea-chest. Seeing Mabel, she pushed these aside, saying, 'I can do this anytime. Do you think you can drag that blanket box over here?'

Straining every muscle in her body, Mabel managed to drag the heavy dark oak chest towards her employer, panting for breath and pressing her hand tight against the pain in her side as the lid was swung open to reveal layer upon layer of clothes. It was soon apparent to both of them that none resembled any of the fashions worn in this century or even the styles still popular at the end of the last.

They were about halfway through sorting the contents when Mabel lifted a heavy velvet hip-length cape from the chest. It was a dark green, faded a little in places but handsome still, the pale green lining in a heavily embossed silk, the deep collar edged with ornate braid. The width of the hem puzzled Mabel for it hung in deep folds until Mrs Grey explained that it would have been made to accommodate a crinoline.

'There's good velvet in that,' she said, fingering the silky pile. 'Perhaps you could make something for your daughter with it?' Mabel had told her about Ellie at the interview, explaining that her niece, who was living with them, would look after her while she was away. Now, eyes shining with gratitude, she was fingering the beautiful material as she replied. 'Thank you very much! Oh, it's lovely, and there's a lady in our street makes things over.'

But there were more wonders to come. At the bottom of the trunk was a hat-box, and when the ribbons were undone and the lid lifted it revealed a green velvet bonnet the material matching that of the cloak exactly, the lining the same brocaded silk, the crown decorated with velvet roses in pink and a paler green, and with a plume of glossy green feathers curling about the brim.

Mrs Grey turned the bonnet around. Then handing it to Mabel, she said, 'Well, you'd better have this as well. It's of no use to me. Your little girl may like it for dressing up. Most girls enjoy doing that.'

Mabel thanked her profusely again. Ellie would be over the moon. Despite the hard work, she had enjoyed her morning. Then, when it was time for her to go home, Mrs Grey wondered if she could come back after lunch? At the same rate per hour of course. Mabel would have skipped home with joy if it hadn't been for her bulk and her already aching limbs. As it was, the streets between Newport Road and Splott seemed to have grown longer as her weary legs took her homewards, carrying the hat-box now tied up with cord, the brown paper parcel containing the cloak clutched tightly to her bosom.

Chapter Seven

That Saturday morning, as soon as Aunt Mabel had closed the front door behind her, Emma set about the task of tidying the room, excitedly anticipating her aunt's delight on her return. The first thing was to keep Ellie busy and out of mischief, so what job could she safely be given to do?

'Would you like to put the polish on the sideboard, Ellie?' she asked, but the girl shook her head.

'Why not?'

'I want to go out.'

'Well, let's get the work done first. Come on, love, we'll dress you up for the job.'

At the thought of dressing up Ellie smiled happily and was soon enveloped in one of her mother's voluminous aprons. Emma brought her the tin of beeswax and some rags for dusters, and soon, tongue between her teeth with concentration, Ellie was absorbed in the task.

'I'm going to sew up that hole in the armchair,' Emma told her, pushing the bulging stuffing back into place and drawing the frayed edges of the material together. Her nan had taught her to sew and the stitches hardly showed. They wouldn't have done at all, she told herself, if the thread had been a better match.

The next job was to remove the stains so she dipped a rag in soapy water and rubbed until her arm ached, but they were stubborn and it was some time before she turned to look at Ellie who was humming tunelessly as she worked. When she did turn Emma gasped in horror for the sideboard was covered with a thick coat of beeswax, the tin now half empty.

'No, Ellie, no!' she cried, taking the tin of polish from her.

It took a good half-hour of hard rubbing to remove the sticky beeswax, and her arms and back ached as she polished the sideboard until it shone. Then, suddenly remembering her aunt's words of warning, Emma took her protesting cousin out to the WC, sitting down on the scrubbed wooden box-seat to undo the calico buttons that fastened Ellie's drawers.

While her cousin sat there, still sulking at being taken from her task, Emma filled the two battered galvanised buckets that were kept outside the lavatory door ready to flush the pan. Then, anxious to get back to the chores, she stood in the doorway, drumming her fingers on the frame.

'Can't go,' Ellie told her triumphantly. 'I told you I couldn't, didn't I?'

Ten minutes later Emma was in the garden beating the coconut matting which she'd hung over the line, when Ellie began pulling her towards the lavatory once more. When this had happened three times in half-an-hour, with no result, she realised that to Ellie it was just a game.

She was scrubbing the worn oil-cloth the next time Ellie tried to drag her out, only this time Emma wasn't having any. Congratulating herself on being firm, she reached the patch where Ellie stood in an ever widening pool, then all contrition, Emma put her arms about her, telling her over and over that it wasn't her fault.

After mopping up the floor, she got her cousin into a clean

pair of drawers and washed the ones she'd taken off. She was hanging them on the line when a voice said, 'Playing you up, is she, love?'

'No! Ellie's been really good. All my fault it was,' she told their neighbour honestly.

'You must be Emma? Mabel's talked about you a lot.'

Emma nodded, hoping what she'd heard had been good.

Mrs Williams was leaning her plump arms on the wall, saying, 'If she gets too much for you, love, send her in to me. Used to Ellie we are, aren't we, cariad?'

'She's helping me clean the room,' Emma told Mrs Williams, and putting an arm about her cousin, added, 'We'd better get on.'

After that she took Ellie to the lavatory every time she asked, noticing the gleam of satisfaction in her cousin's eyes whenever work was interrupted. But at last the mats were back in place, the tarnished brasses almost shone, and instead of stains there were now a number of damp patches on the armchair. Glancing at the clock, Emma brought the stew from the safe on the yard wall, and tipping it into the big soot-blackened iron saucepan, put it on the trivet over the fire, looking forward eagerly to the afternoon when with her aunt at home she could visit Aunt Mattie and perhaps even call at Lizzie's house. Although they had been best friends since the day they'd met at the pawnbroker's, they only ever managed to meet at school.

Looking around her at the tidy room and gleaming sideboard, Emma felt a glow of satisfaction. Aunt Mabel was bound to be pleased, wasn't she? Emma couldn't wait to see her face. By the time her aunt came home the table was laid and the stew bubbling in the pot. Looking around her in surprise, she began, 'Well, it looks really nice here, Emma . . .' But Ellie was pulling at the parcels she carried. When the one wrapped in brown paper came away in her hand, her mother said fondly, 'All right, love, they are for you anyway.'

Ellie was getting more and more frustrated at being unable to undo the knots so Emma, swallowing her own disappointment, fetched the scissors and cut the cord, curious herself to see what was inside.

Ellie tore at the paper to reveal the folds of green velvet and her mother lifted the cloak and set it about her shoulders. But before she could fasten it at the neck, Ellie bent to take the lid from the hat-box and let the cloak fall to the floor in her eagerness to try on the bonnet. As Aunt Mabel went to lift it, an excited Ellie picked it up again, and in an attempt to put it on, flung it wide, narrowly missing the ornaments that crowded the overmantel.

'Lovely!' she cried, stroking the silky pile as her mother tried once more to fasten the braided hook and eye.

When they'd all admired the outfit as Ellie paraded around the room, Mabel rose stiffly from the chair, saying, 'I'd better have my dinner 'cos I've got to get back. You won't mind looking after Ellie again this afternoon, will you, love?'

Bitterly disappointed, Emma said, 'No, of course not.' Her aunt went on, 'You could get me some things at the Maypole, love. The walk will do Ellie good.'

The meal over, Mabel winced as she struggled to pull the boots back on to her swollen feet. Her forehead creased with pain, she said, 'I shall be good for nothing by the time I get back there.'

'Why don't you take a tram?' Emma suggested. 'There's one that goes along Glossop Road. You could get off when it reaches Newport Road. It wouldn't be so far to walk then.'

'Just for once, I think I will,' Mabel said, cheering up at the thought of the ride. She hadn't been on one since the horse trams had been taken off the road a few years ago, and often made a joke about Shanks's Pony getting you there for nothing. Anyway, Mrs Grey had already paid her for her morning's work so she could afford it today.

Before she left, she gave Emma the list of groceries and some money in a purse, adding. 'And there's a penny each for you to spend. I've put enough for the tram in my pocket.'

When her mother had gone Ellie insisted on putting on the cloak and bonnet once more.

'Well, just until we're ready to go out,' Emma told her as she poured water from the kettle into the washing up bowl. When she'd finished she put on her boots before going over to help Ellie off with the cloak.

'No! No!' Her cousin was jumping up and down with rage as Emma tried to undo the ribbons of the bonnet.

'Look, Ellie, you can't go to Clifton Street like that. I'm just going to get our coats. Let's see if you can get them off by the time I get back.'

Emma took the purse and shopping list to put in her pocket and went to the cupboard under the stairs. As she unhooked the coats she heard the front door slam and, rushing to the door, the coats and tams in her arms, was just in time to see Ellie disappearing around the corner. Emma felt cold with dismay as she realised that her cousin was still wearing the cloak and bonnet.

Struggling into her own coat, she let Ellie's fall to the floor in her rush to run after her and bring her back, but when she reached Sanquahar Street Ellie was nowhere to be seen. It wasn't until Emma had turned into Carlisle Street that she saw Ellie again, and when she reached Splott Road with her cousin still well in front her heart was in her mouth as she watched Ellie standing at the curb, about to cross the busy road. Thankfully a woman who was waiting took Ellie's hand. With a sigh of relief, Emma redoubled her efforts to catch up.

When she finally reached Ellie's side her face became scarlet with embarrassment as people turned to stare at the girl's unaccustomed garb. What should she do? It would be much further to go home than to the shops, and she had the purse and the list with her.

'Let's get it over with,' Emma told herself, hurrying Ellie along and staring straight ahead, hoping not to see anyone she knew.

They made good progress until they reached the confectioner's where her cousin stepped into the doorway and refused to come out.

'Come on, Ellie, we've got to go to the Maypole,' Emma begged.

'Want some liquorice with Mama's penny.'

When they entered the shop and the young assistant saw Ellie she began to titter, disappearing behind the counter until she'd composed herself. Gathering all the pride she could muster, Emma asked for a ha'porth of liquorice cuttings, and as the girl took a piece of paper and shaped it into a scoop, told her cousin, 'You can keep the halfpenny change until tomorrow.'

As they left the shop four bare-footed urchins had their noses pressed against the window, gazing longingly at the wonders displayed within. Then their eyes slewed towards Ellie who was stuffing liquorice into her mouth as fast as she could.

'Strewth! It's a duchess, innit?' cried the tallest of the boys, sweeping an imaginary hat from his tousled head and bending low. When Ellie returned the bow they fell about laughing then followed the girls as they hurried up the street.

'Gi's a sweet, youer ladyship,' one of the boys begged with a cheeky grin, and Ellie, her plump face pink with excitement, despite Emma's protest, offered the bag. But when a few moments later, it was returned empty, her wail of despair made all heads turn in their direction. Their fun over, the boys scampered off, but there was even worse to come for crossing the road towards them, her eyes blazing with indignation, was Emma's teacher. Her voice sharp with disapproval, Miss Roberts cried: 'You should have more sense than to let that poor girl make an exhibition of herself, Emma Meredith. I saw that disgraceful incident with those boys.'

Ellie, remembering it had seemed to please her audience before, bowed low, but Miss Roberts was obviously not amused.

'Shame on you,' she told Emma. 'Now take her home and get her out of that ridiculous outfit.'

She was given no time to explain that Ellie had run away from her as Miss Roberts, her thin lips pursed together, back like a ram-rod, swept past them. The unfairness of it all brought tears to Emma's eyes but she brushed them away, took Ellie's hand and turned towards home.

They were in Splott Road before, searching desperately for a handkerchief to stem her tears, her hand encountered the grocery list and purse, but by now wild horses wouldn't have dragged her back the way she had come, not with Ellie dressed as she was.

Ask Mrs Williams I will, to mind her while I do the grocery shopping, she thought.

A little sob escaped her at the injustice of her teacher's words. Instantly Ellie's arms came about her, great slobbering kisses

51

mingling with the tears that rained down Emma's face. Then her cousin too began to sob loudly, and at the heart-rending sound Emma put an arm about her shoulders and quickened her steps for home, Ellie trotting faster and faster by her side.

Chapter Eight

It was the end of summer and by now Emma should have been with her Aunt Clara, but Mabel, fearful of having to give up her job, had begged to keep her a little longer.

Emma's boots had been pinching her toes for a very long time but when at last Mabel noticed her limping, she only said, 'I was going to buy Ellie some new boots next week. I'll get her old ones cobbled for you, love, if you like?'

Horrified, Emma looked down at her cousin's shabby boots which were at least two sizes too large for her, and remembering them being soaked through on that first Saturday that she'd minded Ellie, shook her head, saying, 'Mine are not too bad as yet, Aunt Mabel. I can manage for a while.' And manage she would, she told herself, gritting her teeth determinedly, though she didn't know for how much longer.

And it wasn't just her boots that were too small, she reflected sadly. Her dresses were already almost to her knees and stretched tightly over her budding breasts, but she meant to keep silent about it for Ellie wore an odd assortment of clothes and she didn't want any of her hand-me-downs.

Then came the crisp autumn Saturday afternoon when Clara paid them an unexpected visit. Ellie had been pestering Emma to take her to Clifton Street to spend the penny her mam had given her, but, unable to face the crippling walk, for it was as much as she could do to force her boots on to go to school, she'd pleaded a headache. While Mabel was looking on the top shelf of the pantry for a daisy powder there was a knock on the door. When Emma saw her Aunt Clara standing there and a cab drawing away from the curb her eyes lit up with delight, but Clara was staring back at her niece in shocked silence, remembering how neat and pretty she'd always looked while in her nan's care. The child's face was pinched with pain, and the slippers she wore, obviously an old pair of Mabel's, were falling off her feet, grubby and torn.

Suddenly Clara was overcome by guilt for not having come to see Emma before, for just taking Mabel's word that the child was all right. Anyway, it had made up her mind on one score. Emma would accompany her home when the cab called back. She wouldn't be persuaded to give in this time.

Emma had scrubbed the oil-cloth and tidied the room that morning while her Aunt Mabel was at work but Clara was soon looking about her, lips pursed with distaste as her eyes rested on the shabby stain-spotted armchair and the grubby rug in front of the fire.

Mabel, guessing the purpose of her sister's visit, was silent as she busied herself making a pot of tea.

'Not for me,' Clara said as she watched her warming the pot. 'I've asked the cabby to call back for us in half-an-hour.'

Mabel's voice was heavy with disappointment as she cried, 'You can't mean to take Emma from me? Not yet anyway.'

'If it's your job you're worried about, Mabel,' Clara told her, 'Emma can come to you every Saturday, for the time being anyway.'

'That's all right then.' Mabel sighed with relief, and Emma's heart twisted with pain at this further proof that her aunt's only real interest in her was that Emma enabled her to go to work. Looking at her Aunt Clara, hoping that this time she'd really be wanted, she wondered how she'd got that lovely fashionable shape. Her bust in the crêpe-de-chine blouse was thrust forward and she had such a tiny waist, she looked just like the pictures of ladies in the smart magazines Aunt Mabel had been given by her employer. Neither Mabel nor Mattie were shapely like that. Then Aunt Clara was saying decisively: 'Get your things together, Emma, and put on your best clothes,' and her spirits soared.

As she flew upstairs Ellie lumbered after her. As Emma went to take her dresses from the wardrobe, Ellie flung her arms tightly about her, sobbing and moaning in utter despair. Deeply touched, she drew her cousin down on to the bed, putting her arms comfortingly about the girl and gently drying her eyes, telling her, 'I'll be here every Saturday, Ellie love. We'll have some good times, you'll see.'

'Are you ready, Emma?' came Aunt Clara's voice from the bottom of the stairs.

With the straw holdall in one hand and Esmeralda under her arm, she followed her tearful cousin down the stairs, eyes bright with excitement until she saw her aunt's look of shocked disapproval at her shabby clothes. As she walked into the room, Aunt Clara asked, 'Is something wrong with your feet, dear?'

'I've offered her a pair of Ellie's boots,' Mabel told her defensively.

Just then there was a loud rap on the front door and Emma saw her Aunt Clara pressing money into her sister's hand before kissing her gingerly on the cheek. Emma herself flung her arms about Ellie and then her Aunt Mabel before hurrying to the door and stepping excitedly into the cab.

As the horses drew away towards Sanquahar Street she saw Ellie's woebegone face and waved madly, but her aunt was speaking to the driver, bidding him take them to a drapery warehouse at The Hayes end of town before going back to Duke Street. Staring at Emma, who seemed to be absorbed in the passing scene, Clara was sure she was doing the right thing. She'd felt uneasy about taking her niece back to the shop dressed as she was. First impressions were lasting impressions and she didn't want the assistants pitying the girl. She'd rig her out in something more suitable for the niece of a town draper like Lionel. One good thing about her husband – he was never mean, and she and Emma could have a shopping spree on Monday morning for anything their own store couldn't provide.

Emma was turning to her now, face glowing with pleasure, saying, 'I've never been in a cab before, Aunt Clara.'

'Your uncle's talking of getting a carriage of his own,' she replied. 'Oh, my dear, you must sometimes wonder why I didn't take you home with me when your nana died? There was a very good reason which I can't tell you about now, but I only had your welfare at heart. Anyway we'll see how you get on. Ah! Here we are at the warehouse.'

'Shall I wait in the cab?' Emma asked, hoping she'd be allowed to go inside.

'You'll have to come, Emma love.' Her aunt smiled as she took her hand. 'I want you to try things on.'

Blissfully Emma followed her aunt into the warehouse and up the steep flight of wooden steps, hoping desperately that the things she tried on would include a pair of boots.

The warehouse was a long room filled with merchandise piled on counters, displayed on stands, and hung on hangers.

Emma followed her aunt eagerly across the room to where long rails were hung with coats, skirts, blouses and dresses. As her aunt fingered some of the display a tall man in a dark suit, stiff white winged collar and with a great expanse of cuff showing, was coming towards them, rubbing his hands and beaming as he said, 'How nice to see you again so soon, Mrs Emmanuel.'

'What have you to suit this young lady, Mr Williams? I thought perhaps a blouse and skirt, and maybe a jacket?'

Emma was shown into a small cubicle in which was a bentwood chair, a large spotted mirror and a row of pegs on the wall. Soon she was joined by her aunt carrying several garments over her arm.

'This is just to wear for now, Emma,' she was told. 'There are lots of garments at the shop that will suit. Anyway try this skirt and tell me if you like it.'

A few minutes later, her cheeks pink with excitement, Emma was staring into the spotted mirror. The skirt she was wearing was navy and in a soft wool which fell in folds to her calves; the blouse a simple shirt style in fine lawn with a neat collar and pintucked front.

'You like them, Emma?'

'They're lovely. Oh, thank you, thank you, Aunt Clara!' she cried, kissing her aunt warmly on the cheek then going back to the mirror to twist this way and that, fear in her heart in case her aunt had forgotten the boots.

When she began to undo the tiny pearl buttons of the blouse, her aunt said quickly, 'Don't take it off, child, they're for you to wear home.' And suddenly she understood. The joy died within her and tears sprang to her eyes as she stepped from the cubicle, desperately trying to brush them away. Her aunt was ashamed of her, wasn't she?

'Not so fast, Emma,' Clara cried as she made towards the counter. 'We still have to get your boots.'

Emma dabbed frantically at her eyes before turning, ashamed now of her ungraciousness.

The boots she was given to try on were in soft kid with tiny leather-covered buttons at the side, and she was very thankful to keep these on as she enjoyed the luxury of wiggling her toes about for the first time in many months.

Her old clothes were made up into a brown paper parcel and tied with string. Soon they were back in the cab heading for Duke Street. As they turned into the narrow shopping thoroughfare Emma looked from side to side with interest, at the shop widows chock-a-block with merchandise and the smartly dressed shoppers thronging the pavements. Soon she was following her aunt from the cab, staring up at the impressive brass lettering over the entrance to her uncle's shop: LIONEL EMMANUEL, DRAPER AND HABERDASHER.

Following her aunt into the store, Emma's first impression was of the smell of new wool and linen and of dark wood counters behind which lady assistants in black dresses relieved only by white lace collars, stood serving. A number of customers either stood or were seated on bentwood chairs. A tall pale young woman was unblocking a bale of cloth with a speed and dexterity that belied her delicate appearance. Emma was aware of eyes turning briefly towards her and of welcoming smiles.

By now they were at the foot of the stairs and her uncle was hurrying towards them. He looked so young and handsome, much younger than Aunt Clara, and his big dark eyes were welcoming. Above a high winged collar, his fresh-complexioned face was creased into a smile. His black glossy hair was parted in the middle, and with his equally black waxed moustache, he looked every inch the proprietor. Emma was surprised and pleased at the warmth of his welcome as he told them he'd join them for tea very shortly then walked briskly away, the tails of his cut away morning coat flapping behind him.

Now they were climbing the worn wooden stairs and passing under a wrought iron archway which proclaimed MANTLE DEPARTMENT in curly gold lettering, turning towards a door marked PRIVATE beyond which the polished oil-cloth gave way to soft beige carpets.

In a large room that overlooked the street stood a small table laden with a tea-tray, a plate of dainty sandwiches and another piled with buttered scones. A friendly-looking lady in a big white overall, who was introduced as Martha, smiled at her warmly as she poured Emma's tea. Eyes glowing with happiness, she wanted to pinch herself but instead stared down at her lovely new boots and wiggled her toes about for sheer joy.

Chapter Nine

'You tuck into them scones, cariad,' Martha said, putting a plump arm about Emma's shoulders. 'Just what we need it is, 'aving someone young about the place.' Her voice had the friendly lilt of the valleys and Emma found her cheek pressed against an ample starched bosom until her aunt came into the room, saying with an approving smile, 'Martha's one ambition will be to feed you up, love, until you're as buxom as she is herself.'

Emma glanced nervously towards the housekeeper who, she'd been told, was also her aunt's longtime friend. But she needn't have worried. Warm brown eyes alight with merriment, Martha replied, 'I'm glad I 'aven't got to wear them fancy corsets you wear, Clara. Take more than them it would though to give me a figure like yours!'

Now they both laughed and Emma marvelled at the camaraderie between the two women, so different in looks and personality.

'I don't know what I'd have done without her all these years,' her aunt confided when Martha had taken the tray to the kitchen. 'She's going to love having you here to spoil. I'll show you your room now, Emma, shall I?'

Feeling happy and excited, Emma followed her aunt along

the passage and into the little room that was to be her very own.

Esmeralda was already resting against the satin cushions of the basket chair. A snowy huckaback spread covered the small brass bedstead on either side of which were laid soft rugs in pale cream.

Clara opened the door of an oak wardrobe which matched a chest of drawers on the opposite wall, saying, 'We'll have to choose some clothes for you to put in here, Emma. Go down to the shop we will after dinner, it should be quieter then.'

When her aunt had closed the bedroom door behind her, Emma sat on the edge of the bed for some time looking about her, filled with wonder at this change in her fortunes. Then she remembered her books and the china dogs that she'd used as book-ends, all of which her Aunt Mattie was still minding, and pictured them set out on top of the chest of drawers. Now she'd be able to read her favourite books again. The one she loved best was called *A Peep Behind The Scenes*. It was a lovely story which began, if she remembered rightly, 'Oh, how the rain fell on the fairground on that miserable Saturday afternoon.' But this was a happy Saturday afternoon, wasn't it? The happiest she'd ever spent. Though the warm gratitude she felt towards her Aunt Clara was tempered with puzzlement as to why she hadn't invited Emma to live with her before.

Feeling tired she lay back on the bed and, stretching luxuriously, was suddenly fascinated by an intricate pattern that danced on the ceiling. It was reflected there by sunlight filtering through the lace curtains that stirred gently in the breeze. She must have dozed for she woke with a start to hear a tapping at the door and Martha's voice calling, 'Made a cup of tea I have, cariad, if you'd like to come down.'

On her way down she pushed open the bathroom door and entered a cool green world that gave the impression of being underwater. Autumn sunlight filtered through the green blind, shimmering on the pale green tiles that reached to the ceiling, broken only by a border of embossed yellow lilies about halfway up the wall. The bath with its single brass tap seemed enormous, encased as it was in dark wooden panelling. At the washbasin cream scented soap rested in a pretty porcelain dish and several fluffy pale green towels hung over a wooden stand. As Emma dried her hands she marvelled at their soft thickness, remembering the harsh roughness of the roller towels she'd grown used to using.

After a delicious dinner of tender lamb cutlets, mint sauce, roast potatoes and greens, followed by steamed fruit pudding and custard, Emma helped Martha with the washing up. When she went to the sitting room only Uncle Lionel was there. Dressed comfortably now in a dark green velvet smoking jacket, he was pressing tobacco into his pipe with his thumb. Seeing Emma, he put the pipe aside. He beckoned her over and to her embarrassment lifted her on to his knee. Putting an arm about her waist to steady her, he said kindly, 'I hope you're going to be very happy with us, young lady.'

As she murmured that she was happy, Emma's cheeks were scarlet. She was almost twelve years old and Uncle Lionel was treating her as if she was a little child, but a part of her was glad, for wasn't it what she'd craved ever since Nana died? Someone to love her just for herself? Her aunt and uncle and Martha all seemed to want her here. Perhaps it was too soon for them to love her yet, but they did seem glad to see her.

Just then Aunt Clara came into the room and Emma saw the smile freeze on her face as she cried brusquely, 'Come along, child, we have to go down to the shop and I haven't got all day.'

Was it because she'd been sitting on her uncle's knee? Emma asked herself. But there was no harm in that was there? He was her uncle after all.

Her aunt's voice held its usual friendly tone when she spoke again, telling Emma: 'We'll go to the lingerie counter first. I think the smallest lady's size should fit you.'

By now they were entering the shop and as they approached the lingerie department Emma felt all eyes upon her. She stared in astonishment at the stands topped with wooden knobs on which were displayed chemises and corsets of every shape and description: long with whaleboned fronts, short with hook fastenings, all of them laced at the back, most pink and trimmed with ribbon and lace. Some were a peculiar 'S' shape and it dawned on her that these must be what the fashionable ladies like her Aunt Clara wore, with their tiny waists and bosoms pushed out in front.

'Emma!' Aunt Clara was calling her to the counter where she was talking to the lady in charge.

'Miss Williamson,' she said now, 'I'd like to introduce you to my niece Emma.'

'Pleased to meet you, miss, I'm sure.' Miss Williamson gave her a tired smile. She was tall and sallow-skinned with greying hair, and wanted nothing more than for it to be nine o'clock and the shop closed so that she could add up her bill-book, put the dust covers over the stock and go home to take her boots off, but she put her mind now to serving Mrs Emmanuel who was a kind enough lady, and her niece who seemed to be a friendly little thing.

Out came the tray of chemises and three of the smallest size were put aside. Soon petticoats were added to the pile, then several pairs of drawers, lisle stockings and garters. If Miss Williamson thought it odd that such a well-dressed young lady, for the skirt and blouse the girl wore were obviously of good quality, should be in urgent need of all this underwear, she didn't show her surprise, but smiled pleasantly as she told Clara that she would wrap the things and have an apprentice bring them upstairs before closing time.

On their way to the Mantle Department they passed a boy little older than Emma herself who smiled at them shyly as he attempted to balance two heavy bales of cloth, his thin arms only just managing to span them. His arms and legs seemed to shoot out of his jacket and trousers whose bottoms didn't reach the top of his boots, but he had a nice face and big soulful brown eyes.

'I should get those back to the Manchester Department before you drop them, Bennie,' Aunt Clara said in a kindly voice, then they were climbing the stairs to choose a navy reefer jacket to go with Emma's skirt, then passing on to Millinery for her to try on hats. Emma was relieved to find that her aunt favoured simple styles, like a boater that would do for best wear until the winter set in, and a tam-o'-shanter for everyday wear. Some of the hats on the stand intended for young ladies were elaborate affairs with wide brims and adorned with flowers or feathers, just like the ones the fashionable ladies wore. Aunt Clara did insist on Emma's having a dress for best, but it was made of tartan taffeta and in a simple style with only pintucking for decoration.

Half-an-hour later she was back in her room, opening the parcels an apprentice had brought and putting the things away in wardrobe and chest-of-drawers, savouring each moment as she put lavender sachets Aunt Clara had left between the chemises, drawers and petticoats, and hung the dress and jacket in the wardrobe, lingering over closing the door so that she could take another peek.

Downstairs once more, Uncle Lionel barely looked up from his evening paper and her aunt seemed to be concentrating on her embroidery frame. Emma sensed a strained atmosphere between the two. Her aunt turned to her to say, 'Martha's making cocoa for you in the kitchen, Emma. You'll have to get up early tomorrow, love, to get a tram to school.'

In the kitchen, sipping hot cocoa, Martha was bursting with goodwill as she regaled Emma with tales of her youth.

'Known youer auntie I have ever since we moved to Cardiff,' she told her. 'Lived next-door to each other we did. Course I went into service and Clara came here to work in the shop. Sent for me she did when they got married.'

Upstairs Emma put her candle down on top of the chest-of-drawers and undressed quickly. Snuffing out the flame, she got into bed, savouring the luxury of having it all to herself. The crisp sheets smelt faintly of lavender and sleep seemed very far away as her mind raced over the exciting events of the day.

Somewhere along the corridor a door banged and she heard voices raised in anger which she recognised as belonging to her aunt and uncle.

'I only took her on my knee, for God's sake, Clara. There's no harm in that.'

'Just you remember she's your niece,' his wife replied sharply. 'Emma's not a child any more. She could be leaving school when she's twelve in a few weeks' time.'

She heard another door close with a loud click. Their bedroom must be next to hers for the angry voices went on and on, muffled now, the words unrecognisable. Emma sighed and turned her face into the pillow, her heart heavy with foreboding. It was Aunt Mattie's all over again, wasn't it? For, however unwittingly, she was the cause of the trouble between her uncle and aunt. But why was Aunt Clara so upset over Uncle Lionel taking her on his knee? He'd just been trying to be kind and make her feel at home.

In the quiet of their bedroom Clara and Lionel lay rigidly back to back. She couldn't ever remember going to sleep without his arm about her and knew she'd brought it on herself. She'd known in her heart that there hadn't been any real harm in his cuddling Emma and wouldn't have given it a second thought if it hadn't been for those episodes in the past, though in her heart she'd always known that there hadn't been any real harm in those either.

Like her sister Mattie, Clara would dearly have loved a daughter of her own, and when her mother died had been sorely tempted to take Emma home with her for good. Early in their marriage there'd been two miscarriages. After the second, and the doctor's warning that there should be no more pregnancies her heart had almost broken. Lionel had been bitterly disappointed too despite his assurance that so long as she was all right he wasn't upset. She'd known from the beginning how much he loved children and that he longed to add 'AND SON' to his name in brass lettering over the door.

As the years had gone by she'd become increasingly aware of his fondness for the young lady assistants. It wasn't a serious threat to their happiness for he did nothing more than smile at them, or put an arm about them lightly as he attempted to squeeze by behind the narrow counters, and the assistants were tolerant of him for he was a good and thoughtful employer. Then just before her mam died there'd been trouble when a new assistant had gone home at midday never to return and her brother had come to the shop to complain loudly.

'Don't be ridiculous!' Lionel had said when Clara had tried to have it out with him. 'How can I possibly pass them without some contact? You can't swing a cat behind those counters, you know that.'

Clara had sighed wearily. She'd done everything she could to keep her figure; perhaps enhance it would be a better description. No one but herself knew the relief it was to take off those awful corsets at night, and despite his disappointment, knowing that he would never have a son to carry on the business or a daughter to spoil, Lionel was still a very attractive husband, his weakness for pretty young girls his only foible. He just couldn't seem to resist. Emma was already an attractive young girl with gentle brown eyes and long fair hair that curled becomingly about her pale oval face. Within a few years she would have a quiet beauty and to take her permanently into their home might be a risk. It was because of this that Clara had welcomed Mattie's suggestion that they each take her for four months of the year, for by the end of Emma's first stay she'd have a good idea how things were going to turn out.

Very soon it would be her niece's twelfth birthday and Lionel had already suggested that she should go into the shop as an apprentice which would mean she would stay with them permanently. Clara had been happy about this until tonight when she'd seen her perched on Lionel's knee. Had she been fair or was she just looking for trouble? After all, wasn't it natural for an uncle to be fond of his niece, especially when he had no hope of children of his own?

Lionel was stirring in his sleep, turning towards her, his arm outstretched to encircle her waist. As their lips met and she felt the warmth of his kiss Clara responded eagerly, telling herself she had nothing to fear for he was as loving and thoughtful now as on the day they'd married nearly fifteen years ago.

Chapter Ten

'Go on, open it!' Clara smiled warmly as Emma unfolded the brown paper parcel with eager fingers, exclaiming in delight as she drew the silky folds of the party dress from its wrappings.

Eyes bright now with excitement, she turned to the mirror and held the pale blue dress against her, gazing at her reflection.

'Oh, it's lovely!' she breathed, laying the dress over a chair and flinging her arms about her aunt, adding, 'But it isn't my birthday until tomorrow.'

'It isn't a birthday present,' her aunt told her. 'I bought it for you to wear when your little friend comes to tea.'

No one noticed the colour put there by all the excitement rapidly drain from Emma's cheeks. Lizzie was coming tomorrow, but how could Emma wear this lovely frock? Her friend had taken some persuading to accept the invitation, saying she had nothing but the faded brown merino dress she wore every day. Emma had assured her that she wouldn't be dressing up either, that she'd wear the very same blouse and skirt she wore to school. Even this promise hadn't cheered Lizzie much for since Emma had gone to live in Duke Street she was easily the best dressed girl in the class.

'I'll 'ave to wash it out Friday night and dry it over the guard,' she'd said, the thought of missing the birthday tea making her change her mind. 'There'll only be us, won't there?'

'Only us,' Emma assured her. 'Martha will be looking after us but you'll love her, and she makes lovely pastries and eclairs and things.'

'I'd better get back downstairs.' Clara's words brought Emma's thoughts back to the present. As the door closed behind her, Martha looked at Emma questioningly.

'What's wrong?' she asked. 'Don't you like the dress?'

'It's lovely, really it is, it's just I can't wear it tomorrow.' Emma's eyes were wistful as she gazed at the new frock with its dainty lace collar, the very same lace trimming the row of pin-tucks down the front of the bodice and the hem of the overskirt. But Martha's voice was sharp as she told her, 'Don't disappoint youer auntie, there's a good girl. Planning to take you out she is this afternoon, to buy you dainty shoes to go with it.'

Before Emma could open her mouth Martha had picked up the tea-tray and hurried from the room, and Emma knew that, however much she hated letting Lizzie down, she couldn't hurt her aunt's feelings, not after all her kindness.

For the rest of the day she worried about her dilemma. At the end of the following week she would be leaving school to become an apprentice on the Haberdashery Counter in the store downstairs, but her joy at the prospect and at receiving this morning's surprise present was clouded by the thought of what she was about to do to Lizzie's fragile self-confidence.

I won't see much of her once we both leave school, thought Emma sadly, but wasn't that all the more reason to give her friend a day to remember? Lizzie was to start work on Monday as a scullery maid.

'Had to get myself a job where I could live in,' she'd confided.

'Mama's 'aving another baby and there's already six of us in one bed. The little ones sleep at the bottom and you can't stretch youer legs out in case you kick them.'

Next morning when the birthday cards arrived Emma admired the glossy pictures in glowing colours, some of beautiful girls, some of flowers, all of them edged with gilt or lace. There was one from Aunt Mattie and Uncle Fred, and one from Aunt Mabel and Ellie. The one with dark red roses was from Mrs Davies who had lived in rooms with her nan, and there was even one from old Mrs Thomas, Aunt Mattie's mother-in-law.

When Emma had gone to mind Ellie for the last time her cousin had clung to her tearfully and poor Aunt Mabel had been really upset – that was until she'd opened Aunt Clara's letter and the two sovereigns had fallen out, money that would enable her to pay her neighbour to look after Ellie while she was at work. There'd been presents for Emma too when last she'd seen them: embroidered hankies from Ellie and her mother, lisle stockings and a pair of fancy garters from Aunt Mattie, and chocolates from both Mrs Davies and Mrs Thomas, making her think the old lady wasn't as hard as she made out.

The previous afternoon Aunt Clara had taken her shopping for new shoes after insisting they go up to the Mantle Department to choose a full-length winter coat.

'Your reefer jacket's fine with a warm skirt,' she'd told Emma, 'but you'll need a long coat to wear with your dresses. Soon it will be much colder.'

But Emma had already made up her mind that somehow she would wear the old coat she had brought with her when she went to meet Lizzie tomorrow.

The following day, buffeted by a high wind that tore at her skirts and made her hold tightly to her tam-o'-shanter, she met

Lizzie at the tram-stop. Her friend's welcoming smile froze on her lips when she saw the froth of party dress showing beneath Emma's old coat. Before Emma could explain Lizzie said sadly, 'Dried my dress too quickly over the guard I did,' and opened her coat to show how the shrunken dress clung now to her skinny figure.

She seemed to understand Emma's predicament when it was explained. Emma herself was as warm as toast in the cardigan Martha had knitted for her and pleased that even with her coat off it would cover up most of her pretty dress.

The table was laid ready with an iced birthday cake with twelve pink candles waiting to be lit, trifle, plates of dainty sandwiches, a covered dish which Emma knew contained hot sausage rolls, and a two-tiered cake-stand piled high with delicious-looking cream horns and chocolate eclairs.

As they sat down and Emma unfolded her napkin, Martha brought in a dish containing dainty triangles of hot buttered toast on which was piled mounds of fluffy scrambled eggs.

Lizzie watched Emma anxiously to see what cutlery she took and all went well until the pastries were handed around.

'Take a cream horn as well,' Martha urged as Lizzie chose a chocolate eclair. So intent was she on taking a large bite she didn't notice Emma cut a manageable slice of hers with her pastry fork. As Lizzie's teeth sank into hers she never tasted the cream for to her consternation it oozed from the pastry and fell with a splodge on to the snowy damask cloth.

'Oh! I'm sorry!' Lizzie's face was scarlet with embarrassment. Martha, while muttering, 'Don't worry, love, it'll come out,' quickly settled a saucer of hot water under the offending patch after scraping off the worst, then putting an arm about Lizzie's skinny shoulders, told her, 'Messy things them cream horns. Come on, take another or I'll be thinking something's wrong with my cooking.'

Despite Martha's kindness, Lizzie was obviously ill at ease. She took tiny pieces now, separating them carefully with the cutting edge of her pastry fork, then transferring them very carefully to her mouth, and Emma felt grateful to her nan who had been in good service before her marriage and had taught her what cutlery to use, although they'd used only the basics most of the time.

They hadn't long finished tea when Lizzie announced that it was time she went home.

'Got to get back in time to get the kids to bed,' she said.

'But it's only just gone four.'

'Well, by the time I catch a tram, and I've got to walk a good way after.'

Seeing that her friend was determined, Emma went to tell Martha they were going for a walk. It was true in a way and she didn't want her to know Lizzie was leaving so soon.

'Don't you hang about on youer own after she's gone now, Emma. Anyway, tell your friend to wait a minute while I get some bags.'

Into one bag went cream horns and chocolate eclairs, into another the cooling sausage rolls. Tongue-tied with gratitude, her usually pale face flooded with colour, Lizzie took them from her and Martha said, 'Emma tells me youer going into service?'

Lizzie nodded.

'If you wait a minute, cariad, I still got my dresses and aprons upstairs. To think I was almost as thin as you in them days and just look at me now!' She chuckled until her plump shoulders shook and her arms wobbled.

When the strong calico dresses and holland aprons were

brought down and shaken from their folds, there was the fragrant scent of lavender. Overcome with gratitude, Lizzie stretched up to kiss Martha's cheek, saying, voice trembling with emotion, 'At her wit's end Mama was. Going to pawn 'er wedding ring.' Then realising what she'd said, her face grew scarlet again.

Martha, ever generous, told her, 'See what else I can find when I've got time. Anything that fitted me 'fore I came here to work certainly won't fit me now.'

When they reached the stop the tram was waiting, the conductor about to clang the bell, and as Lizzie stepped on and took her seat it drew noisily away. Deciding it was too early to go home, for Aunt Clara would surely want to know why Lizzie's visit was so short, Emma decided to look around.

By the time she reached the stalls set out on The Hayes by the Central Library it was beginning to get dark and the squally wind that had made her button her coat to the neck and keep her hands deep in her pockets was tearing at the flimsy canvas roofs, forcing them noisily up and down, the lanterns lighting the scene squealing and groaning as they swayed wildly to and fro.

Leaning against the spiked iron railing of the new underground lavatories, Emma watched the milling crowds: women with shawls clutched tightly about them, long skirts brushing the garbage underfoot, some using the wicker baskets on their arms as battering rams to reach their goal at the front of the stalls.

Suddenly her heart leaped into her mouth as a hand gripped her arm and a hoarse voice, breath smelling strongly of beer, cried: 'Giss a penny for a cuppa, miss, I ain't 'ad one all day.'

'I-I haven't got any money,' she stuttered, trembling with fright. A long dirty grey beard was thrust into her face as, tightening the grip on her arm, the beggar demanded, 'Wot you doin' 'ere then?'

As he was about to plunge his free hand into Emma's nearest pocket it was wrenched away and he was flung against the railings. Suddenly Emma was engulfed in a warm embrace and Martha's voice, sharp with anxiety, scolded, 'What you doing down here on youer own? Didn't I tell you . . .?'

When Emma broke into sobs of relief she was drawn closer into welcoming arms. Voice gentle now, Martha said: 'There, there, cariad, better get home we had. I'll get the rest of the things later in the market in St Mary Street. Youer shivering, child. Why aren't you wearing youer lovely new coat? But I don't need to ask. It's because of Lizzie, isn't it?'

With Emma clinging tightly to Martha's arm they turned the corner and found themselves walking behind a small barefoot boy carrying a heavy wooden pail of water in each hand which slopped over his legs and feet at every step. Pieces of grubby flannelette shirt protruded from the ragged elbows of his jacket and the equally ragged seat of his trousers, and, as he turned a corner Martha let out a sigh, saying feelingly, 'Pooer little devil, there's not even a pump in some of them courts. Got to cart all their water from St Mary Street they have, and there's only four lavvies between all the houses. Smell them from here you can, when the wind's the right way.'

As they neared Duke Street she said anxiously. 'Don't you say anything to worry youer auntie now, Emma. Just tell her that when you left Lizzie, you met me and came shopping. Don't you ever go wandering like that again. Promise me now!'

Chapter Eleven

On the morning she was to start work, wearing a neat black dress with a white lace collar and cuffs, Emma followed her uncle downstairs. When they arrived at the Haberdashery counter and she'd been introduced to Miss Coles who was in charge, she heard her uncle murmur, 'She's to be treated exactly the same as the other apprentices. No favouritism, you understand?' Then with a brief smile in her direction he clasped his hands once more beneath his coat tails, causing them to bounce with every step as he made his way towards his office.

Emma glanced about her nervously, watching as staff arrived and made for the cloakroom upstairs. Last night as she'd lain awake thinking of today she'd wondered if she might find herself a new friend for there was at least one apprentice on each counter, but now they all passed her with barely a glance and she reminded herself they'd be anxious to take their place behind the counter before Uncle Lionel sent someone to unbolt the big double doors.

Miss Coles was a bustling little woman with a fresh complexion and black eyes; her dark hair, streaked with grey, was plaited and twisted into a bun. Pointing to the drawers she told Emma what each one contained. Lace collars, ribbons, elastic, pearl buttons, buckram, hooks and eyes, sewing thread, embroidery silks, crochet hooks . . . the list seemed to go on and on. Emma was relieved to see that each drawer was labelled anyway.

'When you have to cut a length of anything the scissors are kept here,' Miss Coles went on, pointing to them dangling from a cord attached to the counter. 'And the measure is here.' She rubbed her finger along the brass rule set into the edge. 'Every morning your first job will be to polish the brass and then the counter. The polish and cloths are kept in this cubby hole.'

As Emma nodded, Miss Coles said brusquely, 'Well, as I said, that is your first job so get on with it now.'

Just then a young woman joined them and was introduced as Miss Evans. She seemed to be a few years older than Emma and was plump and pretty. Emma felt envious of her rounded breasts and hips for at twelve the black dress did little to show up her own budding curves.

Miss Evans immediately began to cut pieces of brown paper ready for stringing until Miss Coles told her: 'Best leave that for our new apprentice, Eva. You know he'll expect us to keep her busy.'

When Emma looked up inquiringly, Miss Coles said, 'Finish the job you're doing first. There'll be plenty of time to string paper. You have to be kept busy and there's a long day ahead.'

It was easily the longest Emma had ever known. Being a Monday, business was slack yet everyone seemed to be doing something, bustling back and forth, rearranging stands that didn't need doing, polishing counters and the glass display cabinets over and over again, stringing up yet more brown paper although on Haberdashery at least not a single piece had been used.

Emma found herself trying to suppress a yawn. When she

yawned the second time she looked anxiously towards Miss Coles but her superior was busy marking up lace collars, her eyes on her task, and Emma found it prudent to do the same for at any moment Uncle Lionel could appear around the corner of the fixtures on his regular patrol of the shop.

She'd had a busy time at the weekend, getting ready for today, taking up the hem of the shop dress she'd been given to wear and tacking on a new white collar and cuffs for these would need to be changed frequently. She'd washed and brushed her long hair until it gleamed and rippled down her back and taken her weekly bath in the freezing bathroom, having first to heat and carry two galvanised buckets of water plus the big iron kettle, but even with the cold water from the bath-tap it was still only a few inches deep. Covered in goose pimples she'd sat in it, soaping herself hurriedly, thinking longingly of the tin tub in front of Nana's kitchen range, with her clothes deliciously warm at one end of the guard and the fluffy towels at the other.

Martha had soon imparted her views on the inconvenience of this modern convenience.

'Not worth all the palaver,' she'd told Emma. 'Daft I call it. Pity we can't use a tub like everyone else, but with no yard, where would you empty it? Manage with a big bowl I do but I got to wait until youer all in bed. Too much trouble lugging all that hot water and it gets cold before you get in.'

'Couldn't they have put in a hot water tap?'

'That bath was 'ere long 'fore youer auntie came. She had it all tiled not long ago but apparently hot water was too difficult. Something to do with the boiler and the pipes.'

'Don't string any more paper, Miss Meredith, you've done enough already to last us a week.'

Emma blushed as she looked down at the mound of paper,

knowing her mind had been elsewhere. Half-an-hour later it was her turn to go up to the staff tea-room which was at the top of the stairs on the opposite side to their own living quarters. None of the staff lived in at Emmanuel's Drapery Emporium but the long hours they spent in the shop made it necessary to have a tea-room cum rest-room, and a cloakroom with conveniences. Now Emma climbed the stairs with some trepidation for although she would dearly have liked to be friends she hardly knew a soul. Even Miss Evans who wasn't that much older than herself had been helpful but distant.

When she entered the room there was a group of girls making toast by the fire, which, being the only means of heating the room and boiling the kettle, was kept replenished by the apprentices until after the tea break when it was allowed to go out. The girls were laughing over something but stopped when she entered the room, eyeing her cautiously it seemed to Emma as they introduced themselves. When she attempted to do the same, one of the girls said with a short laugh, 'Oh, we all know who you are, miss. Youer the boss's niece.'

As the months passed Emma's slim body developed gentle curves and her cheeks took on a becoming tinge of colour. Both her aunt and Martha often remarked on how bonny she looked and sometimes she would be aware of her uncle's warm gaze, but ever since the day she'd arrived when there'd been a fuss about him taking her on to his knee he hadn't so much as rested a hand on her shoulder.

In the shop conversations would stop suddenly as she passed and she knew that her hopes of finding a real friend amongst the apprentices were slim for they obviously didn't trust her not to tell tales. But what was there to tell tales about? she asked herself. She'd soon found out they had a pet name for Uncle Lionel but it was used with affection. Anyway 'Dapper' suited him very well, Emma thought, with his meticulous morning suit, freshly starched high winged collar, smooth pink cheeks and glossy waxed moustaches. The big dark eyes, though ever watchful, were kindly and she soon suspected that some of the older staff had what Martha would call 'a soft spot' for him.

Emma soon found the long hours behind the counter hard on her legs and feet for the knotted boards in the narrow space had been worn into an uneven rut, but when at last she was allowed to serve customers she put her whole heart into it, whether it was selling a yard of elastic or a collar and cuffs of delicate Brussels lace. Most of them were pleasant to serve, whether they were fashionably dressed or wore a shawl, but occasionally there were awkward ones and these often came in pairs. They would sit on the bentwood chairs discussing the merits or otherwise of this or that piece of merchandise until all the stock was displayed, then one would say something like, 'I don't think they have anything to suit us here, dear. Shall we try David Morgan's?' As they made for the door one of the gentleman assistants would rush to open it for them, leaving Emma fuming as she put away the stock for Uncle Lionel would likely have noticed the lack of a sale and never failed to ask the reason.

Chapter Twelve

In the autumn of 1911 Emma was nearing her seventeenth birthday when something happened to trigger events that within a few months were to alter the whole course of her life. By this time she was no longer an apprentice but had been made responsible for training a school-leaver, making sure she was kept busy and taught her trade.

Early one morning in October, Eva, who was still second sales, suddenly dashed from the counter and up the stairs. When she'd disappeared from sight, Miss Coles turned to Emma. Her voice sharp with annoyance, she said, 'Go up and see what's happening, Emma. She dashed off yesterday while you were in the basement and not a word of explanation afterwards.'

Emma left what she was doing and hurried upstairs. There was no sign of Eva in the rest-room, but as she opened the cloakroom door she heard the sound of retching coming from one of the lavatories.

'Is that you, Eva?'

There was no answer but a few minutes later the door opened and Eva came out, mopping her mouth with a handkerchief. Giving Emma an uncertain smile, she walked on wobbly legs towards the sink. When she'd dried her hands, Emma guided her to a chair, asking with concern, 'Was it something you ate?'

This brought a wan smile to Eva's face as she confided, 'It's going to mean the sack if they find out but you'll know sooner or later, Emma – I'm going to have a baby.' Then, seeing Emma's look of pity, she hastened to add, 'It's not what you think. Harry and I were married over three months ago.' Unbuttoning the neck of her dress, she disclosed a wedding ring hanging from a thin chain. 'The truth is, Emma, I'd no intention of getting caught for a baby so soon.'

'But that's wonderful!' Emma enthused.

Eva replied bitterly, 'No, it's not! If Dapper finds out I'm married I'll get the sack right away, and with the baby coming I need to work as long as I can. It was easy at first to keep it a secret, but with this sickness I'm sure Miss Coles is beginning to suspect.'

'Well, she won't find out from me, and nor will anyone else,' Emma assured her. 'Couldn't you say you forgot to bring something down from the stock-room yesterday and you went up to look for it?'

The colour was returning to Eva's cheeks as she answered with a smile, 'Well, I should have brought down a box of button-hooks.'

'I'll go and tell Miss Coles you're looking for them, shall I? And I'll find some excuse next time you've got to dash upstairs.'

'You're a good sort, Emma. I should have trusted you before. Ginny and Elsie know already.'

Emma didn't know whether Miss Coles believed the excuse she gave for Eva's absence for just then the door opened and a lady wearing a large beflowered hat, her long braided skirt sweeping the floor, made straight for Haberdashery and Emma was hurriedly instructed to offer one of the two bentwood chairs while Miss Coles came from behind the counter to purr, 'How wonderful to see you, Lady Winterton, and how may I help you this morning?'

Glowing with pleasure at serving one of her most illustrious customers she didn't even notice Eva's return with the box of button-hooks.

By the time Eva left on Christmas Eve she and Emma had become close friends. Though sad at her leaving, Emma had soon found the other girls taking her into their confidence, the way she'd helped Eva obviously allaying their own fears.

Today it was New Year's Eve and she had never felt so happy. She'd taken Eva's place as second sales, but even more important there was no longer dead silence when she entered the staff-room. She'd felt a special glow of satisfaction when she'd been the one to be asked to collect for Eva's leaving present, especially when Elsie added, 'You were a good friend to her, Emma.'

Tonight her aunt and uncle were to go to a dinner to celebrate the New Year, and she and Martha were going to stay up to see it in together. Martha was making it quite an occasion judging by the plates of sandwiches and fancy cakes she'd prepared. The shop had been closed for about half-an-hour when Clara came wearily up the stairs, shivering as she held her outstretched hands towards the fire, saying, her voice sounding hoarse, 'My throat is getting worse, it feels on fire. I don't think I can go with Lionel tonight, Martha.'

'Does he know?' Martha asked, draping a shawl about Clara's shoulders.

'I'll tell him when he comes up.' She shivered once more. 'Think I'll get into bed.'

'Hang on a tick while I light the fire and put a bottle in.'

'I'll fill the bottle,' Emma offered, needing to be helpful.

'You do that, cariad.' Then Martha turned to Clara, saying firmly, 'Youer not going to bed until you've something warm inside you.'

By the time Clara was ready orange flames were devouring the coals, bathing the bedroom in a cosy glow. When Clara was settled under the eiderdown, Martha took the empty toddy glass and gently closed the door.

It was business friends they were to dine with so Lionel, disappointed, went alone in the carriage, promising not to be late. Martha and Emma sat either side of the fire yawning occasionally though it still wanted two hours till midnight.

'She must be poorly not to have gone,' Martha said worriedly. 'Lionel being so much younger than her, she likes to keep up.'

Presently, stifling yet another yawn, she said: 'What say we celebrate now?' and Emma was only too glad to agree.

The unaccustomed glass of port made her head swim and when she nodded off with her sandwich only half eaten Martha insisted she leave the dishes and get into bed. The fire in her room had died down but it was pleasantly warm. Blowing out the candle and drawing the curtains back, Emma was surprised to see soft white flakes of snow whirling madly about lightning the darkness.

Although she'd been dozing off in the kitchen, sleep now seemed far away as she lay in the warm bed staring up at the ceiling. She was still awake when the clamour of church bells began to ring in the New Year. Just after they'd stopped there was the sound of laughter and scuffling from the street below and she pulled on her warm velvet dressing gown, one of her Christmas presents, in time to see a group of young men pelting each other with the still watery snow. When they'd gone on their way she climbed back into bed and was just feeling pleasantly drowsy when there was a new sound coming from somewhere just below. Looking out of the window, she saw a carriage drawing away from the curb, steam from the horses rising on the frosty air.

There was the scratching sound again. At the realisation that it was her uncle trying to get his key in the lock she pulled her dressing gown about her once more, lit the candle and hurried downstairs.

Reaching the side door she called softly, 'Is that you, Uncle Lionel?'

'Of course it is. Let me in, there's a good girl.'

As she opened it wide he almost fell inside, laughingly explaining, 'Been celebrating a bit too much, Emma,' then leaving her to bolt the door, he lurched upstairs. When she followed him up she found him in the sitting room, standing with his back to the fire.

'Would you like a hot drink?'

'I think I've drunk enough, don't you?' he laughed.

He hadn't taken his eyes from her face since she'd entered the room. Embarrassed by the warmth of his gaze, she dropped hers but next moment they flew to him again as he told her, his voice a little slurred,' I've got a surprise for you, Emma. I was going to keep it till the morning, but hang it all. It is morning isn't it? It's New Year's Day.' A wide grin on his handsome face, dark eyes merry, he sank unsteadily on to the sofa.

'What's the surprise, Uncle Lionel?' Emma couldn't keep the eagerness from her voice.

'Well, it's like this. I'm going to promote Miss Coles to head of Mantles – she's always wanted to work there. And you, little Emma, will manage Haberdashery just as soon as I've chosen someone to take your place as second sales.'

Impulsively she flung her arms about him, crying, 'Oh, thank you, thank you! That's wonderful.' But when she unclasped her arms he held her tight, pulling her down to the sofa, his lips seeking hers, hands caressing her hair. An emotion she'd never felt before welled up in her; her heart beat fast at the strange feeling of excitement that gripped her. Shocked at the tumult within her which his kisses had evoked, she drew quickly away, pulling at his hands to loosen their hold. Despite her struggles his grip was gentle but firm, his voice charged with feeling as he told her: 'You're so lovely, Emma, and never more than now. Don't you know I love you?'

A gasp from the direction of the doorway made them turn startled eyes towards Clara who stood there, white as lint, her eyes seeming to bore into Emma's own. A sob rose to her throat, then another. They seemed to be torn from her heart – and tore at Emma's too.

Before she could rise and go to her aunt the door slammed shut, and the bedroom door too. There was a shocked silence before Lionel, sobered now by what had happened, face scarlet with embarrassment, said, 'Forgive me, Emma, I had no right. It must have been the whisky loosening my tongue. My God! This is going to take some explaining.' Sighing deeply, he made for the door.

Emma stared miserably into the dying embers of the fire. Why had she been so stupid, flinging her arms about him like that? Whatever had possessed her? Poor Aunt Clara, what must she be thinking? Turning off the gaslight she went to her room and lay there in the darkness, listening to the muffled voices: Aunt Clara's harsh and accusing, Uncle Lionel's placating. Tears misted her eyes at the thought of the misery she'd unwittingly brought about.

Presently she got out of bed and went to the window once more. The wind must have died down for the snowflakes no longer whirled madly about but fell gracefully to the ground, the lamplight turning them to gold. Peering at the gilt clock on the dressing table, she saw that it was four o'clock. Lying in bed, she'd made up her mind to leave as soon as the trams started up. She couldn't stay here now with her aunt's hurt eyes watching her constantly and an embarrassed Uncle Lionel not able to meet her gaze, but she'd have to creep out before Martha was up and about.

Sometime during the night an idea had come to her. If only she could find out where Lizzie worked now, perhaps she would know of a vacancy, somewhere in service where she could live in? But she knew it was a slim hope for girls started young and she had no experience to offer. But she couldn't stay here, not after last night.

At about five o'clock she washed and dressed quickly and put a few things into the holdall she'd brought with her, wondering what time the first trams would run.

When she was dressed in her coat and tam she wound a warm scarf about her neck and looked regretfully towards Esmeralda, knowing that if she wasn't to draw attention to herself she must leave the doll behind. Brushing tears from her cheeks, she closed the bedroom door quietly behind her and, boots in hand, crept downstairs. Passing Martha's room she'd thought she heard her moving about and quickened her steps, knowing there was no time to lose.

Outside in the street she looked up and down. A few lights were on in the rooms above the shops. It had stopped snowing and the glistening pavement was unsullied until her boots sank in at every step. Turning the corner, she joined the early risers on their way to work. A tram was standing at the stop in Queen Street, the burly conductor stamping his feet and thumping his mittened hands about his body in an effort to get warm. Sitting on one of the slatted wooden seats, Emma proffered her penny for he'd followed her on.

'Where to, miss?'

'Clifton Street, please.'

'Happy New Year, miss.' He smiled as he passed on up the tram. There were about half-a-dozen workmen, their fustian trousers tied with string, smoke billowing from clay pipes, and a woman sat in front of Emma, a bag of cleaning things by her side, shawl pulled tightly about her.

What would she do, she thought miserably, if she couldn't get a live-in servant's job? She could probably find another position as a drapery assistant, even one where she could live on the premises, but her uncle was well known in business circles and she would soon be taken back to Duke Street to live under sufferance with Aunt Clara's accusing eyes always upon her, and she couldn't bear that.

The tram was drawing noisily away from the stop, taking her from the life she'd grown to love. When Emma had left Duke Street behind she'd glanced back at the Castle, its stout grey walls imposing even in the murky half-light of this freezing dawn. Martha had always been so proud of them having a castle almost on their doorstep, and had told Emma all about the Bute family who lived there. Emma and Martha had often wandered about the town; everyone called it 'town' though Cardiff had been a city since 1905. Together they'd explored every nook and cranny from Temperance Town to Crockherbtown. On warm summer evenings they'd rested their elbows on the canal wall near Mill Lane and watched the barges drifting by, or sometimes wandered through the arcades with their high vaulted glass roofs which kept you cool in summer and in winter kept out the wind and rain.

Tears welled again at the thought of all the things she was going to miss, including the companionship of the staff at the shop. Only last week she'd gone to the Empire Music Hall with Elsie from Millinery, and they'd been escorted by Tom and Artie from Gents' Outfitting. During the show Artie had held Emma's hand firmly in his until the lights went up. It had been a wonderful night, the theatre itself the last word in luxury with elegant potted plants in the carpeted foyer and beautiful hangings and upholstery.

The September evening she'd gone to the Empire with her aunt and uncle and Martha came to mind. It was Martha's birthday treat and she'd dressed for the occasion wearing her very best hat which, except for Sundays, lay undisturbed in a large hat-box on top of her wardrobe. It was a deep blue felt with a wide brim decorated with an enormous ostrich feather which needed a good twelve inches of clearance at the back. When a lady behind them complained that it was not only tickling her face but obscuring her view, Martha had reluctantly removed it and put it on her lap.

Oh, if only she'd stayed in bed last night and left it to Martha to let her uncle in! Emma's cheeks grew hot as she recalled flinging her arms about him. She'd been so excited about his wonderful news, she'd just thrown caution to the winds. If Uncle Lionel had been himself he'd have just laughed it off, not kissed her and told her he loved her, and it must have been the whisky talking for you only had to see them together to know that he loved Aunt Clara very much. As it was, that moment's foolishness had cost her dearly for already her heart ached to be back at the shop with the three people she'd grown to love so much.

Chapter Thirteen

At the Emporium in Duke Street New Year's Day dawned anything but happily. Having heard the rumpus in the early hours, Martha assumed that Lionel had been celebrating too freely and didn't suspect that Emma was in any way involved.

'Kept her awake half the night as well by the looks of it,' she murmured to herself when the girl didn't as usual come to the kitchen to help with the breakfast. 'Take her a cup of tea I will as soon as Clara's had her tray.'

When she went into the bedroom with the breakfast tray Clara looked poorly as she lay back amongst the pillows and waved the tray aside.

That dratted cold has taken away her appetite, Martha thought worriedly. But it had taken a lot more than just a cold to make her eyes red and swollen and her face so blotched and puffy. In reply to her gentle, 'How are you feeling this morning, cariad?' the tears flowed once more as Clara dabbed her eyes with an already sodden hanky.

Cradling her in her arms, Martha told her, 'I don't know what all this is about, love, but things are seldom as black as they seem.'

'Oh, but they are, Martha. They are!' Then, as though she'd already said too much, Clara turned away and pulled the bedclothes about her, closing her eyes once more.

'Bring you some fresh tea I will, soon as Lionel's had his breakfast,' Martha told her making for the door.

'Martha!'

'Yes, cariad?'

'I've got to tell someone. Emma will have to go. It isn't her fault, I know, but Lionel loves her. I heard him tell her so last night.'

'You must be mistaken, Clara. Of course he loves her – she is his niece after all. Anyway it was probably the drink talking. I expect he had a drop too much, especially as he was on his own.'

Clara's eyes were filled with sadness as she said, 'It must be what he really feels, Martha. I am ten years older than him. It didn't seem to matter at first . . .'

'And it doesn't matter now, cariad. Why, you're the prettiest woman I know. Thirty-seven is no great age when a woman looks like you.'

Clara dabbed her eyes with the lace-trimmed hankie Martha had fetched from the drawer. Her head ached and her eyelids seemed to be stuck together.

'Pass me the looking glass, Martha.'

Taking the silver-backed mirror into her hands, she gazed at her reflection, managing a wan smile as she told Martha, 'You must be blind.'

'There's nothing that bathing your face and getting rid of that cold won't cure,' Martha assured her. 'Get you a daisy powder I will, and a fresh cup of tea.'

'That won't alter anything, will it?'

'For goodness' sakes, Clara, the girl's only seventeen.'

'The same age Lionel was when we met. I was ten years

older. Now he's that much older than her.'

Gripping Martha's hand, she asked plaintively, 'How am I to tell Emma she has to go?'

'It'll all blow over,' Martha told her, 'you'll see.'

Knocking on Emma's door and receiving no answer, Martha pushed it open and glanced inside. The bed had been neatly made up and the wardrobe door had swung open to reveal empty hangers and a gap where garments had hung. Martha's eyes flew to the top. Finding the holdall gone, she clapped a hand to her mouth and sank to the bed, crying, 'Oh my God!'

Poorly or not Clara would have to be told. Her thoughts in turmoil, Martha hurried back to her room.

'Gone?' Clara cried. 'But where? I'd better get up, she'll have to be found.'

'But you just said she'd have to go.'

'Oh, but not like this, Martha. I thought perhaps she could have gone back to Mabel for a while and Lionel could use his influence to get her a good job.' She pushed back the bedclothes and swung her feet to the floor.

'Youer not going anywhere. Come on, back into bed with you or you'll catch youer death of cold.'

'Oh, Martha! What can we do?'

'See what Lionel thinks.'

'I'm not talking to him!' For a moment Clara's eyes flashed with the old spirit.

Martha was about to leave when Lionel appeared in the doorway. Looking shamefaced, he went towards the bed.

'How are you feeling now, Clara?'

When she didn't answer but turned her head away he went on, 'Look, I'm really sorry, love. It must have been the whisky talking.'

'Tell that to Emma – when you find her.'

'She's packed her things and gone,' Martha told him, moving discreetly towards the door. As she turned to shut it behind her she saw the colour drain from his cheeks as he said anxiously, 'Dear God, and in this weather! Poor little soul.'

Messages hastily sent to Mattie and Mabel proved fruitless. Neither had seen Emma since before Christmas when she'd brought their presents.

As the hours passed Lionel grew more agitated, Clara more and more upset. Martha, her heart heavy, stared out of the window watching a fresh flurry of snow whirl past, racking her brains for an answer but could think of nowhere the girl could have gone, for all her friends were here at the shop.

If she's lucky enough to find work, she told herself, it will have to be somewhere she can live in. A drapery store, perhaps, or service? But she had no experience of service and Lionel was well known and respected in the trade, and would soon be informed of her whereabouts if she found work in a draper's.

Martha's eyes misted with tears at the thought of Emma alone out there. She'd loved her from the moment Clara had brought her home: a skinny twelve year old with big warm brown eyes in a pale oval face, and still loved her dearly for Emma had become to her the child she would never have. Now that child had grown into a lovely young woman, her long, wavy hair like spun gold, cheeks tinged with colour. Warm-hearted and trusting, she'd never been prepared for a hostile world.

Where would she sleep tonight? Martha's fears were the same as any mother's anxious for her child. If only Emma had left some clue! Sitting there, thinking back over the years, Martha was remembering the day young Lizzie had come to tea. The child had been going into service and she'd given her the calico

98

dresses she'd hoarded for years.

I've got her address somewhere, Martha thought. I sent a parcel of things to her mam when I was clearing out. I kept it in that old purse I put away when Emma bought me a new one. Suddenly filled with hope, she searched for the slip of paper, cautioning herself that it was unlikely they'd kept in touch all these years.

But it's worth a try, she told herself. Fetching her stoutest pair of boots, warm winter coat and hat, she dressed quickly and wound a long woollen scarf about her throat. Lionel was still out searching the streets and she could hear Clara moving about, probably getting dressed. Martha wondered frantically what plausible excuse she could give for her journey. In all probability it was just a fool's errand and she didn't want to raise Clara's hopes too high . . .

Chapter Fourteen

Turning into the street where Lizzie had lived, Emma was remembering that warm autumn day when she was eleven, the one and only time she had ever called on her friend. The street teemed with life then: old ladies wearing their husband's flat caps, some sucking on stained clay pipes, sat on kitchen chairs or stools outside their houses watching their charges; babies crawled on the pavements; noisy games of marbles were going on in the gutter, even noisier ball games in the road.

Lizzie's door had been shut and it was some time before she'd answered Emma's knock, her mother's sacking apron about her waist, a screaming baby resting on her hip, toddlers clutching her skirt on either side. Her face red with embarrassment, she'd pulled the door quickly to behind her but not before Emma had seen the bare boards.

'I can't come out,' she'd told her friend. 'I'm feeding 'im.' She'd hitched the baby a little higher on her hip. 'He won't shut up till I give 'im the bottle back.' She was already closing the door, making Emma wish she'd never come.

Today the narrow street was deserted, road and pavement one expanse of as yet pristine snow, every door shut tight. This time Emma's knock was answered by a thin harassed-looking woman.

'Are you Lizzie Ball's mother?' she asked nervously.

The woman nodded. 'You a friend of 'ers then?'

To which Emma replied, 'Yes. An old friend.'

'Better come in,' Mrs Ball told her, 'we can't stand talking in this weather. Ouer Lizzie's in service, she doesn't live 'ere no more.'

Emma nodded. 'I was just hoping you'd give me her address.'

She stepped into the narrow passage. A shabby pram smelling faintly of urine barred the way. A baby slept in it under a pile of blankets. They flattened themselves against the wall to pass it. Children's voices shrill with argument were coming from the kitchen. As they descended the two steps that led to it, the noise stopped abruptly and all eyes were turned in her direction. It was a small room that seemed to be filled with children, kneeling at the table, rolling about on the pegged hearth-rug, watching Emma with interest from the sofa that took up all of one wall.

Mrs Ball lifted a protesting child from its chair by the table to offer Emma a seat but she shook her head, saying, 'My coat is soaking wet.'

'Take it off, girl. Hang it on the end of the guard, it will soon dry.'

As she did so, Emma explained, 'We were friends at school, Lizzie and I.'

'Youer the girl who went to live in her uncle's shop in Duke Street?'

'Yes. Lizzie came to tea once.'

'She talked about that for a long time. I remember how good to us someone called Martha was.'

The noise had started up again: spoons dipping into porridge already growing cold, the baby in the shabby wooden high chair yelling its disgust at being kept waiting. Emma blinked back the hot tears Martha's name had evoked. For a moment she saw the shining kitchen with bread and cakes cooling on the table and heard Martha's apron crackling with starch as she worked. An arm came gently about her shoulders and the children stopped eating again to stare at the tears she couldn't prevent from falling.

'What's troubling you, love?'

'It's nothing. There was a misunderstanding and I had to leave home.'

'You looking for work?'

Emma nodded. 'I thought perhaps Lizzie might know—'

'In service, do you mean?' Mrs Ball shook her head. 'Not at youer age, love. Likes them straight from school they do. You were working in youer uncle's shop. Why don't you try one of those? There's one in Clifton Street where they live in.'

A knock on the door saved Emma having to answer. A few minutes later a plump, middle-aged woman was following Lizzie's mother into the kitchen.

'This is a friend of Lizzie's, Blod,' Mrs Ball introduced them. 'Ah! That kettle's boiling at last. I'll make us a fresh pot of tea.'

The children, three boys, two girls and one in petticoats who could have been either, had got down from the table and were pushing each other around, their eyes on Emma. She was relieved when their mother cried, 'Scoot, you lot! You better put youer coats on and play in the front room.'

As they trooped noisily along the passage Emma took a hot cup of tea in her hands and sipped gratefully. It was strong, almost black, and sweet, but at that moment it tasted like nectar. Very soon she was enjoying a second cup and a thick wedge of toast spread thinly with margarine.

'This young lady's lookin' for a job, Blod,' Lizzie's mam told her friend. 'Somewhere where she can board. She thinks ouer Lizzie might know of something.'

'You been in service before?' Blodwen asked.

'No. Mrs Ball was just telling me I'd need experience.'

'I think you will, love. The place where my sister works as a char wants someone to help in the nursery, but I expect they want someone who's just left school or 'as experience.'

'Could I try for it, do you think?'

'Well, you could try. There wouldn't be no 'arm done, would there?'

''ave another round of toast and a warm by the fire first,' Mrs Ball said kindly.

Emma looked at the loaf already down to its heel and shook her head.

'I'd better go while there's a chance.'

Taking her steaming coat from the guard, she put it on, glad that for the first time today she felt warm inside.

'Thank you, Mrs Ball,' she said gratefully. 'Thanks for everything. And thank you, Mrs . . .'

'I'm Blod to everyone.'

'Well, thank you, Blodwen. It's worth a try anyway.'

'I'll just copy the address for you,' Lizzie's mother told her, taking a stub of pencil from a drawer. When she'd scribbled it on to a scrap of paper, together with Lizzie's place of employment, Emma picked up her holdall and made for the door.

'You come back 'ere if you don't get any luck,' Mrs Ball said. 'You can make do on the couch just for tonight.'

When the door closed, filled now with apprehension, Emma

picked her way up the street. What a fool she'd been to leave home without first finding a job and somewhere to live, and on such a day as this! Thankfully it had stopped snowing but an icy wind tugged at her scarf and tam.

It was a genuine desire not to cause any more trouble that had made her decide to leave. Oh, why had she been foolish enough to throw her arms about her uncle in gratitude at being made head of the haberdashery counter? It had been that and the whisky he'd drunk celebrating the New Year that had started him off. If only Aunt Clara hadn't witnessed it all everything might have blown over. As it was she had to prove that his unfortunate declaration of love for her had no echo in her own heart. She did love her uncle, of course she did, had loved him from the very first day – which was only natural seeing all he'd done for her. Despite the cold Emma's cheeks grew hot as she remembered the strange emotions that had stirred in her just before she'd pushed him away.

The house where she hoped to find work was right at the beginning of Queen Street. If she was lucky enough to get the job would she be likely to bump into Martha and be taken back home? But Martha always shopped at the market or around The Hayes area, and Emma herself wasn't likely to have much time to wander around town.

When she stepped down from the tram and gazed up at the tall narrow grey stone houses the feeling of apprehension increased. What did she know about service of any kind, let alone looking after children? Her only experience of them was minding David or poor Ellie.

Her knock on the side door was answered by a flustered little maid who told her to wait while she asked Mrs Wren. A few minutes later Emma was being shown into the hall of the servants' quarters while the mistress was contacted. Ten minutes later the maid was back to lead her along a passage and through swing doors and so to the front hall.

'Mistress says to put you in the morning room,' she told Emma, opening a door on the right. Leaving her holdall outside, she stepped into the room and the door closed behind her. It was a long room and comfortably furnished with heavy plum-coloured drapes at the windows and a high ornate ceiling. Clasping and unclasping her hands in her anxiety, Emma stared longingly at the glowing fire.

When the door opened a tall middle-aged lady came into the room.

'Come and sit down, my dear, over here by the fire. If it's the nurse-maid's position you've come about I can tell you now that I would prefer to engage someone with experience. But tell me, how did you hear about it? The advert was only taken into the newspaper offices this morning.'

'A lady who works for you in the mornings told her sister.' Emma didn't know Blodwen's second name, but it seemed that it didn't really matter. She was rapidly losing any hope of getting the job.

'Perhaps then you have some experience?' The grey eyes surveyed her kindly.

'I haven't any, I'm sorry,' Emma admitted, rising to go.

'Sit down a minute. What sort of work are you used to then?'

'I was a drapery assistant.'

'Why did you leave?'

Stumblingly Emma explained that she'd worked in her uncle's store, there'd been a misunderstanding and she'd felt she must leave.

'Was it to do with your work?'

'No. In fact I was to have been made head of my counter. My uncle was very kind and generous. The misunderstanding was something personal that made it impossible to accept his charity any longer.'

'And you can assure me this had nothing to do with your work?'

'Nothing at all. We haven't even quarrelled.'

'Are you fond of children?'

'Yes. I have a little cousin, I loved looking after him.'

Mrs Bishop was remembering the girl she'd interviewed not half-an-hour since. She'd been the right age and had seemed willing enough but she'd barely stopped scratching her head. Her hair had been matted and badly in need of a wash; in fact all of her had been in need of a wash for there'd been a sour smell to her clothes. She'd have needed delousing and her own clothes burnt before she could be allowed near the children, but then she'd probably have gone home on her half-day and got infested all over again. This girl looked very clean; her pale hair shone with cleanliness. Although her clothes were wet, she'd removed her coat and it was hanging in the hall. Mrs Bishop couldn't help noticing the quality of it, and of the skirt and cardigan the girl wore. She was desperate for someone to help Nanny Morgan. Doctor Henderson had told her only this morning that Nanny's heart was tired, and looking after the new baby as well as the other two was too much for her. She could train this girl to do the hard work and take it easy herself. Turning to Emma, she said, 'You can furnish references, of course?'

Emma's heart sank and she shook her head, saying, 'I don't want to tell them where I am. My uncle might come and insist I go home.'

Mrs Bishop's kindly grey eyes wore a worried expression.

'It's highly unusual to take on anyone without references,' she said. 'But I'm inclined to believe you and I'm willing to give you a trial. For a month, shall we say? When can you begin?'

'I have my bag with me now,' Emma told her, giving a sigh of relief.

'I want you to help Nanny all you can, especially with the tiring jobs. She hasn't been well, Doctor says she must rest. We have a daughter a year or so older than you and a boy of fourteen who's away at school. There are three in the nursery now. The two older children are missing their exercise and getting to be a handful. Gwladys will show you up, and I'll be coming up to see Nanny in about five minutes.'

Mrs Bishop tugged on a braided bell-pull at the side of the wide hearth and a few minutes later the little maid bobbed a curtsy as she came into the room.

Chapter Fifteen

As Emma followed the maid through the baize doors and up a flight of stairs Gwladys chattered non-stop. The springy curls had escaped the confines of her lace-trimmed mob-cap which was now awry, her round cheeks were bright with colour, and although the cotton dress and starched bib apron were several sizes too large, she was a cheering sight and balm to Emma's anxious fears.

'Nice the mistress is,' she was saying now. 'Mrs Wren, that's Cook, keeps you at it all the time. She ain't really a Mrs. It's just 'cos she's Cook, you see, she 'aven't got a ring. Rushed off my feet I am sometimes, but Mam says I got to count my blessings.'

By this time they were at the nursery door. First tapping loudly then flinging it wide, Gwladys cried, 'Brought you the new nursery-maid I 'ave, Nanny Morgan,' and scuttled away, leaving Emma still outside the door.

'Come in! Come in, girl,' Nanny called a little testily. 'That child will never learn to show people in and introduce them properly.'

Emma quietly closed the door behind her and stepped into the room, her eyes taking in the two well-upholstered armchairs on either side of the fire. Nanny, a stout lady in her fifties, Emma guessed, reclined in one, greying hair drawn tightly back into a bun, face pale and drawn, but it was a pleasant face despite the pallor. Emma's eyes had travelled as far as the oblong deal table on which brightly coloured building blocks were scattered and a small rag doll stared ceilingwards, when Nanny said, 'Come and sit down, girl, and I'll explain youer duties. But perhaps the mistress has already done so?'

Emma slipped into the armchair, thankful for the warmth from the fire, saying, 'Mrs Bishop did tell me a little. She's coming up to discuss it with you.'

'One good thing,' Nanny told her, 'at youer age you'll have had some experience and that's what I need right now.'

Licking dry lips, Emma nervously admitted she'd never worked as a nurse-maid before.

'Well, that's a pretty kettle of fish!' Nanny sounded aggrieved. 'How am I to rest and get well when I'll still have to do everything myself?'

'I can learn very quickly,' Emma assured her. 'I'll do all the heavy lifting, the baths and things.'

While they'd been talking she had been taking in the rest of the room. Against one wall was a long green leather couch piled high with chintz cushions, and a dresser filled with brightly patterned china stood between the two long windows. In the middle of the room was a large rocking horse with a silky brown mane.

Slightly mollified, Nanny was saying, 'I suppose it could be worse . . .' Her words were cut short by a tap on the door which opened immediately. Mrs Bishop came in.

'How are you feeling now, Nanny?' she asked. 'Did Cook send you the beef tea I ordered?'

'Yes, thank you, madam. Miss Vera took the children about

110

an hour ago. Amusing them in her room she is.'

Turning to Emma she said, 'You could fetch them back to the nursery now. Miss Vera's room is on the next landing down, to the right of the stairs.'

She wants to speak to the mistress alone, Emma thought with a sinking heart. Would Nanny tell her that she was unsatisfactory? If only they'd give her a chance, she'd soon prove how useful she could be.

But Mrs Bishop was turning to her, saying, 'Oh, Emma, they've found a uniform that will do you for now. Gwladys was to fetch it from the linen store. She will show you your room and you can change before you fetch Huw and Amy.'

When she opened the door Gwladys was coming up the stairs, a lavender cotton dress and starched bib apron over her arm.

'These are for you, miss, and I got to show you your room,' she told Emma importantly.

The room was in the attics, small and barely furnished with a sloping ceiling. There was a single bed covered by a white huckaback spread, a wicker armchair, a dark oak chest-of-drawers and a row of pegs to hang her things on the wall. Changing into the dress and apron, both of which were on the small side, Emma hung up her clothes and went downstairs.

She could hear the children laughing long before she reached the door and tapped on it.

'Come in!'

Pushing it open, Emma took in the scene. A young woman sat in an armchair drawn up to the roaring fire, an open book in one hand, a little girl with long fair hair curled up on her lap while a ginger-haired boy stood by her side, his arm about her shoulders.

'I've come for the children, Miss Vera.' She got no further

before there were loud protests from the boy and girl.

'Oh, no! I want to know if the prince married her, Vera,' the boy pleaded, while the little girl kissed her cheek, saying, 'Amy wants to hear the end.'

There being only two pages to go, Emma was invited to sit down and was glad to for she didn't want to start off on the wrong foot with her young charges. There was time now to study them. There was a pretty little girl in a blue velvet dress and broderie anglaise pinafore, her fair curls tied back with a blue ribbon, her brown eyes thoughtful as she listened to the tale. The boy was short and sturdy, his hair a flaming cap of curls, face lightly freckled. He was dressed in a navy blue sailor suit. And Vera herself, straight fair hair drawn back and twisted into a loose bun, looked to be about twenty. When she closed the book and turned to Emma, the grey eyes were friendly, cheeks dimpled into a smile, but the set of her jaw was strong.

'There you are then,' she said, lifting the girl from her lap. 'Now scoot, you two, and give me a bit of peace.' Turning to Emma again, she added laughingly, 'You're welcome to them.'

When Emma got back to the nursery with the children and had settled them to play at the table it was time to top and tail the baby and take her to the mistress's room to be fed.

'When you come back,' Nanny told her, 'you can take those two pails of nappies down to the washer-woman. She'll be here all day today.'

So on her return Emma carried the heavy buckets down several flights of stairs to the wash-house which was at the back of the house beyond the scullery and reached by going out into the yard.

She stepped gingerly into the snow, slushy here from the

warmth of the steam which billowed through the open door. Thankfully she set the buckets down and waited for the woman to turn around. She obviously hadn't heard Emma for, wreathed in steam, she continued to bend over the tub, soaping and rubbing clothes on the wash-board. When Emma tapped the door she turned a damp red face framed by damp grey hair towards her, saying, 'Oh God! Another bleedin' lot I gorrw do. 'Ow am I goin' to dry 'em all in this weather?'

Back in the nursery it was time for lunch and Nanny wanted the table cleared and laid. As Emma began to collect the bricks there was a shriek of rage from Huw who sent the pile he'd been building flying with the back of his hand.

'Shame on you, Master Huw,' Nanny said sternly. 'We'll have to learn to curb that temper before we're much older won't we?' Turning to Emma, she whispered, 'A chip off the old block if ever I saw one. The spitting image of the master he is, temper an' all.'

It seemed no time at all before the baby had to be topped and tailed again and put into yet another clean daygown before being taken to its mother to be fed. Each time Emma had changed little May, Nanny had fussed around her.

'Support her like this,' she said now, taking the child and demonstrating how she wanted it done, then again when Emma was dressing the child, 'Never pull the baby's arm through the sleeve. Always pull on the sleeve, see!'

When she got back to the nursery, after leaving little May with Mrs Bishop, Nanny said, 'Might as well take the rest of that washing downstairs,' and Emma's heart sank at the thought of the extra burden she'd be putting on the poor washer-woman. She wished she knew the woman's name so that she could call her by it. It would seem a lot more friendly.

113

Passing through the servants' hall, she met Gwladys about to climb the stairs.

''Er name's Flo,' Gwladys told her. 'Works awful 'ard she does. Washes for another 'ouse as well.'

This time when Emma dumped the buckets on the flag-stoned floor and tapped on the open door, she said as the woman turned around, 'Sorry, Flo, but Nanny thought they ought to be brought down.'

'She ought to 'ave to blooming well wash them!' Flo grumbled, attempting to push back a strand of damp grey hair that was stuck to her glistening face. ''Tain't natural changing a kid so often. Look at this gown. Only 'as a bit of dribble on it, and them back flannels is 'ell to get dry.'

Emma noticed now the clothes rack drawn up towards the ceiling filled with drying clothes. Looking into the tired eyes Emma wished she could have stayed to help, but Flo had already turned back to her tub.

'Fancy a cup of tea?' Nanny asked when she got back to the nursery. 'The tea-cups and things are on the dresser and the milk's in the pantry. You could get the children a glass of milk and a biscuit, it's a while till tea.'

When she'd brought in the tray Emma wished she could have offered a cup to Flo. She probably had a family of her own to look after when she got home, poor soul.

It was nice sitting by the fire with a cup in one hand and a biscuit in the other, but her rest had to be cut short for soon it was time to fetch May.

It grew dark quite early, and although it hadn't snowed since morning, the garden was a white wilderness, the bare branches of the trees bowed low with snow as Emma drew the curtains shutting out the wintry scene. The nursery was warm and cosy now in the mellow gas-light. May lay in the wicker bassinet kicking her legs as far as she could in all those cumbersome gowns, and the children lay on their stomachs on the hearth-rug in front of the guard, turning the pages of their picture books. Nanny had closed her eyes and, head back on the cushions, was snoring gently. Soon it would be time for nursery tea, then to prepare the baby's bath and take her to her mother once more. Nanny had told Emma they had their main meal later on when the children were tucked up in bed.

When nursery tea was over it was time to bring in the baby's bath and put it on its stand. Nanny had already hung the tiny garments over the guard to keep warm but she'd closed her eyes again and Emma looked apprehensively towards the clothes: a little woollen vest, napkins, a back flannel, another flannel garment Nanny had called a pilch, a flannel gown, a cotton gown, and a little jacket, thinking that if only she'd been brought up in a family of children she'd have mastered the art of putting napkins on by now. She was relieved to see Nanny open her eyes and tell her to hurry with the water and not forget to test it first.

Soon it was time to bathe the children in front of the fire – a much more boisterous affair. When Amy and Huw were tucked into bed, she and Nanny sat either side of the fire and she found herself longing for the moment when she could escape up to her own little room. All day she'd been troubled by the unhappiness she'd caused her aunt and uncle and Martha. Aunt Clara must think her very ungrateful, and as for Martha . . . remembering how kind and patient she'd always been Emma's eyes swam with tears, but Nanny was speaking to her, words bringing dismay.

'Go and bring your nightgown down ready,' she told Emma.

'Our supper will be brought up soon then I'm off to my bed. There's books in the cupboard if you want to stay up a while and read.'

'But my room is upstairs,' Emma began.

'Of course it is, girl, and you need a room to keep your bits and pieces and for your time off, but someone has to stay with the children and just now I need my rest. There's a bed behind the curtain in the children's room and you'd better take my alarm clock so you'll wake for baby's feeds. But don't let it ring, it makes an awful din.'

After supper, the fire banked down, Emma took her night things, lit a candle and crept into the room where the three children slept. Lying in the darkness listening to their even breathing, she knew nothing more until she was awakened suddenly, but it wasn't the clanging of the alarm that tore her from her exhausted sleep but baby May, her crying ever louder. Emma sprang from the bed and, barefoot despite the chilly oilcloth, rushed to the cot to lift a very wet baby before the other children were disturbed.

Chapter Sixteen

Just after ten o'clock that morning Gwladys tapped on the nursery door, saying, 'I've got a note 'ere for you, miss.' When Emma saw her name written in Martha's familiar loops and curls her heart beat fast and she tore the envelope open with eager fingers, wondering how Martha had known where to send it. Nanny was in the children's bedroom seeing to baby May so Emma unfolded the note immediately and read:

Dear Emma,

    Lizzie's mother said she could get this letter to you but wouldn't give me your address. She assures me you are safe and well and that you've managed to find a job.

    We've been so worried about you, and your uncle tramped the streets all day yesterday looking for you despite the weather. He's told your aunt he's very sorry for whatever happened and I know poor Clara is worrying about you.

    When you get some time off, could you meet me somewhere? Perhaps then I can persuade her that you are all right. We'd love you to come home, but whatever happens let us keep in touch.

With love,
Martha

Her eyes misted with tears, Emma folded the letter and put it into her apron pocket. Dear Martha, how she'd love to see her, but there'd been no mention as yet of her having time off, and with Nanny Morgan still not well enough to cope on her own it would be difficult to arrange. One thing she was determined about: much as she'd like to she wouldn't go back, for even though she hadn't been to blame, her being there had caused trouble for Aunt Clara who had shown her nothing but kindness.

'Take the baby, Emma, and change her while I put the kettle over the coals ready for a cup of tea,' said Nanny, putting May into her arms.

That evening, begging paper and pencil from Nanny, Emma wrote to Martha without giving her address, and told her she'd love to meet her and would let her know as soon as she had time off. But it was over a week before the opportunity arose.

Vera sent a message that she wanted to take her little brother and sister visiting the next day and would Nanny see that they were ready by two o'clock? It was Nanny Morgan herself who suggested that this would be an ideal opportunity for Emma to take some time off.

'May is sure to sleep after her feed,' she told Emma. 'Besides, I'm feeling much better, thanks to you being here.'

'I would like to meet a friend,' Emma admitted. 'If I wrote now she'd get it first post.' Then she realised that she still had neither writing paper, envelope nor stamp, but Nanny was already taking them from a drawer, saying, 'This will tide you over. You'll have a chance to get some while youer out.'

The letter was written and posted before lunch and Emma felt sure Martha would receive it in time.

The next day, dressed in her dark blue coat and wearing the

navy blue velour hat with its brim turned up at the back that Mrs Bishop had given her ready for when she took the children out, she set off for the arcade at the bottom of The Hayes and the tea-shop where she'd arranged for them to meet.

As she opened the door and the bell tinkled she saw Martha at a table in the corner and hurried over, but Martha was already on her feet, arms outstretched towards her, crying, 'Emma. Oh, Emma! How I've missed you, girl.'

'I've missed you too, Martha. Oh! It's lovely to see you. Shall we order now then we can talk? How is Aunt Clara? And – and Uncle Lionel? Oh, I'm sorry to have been the cause of all this trouble, honestly I am.'

'Well, by youer uncle's own admission, you weren't to blame in any way. It was just you looking so bonny and him having a drop too much, but according to him you soon put him in his place.'

Emma was thankful that he thought that, it would at least make it easier if they were to meet again, but would Aunt Clara agree with him? The memory of that night still made her blush.

'Are you happy, Emma?' Martha's words brought her mind back to the present. Emma was very glad she couldn't read her thoughts.

'Yes, I'm helping to look after three little children. They've got a nanny but she isn't very well.' There seemed no harm in telling Martha what she was doing.

'You've never had any experience in that line, cariad. Still you must be coping. And youer looking very well.'

'Is Aunt Clara over her chill? I felt awful leaving like that, Martha, but I heard them quarrelling and it was over me. I just wanted them to make up and be happy again.'

'Youer uncle, bless him, could never take his drink. Always

goes to his head it does. Sorry he was afterwards, I can tell you.'

'I felt awful about Miss Coles too. I hope I didn't spoil her chance of going to the Mantle Department?'

'Youer uncle is a very fair man, Emma,' Martha broke in, 'and he always keeps his promises. Upset as he was he transferred two girls to Haberdashery, one to be trained as second sales, the other to learn to manage the counter.'

As Martha's words reminded Emma of all she'd sacrificed by leaving home, disappointment welled afresh, but it was too late now. She glanced anxiously at the long-cased clock on the wall. She must return before the children got back. Martha looked so upset when she said she'd have to leave that Emma threw caution to the winds and told her where she was working, adding, 'Keep it to yourself for now, Martha, but at least you'll know where I am if I'm ever needed.'

'Youer needed now, Emma. Come back with me, love. It'll be as though you never left.'

But Emma knew that it wouldn't. She was terrified of facing her aunt after what happened, and the staff must be curious and wondering why she'd left her job so suddenly, and they'd expect an explanation if she was to work with them again.

She got back to the house before the children returned, offering Nanny the stamps, paper and envelopes she'd provided her with, but Nanny Morgan shook her head, pushing them back towards Emma as they sat at the table enjoying a cup of tea.

'You keep them, cariad,' she said. 'You'll be needing them more than me. Did you meet youer friend?'

There was the sound of footsteps running up the stairs and children's voices high with excitement, then the door burst open and Huw ran into the room. Nanny warned, 'They're going to take some calming down tonight.'

Martha left the tea-rooms feeling happier than she had for some time. She'd loved Emma from the moment Clara had brought her home, a pale, skinny eleven year old with big soulful brown eyes. The lovely young girl she'd met today bore little resemblance to that puny-looking child but Martha knew that she was still as sensitive and vulnerable to being hurt. Still, thankfully she seemed to have been very lucky in the employment she'd found, but it could have been so different, for good employers were few and far between.

When she told Clara she'd had tea with Emma, making it sound as though their meeting had been casual, Clara said, 'Well, that's a relief, to know she's all right. We can stop worrying now, Martha, and so long as she's happy it's probably all for the best.' Then, giving a dubious little smile, she added, 'I'd have watched her like a hawk if she'd stayed here. But we must keep in touch. You do have her address?'

Martha didn't answer. She was feeling a little guilty about assuring Emma everyone wanted her home. It was obvious now that Clara still felt her niece was a threat to her happiness, but seeing how attentive Lionel had become since that awful night, Martha was sure Clara had nothing to worry about.

The following afternoon Emma had just put May into the bassinet and had settled the children with picture books at the table when there was a rap on the door, and when Emma opened it Gwladys beamed at her, saying, 'Someone to see you in the kitchen there is, miss. Cook said to ask 'er in an' she's offered 'er a cup of tea.'

Surely Martha hasn't broken her promise? Emma wondered uneasily. But if it wasn't Aunt Clara then who could it be?

With Nanny's permission, her heart beating fast, she followed Gwladys down the stairs. When she opened the kitchen door and saw a neatly dressed young woman she was puzzled, but only for a moment. Then she was rushing towards her with open arms, crying, 'Lizzie! Oh, Lizzie! There's lovely to see you.'

'And you, Emma love, though I'd hardly have recognised you. I know youer working, and anyway I can't stay, but I just had to see you. Just left my mam's I have, and on my way to meet Arthur. Engaged we are.' And she held out her left hand for Emma to see the ring with its five small diamonds in a gypsy setting.

'Congratulations! When will you get married?'

'When we can find somewhere to live. There's no room for us with my mam.'

'Why don't you two talk in the hall?' Cook suggested. 'That's if Nanny Morgan can spare you any longer.'

Knowing that Cook wanted them from under her feet, though she appreciated her giving Lizzie a cup of tea, Emma drew her friend through the door and along the corridor but Lizzie was already pulling on her gloves, saying, 'I've promised to meet Arthur at four o'clock in St Mary Street. We're going to have tea then on to the Empire. We can't afford to go every week now we're saving up.'

'You look very nice, Lizzie. I like your coat and hat.'

'The mistress is very good to me, gives me things for my mam to cut down for the kids. Mam's friend made the coat to fit me and altered the hat. Originally it was covered in silk roses but she took them off and put on a plain petersham band.'

Lizzie was no longer skinny: she'd grown tall and had a good figure, and a confidence about her that she'd never had as a child. As she moved towards the door Emma said, 'Perhaps we could meet sometime? Only I don't have a regular half-day as yet.'

But Lizzie told her, 'I always go to Mam's and then on to meet Arthur. It's the only time we can see each other except for church on a Sunday.'

When Lizzie had gone, worried at being away so long Emma took the stairs two at a time. She was relieved to find the nursery quiet and Nanny Morgan sitting with her eyes closed. That was until Emma had sat down too, when she opened them, saying, 'Miss Vera's taken the children, bought them a new story book she has and wants to read it to them. She says can you fetch them in time for nursery tea?'

This time when Emma entered Miss Vera's room the children were still absorbed in the tale so Emma too sat down and listened while she looked about her. It was a very feminine room with a rose-coloured satin spread covering the bed and deep rose tinted oil-lamps set on matching tables to either side, their glow bathing everything about them in warm colour. There was a bookcase and a small sloping desk with drawers in the side in the same dark wood as the little tables, and bed-head and foot were of brass, reflecting the dancing flames of the fire. The armchair she sat in and the one occupied by Vera and the children were the only other pieces of furniture. The Turkish-patterned carpet, its colours a little faded, was covered in front of the fire by a cream bearskin rug.

Now, as Vera's musical voice conjured up images for the children, Emma's thoughts turned to Lizzie's engagement. They were near enough the same age but already Lizzie was planning her marriage while Emma herself had never had a serious young man. In fact, the only ones she'd met since leaving school had worked at the shop, and although Artie had accompanied her whenever the four of them had gone to the music hall, and they'd often held hands, he'd always seemed to hold back, probably conscious of her relationship to his employer.

Anyway Emma had never felt anything but friendship for him; he'd been a good sort and fun to be with. She'd never known any other feelings until Uncle Lionel had kissed her that night. She wasn't likely to meet any young men here either, confined as she was to the house for most of the time.

Suddenly she became aware that Vera was speaking to her while her own thoughts were far away.

'Sorry, Miss Vera,' she mumbled. 'I didn't hear.'

'I was only telling you the children are ready to leave.'

She got up and took Amy's hand while Vera was saying, 'Emma, do you know anything about the suffragette movement?'

The question took her by surprise but she answered, 'Yes, I've read about it in the newspapers. They're trying to get women the vote.'

'That's right. I was wondering . . .' Then Vera seemed to change her mind for she went on, 'Tell Nanny I'll be taking the children visiting again next week, but the week after that my friend will be visiting me and bringing her two little brothers. They'll be sharing nursery tea.'

As she walked along the corridor with a child on either side Emma wondered what Miss Vera had been about to say. She'd mentioned the suffragettes and there'd been a lot about them in the newspapers. The cause they supported was a good one but they had stirred up a lot of trouble. Just before Christmas some of them had daubed the window of a shop near them with the slogan 'Votes for Women', and landed up in prison. Why had Miss Vera asked if she knew anything about them? Surely she didn't think that Emma was involved with them?

I wouldn't be brave enough, she told herself, I'd be afraid to get into trouble even for a good cause. I'm no more fitted to become a suffragette than Miss Vera herself.

Chapter Seventeen

With the lengthening days of spring Emma began taking the children to the park or for walks, with Huw and Amy on either side of the bouncy pram holding on to its handle. Huw, easily bored, was inclined to sulk, but little Amy, who seemed to have inherited her mother's sunny nature, chatted happily to Emma or baby May.

On a warm afternoon towards the end of June they were just leaving the park when, distantly at first, they heard the tramp of marching feet. Huw, glad of anything that broke the monotony, stopped and turned round. Herself a little curious, Emma turned the pram, amazed that the colourful procession coming towards them were all women, and well-dressed women at that, wearing pretty summer gowns, many with their eyes shaded by the brims of straw hats. Each seemed to have a large identical poster slung about her neck with the slogan 'VOTES FOR WOMEN' printed on it in large black capitals.

So these were the suffragettes Miss Vera had spoken about. Emma watched with interest as the marchers drew near, seeing that some were also carrying aloft colourful banners in shades of purple, white and green. These had the letters WSPU embroidered on them, and below 'WOMEN'S SOCIAL AND POLITICAL UNION', with underneath this again 'CARDIFF

AND DISTRICT WOMEN'S SUFFRAGE'.

A lady was approaching Emma holding a magazine towards her.

'Oh! No, thank you.' She shook her head. When Emma was able to give the marchers her full attention again she saw that one of them was holding aloft a circular banner in colours of purple, white and green on which was superimposed an angel, at least it looked like an angel, blowing a trumpet and carrying a banner with the word 'FREEDOM' on it.

The young lady turned her head towards Emma's side of the road, and, hardly able to believe her eyes, she found herself returning Vera's startled stare. Thankful that neither Huw nor Amy had seen their sister, Emma licked dry lips and tried to gather her thoughts, hardly noticing that the marchers were fast disappearing into the distance.

Turning the pram once more towards home she was dismayed to find that May was fast asleep, plump cheeks pink from all the fresh air, ginger-gold curls escaping the confines of her bonnet. Nanny Morgan wasn't going to be very pleased for the baby had already had her afternoon nap and would now be wide awake at bedtime.

Emma was wondering if what she'd seen had anything to do with Miss Vera now staying with her friend overnight and so not taking the children with her when she visited? Poor Huw had so looked forward to those visits to the two little boys. Emma had come to feel sorry for him and tried to understand his naughtiness and frustration, knowing that if he'd been brought up in the streets she'd lived in as a child he'd have played ball games in the middle of the road, made hair raising journeys on bogeys made from old pram wheels and a plank of wood, and rolled marbles in the gutter. As it was he was expected to keep his smart knickerbocker suit clean, and to play quietly. It was so much easier for Amy to be good. She had a favourite rag doll from whom she was rarely parted. Nanny Morgan sat for hours making little garments while Amy waited impatiently for the moment when she could try them on her precious dolly. Soon Nanny would teach her to knit and sew, then she would make her own doll's clothes.

Thinking about dolls, Emma found herself wondering if Esmeralda still sat in the basket chair in the little bedroom above the shop in Duke Street. She must remember to ask Martha for one day she might have a little girl of her own. It didn't seem very likely though for how was she to meet someone, fall in love and get married, when the only places she went were the park with the children and an occasional meeting with Martha for tea and crumpets at the tea-rooms in the arcade?

I'd like to meet Aunt Mattie and Aunt Mabel again, she thought, and there was really no reason why not, though leaving the shop so suddenly was going to take some explaining. She was remembering Ellie on the day she'd gone to live with Aunt Mabel and the way she'd clung to Esmeralda. Soon Ellie would be twenty; it was sad that in her mind she would always be a child. She had grown very fat and would sit in a chair rocking a rag doll just as though she really was only eight years old. Poor Ellie. Poor Aunt Mabel.

When the children were in bed, Emma settled down with some darning while Nanny opened her knitting bag and began to turn the heel of a sock. She put it down to say, 'The mistress told me today that Master Huw is going to have a tutor, and not before time either. Needs some discipline that boy does.'

'Oh, I'm glad.' Emma moved her sewing a little nearer the

lamp. 'Huw will be a different boy with something interesting to do.'

Nanny Morgan had been part of the household ever since Miss Vera was born and in Nanny's eyes the girl could do no wrong. Emma wondered what she'd say if she knew her favourite was an active suffragette? She wondered too what the children's nurse had done during the long gap between looking after Master Eddie, the boy who was away at school, and young Huw? Nanny's eyes grew sad and tears glistened on her lashes when Emma asked the question.

'There was a little girl called Phyllis in between.' Nanny wiped her eyes with the hem of her calico apron. 'A little angel she was, with all she had to suffer. She was a delicate child from birth, bless her, and spent her life in an invalid carriage. Passed away just after Master Huw was born she did.'

To save Nanny further distress Emma changed the subject, asking, 'When will the tutor be starting?'

'The spare room next door has to be got ready. The young man will only teach Huw in the mornings to begin with. They'll have to put in a blackboard and easel and a desk – but they're going to distemper the walls first.'

There was a tap on the door and Vera put her head around to ask, 'Can I borrow Emma for half-an-hour, Nanny? I'd like her to help me sort out my wardrobe.'

She wants to talk to me about this afternoon, Emma thought. Wants to make sure I don't tell anyone I saw her.

Vera chatted about the children until they reached her room. There were two pretty dresses draped over the back of a chair but the wardrobe doors were closed and she made no move to open them. Instead she turned to Emma, her eyes pleading, saying anxiously, 'You haven't told Nanny you saw me today, have you, Emma?' Then as Emma shook her head, 'You won't mention it to anyone, will you? If Father found out, I'd be in real trouble.'

'I won't tell anyone, Miss Vera, it isn't my business.'

'If you believe in something you've got to take risks for it.' Vera's voice was more confident now. 'The women in the WSPU are wonderful people. Look, I've got some posters here from our offices in Windsor Place but I daren't put them up.'

Emma looked down at the topmost poster. The caption was written in large capitals:

THE RIGHT DISHONOURABLE DOUBLE FACE ASQUITH

then underneath a scene she didn't understand, the words

VOTES FOR WOMEN

She could see Emmeline Pankhurst's name at the bottom together with another Emmeline whose surname she didn't recognise from the newspapers.

Vera took the posters over to a drawer and hid them between some linen, saying, 'It's a shame because they won't do any good here. I'd like to do a lot more for the cause, but living with Mother and Father it's impossible to have a life of my own.'

Emma searched her mind for something to say, but picking up the dresses and holding them out to Emma, Vera went on: 'I was wondering if you'd like to have these? Perhaps you know someone who could alter them to fit?'

Emma didn't need the dresses. The wardrobe in the little room upstairs in the attics was bulging with clothes for every time she and Martha met now her friend would bring some of the things she'd left behind. At first she'd refused but Martha had told her it was only common sense for they wouldn't fit anyone else. But Miss Vera looked so pleased as she pressed the frocks on Emma there was nothing to do but murmur her thanks and settle them over her arm.

Turning to leave, she'd almost reached the door when Vera called her name. She turned to see the girl's face redden with embarrassment as she said, 'There's a favour I want to ask of you, Emma.'

'Anything I can do, miss.'

'Could I rely on you to come downstairs and let me in by the side door if I go out on an assignment?'

Emma's heart sank. Had the dresses been a sort of bribe? And by 'assignment' did she mean daubing buildings with the words VOTES FOR WOMEN, or even perhaps tying herself to some railings? But how could she refuse with the beautiful dresses she'd been given lying heavily on her arm?

'Oh, Miss Vera,' she couldn't help saying. 'You'll be taking an awful risk.'

'That's what's exciting about it,' Vera replied. 'It's a great injustice that women haven't any say. But will you do that for me, Emma? You've only to unlock the side door.'

When she got back to the nursery, Nanny said, 'Always was generous, our Miss Vera. I can't see you wearing them though, Emma. The only time you go out is to take the children to the park or meet your friend for tea.'

Work went ahead on the schoolroom. The walls were distempered and the smell of the paint pervaded the nursery floor for days. Then a deal table and chair and the blackboard, easel and school desk were brought in, after Gwladys had scattered damp tea-leaves on the faded Turkish carpet and brushed them up with a stiff brush. Huw was looking forward impatiently to his lessons. He was already a fluent reader, thanks to Vera. Now he sat importantly at the desk, trying it for size, and begged to write something on the blackboard with the squeaky chalk.

It was on the Friday morning that Vera waylaid her when Emma was taking the washing down to Flo. Drawing her to a secluded corner of the landing, she whispered, 'Will you let me in tomorrow night? It will be somewhere around twelve to one o'clock. I'll loan you my alarm clock to wake you up.'

'But I sleep with the children. The noise would disturb them.'

'Put the clock underneath the bedclothes, that will muffle the sound. I'll bring it down to you later when Nanny's gone to bed.'

Disturbed by the conversation, Emma went on her way. In the wash-house Flo was bending over the tub, wreathed in steam, rubbing something on the board just as though she'd never moved since Emma's last visit. Turning a red, perspiring face towards her, Flo said, ''Ello, love.' Then seeing the large bundle of clothes and the heavy bucket that Emma had brought down, she straightened her aching back and pushed the damp hair from her forehead, crying, 'Not another bleedin' lot! 'Ave to get another sodden line they will at this rate 'cos both of them is full. Wouldn't be so fond of changing the kids' clothes, would they, if they 'ad to wash 'em themselves?'

Feeling guilty at adding to the washer-woman's load, Emma asked, 'Can I peg anything out for you, Flo?'

'No room, love, like I said. Got this line full an' all.' She pointed to the rack drawn up to the ceiling and barely visible through the steam.

As soon as Emma left the wash-house her thoughts turned worriedly to Saturday night and her promise to Miss Vera. She was lucky to have a warm dressing gown; it had been a present from her aunt and uncle and Martha had brought it to the tea-rooms the second time they'd met there. But how could she leave the children alone all that time? Supposing May began to cry or one of the other two woke with a pain?

When, waiting until Nanny had gone to bed, Vera brought the alarm clock, Emma confided her worry.

'Make it dead on one o'clock then. I'll just have to hang around if I'm back before,' she replied. 'Or how about if I hoot like an owl under the nursery window if I get back earlier?'

'Be careful, miss,' Emma found herself saying. But, eyes shining, Vera replied with a laugh, 'Do you know? I'm more afraid of Father finding out than I am about tomorrow night. And just think, Emma, you'll be doing this for the cause.'

All next day her thoughts were on the night ahead. She took the children for their walk, prepared nursery tea, bathed them and tucked them into bed, but all the time her heart was filled with dread. There was only a flimsy curtain between her bed and the children's and she'd no idea how loud even a muffled alarm could be, and then a creaking stair or a squeaking door could disturb Cook or Gwladys. What possible excuse could Emma give them for being downstairs?

The summer evening had turned chilly and a stiff breeze rustled the leaves of the oak trees just yards from the bedroom window. Emma drew the curtain back and looked out, watching the branches dip and sway in the moonlight like crazy ballet dancers. Before getting into bed she set the alarm and tucked the clock well down under the bedclothes. Shivering at the thought of her role in the night ahead, she undressed quickly and blew out her candle before creeping between the coarse linen sheets. Usually sleep came as soon as her head touched the pillow but tonight she lay taut, waiting for the moment when she'd hear and feel the vibrations of the alarm clock or the eerie night cry of an owl.

She must have dozed after all for she jumped up with a start, puzzling over what had woken her, but there it was again.

'Tu-whit-tu-whoo!'

And jumping out of bed, Emma dragged on her dressing gown. She lit the candle, pulled the door to quietly behind her. It wasn't until her feet touched the cold oil-cloth that covered the stairs that she realised she wasn't wearing her slippers, but it was too late to go back.

When she forgot and trod on the creaking stair her heart beat fast but she hurried on, her feet skimming over the stone tiles of the hall, only to be tortured by the prickles of the mat she had to stand on to pull back the heavy bolts with stiff fingers.

'Tu-whit-tu-whoo!' There it was once more. Why didn't Miss Vera shut up? She'd have the whole household awake at this rate. As Emma drew the heavy door back and the wind whistled about her feet she expected Vera to rush past her but there was no one in sight, and when after about a minute the cry of an owl came again, and from the direction of the trees, she knew with a sickening certainty that it was the real thing. What time was it? She hadn't thought to look. Cold and fed up, she closed and bolted the door, and taking the guttering candle she'd left on the stairs, tip-toed back upstairs. By now stiff with cold she got back into bed. Lifting the alarm clock from its nest, she peered at the dial. It still wanted ten minutes to eleven o'clock.

Next time it was the throbbing of the alarm that woke her from a troubled sleep. Tip-toeing to the window she watched for any movement from below but apart from the rustling of the leaves as the branches swayed this way and that there was none. May stirred in her cot but made no sound and Emma waited

135

anxiously for her to settle. Carefully avoiding the creaking stair she put the candle down and stood on the mat to stretch up and release the heavy bolt. Swinging the door back gently she peered out but Vera wasn't there yet. And as Emma closed the door once more the flame of the candle flared wildly and went out.

As the darkness closed in she gave a little sob of despair. She huddled against the wall near the door, shivering with fright, sure she could hear mice scuttling across the floor, longing with all her heart for Miss Vera's return and her own ordeal to be over. As the minutes passed and she lost track of time her fears grew. Where was Vera? Emma's ears strained for any sound.

Presently she heard running footsteps scuffling to a stop outside the door. As she opened it and Miss Vera rushed past there was a new sound, a shrill whistle that came again and again, growing ever louder as it neared the house.

'The door! Police . . .' Miss Vera cried breathlessly.

'The candle's gone out, miss,' Emma told her as she closed it.

'Matches in . . . table-drawer . . .'

As she struck one and the candle flared into life Emma saw that Miss Vera's clothes were torn and covered in mud, and as her eyes went to the girl's white face she saw she'd lost her hat and the pins had fallen from her hair which straggled damply about her face.

Chapter Eighteen

'Whatever's the matter with you this morning, Emma? Didn't you get any sleep last night?' Nanny watched as she stifled yet another yawn.

'I couldn't get off,' Emma told her, and it was true, for, after Miss Vera had closed the door, she'd regretted the promise she'd felt bound to make when that young lady had begged her to try to repair the skirt of her dress and take it and the petticoat down to the washer-woman, at the same time pressing a half sovereign into her hand for her to share with Flo.

How was she to repair it without Nanny seeing unless she did it in the bedroom by candlelight? And Flo too, if she agreed, would have to be equally discreet. Emma had brought the things with her last night and hidden them in the cupboard in the children's room. This morning she'd dashed in there every time May whimpered, terrified that Nanny would find the bundle and demand an explanation.

Tomorrow morning Huw was to start his lessons with his tutor Mr Thompson and already he was restless with excitement. It was a lovely sunny morning, a day for a boy to be running about in the fresh air, but when Emma had suggested that he play in the garden Nanny had said that it was Sunday, wasn't it? But even if it hadn't been it was too far down for them to keep an eye on him, and anyway Emma would be taking the children to the park after lunch.

Poor Huw, how he hated hanging on to the pram while other little boys ran past them with their hoops and crops.

That night Emma sat on the side of her bed and mended the muddy garments by the flickering light from the candle. Vera had given her the needle, thread and scissors from her sewing box. Even though she'd shaken the skirts out of the window little clods of dried earth were still falling on the coverlet. Emma wasn't happy about the job she'd made of repairing the dress but it was the best she could do. Tomorrow she'd have to wait for an opportunity to take them down to Flo.

Monday was the main wash day and when Emma saw the mounds of washing awaiting Flo's attention it made it all the harder to ask but she couldn't risk them hanging about in the nursery any longer.

'Flo, I've come to ask you a favour,' she said to the washer-woman's back.

'What's that, miss?' Flo turned to eye with suspicion the things hanging over Emma's arm.

'It's a dress and petticoat belonging to Miss Vera. She had a fall when she was out in the rain but she doesn't want her parents to know, so you won't say anything about it, will you?' Emma opened her palm to display the bright half sovereign, deciding to forgo her own share as Flo would have by far the hardest task.

Flo's eyes opened wide. Staring at the gold coin she asked, 'Is that all for me?'

Emma nodded, warning her again, 'But you'll have to keep quiet.'

'Let's 'ave a look at 'em then. Dresses don't usually come to me to be cleaned.'

'No, and it was lucky her coat was shorter and was all right with a brush.'

Turning the dress this way and that Flo said, 'It'll want a good shakin' first. No one comes out 'ere once the washing's all down until Gwladys brings me a cuppa about eleven.'

Relieved to be rid of the dress and petticoat Emma went back upstairs where Nanny waited impatiently to tell her, 'You have to take Master Huw into the schoolroom by nine o'clock.'

'I know. I got him all ready before I went down with the baby's washing.'

Huw was already at the door, opening it hopefully and peering into the corridor then closing it again in disappointment. When five minutes later she heard someone talking to Gwladys at the foot of the stairs, Emma quickly took his hand and went next-door.

A tall, good-looking young man with the bluest eyes she'd ever seen stood in the doorway for a moment then came across to where she stood by the window and introduced himself. 'I'm Daniel Thompson, the new tutor, and this must be Huw?' he said, smiling at the boy.

'Yes, sir,' Huw answered importantly. 'This is Emma.'

'Emma Meredith, nurse to the younger children,' she introduced herself.

The tutor's blue eyes were having a strange effect on Emma. Her heart beat fast and she seemed unable to lower her gaze, but Mr Thompson as she thought of him, was turning away, putting the books he'd brought on to the table. Forcing herself to move, Emma asked if he had everything he needed, and being assured he had, left the room.

As she stepped into the corridor she saw that Gwladys was at the nursery door but seeing Emma she came towards her, saying, 'I wanted to see you and Nanny Morgan, miss.' Her brown eyes were wide with importance as she went on, 'I got to tell someone. You know Flo what does the washing?' Emma's heart sank in anticipation of what she thought was to come, but she nodded and Gwladys continued, 'Well, I wouldn't 'ave believed it if I 'adn't seen it with my own eyes – stuffin' a frock in 'er bag she was. Looked like one of Miss Vera's it did, and I asks 'er outright: "She give you that, Flo?" 'cos I didn't think she 'ad.

'"No, she 'asn't given it to me, Gwladys," she says, brazen like, but she didn't give no explanation so I thought: "I'll tell Miss Emma and Nanny 'cos they'll know what to do." I could 'ave told Cook but there'd 'ave been 'ell to pay then.'

Thankful that Nanny Morgan hadn't come to the door, Emma guessed what had happened. Flo had probably decided that taking the garments home to do them would be safer than hanging them on the line here. But Gwladys was looking at her with a puzzled expression. Emma's reaction to her news had obviously not been what she'd expected. Emma thought quickly, realising that she had no alternative but to tell her part of the truth, so she said, 'I know about the dress, Gwladys, I took it down to Flo myself. Can you keep a secret?'

Eyes alight with interest, Gwladys nodded her head.

'Miss Vera fell in the mud and spoilt her dress. She didn't want the master and mistress to know, they don't approve of her going out on her own, so don't tell anyone what you saw. Anyone, mind. Flo's going to take the dress home, see what she can do with it. It'll be back with Miss Vera in a few days.'

The drama and excitement of the incident now well and truly over, Gwladys looked disappointed but said, 'Well, Flo's a dab hand at gettin' things clean. I won't tell no one, miss. No one at all. And to think I was sure Flo was walking off with that dress! You won't tell 'er, will you, miss?'

'She won't hear it from me, Gwladys, so long as you keep quiet too.'

'I won't breathe a word, miss, honest I won't,' she answered with conviction.

Sighing with relief Emma opened the nursery door to be greeted with: 'I recognised young Gwladys's voice. What was she on about?'

'Oh! She was telling me some tale about Flo and the washing. Better than the *Echo* that girl is at keeping you informed.'

'You're right there, Emma, but she'll have to calm down if she's to get on in service. Cook says she's like a blue-arsed fly, always flitting from one unfinished job to another. Says she often has to give her the length of her tongue.'

As the days passed Emma always tried to be in the corridor about the time of Mr Thompson's arrival. He would hardly stop long enough to discuss the weather but it kept Emma going until one o'clock when she would watch from the window for him to come around the side of the house and walk down the short path to the gate. He never looked up and she'd have felt embarrassed if he had, but something irresistible drew her there every working day at that time. Soon Huw would come running into the nursery carrying his books, and until well after lunch every sentence he uttered would begin, 'Mr Thompson says . . .'

The weather continued warm and bright and Emma dreaded meeting Miss Vera in the corridor or on the stairs in case she was planning to go out on another assignment and wanted Emma to let her in, with all the attendant risks of being found out. One day Huw was much more excited than usual when he came in to lunch. He could hardly wait to tell them, 'Mr Thompson has asked Mama if he can take me down to play ball games in the yard for the last half-hour before he goes home. We're going to start tomorrow.' Then, going over to Nanny Morgan, he asked, 'Do you know where the blue ball Aunt Phoebe gave me is now, Nanny? Remember Father took it away when I broke that vase?'

Nanny did know but was adamant that it would stay where it was until they were actually going down to the yard, and with this Huw had to be content. Now there was an added joy for Emma to look forward to for, under the pretext of watching Master Huw's prowess with the ball, she gazed down on Mr Thompson, shirt sleeves rolled up to show a glimpse of rippling muscle, running around lithely, his face flushed with effort. When at lunchtime the boy came in hungry and glowing with health, it was obvious that the new introduction to the curriculum was an unqualified success.

Emma hadn't seen Aunt Mattie or Aunt Mabel since before Christmas when she'd taken them their presents, and although she would dearly have liked to see them again, she kept putting it off because of all the explaining she'd have to do about why she was no longer living and working at the shop.

I'll just tell them we had a bit of a misunderstanding, she told herself, hoping they wouldn't ask what it had been about.

When her next half-day came it was warm and sunny, and as soon as she got off duty she went upstairs. Closing the curtains in the little attic bedroom that was hers but in which she'd never slept, she poured water from the flowery jug into the matching bowl and stripped to the waist before rubbing her flannel with the scented soap, rinsing herself quickly for the water was icy cold.

Choosing a dainty muslin dress that she'd brought with her, she combed her hair and tied it back with a fresh ribbon, put on her straw boater and took a clean hankie from the drawer. She went downstairs feeling a little apprehensive about visiting her aunts after all this time.

Aunt Mattie had for once finished her chores early, and after kissing Emma warmly on the cheek she put the kettle over the coals, glowing even on such a warm day, and set the cups and saucers on the table, saying, 'Tell me all about your new job, Emma? I never could understand why you left our Clara's. You'd fallen on your feet there.'

'I'm nurse-maid to three children and it's a very nice place,' she began, ignoring her aunt's question, but Aunt Mattie wasn't put off so easily.

'But why did you leave the shop?' she asked again. 'Last time I saw you, you loved the work, and had made a lot of new friends.'

'We had words over something, but Aunt Clara and Uncle Lionel have been marvellous to me always. After all, I was with them longer than with you or Aunt Mabel. I'm old enough now to stand on my own two feet.'

'What sort of words?'

'Aunt Mattie, it's over now and we're all good friends again. It's finished as far as I'm concerned. How are Uncle Fred and David? Oh, and Mrs Thomas?'

'Fred and David are fine. Mother-in-law's all right. Whenever she gets my back up and I complain to Fred she does something generous and makes me feel bad, but her tongue is as sharp as ever.'

'Like the time she cleared out the spare room for David?'

'Yes, called in a dealer she did and bought him a new bed with what she got, and a second hand chest-of-drawers and a little table to do his home-work on. Of course Fred went around saying "I told you so" and I had to eat humble pie, but that's how she is. Then she makes some remark that gets me annoyed and we're at it again.'

Emma laughed, saying, 'I can remember some of the ding-dongs you used to have, but I think she's fond of you, Aunt Mattie, and you keep the place spotless just like her.'

They heard the front door open and a moment later David came into the room. Looking at the tall boy with cropped curly hair Emma was remembering the little one she'd nursed all those years ago. He seemed glad to see her but after a few minutes went to the kitchen to talk to his nan, then before he went upstairs with the comic the doting old lady had given him, he poked his head around the middle room door to say, 'Nan says not to forget to look in on her before you go, Emma.'

Mrs Thomas sat at the table, a spotless white starched pinny over her dark grey dress.

'I hear youer looking after young children now?' she began. 'A change from working in a draper's, I should think.'

Again Emma was not to be drawn.

'They're nice children,' she said. 'I'm very lucky. But how are you feeling, Mrs Thomas?'

'Oh, I'm all right. Have you seen ouer David? He's getting so tall. He's a fine boy, isn't he?' Her dark eyes glowed with pride.

Emma couldn't stop to see Uncle Fred. Sending him her love, she set off for Aunt Mabel's, expecting her to be equally curious about her niece's reason for leaving Duke Street.

Ellie opened the door, and when she saw who it was her plump face broke into a smile. With a squeal of delight she flung her arms about Emma and rained kisses all over her face. Emma was relieved when Aunt Mabel came into the passage to see who was at the door and pulled her daughter away, saying, 'Give over, Ellie. Let Emma get inside.'

As soon as she had hung her boater on the hall-stand Ellie lifted it from its peg and paraded around in it. Then, still wearing it, she sat down with her doll and began to rock to and fro. In the passage with Ellie's arms about her Emma hadn't noticed the state of things but the room was scruffier than she'd ever remembered, and when her aunt laid a newspaper on the table and put the chipped cups on top ready for when the kettle boiled, she wished there was some way of refusing the drink without hurting her feelings.

'Saves washing,' her aunt explained, glancing over to where Ellie sat, 'and anyway the tea-pot dribbles something awful.'

No wonder, Emma thought, glancing in horror at its broken spout.

Aunt Mabel still worked for Mrs Grey for a few days a week but seemingly had no energy left for tidying her own place. Ellie was nineteen now and had put on a lot of weight. What a shame she was as she was. How different life would have been for them if Ellie had been all right. Her father would probably not have left them then, though Emma didn't think much of a man who could leave his wife to struggle on alone. She looked around the room, her fingers itching to clean and scrub. Nan had been houseproud just like Aunt Mattie. How upset she would have been to see the state of her youngest daughter's home. Emma was sure Ellie could have been taught to help if only Aunt Mabel put her mind to it.

Mabel didn't question her about why she'd left Duke Street but talked all the time about the house in Newport Road where she worked, and about Mrs Grey, her employer. When Emma told her she was now a nurse-maid and that she liked the job, her aunt didn't ask any questions but said, 'Well, that'll be helpful when you get married and have little ones of your own.' Then she looked at Ellie and her expression was sad as she said with tears in her eyes, 'She's the only company I've got. I'd be lost without her.'

Emma went across and put her arms about Aunt Mabel, and putting her doll down on the chair, Ellie did the same.

When she left they both waved from the doorway. Emma walked through Adamsdown and past the Royal Infirmary, now called the King Edward VII Hospital. She was remembering the day early in May 1910 when the shop had been plunged into mourning for the King. As they'd decorated the departments with black crêpe paper and wide black satin ribbons some of the girls had been in tears, for many had had a genuine affection for the portly monarch who'd come to the throne so late in life and seemed such a friendly figure after the remoteness of Queen Victoria.

But soon Emma's thoughts were of Daniel. These days he was never far from her mind. He was always friendly when they met but seemed totally unaware of the turmoil his presence stirred in her. His blue eyes and strong jawline were imprinted on her mind but still she hung about just to catch a glimpse of him when he arrived. As he passed her he would make some remark about the weather or Huw's progress while that young

146

man waited impatiently at his desk, and then Emma would go back to the nursery to torture herself with the thought that he might already have a sweetheart, perhaps even a wife. If he did, she wasn't at all sure she wanted to know!

Chapter Nineteen

'Will you let me in on Saturday night, Emma?' Vera whispered, stopping her on the stairs, and Emma nodded miserably.

It was an August day in 1912 and Vera was by now an old hand at what she called her 'assignments', but she'd have had to be both blind and deaf not to know that Emma was less than willing to perform her part.

We all have to make sacrifices, Vera told herself, choosing to ignore Emma's lack of enthusiasm for without the girl's help in letting her in through the servants' hall she couldn't have carried on.

She'd been detailed for something called 'fly-posting' which was simply pasting WSPU notices on letter boxes, church buildings, walls, hoardings . . . anywhere they'd stick and could be seen. Seems fairly easy so long as I don't get caught, she thought.

'I should be home by half-past twelve,' Vera told the grudging girl who, anxious to be away, had her hand on the knob of the nursery door. Drawing Emma a little way along the corridor, she went on in a low voice, 'Why don't you come along to our headquarters in Windsor Place on your half-day? There's always a warm welcome and a chat over tea and biscuits. They'd be delighted to meet you, Emma, especially as I've told them how vital your help has been.'

'Oh, no! Please, Miss Vera, I don't want to get involved,' Emma whispered anxiously. 'I'd be in real trouble if the master found out what I was doing. You should be more careful yourself, miss. I read in the *Echo* only last week about some suffragettes who were sent to prison.'

'Yes, well, we all have to take risks,' Vera told her with a nonchalance she was far from feeling for the fear of being caught was never very far from her mind. She'd been more than lucky so far though there'd been a number of narrow escapes, but the thought of her father's wrath if he should find out what she was doing sent her into a cold sweat. He was a devout Liberal, a great admirer of Mr Asquith, and never missed a chance to pour scorn and contempt on the suffragettes.

It had been the boredom of her uneventful life that had driven Vera to join the movement. A lot of people would say she should be thankful for her comfortable life-style, but she'd longed to meet people and had begged her father to let her take a job. He'd poured scorn on that too, saying in a voice heavy with sarcasm, 'And tell me what work you think you're fitted to do, young lady?' adding in rare acknowledgment of his own humble beginnings, 'My mother had a couple of children and a miner husband to look after at your age, Vera, and not even running water in the house – that is, except for the damp that ran down the walls. And you, you ungrateful girl, have never had to lift a finger! All you've got to do is to wait until Mr Right comes along to marry you and keep you in the manner to which you're accustomed.'

Vera's anger rose swiftly at her father's assumption she couldn't earn her own living, but in her heart she knew he was probably right. While the two boys had had tutors, and Huw would eventually follow Eddie to boarding school, she'd been sent to a dame school where she'd been taught fine needlework, deportment, and the manners of a bygone age. There'd been only a smattering of the three Rs or any other subject that might have equipped her to earn a living. And as for her meeting Mr Right, as Father so coyly put it, there seemed little hope of that for they rarely entertained, and when they did it was always Father's middle-aged business associates and their wives, and he'd made a strict rule that she should speak to no man unless she'd been properly introduced.

Because of Father's strong views, almost hatred of the suffragettes, Vera had tried to avoid the limelight but it was that very limelight that was needed to publicise the cause. She would love to do something really brave, even foolhardy, that would land her in prison and earn her the admiration and respect of all her friends, but she knew it wouldn't be just herself who'd suffer but her gentle, long-suffering mother as well.

Later, over tea and buttered scones at headquarters, the main topic of conversation was the march from Edinburgh to London that was to take place in October. It was a lively discussion with some speculation as to who would represent the Cardiff branch. Feeling a bit of a fraud, Vera made no comment. The march would attract a lot of publicity, and if she took part and he found out about it her father's rage would be devastating.

One morning a few weeks later Emma hung about as usual, anxiously waiting for the tutor to arrive. As she watched from the nursery window, she saw Daniel come around the side of the house and up the short path to the side door. Even from this distance there was a dejected look about him as, head down, he waited to be let in. Concerned, she hurried to the landing, staring down over the banisters to where a chattering Gwladys was opening the door, but with a brief nod in the girl's direction Daniel made for the stairs. Pretending to busy herself at the linen cupboard, Emma turned to remark, 'It's a nice day after all that rain.' But seeing the young man's eyes filled with sadness her heart gave a little lurch as he answered, 'Sorry, Emma, I hadn't noticed,' and went into the schoolroom and closed the door.

Feeling apprehensive she pondered on what could have happened since Daniel had left the house yesterday. Could there have been a bereavement in the family? But surely if there had and it had been a close relative then he wouldn't have come to work today? Emma couldn't bear to see him so unhappy and longed to comfort him, but Daniel seemed hardly aware of her except to exchange pleasantries while Emma had seen to it that they met as often as possible, but it had made no difference. He seemed quite unaware of the turmoil he stirred in her breast.

When, at twelve o'clock, she heard him going downstairs with Huw she hurried to the window that overlooked the yard. As they began kicking a ball about she could see his heart wasn't in it, and when presently a subdued-looking Huw came into the nursery for lunch, she hurried to the window once more in time to see Daniel closing the gate, shoulders bowed, and starting off for home.

The march from Edinburgh to London had been a great success. Suffragettes who'd taken part told of their experiences in glowing terms. Listening to them, Vera felt ashamed of her own timidity.

'Crowds thronged the route all through Edinburgh as far as Portobello,' one woman told them, and others who'd been there nodded their agreement.

'Who headed the procession?' someone asked, and was told, 'Miss Byham of Sussex and Miss Brown of Edinburgh. They carried the Appeal of Womanhood.'

Vera knew this referred to a handsome and cherished banner carried on special occasions.

'Butterfly drew the van as far as Finchley,' the woman went on. 'You were selling copies of *Votes for Women*, weren't you, Mabel?'

'Yes, and we got people to sign the petition all along the route.'

Vera herself had signed this plea:

WE THE UNDERSIGNED PRAY THE GOVERNMENT TO BRING IN A BILL FOR WOMEN'S SUFFRAGE THIS SESSION.

'We never missed a chance, did we?' the women continued. 'Whether they were digging holes in the road or sweeping the gutters. Hardly any refused.'

Vera could see it all in her mind's eye. The women smartly dressed in the WSPU colours of purple, white and green, marching with heads high, encouraged by a cheering crowd. Yet only too often she'd seen a different picture, for when one of them jumped on a soap box here at home, whether it was on a street corner or in the park, there were jeers as well as cheers from the audience.

The opportunity for Vera to prove her own worth came one bitterly cold day in January when volunteers were required to heckle a Liberal Party meeting.

They were to infiltrate the audience dressed demurely but with small white banners proclaiming 'VOTES FOR WOMEN' hidden beneath their coats.

When she had taken her place Vera licked dry lips and looked

around her, frantically seeking her accomplices. But hidden in
the crowd, with wide-brimmed hats shading their eyes, they
were unrecognisable amidst the sea of unfamiliar faces. She
was to be the third suffragette to jump up and display her banner
while crying 'Votes for Women' but the thick-set body of the
man in front of her, his broad backside taking up two chairs
and sitting tall in his seat, was going to spoil everyone's view.

I'll stand on a chair, Vera told herself bravely, but it was
only Dutch courage for by now she was shivering in her shoes.

When the speakers were introduced Vera wished she'd taken
a greater interest in politics and politicians, especially the Liberal
variety for she didn't recognise anyone on the platform. The
first speaker had just got underway, waving his arms about to
emphasise some point, when one of Vera's colleagues sprang
up, crying in a strong voice: 'Votes for Women' and waving
her banner wildly. There was instant uproar as stewards dragged
her protesting from her seat. As the door slammed behind her
the meeting gradually settled down but half-an-hour later the
second suffragette jumped up. With uproar all around her as
the second woman suffered the same fate, Vera found herself
getting more and more nervous by the minute. But when the
oversized gentleman in front turned to her to remark, 'Prison's
too good for those hooligans,' her blood boiled and anger
strengthened her resolve. But the last thing she wanted just now
was to draw attention to herself before time so she remained
silent.

Vera hoped fervently that when the time came she'd be able
to mount her chair quickly and with dignity. She was so worried
about this that she almost missed her cue, but as the third speaker
waxed eloquent, obviously taking the audience with him, she
climbed quickly on to the chair, banner at the ready crying,

'Votes For Women! Votes For Women!'

There were audible gasps all round as the stewards closed in on her, their arms outstretched, but just before they hustled her from the seat her eyes met those of a man two rows in front of her and she froze as she looked into the familiar face of her father, distorted now with anger, his ginger beard quivering. He made no move as she was dragged from her perch, hustled towards the door and thrown unceremoniously into the street. There were several policemen standing in a group but as they moved towards her a cab drew up, its door open, and an urgent voice told her to get in. Then they were away, the police running after them, and unable to believe her luck, Vera was telling the driver where to go.

'However did you manage to be there just then?' she asked the man at the wheel.

'My wife's one of you,' the cabbie volunteered. 'Took the first lady I did but the second one got caught. Won't be able to do it again though, they'll know the cab next time. Makes me sick it does the way you people are treated.'

For the rest of the journey Vera was preoccupied with her own worrying thoughts. The unthinkable had happened and she was filled with apprehension for the ordeal to come when she came face to face with her father again. As the cab drew up she paid the driver quickly, adding a generous tip despite his protest. Hurrying up the path she knocked twice on the door, praying Emma would be waiting. Thankfully she was for Vera had told her she expected to be home as soon as she'd made her protest.

'Oh, Miss Vera, I'm glad you're back,' Emma told her with a sigh of relief. 'Cook and Gwladys are still in the kitchen. What shall I tell them if they ask why you came in this way?'

Emma never found out for in the very act of closing the door it burst open, pinning her against the wall, and Mr Bishop strode in, looking wildly around. On seeing a terrified Vera running up the stairs he took them two at a time and dragged her back to the hall.

'I never thought a daughter of mine would behave so disgracefully!' he cried, voice vibrant with anger. 'You'll stay in your room, miss, until we can arrange to send you to Aunt Phoebe and your uncle at the vicarage. Being a man of the cloth, he can maybe talk some sense into you, you wicked stupid girl!'

The rumpus in the hall had brought Cook and Gwladys to the kitchen door, but seeing it was the master they retreated hurriedly to speculate on what Miss Vera could possibly have done to make her father so angry.

A badly frightened Emma was just about to climb the stairs when she found her way blocked as Mr Bishop towered over her, yelling, 'And you're the one who made it possible for Miss Vera to work for these lunatics, aren't you? You've been letting her in. Well, it's finished now. You can pack your bags this minute and I'll wait down here to see you out, you deceitful hussy.'

'Not tonight, dear, you can't turn a young woman out at this time of night whatever she's done.' Neither of them had noticed Mrs Bishop coming through the green baize door. Now she went on soothingly, 'Whatever it is we can discuss it properly in the morning. I'll go up and have a word with Vera now.'

'The girl is going . . .'

'Please, Father! It's not Emma's fault.' Vera had come out on to the landing to protest.

'Don't you speak to me, girl . . .' But taking his arm, his wife led him towards the baize door, turning to say to Emma, 'Go to bed, we'll discuss it in the morning.'

'I shan't change my mind,' Mr Bishop warned as the door began to swing slowly to behind them, and Emma heard his voice, loud with anger, crying, 'Blasted suffragettes! Trouble makers! They ruined the meeting tonight. Never be able to raise my head again if they suspect she's my daughter, the wicked girl! Must have been other times and that little skivvy made it possible.'

'She's not a skivvy, dear, she's a nursemaid, and a very good one too. The children are very fond of her . . .'

'She's going first thing, and Vera will be packed off tomorrow too. A stay at the vicarage with those do-gooder relations of yours will soon calm her down.' His voice was muffled now and Emma didn't catch the mistress's reply. Tears streaming down her face, she went upstairs to the nursery floor, half expecting Miss Vera to come out of her room on the next landing but even from here she could hear her sobbing wildly.

With heavy heart Emma crept between her coarse calico sheets. She loved this house and looking after the children. She'd grown very fond of the three of them. Little May was beginning to walk now, her chubby cheeks rosy, blue eyes wide with wonder at her achievement, stumbling towards Emma before falling into her arms or flopping down on her fat little bottom to finish her journey with a crawl. And dependable Amy, always so anxious to please. She didn't spend so much time with Huw since Daniel came . . . At the thought of Daniel Emma buried her face in the pillow and sobbed her heart out. How was she to bear never seeing him again? And where would she go? And Nanny Morgan and Gwladys, Cook and Flo . . . they were all her friends. Then she thought of a new worry which brought her near to despair. How would she ever get a job without a reference? In the mood Mr Bishop was in, she was unlikely to get one.

Chapter Twenty

The mistress came to the nursery before breakfast, the expression on her face sad and defeated as she told Emma, 'I'm sorry, my dear, but I haven't been able to persuade the master to change his mind. The children are going to miss you, and I don't know how Nanny Morgan will manage.' Then taking Emma's hand, she pressed a small brown envelope into it, saying, 'There's a little extra besides your wages, Emma, and I wish you well, my dear.'

The little extra proved to be three whole sovereigns. Emma had never had so much money in her life, but would gladly have done without it to have stayed.

Nanny Morgan hadn't yet come into the nursery and Emma dreaded having to explain. She'd got the children ready and was bathing little May, lingering over the task, savouring every moment, when Nanny came into the room, her face anxious. 'What's this about you leaving, Emma? I've been talking to the mistress and she's very upset. Miss Vera wants her bottom smacked, big as she is, for involving you like that.'

'I couldn't very well refuse, Nanny. He must have guessed I'd done it before. Let her in through the servants' hall, I mean.'

'Which is why she should have had more sense!'

For Nanny to speak about her precious Miss Vera like this

showed how upset she was. Emma found herself comforting the old lady and making her a much needed cup of tea.

After breakfast the master stood just inside the baize doors in the servants' hall, waiting to see her leave. If anything he looked angrier than on the previous night and if Emma had had any thought of begging him to let her stay, looking at his glowering face she knew she didn't have the courage.

A cutting wind met her as she opened the door and stepped on to the path. Turning to close it behind her, she saw the master, mission accomplished, disappearing through the baize doors. Round the side of the house, out of sight now of the windows, a breathless Gwladys caught up with her, saying tearfully, 'Oh, miss, me and Cook are real sorry youer going, an' I knows Flo will be when she finds out. Ooh, look! Nearly forgot I did. Miss Vera said to give you this. Cryin' she was an' all.'

As Emma felt the round hard pieces pressing into her palm through the envelope she thought bitterly, Conscience money! But it would be churlish to refuse it, and anyway she should be grateful for without references it might be some time before she got another job.

Gwladys, her face tear-stained, her cap as usual awry, was glancing anxiously towards the door. Emma hugged her warmly. The maid scurried back to the house. Emma walked to the gate where she turned and glanced up at the nursery window to see Nanny Morgan with little May in her arms, the children by her side, all waving forlornly. As she waved back, a tear rolled down Emma's cheek. Unable to stem the flow, she closed the gate and turned away, wondering which way to go.

The rough wind tore at her scarf, whipping it away from her face. As she dabbed at her eyes a voice she recognised as

Daniel's asked anxiously, 'Whatever's wrong, Emma?' Then glancing at the holdall at her feet, he added, 'You're leaving? But why?'

She hadn't seen him approaching the house. Looking into his worried face she quickly explained, anxious to keep him with her even in her troubled state. Looking thoughtful, he asked, 'Have you anywhere to go?'

Knowing it would put poor Aunt Mattie in an impossible position if she turned up on her doorstep, Emma shook her head. Aunt Mabel would probably welcome her with open arms as minder for Ellie, but fond as she was of her backward cousin Emma shuddered at the thought of sharing her bed and enduring all those slobbering kisses which people had found endearing when she was young. She'd only be a drudge in that unkempt house while Aunt Mabel went to work.

'I'm sure you'd be welcome at our house for a few days until you sort yourself out,' Daniel was saying. She was about to refuse, telling him she couldn't impose on his mother, when he added: 'I'll be home myself about one o'clock. I'll look in Lacey's window on the way home. There are often notices advertising for domestic jobs.'

Suddenly all that mattered was the chance of seeing Daniel again. Thanking him, and saying she hoped his mother wouldn't mind, Emma listened to the address, surprised to find that it was only a few streets away from Aunt Mattie's.

The thought sustained her until the tram reached Clifton Street when, sitting on the slatted seat, her shabby holdall beside her, she realised she'd have to get off very soon and wondered anxiously just how she was to explain herself to his mother? To turn up unannounced expecting to stay until Daniel arrived home seemed a bit of a nerve, but she'd committed herself now.

As the tram rattled towards the Royal Oak she wondered just what she could say.

The streets off Broadway were familiar to her and the sight acted like balm to her troubled thoughts, but when she'd reached Daniel's house and stood outside number twenty-two with its gleaming brass knocker and letterbox, crisp curtains of Nottingham lace at the parlour window, she felt numb with anxiety. It sounded odd even to her ears to say, 'I've lost my job, your son told me to come.'

When the door opened and a neat rosy-cheeked woman in a spotless white apron looked at her in friendly enquiry, Emma's tongue seemed suddenly to be as frozen as her fingers and toes, but when she saw the woman's expression slowly turn to puzzlement she managed to blurt out, 'Daniel said to come.'

'Well, you'd better come in then. No sense in us both freezing to death.' The woman's smile was encouraging as she added, 'I'm Daniel's mother.'

'Emma Meredith.'

'Ah, yes, I've heard him speak of you. Aren't you the nurse-maid to the young sisters of the boy he teaches?'

'I was,' she replied sadly. 'I've – I've had the sack.'

'Oh, my dear.'

And so, sitting by the glowing kitchen range, watching the firelight dance and twinkle amongst the brass ornaments on shelf and window ledge, Emma told the older woman the whole story, adding, 'Daniel thought you might know of some work? I'll try anything so long as it means a roof over my head, but I do love being with children.'

But Mrs Thompson was shaking her head, saying, 'I don't know of anything, love, but we could look in the newspaper. We'll get Daniel to get one this afternoon.'

She felt well disposed towards this gentle-looking girl. Her face had been pinched with the cold when she'd first come in, but she was getting a little colour back now. The lovely wide brown eyes had looked hopeful until she'd said she knew of no work. And it was good that Daniel was taking an interest in someone else's misfortunes instead of wallowing in his own as he had done since that Cissie left him the note returning the ring.

'My son hasn't been himself lately,' she told Emma.

'He's looked very sad,' she agreed.

'Well, he was courting Cissie for nearly five years. Getting married next year they were.'

'Has something happened to her?' Emma asked sympathetically.

'Oh no! I thought you knew, my dear? Perhaps I shouldn't have said. I'll have to tell you now, won't I? Cissie sent a note saying she was marrying someone else. Broken-hearted he is, though the way she never wanted to set a date for the wedding made me wonder.'

'Poor Daniel,' Emma murmured, yet couldn't help a little flutter of hope.

'Best not to say anything,' his mother told her. 'Better let it come from him. Well, I'd better start on that stew. We'll be needing something hot on a day like this. Got another pupil to go to after lunch he has.'

'Please can I help?'

And so they worked together, Emma peeling vegetables, Mrs Thompson chopping the lamb into small cubes, then, when it was bubbling and gurgling in the big iron saucepan on top of the range and Emma had added the dumplings she'd been entrusted to make, they sat down once more and over another

163

cup of tea Daniel's mother said, 'You know, Emma, youer welcome to stay for a few days. It will give you a chance to look around.' And she replied, 'Only if I can pay towards my keep, Mrs Thompson.' To which Daniel's mother answered, 'We'll have to see about that, but not yet.'

Daniel came home with the *Western Mail* but although they looked eagerly through the vacancies column there was nothing remotely suitable for Emma.

'We've still got the *Echo* to come,' Mrs Thompson told her optimistically.

Daniel said Gwladys had overheard the mistress and master having ructions over Emma's dismissal. 'Said she'd never known the mistress stand up to him before. Oh, and Miss Vera's been sent away.'

Poor Miss Vera, thought Emma. For all her hopes and ideals over women's emancipation she was as powerless as her mother in her own home. Outside the leaden sky promised snow as Daniel left for his afternoon pupil, dressed in a warm greatcoat with a long woollen scarf wound about his neck, and Emma was reminded that it was in weather like this just over a year ago that she'd left the shop in Duke Street. Now, as they washed the dishes, she felt grateful to Daniel and his mother. Mrs Thompson's kindness had made her welcome but Emma had no intention of putting on her. If her search for a job proved fruitless after a couple of days she would go to Aunt Mabel's, there was nothing else for it.

When two days had passed, and neither the columns in the *Echo* nor signs eagerly scanned in shop windows had yielded any possibility of a live in job, she made up her mind that if there was nothing in the paper Daniel brought home that night then she would go to see her aunt. Emma felt guilty about keeping her aunts in the dark but dreaded having to tell them she had neither job nor home. Aunt Clara might feel obliged to have her back, and although she'd never actually said so Emma knew she didn't really want her again because of what had happened that New Year's Eve. She knew too that Aunt Mattie, generous soul that she was, would feel unhappy over not being able to offer her a bed.

By tea-time she was wondering whether to keep to her decision when Daniel came in to tell her there was a notice that might interest her in the newsagent's window. Someone was required to look after a widower and his two children.

'Sounds right up your street, Emma,' Daniel's mother told her. 'Why don't you go and find out about it? Did you notice the address, Daniel?'

'There wasn't one. It said to ask inside.'

When the newsagent had lifted the card from the window to see the address on the back it proved to be quite near where Emma was staying and she decided to go there right away. The house looked neat enough with a small garden in front surrounded by iron railings. Both knocker and letter-box were badly in need of polishing but you'd expect that from a man on his own, Emma thought. She couldn't imagine either Uncle Lionel or Uncle Fred caring twopence about the brass being polished.

After she'd knocked Emma closed her eyes for a moment, taking deep breaths to steady herself. When she opened them a tall, quite young-looking man was standing in the doorway, and when blushing with embarrassment she looked up at him, her gaze encountered the saddest eyes she'd ever seen.

'You have an advert in the paper shop for a housekeeper?'

'Come inside,' he said, ushering her in. As she walked behind him she was aware of soft pile rugs underfoot instead of the usual coconut matting and when they reached the kitchen here too there were rugs on the diamond-tiled floor. But there was an air of neglect about everything, a layer of dust coating shelves and dresser, yesterday's ashes piled up in the grate. There was a sense of desolation too about the two little girls huddled together on the edge of the brown leather sofa, their long hair uncombed and pinafores badly in need of a wash. Emma's heart went out to them as their eyes nervously met hers.

'Daisy and Dorothy,' the man introduced them. 'Daisy's the eldest,' he told her, and looking at the child, her pale face lit by deep blue eyes, Emma judged her to be about eight years old, and the younger one about five or six.

'Samuel Evans,' he introduced himself, but his next words dashed Emma's hopes as he said, 'I really wanted someone much older, someone middle-aged.'

'I've had experience of looking after children,' Emma assured him, praying he wouldn't mention references. He didn't, merely repeating what he'd said before, adding, 'Looking after a house and children is a big responsibility. Besides, if someone as young as you stays here without another woman in the house the tongues will begin to wag, you can be sure of that. Still, as you can see I am out at work all day and I just can't cope. I never was very domesticated – left all that to the wife. The place looked like a palace. She was a wonderful woman. Break her heart it would to see the place like this.' His voice faltered and he took out a grubby hankie and blew his nose loudly.

Emma turned to the children who had gradually edged closer and were watching her with interest.

'Do you both go to school?' she asked.

'Yes. It's in Stacey Road,' Daisy answered.

'Are you coming to look after us?' Dorothy asked hopefully.

'I'd like to,' Emma told her, hoping it would help their father to make up his mind.

'Look, you can stay if you like, see how you get on. I'm afraid I'm not much company for anyone since Sarah died. But you'll be good for the girls, I can see that.'

'When shall I start?'

'Tonight if you want to. We'll come to an agreement about wages as well as your board. But I warn you, since my wife died I'm not very sociable. I like to be left alone.'

'I'll just get my things,' Emma told him. She was really looking forward to looking after the little girls and was eager to start.

Daniel's mam had kept her meal hot but Emma felt keen disappointment that there was no sign of him.

'Marking papers he is,' Mrs Thompson explained.

When she was ready to leave and had thanked his mother warmly it was time to say goodbye to Daniel himself. Tapping on the parlour door Emma thought she heard him call: 'Come in!' Opening it, she found him not at the table where books and papers were spread out, but in the armchair by the fire, his head in his hands.

'Oh, Emma!' He sprang up in some embarrassment, evidently expecting his mother, and as she looked into his face, which over the months had become so dear to her, Emma saw deep anguish in his blue eyes, and her own heart swelled with pain for him for didn't she herself know the heartache of loving someone who hardly seemed to know she existed? She'd hoped for so much from the few days she'd spent here at his home, but Daniel was still pining after someone unattainable, and wasn't she doing the very same thing?

Chapter Twenty-One

Arriving back at the house, Emma found the door ajar. When there was no answer to her knock, she pushed it open and made her way to the kitchen where the two little girls still sat on the sofa, just as they had when she left, the older child looking at a picture book, the younger one yawning widely. Emma felt a pang of guilt for being away so long.

Taking her apron from the holdall, she put it on and stirred the fire into flames before putting on the big iron kettle to boil. Smiling at the girls, Emma told them, 'It'll have to be a lick and a promise for tonight,' while assuring herself that by this time tomorrow they'd be bathed and their hair washed, in clean clothes and with beds made up with fresh linen.

As soon as the kettle was hot enough Emma sat them in turn on the table, washing down to the waist then legs and feet in warm soapy water. The only towel she could find was rough and grey and her mind leaped forward to tomorrow morning when she meant to get up with the dawn to fill the copper in the wash-house, light the fire beneath it and start the mammoth task of tackling the washing that had accumulated.

When Daisy told her where linen and underwear could be found, Emma was surprised to find drawerfuls of beautifully laundered bedding and undergarments. Was the children's father so heartbroken he didn't notice their needs? And how had they managed for meals? As though reading her thoughts Daisy was saying proudly, 'I help Daddy with the cooking. I can boil eggs and make toast on the toasting fork. Daddy boils potatoes and things when he comes home.'

Soon the girls were sitting at the table, sipping mugs of steaming cocoa, hair brushed until it rippled down their backs, faces pink and glowing from soap and hot water. When Dorothy yawned again Emma lit a candle and led the way up the carpeted stairs, the dancing flame casting weird shadows before them, hesitating on the landing until Daisy opened a door. Going to the bed she knelt on one side of it while Dorothy sank to her knees on the other. Hands pressed piously together, they began their prayers to Gentle Jesus. When they'd finished and had asked Him to take care of their daddy and look after their mam they climbed into bed and looked at Emma uncertainly. Remembering her own need for love when she'd been young and had lost her nan, Emma put her arms around them and kissed them tenderly, her heart touched when two pairs of arms came up tightly about her neck.

Tucking them in and finding another candle on top of the chest-of-drawers, she lit it to leave with the children and went to find her own room which she'd been told was the next along the landing. She was very pleased to find it a comfortable place with a small wardrobe, chest-of-drawers and blanket box in dark oak, and a marble-topped wash-stand on which stood a jug, basin and soap-dish all with the same rosebud pattern. On the bed, which had yet to be made with sheets and pillow cases, was a brightly patterned patchwork quilt.

Going back to the children's room and finding them both asleep, Emma blew out the candle and went downstairs. Hearing someone moving about as she passed the door at the top of the stairs, Emma wondered if Sam Evans had gone to bed or would be down to supper? As she tidied the kitchen then sat down by the fire she thought gratefully now of the three aunts who had each given her a home when she'd been left all alone. Where were these children's relatives? she wondered. Where were the caring neighbours? In the streets she'd been brought up in there'd always been someone to help out, someone to bring offerings on a tray covered with a snowy cloth, someone to show they cared.

The kettle boiled and the table laid, she wondered whether to tap on Mr Evans' door. Best not, she thought, remembering his warning about his need to be left alone. Then, just when she'd decided to make herself a cup of tea, she heard footsteps on the stairs. But when the kitchen door opened there was no answering smile to hers as he came towards the fire and stood staring into the glowing coals, saying, 'This is the worst part of the day for me, Emma. We used to sit for hours in the firelight just talking, making plans for the girls. People try to tell me time will heal, but it only gets worse. No, I don't want any supper, thank you, just a cup of tea, then you get off to bed.'

'Do you have to leave early for work?' Emma needed to know.

'I don't leave until about eight. I manage an ironmonger's in town.'

'Will you be home for lunch, Mr Evans?'

'Call me Sam, and if it's all right with you I'll call you Emma. And, no, I won't be home midday. I did have to come home to see to the girls and my boss was very understanding. With you looking after them, things should be a lot easier.'

He drank his tea in silence. As soon as Emma had washed

the dishes and put them away, he said, 'Why don't you go up to bed? I'm sure you must be tired.' It was a dismissal. He evidently wanted to be alone with his thoughts. She had her hand on the doorknob when he spoke again, his voice rough with emotion, saying, 'That was her Emma, that was my Sarah.'

He'd lifted a silver-framed photograph down from the mantelpiece and put it into her hands. Looking down at the sepia picture, Emma saw the face of an attractive young woman, eyes wide and smiling, silky hair worn in a low bun.

'She was very pretty.'

'She's still here. I can feel it.'

His words brought a chill to Emma's heart. In the uncomfortable silence that followed she lit a candle, closed the door quietly behind her and went upstairs, deeply disturbed by the depth of his grief.

Finding sheets and pillow cases in one of the drawers in the chest, Emma made her bed, thankful for the thick flannel blanket she found beneath the quilt. Putting out the candle, she got into bed, conscious of a murmuring coming from below. Just as though Sam's talking with someone, she thought with a shiver. At first, her mind busy with the events of the day, sleep wouldn't come but she must have slept at last for she was torn from a dream by a piercing scream that went on and on. Jumping out of bed, thinking for a moment she was still at the house in Queen Street, Emma made for the nursery, rudely awakened to her change of abode when she knocked her shin painfully against the chest-of-drawers. Then, remembering, her heart filled with fear for the screams were getting louder. She lit the candle with shaking fingers and made for the room next-door.

Both girls were sitting up in bed with Daisy's arm about

little Dorothy whose screams seemed to increase in volume the nearer Emma got to the bed.

'Go away! I don't want to come with you!' she gasped out between screams as Daisy cwtched her closer, saying, 'It's only Emma, Dorry.'

Then Emma's arms were about her and she was rocking her to and fro while Daisy explained: 'She thought you were Mama come to fetch her.'

At that moment their father appeared fully dressed in the doorway, asking, 'What's wrong with her this time?'

'It's the nightmare, Daddy. The one she always has.'

"Why isn't the gas lit? You know I always leave it dimmed.'

'I'm sorry, I didn't know,' Emma told him. 'I'll leave it on in future.'

Going downstairs to get the child a drink, she wondered about Dorothy's fear. Surely she couldn't be afraid of that gentle-looking woman whose photo stood on the mantelpiece? The children had confided how much they loved their mother, so what could have triggered such terror? Sam's obsession with his dead wife can't be good for the children, she thought worriedly. They have to live with his grief every day.

When the girls had drunk their milk, for she had brought some for Daisy as well, Emma turned the gas low and went back to her room, her mind filled with questions.

Two of them were answered next day when she met their neighbour for the first time. Despite her disturbed night Emma had got up at six o'clock to light a fire under the copper in the wash-house and while it was heating the water she blackleaded the grate and rekindled the coals which were still glowing, telling her that the children's father could not have been long in his bed. By half-past seven, the girls washed and dressed in clean frocks and pinafores, Sam had come down. She spooned porridge into dishes and made neat triangles of toast, but it seemed Sam had no appetite. He only nibbled at some toast and drank his tea. Then, buttoning his coat and winding a woollen scarf about his neck, he left for work.

With the children off to school, anxious as she was to start on the washing there was also the midday meal to prepare and the evening meal for Sam when he came from work, so Emma put on her coat and tam and went to the butcher's in Broadway. It was a raw morning towards the end of January, the pavements black and shining from a recent fall of sleet. Just the day for a tasty stew, she thought, thankful she'd always insisted on helping Martha in the kitchen when she was living above the shop in Duke Street and had a number of tasty recipes to fall back on.

Now, as Emma paid for the stewing steak and went next-door to buy vegetables, she thought again that Sam Evans had been more than generous with the housekeeping allowance and she meant to see that he had good tasty meals in return. But today there was no time for further shopping. There was washing to be done, and with all the dampness in the air it wasn't likely to dry soon.

The stew was simmering gently at the back of the range, the washing bubbling in the copper, when, prodding the garments down and putting on the lid, she went out with a damp cloth to wipe the line clean. As she moved the cloth along its length a plump middle-aged woman came up to the dividing wall. Resting her arms on top and her chin on her arms, she gave Emma a friendly smile and asked, 'How are you getting on then, love?' Then, without waiting for an answer, 'Got time for a cuppa, 'ave you?'

As neither stew nor washing was likely to suffer, Emma thanked her while looking dubiously at the high wall.

'You'll find a butter box down there behind the rhubarb,' their neighbour told her with a chuckle. 'Sarah used to use it to get over 'ere. One this side too there is.'

So Emma climbed over and followed her into her kitchen where, settling her visitor at the scrubbed wooden table, she said, 'Call me Maud, everyone does. What's youer name, love?'

'I'm Emma,' she said, watching as Maud poured two cups of strong tea from a pot that had been stewing at the side of the range and sweetened them with generous spoonfuls of condensed milk.

'Heard Dorothy screaming again last night I did,' Maud remarked, cutting her a generous slice of fruit cake made on an enamel plate.

'She had a nightmare,' Emma told her worriedly.

'And no wonder, pooer little soul!' Maud broke in. 'Scared out of 'er wits that child is. I was there myself, Emma, when he brought the girls in to see their Mam. So's they'd remember 'er, 'e said. There was Sarah lying in her coffin on the parlour table, candles flickering all round her. Asked me in to pay my last respects, 'e did, then 'e brings the two girls. Scared stiff they looked an' all, I can tell you. Then 'e took them over to the coffin and said, "Say goodbye to youer Mam for now, girls, but it won't be for ever. One day when God 'as made 'er an angel and the time is right she'll come and fetch us one by one and we'll all be together again." That Dorothy was white as a sheet, 'er eyes likes saucers. Daisy was upset but she's made of tougher stuff. The little one's sensitive like 'er mam was.'

Now she understood Daisy's words: 'She thinks you're Mama come to fetch her.' That's what she must have looked like to the child in her long white nightgown with the candle casting shadows.

But Maud was continuing, 'Everyone in the street wanted to help. Good sorts most of the neighbours are. I offered to 'ave the girls dinnertime when they come from school. Need a hot meal they do, especially this weather, but he wouldn't have any of it. Just said, "Thanks, Maud, but we'll manage." But it's no life for those girls, the way 'e's carrying on.'

'I'll have to go,' Emma told her regretfully. There was still the washing to hang out and the dumplings to put in the stew.

''E's lucky to 'ave found someone conscientious like you,' Maud told her. 'Some of the women are saying youer too young, but I told them, the girls need some young company to take the sad look from their eyes.'

She didn't tell Emma what one of the more spiteful neighbours had said, someone who ought to have known better for everyone in the street knew of Sam's devotion to Sarah's memory, and you only 'ad to look at this young girl to see that she was a thoroughly decent sort. Anyway she'd given that Lena Brown the length of 'er tongue when the cow 'ad the nerve to say, 'I wonder if it's a 'ousekeeper Sam really wants or someone to warm 'is bed?'

Chapter Twenty-Two

Her aunt's reaction to Emma's change of circumstances was predictable. Aunt Mattie said her dismissal from her last job was a crying disgrace and she'd a good mind to go and tell them so.

'And you shouldn't be living in that young man's house unchaperoned,' she told Emma worriedly. 'Your Mr Evans may be a decent sort but tongues are bound to wag.'

Aunt Mabel said Emma must have known she'd be welcome to live with them.

'I can't understand why you didn't come to us right away,' she went on. 'Ellie would have been over the moon to have you back, you know that.'

She didn't get as far as Duke Street, but Aunt Clara wrote to say that she'd heard Emma had changed her job and hoped she'd be very happy. There'd been a post-script at the bottom: 'If there's anything you need, Emma, just let us know.'

There'd been a note from Martha in the same envelope, begging her to come to see them soon and sending all her love.

Aunt Mattie had insisted on coming round to the house to see everything was above board, but Sam had been at work at the time. She'd looked around her with approval at the newly blackleaded range, shining brasses, and matching plum-coloured mantle-cloth and cushion covers, all freshly washed and ironed, then up at the airing neatly folded over a line which stretched across the width of the kitchen about two feet below the ceiling, on which hung the little girls' dresses, starched pinafores and lace-trimmed petticoats and drawers. Mattie nodded with satisfaction.

As the weeks passed Emma found she was really enjoying looking after the children and the house, especially cooking the meals. The little girls seemed happier and more relaxed each day; even Dorothy's nightmares were now few and far between. But their father still sat up night after night, his voice muffled by distance as it droned on and on, talking to someone who wasn't there, and the memory of his words on that very first night echoed in her mind.

'She's still here, Emma, I can feel it.'

Her heart would be full of foreboding, not at the thought of Sarah's disembodied spirit but at the strength of Sam's delusions and where they might lead.

In the morning, with early-spring sunshine bathing the breakfast table and Sam off to work, she'd try to forget his grey face and hollow eyes and laugh with the girls as they got ready for school, attempting to bring some normality into their lives.

Under her tuition Daisy was getting to be very handy about the house and both the girls loved the cooking sessions when they'd have aprons tied about their waists and their hands washed before being allowed to sift flour, whisk eggs, or cream together butter and sugar in the big mixing bowl. Then they'd wait about impatiently for the cakes to be taken from the oven, and were even more impatient for them to be cool enough to eat.

Over the months Emma had paid frequent visits to the

Thompsons but to her great disappointment she rarely saw Daniel. His mother had confided her worries to Emma at the way he shut himself away either in the parlour or his room.

'The girl's married now, and to be honest with you, Emma, I never did think she was much cop. Led him a pretty dance she did.'

But Emma knew from experience just what Daniel was going through. And it must be much worse for him, she thought. After all, they were engaged.

On a fine Saturday early in May she decided to take the girls on their first visit to Aunt Mabel's. Her conscience had been troubling her over not going to see Ellie, so as soon as the midday meal was over they set off, the girls in their favourite dresses of fine blue merino wool, covered by starched broderie anglaise pinafores, and of course their warm coats. 'Ne'er cast a clout till May is out' her nan used to tell Emma, but it was a warm day and they hadn't gone far before they had to take them off.

Ellie was standing by the open door of the house as they turned into the short street. Emma had already explained to the girls about her cousin, saying, 'Ellie will always be a child, but she's friendly and kind, I know you'll both like her.'

But her words hadn't prepared the girls for the way Ellie rushed to meet them, flinging her arms about them in turn and showering them with kisses even though they'd never met before. Then, taking their hands, she rushed them towards the house with Daisy and Dorothy looking anxiously back over their shoulders. Once in the house Ellie went straight to the cupboard at the side of the range and brought out two battered-looking dolls, one for each of the girls to hold, and as Emma sat down in the armchair by the fire she began to show them how to undress then dress them, just as Emma had done for her all those years ago.

Thinking of Esmeralda, the lovely doll that had belonged to her mother, Emma wondered if it was still sitting in the basket chair in her old bedroom above the shop in Duke Street. The girls would love to see it. She'd have to find a way to bring it home.

Knowing Aunt Mabel's circumstances, Emma had brought some cakes she and the girls had made that morning. Now, as she removed the tea-towel and set them out on a plate, she said, 'You sit down, Aunt Mabel, and I'll make us a cup of tea.'

She was relieved to see that the cracked and dribbling tea-pot had been replaced by one of strong brown earthenware. Even the chipped cups had gone and as she brought out the dainty ones that somehow seemed familiar, ignoring the thick mugs that were obviously for everyday use, Aunt Mabel told her, 'Clara gave me those, Emma, when she had a new tea-set. But you'd better give Ellie a mug.'

She was so happy showing off her small treasures to the girls that she didn't complain, and remembering how she used to create if something upset her, Emma was thankful.

When she'd exhausted the contents of her toy cupboard, a motley collection comprising a teddy bear with only one ear, the two dolls, one armless, the other fast losing the stuffing from its kid body, a box of paints with most of the colours used, and a colourful spinning top that would no longer spin, Ellie dashed upstairs full of purpose and came down wearing the old-fashioned bonnet and cloak that Aunt Mabel had brought home for her to dress up in. Emma found herself remembering that awful Saturday, long ago, when Ellie had slipped out of the house wearing the outfit and she'd had to chase her all the way to Clifton Street.

Now, as she paraded up and down in front of them, the girls began to giggle and Ellie giggled with them. You could always rely on Ellie to laugh or cry with you with equal gusto, Emma thought, marvelling at how this woman-child was enjoying the girls' company. Poor Ellie. Children in the streets around wouldn't have thought to invite her into their games, yet she had nothing in common with those her own age.

Suddenly Emma was thinking just what it must have been like for Aunt Mabel all these years. The dreadful realisation that her pretty little daughter, for it seemed Ellie had been bonny as a baby, would never grow up. The double blow of finding her husband wasn't strong enough to take responsibility for her, and the grinding poverty she'd had to endure when left on her own.

Ellie and the girls had taken a piece of rope into the tiny garden, but being so heavy herself Ellie held the end of the rope for Daisy and Dorothy to take turns skipping.

'I've never known her so happy, except years ago when you were here,' Aunt Mabel told Emma. 'Still I can see those girls need you, poor little souls.'

When they left for home Ellie insisted on coming to the corner where their road met Sanquahar Street, then waved to them until they were out of sight.

'She's nice, isn't she, Dorrie? We'll take some of our toys next time. Won't she never grow up?'

'Ellie's happy as she is,' Emma told her, and Dorothy said, 'I'm going to take her my best doll 'cos most of her toys are broken, poor thing.'

And Emma marvelled at the way the little girls had accepted Ellie for what she was.

When they'd turned into their own street the children ran on towards the house, leaving Emma to walk alone.

''Ello! Aren't you Sam Evans' new 'ousekeeper?'

Emma had been wondering whether to speak as she passed the woman who'd been standing by her gate, arms wrapped in a grubby apron.

'Yes, I am,' she said, smiling at the neighbour. 'I'm Emma Meredith.' And she put out her hand. Shaking it, the woman said, 'I'm Lena Brown. How are the girls? Looked happy enough they did when they ran past just now.'

'Yes. They still miss their mam but they're slowly getting over it. It's a good job they've got each other.'

'I suppose Sam's gettin' over it too? Won't be lonely, will he, with you there?'

Emma wasn't quite sure how she was meant to take this remark, but the woman had seemed friendly enough so she said, 'He's still grieving after his wife. It's sad she died so young.'

'Shouldn't think he's missing her much with you around.' The tone of voice was suddenly sarcastic, leaving Emma shocked and bereft of words. She was distressed too by the spiteful gleam in the woman's eyes which left her in no doubt as to her meaning.

'You rotten bitch!' cried a voice vibrant with disgust. Neither of them had noticed Maud's chubby figure coming down the street towards them. Next moment she was shaking skinny Lena like a dog would a bone.

'Don't, Maud, please!' Emma cried anxiously. 'Just leave her alone.'

Maud let go of her opponent so suddenly she fell back against the iron gate.

'I 'ope for youer sake, you rotten sod, that Sam never gets wind of what youer saying!' Maud cried. 'Ought to be ashamed of youerself you did, Lena Brown, saying such wicked things while that pooer man's nearly out of his mind with grief. And let's hope this young lady's fiancé doesn't get to hear what you said. Big 'efty chap 'e is.'

Emma's eyes had widened in surprise at this last remark, then realising it had been said for effect, she thanked Maud warmly as soon as they were out of earshot. Her neighbour chuckled as she said, 'I don't know if you've got a young man, Emma. I expect you have, a pretty young girl like you. Anyway, if you 'ave I 'ope 'e's a big fellow. I wouldn't like to disappoint that old bugger!'

Emma laughed although she was still feeling upset. This must have been just what Sam had meant when he'd warned her that without another woman in the house the tongues would begin to wag. And hadn't Aunt Mattie said much the same?

Chapter Twenty-Three

Remembering the grapevine that could be relied upon to spread gossip amongst the surrounding streets faster than the wind, Emma was worried that Aunt Mattie might hear about the fracas between her neighbour and Lena Brown, and especially the reason for it. The way the houses were built, not only side by side but back to back with those in the next street, meant any juicy titbit would quickly spread as women talked over the garden walls.

She wasn't really surprised when, just after the girls had left for school, Aunt Mattie knocked on the door, her face wearing a serious expression.

'I've just heard about what happened on Saturday,' she said as soon as the door had closed behind her, 'and you can't say I didn't warn you, Emma. Best give your notice in right away, you had. I know our Mabel will be pleased to have you.'

'But I couldn't leave the girls, Aunt Mattie, they rely on me now.'

'He can get someone else. You should never have come here. People will always talk even when there's no truth to their gossip.'

'It's only that spiteful Lena Brown.'

'They'll listen to her, cariad, more's the pity.'

'I'm not going to let them down.'

Seeing the stubborn expression on Emma's face, Mattie decided to change the subject for the time being.

'How's Mr Evans? Is he any better?'

'He seems to be getting worse,' Emma had to admit. 'He hardly ever goes out after he comes home from work, and as soon as he's had his meal he goes up to his bedroom and closes the door. I call him for supper, and after I go to bed he stays downstairs half the night. That's why I can't leave the girls, Aunt Mattie. Anyway you've nothing to worry about. He hardly speaks to me. It's as though I wasn't here.'

'Well, you'll have to put up with the gossip then, but I warn you, that Lena Brown's a troublemaker.'

When Emma didn't answer, she went on, 'I have to admit you're making a good job of it, Emma. Saw Daisy and Dorothy on their way to school I did and they looked a picture. But you think about what I've been saying, girl.'

As soon as her aunt had gone Emma went back to the wash-tub. Vigorously rubbing linen on the board, she tried to put Mattie's warning out of her mind. Come what may, she was going to stay. The girls were happy and she liked the job, and it was near enough to Daniel's home for her to hope to see him sometimes. Also she had a very good neighbour in Maud. As though to prove this last point, just as she'd poked the last of the whites down into the boiler and put on the lid there came a call from the next garden.

'Emma! Emma! Just made a cuppa I 'ave.'

And when she emerged from the billowing steam of the wash-house and stepped on to the butter box to look over the wall there was Maud waiting, her face bright pink and moist from bending over her own wash-tub.

Following Maud to the kitchen and closing the door behind her to keep out the steam, Emma sat at the table while her neighbour poured the tea. Handing her a cup, Maud said thoughtfully, 'Youer not still worrying about what 'appened yesterday, are you, cariad?'

'No,' said Emma stoutly, knowing at the same time that she was.

Maud couldn't have believed her either for she went on, 'That's just what that nasty bugger would like – to upset you. Jealous she is, Emma. Apparently she asked Sam a while back if 'e wanted someone to come in and do for them during the day, but he said no so she must be feeling spiteful. And it's lucky for the girls he did say no 'cos she don't even look after 'er own.'

The following Saturday being another warm sunny day, Emma decided to finish the cleaning as quickly as possible and get the girls ready to go to Roath Park to feed the ducks and swans that swam so gracefully on the lake.

The girls looked very pretty in straw bonnets she'd found put away in a hat-box on top of their wardrobe, and blue taffeta frocks that they would soon outgrow. Her own concession to the warm weather was her boater, which sported a new ribbon, and a white blouse in fine lawn with a jabot of lace.

When they were ready she picked up a parcel of bread for the ducks and a plate she must return to Daniel's mam and shut the door behind them, her heart filled with hope that today he would be there.

His mother opened the door, exclaiming, 'My! You girls do look smart. Going somewhere special, are you?' at the same time closing the door behind them and ushering them into the kitchen where to Emma's delight Daniel sat at the table with a cup in his hand.

'We're going to Roath Park,' Emma told her.

Turning to Daniel, his mother said, 'Why don't you go with them, son? The fresh air would do you good.'

Emma held her breath, her finger-nails digging painfully into her palms as she waited for his answer.

He's embarrassed, she thought, her heart sinking. He's going to say no. But then Daniel put down his cup and got up, saying, 'I won't be long Emma, I'll just get my jacket and cap.'

She could hardly believe her luck as his mother told her, 'Glad to get him from under my feet I am. He's been moping all morning.'

As they went up the street and along Broadway and so into Newport Road, with the girls skipping hand in hand in front of them, Emma wished desperately that Lena Brown could see her with such a fine young man. It might silence her spiteful tongue! As they reached the high white-washed wall that surrounded Roath Court, Daniel was telling her, 'It's not the same at the house now. Miss Vera's still away. Huw will be going to school in the autumn and they're going to have a governess for Amy, and May when she's old enough to join in. I shall be leaving them at the end of the summer.'

'How's Nanny Morgan? Who helps her now?'

'Oh, she's just the same. They took on a girl in your place. Gwladys told me she was hopeless at first, but I think she's getting better. Nanny Morgan's had to do a lot more than when you were there.'

It was a long walk to the park and several times on the way Emma ran out of conversation. Her mouth dry with anxiety, she searched her mind, desperate for something to talk about, but Daniel, lost in his own thoughts, seemed unperturbed.

The park was crowded on this lovely day with people strolling amid the spring flowerbeds: Dad in his best suit and bowler, Mam in her summer straw, the children dressed in their best, walking sedately in front. Occasionally there was the soft rustle of silk as a lady passed by, a parasol shading her face.

As they neared the Pleasure Gardens the strains of a Strauss waltz came to them, the music louder and louder as they neared the ornate band-stand with pagoda-shaped roof, resplendent with musicians in red uniforms and peaked caps trimmed with gold.

Now, as they stood watching, the band began to play 'The Blue Danube' and Emma couldn't stop her toes tapping to the tune. But they were all hot and tired after their long walk so when Daniel led them to an area shaded by trees she was only too thankful to flop down on the sweet-smelling grass.

For a while Daniel played 'I Spy' with the girls while Emma lay back, her hands cushioning her head, staring up at a pale blue sky hung with billowing white clouds, remembering her nan telling her about the day this lovely park was opened. The ceremony had been performed by the young Earl of Dumfries, eldest son of the Marquess of Bute, on 20 June 1894 which had been his thirteenth birthday.

'A few months before you were born it was, Emma,' her nan had said. 'Alderman Trounce asked all the shopkeepers in Albany and Wellfield Roads to shut their shops and decorate the front with bunting. There were crowds watching the procession. The horses and the wagons and brakes they pulled were decorated with flags and rosettes. It was a day to remember, I can tell you.'

'All right if I take the girls to see that old oak?' Daniel interrupted her thoughts. 'It's over there, look. They say it's between six and seven hundred years old.'

Emma looked in the direction he was pointing where a large oak tree spread its branches wide, wondering whether to go with them, but the girls were already almost there and Daniel was running, trying to catch up with them. When they came back Daisy and Dorothy wanted to explore but Daniel groaned and dropped down on to the grass, pretending to be exhausted.

'Don't go far,' Emma warned them. 'Remember we're near the bandstand.'

Daniel had folded his jacket and put it beneath his head and was staring up at the sky as she had done a short while ago. Even as she began to say, 'We'll feed the ducks as soon as the girls get back . . .' she saw he was asleep. He seemed to be enjoying the day. Things were going better than she'd dared to hope. He'd been good with the girls too, keeping them interested. Emma's own eyes felt heavy with drowsiness but she wouldn't give in. It was wonderful to sit here and watch Daniel's dear face, the frown he'd worn lately smoothed away by sleep. She wanted to touch him, to rest his head in her lap, but she was grateful just to be near him, listening to his gentle breathing, her heart swelling with love.

The girls running towards them, giggling happily, broke the spell. As they flopped down on the grass Daniel woke. Looking embarrassed, he said, 'I'm sorry, Emma, I'm rotten company.'

'I fell asleep too,' she lied to put him at his ease.

'The ducks!' Daisy cried. 'When are we going to feed the ducks?'

Getting up and shaking the grass from his coat, Daniel put it on, then held out his hand to help Emma to her feet.

On one of the narrow paths between the flowerbeds it was a job to keep together as the crowds jostled, going in different directions. When Daniel tucked her arm under his Emma was overjoyed.

As they neared the lake the girls ran ahead with Daisy carrying the bag of crusts that had already been broken up, but Emma, wanting to prolong the moment, dawdled by Daniel's side. Suddenly his arm stiffened against hers, then he dropped it to his side and stared as though mesmerised at a couple who were approaching them on the other side of the path. The young woman was fashionably dressed and hung on the arm of an equally smart young man, looking up at him adoringly.

Daniel continued to stare as though he couldn't take his eyes from her but the couple had passed by and hadn't taken their eyes from each other. Was this Cissie, the girl Daniel had been engaged to?

Just then, matching the change of mood, the sun disappeared behind a big black cloud.

'We'd better make for home,' Emma said, trying not to show she was upset.

The last piece of crust was thrown into the water. A couple of ducks snapped at it then began to quarrel. When they'd swum away and the ripples had settled the girls unwillingly turned away and they all made their way towards the exit.

'Can we come again next week?' Dorothy begged.

'We'll save all our crusts, Dorrie,' Daisy told her sister.

'You'll eat all your crusts,' Emma said firmly. 'Anyway they'd be stale.'

To Emma's disappointment Daniel's arm remained stiffly by his side. A tram was waiting at the stop, one that would take them most of the way home. The girls sat facing them on the slatted seats, tired now from all the fresh air. Daniel was silent, wrapped in his own thoughts, but Emma, determined not to let the day be spoilt by that chance encounter, said, 'It's been lovely, hasn't it?'

And he smiled at her and said, 'Yes, I did enjoy it, Emma, especially the band.'

'Will you come next week, Uncle Daniel?'

Emma was grateful to Daisy for asking the question, especially when he answered right away, 'I'd love to. If you'll have me?'

Chapter Twenty-Four

The thought of Daniel's accompanying them again kept Emma happy until the following Saturday morning when she woke to torrential rain. Perhaps it will stop soon, she thought hopefully, but it grew steadily worse, bouncing off the pavements, roaring through the down-pipes, racing along the gutters which were soon in flood as drains failed to cope.

After breakfast two disconsolate little girls stared out of the streaming parlour window, elbows resting on the sill, chins cupped in their hands, until Emma, taking pity on them, said, 'Shall we make some toffee?'

They jumped up eagerly, weather forgotten for the moment as they ran before her to the kitchen.

'Perhaps it will stop by the time we've finished,' Daisy said hopefully, fetching the tin of treacle from the pantry, but it didn't seem likely, especially when ten minutes later Emma had to light the gas for the kitchen was suddenly as dark as night. But when thunder rumbled overhead the girls were so engrossed in stirring the toffee they didn't even notice.

That night Emma was wakened by one of them coughing, but as she got out of bed and pulled her dressing gown around her the sound stopped so she got back into bed after lighting the candle to look at the clock. It was ten past three. Blowing out the flame she lay back, but before she could settle down she heard Sam's heavy footsteps on the stairs then his bedroom door opening and clicking shut.

No wonder he looks so tired, she thought. Doing a hard day's work then staying up for most of the night. But today being Sunday he could have a good lie-in.

She seemed hardly to have dozed off when the coughing started once more, this time raucous and persistent. Shrugging into her dressing gown again, Emma hurried to the girls' room.

Dorothy sat up in bed, eyes bulging, face red as she gulped for air. When at last the coughing eased she lay back against the pillows, exhausted, but had to sit up again right away as she struggled for breath. By this time Emma's arms were around her.

'I'll go down for the cough mixture, Dorrie,' she soothed, unconsciously using the name Daisy had given her sister and which seemed somehow to convey the love and affection she felt for the child.

A rudely awakened Daisy was watching her sister with frightened eyes. As Emma rose from the bed to go downstairs Daisy put her arm about her little sister and cwtched her close. When Emma returned with the bottle of medicine Sam sat beside Dorothy, looking concerned. When Emma had settled the child and turned the gas low, he said, 'I think you'd better take her to the doctor on Monday morning, Emma. Dorothy's not a strong child. We don't want to take any risks.' And she felt pleased that Sam had roused himself from his apathy enough to care. But when Monday came Dorothy seemed feverish and Daisy had to deliver a note on her way to school asking Doctor Armitage to call.

There were mounds of washing waiting to go into the boiler which was bubbling away, but Emma was too worried to care as Dorrie tossed and turned in bed, her small face flushed, eyes unnaturally bright. When the doctor came at last he didn't seem unduly concerned. Giving the child something that would help bring down her temperature, he said, 'Could you come to the surgery about one o'clock? I'll be back from my rounds by then. There'll be a bottle of linctus for her cough and something to cool her down.'

Then, his hand on the doorknob, Doctor Armitage turned to Emma to enquire, 'Is the child worrying about anything, do you think? School perhaps? Her temperature isn't high enough to warrant all this restlessness.'

Emma shook her head for if she told Doctor Armitage what Dorrie was really worried about it would implicate Sam and would only cause trouble.

The doctor had gone and she was bathing Dorrie's face when a plaintive voice asked: 'Will you stay with me, Emma? I'm frightened.'

'But there's nothing to be frightened of, cariad.'

'Will my mama come and fetch me now I'm ill?'

'Fetch you? Your mama!' She tried to make the idea sound ridiculous but could tell by the child's eyes that she wasn't convinced.

'Your mama loves you very much, she wants you to get better quickly and to stay with Daisy and your father. What your dadda meant about being together one day was when you're a very old lady, and tired. You'll be glad to go to her then, I expect.'

'But I'd be older than Mama by that time.'

'Oh no you wouldn't!' Emma had suddenly decided to give

her imagination full rein. 'I think everyone must be young again when their spirit gets to Heaven. You never see statues of elderly angels, do you, love?'

Dorrie seemed satisfied and settled down to sleep. By next morning her temperature was normal but the cough was still harsh and Doctor Armitage suggested that it would be easier for Emma and company for Dorothy if she rested on the couch in the kitchen. When she was settled against the cushions with a shawl about her shoulders and a blanket tucked about her, her favourite picture books by her side, Emma was at last able to get on with the washing with an easy mind.

To Emma's joy Dorrie's illness, instead of keeping Daniel away, brought them closer, for as soon as he heard the doctor was calling he came around to see if there was any shopping to be done. But Maud, good neighbour that she was, had taken care of that chore. As soon as Dorrie was brought downstairs he came whenever he could to play dominoes or simple card games, or just read to her to keep her amused, and soon they were planning their next day out. But once again when the longed for Saturday came the weather was dull and overcast. With Dorrie's recent illness in mind Emma regretfully decided they couldn't risk it although she was doubly disappointed, having planned to wear her new straw boater and cornflower blue muslin blouse.

'I think I've managed to shut up that Lena Brown for good,' Maud told her with satisfaction the next time they had a cup of tea together. 'Scuttles back into her house she does whenever she sees me coming.'

'I've never thanked you properly for what you did,' Emma told her gratefully.

'Just seeing those girls looking so bonny and happy is enough for me. 'Sides I'm not the only one who's told her she's a spiteful interfering bugger!'

Emma laughed at her friend's vehement words, knowing that the swear word was the only way Maud could express her feelings where their unpopular neighbour was concerned.

'By the way, Emma,' Maud said now, 'I'm goin' to see a fortune teller tomorrow after tea. 'Ow about you comin' along?'

'I'd love to but I can't leave the girls.'

'Youer Daniel will keep them amused.'

'But if it's in the evening like you said, Sam will be home,' Emma told her, wishing that he was her Daniel, for although they were the best of friends he certainly wasn't hers.

When Emma told him she'd like to go out for an hour with Maud, Sam said, 'Well, I'm here if they need me, and you say you won't be very long.'

The girls were playing with some dominoes at the table when Maud knocked on the door. As they walked up the street Emma felt a surge of excitement at the thought of having her fortune told, though Maud had already warned her, 'It may be a load of old rubbish so don't take what she says to heart.'

They had each come with some silver. Emma had several threepenny and sixpenny bits in her purse for Maud had said you had to cross Madam Rose's palm with silver before she looked at your hand or laid the cards on the table.

'"Madam Rose" she calls herself,' Maud said with a chuckle, 'but she was plain Rosie Smith before she married that Archie Stubbs.'

Although she laughed with Maud, Emma knew that she was hoping to be told that Daniel would one day love her enough to ask her to marry him, but after what Maud had just said, could she believe it if she was?

197

When they reached the small terraced house and had knocked, the door was opened by a lanky boy who ushered them into the narrow passage, yelling, 'Mam! Youer women 'ave come,' and disappeared upstairs.

They stood for a moment, staring up at a faded print of 'The Stag at Bay', then the kitchen door opened and a small, thin woman, still untying her apron strings, came towards them, saying, 'Youer early for youer appointment, but no matter.' And opening the parlour door, she stood aside to let them pass.

'I'd better explain,' she went on, 'I can only deal with one client at a time. The other must wait in the passage. You can sit on the stair if you like.'

Remembering the worn and dirty oil-cloth she'd noticed when they came in Emma decided to stand outside the door while Maud took her seat at the rickety table and produced her silver coins.

It seemed a long time to Emma as she studied the two prints that hung on the wall, for there was one of Joan of Arc at the stake as well as the Stag at Bay, all the time trying to suppress mounting excitement at the thought of what she might be told.

When at last Maud came out she was smiling but nothing was said as Emma went into the room and took her place at the table. Having crossed Madam's palm with silver, she had her own palm turned over for the fortune teller to stare at intently. Emma couldn't help feeling a little disappointed. She'd imagined a woman dressed in gypsy clothes and there wasn't even a crystal ball on the table, no colourful dress, no jangling ear-rings. The woman's face was sallow and lined, her eyes looked tired, but they held a kindly expression and Emma warmed to her.

'Youer going to have a long and healthy life, love,' she told

Emma, 'but there's no man as yet though you'd like there to be, am I right?'

She was staring now at the cards she'd dealt which lay face up on the table. 'But wait,' she said. 'It looks as though in the not too distant future you will have a proposal of marriage from a man who has dark eyes and dark hair, but he isn't the one you want to propose to you. It isn't a good match for you. You must follow your heart.'

Emma stared at her in dismay. It was Daniel she'd wanted to hear about, Daniel whom she'd hoped to be told would eventually propose. Daniel with his deep blue eyes and fair complexion. She didn't want to think about marrying anyone else. The woman must be wrong. Daniel would notice her one day, she'd just have to be patient.

Overwhelmed with disappointment, Emma got up. Giving the woman a watery smile, she went to join Maud.

Chapter Twenty-Five

It had been a wonderful summer. Daniel's haunted look had gradually disappeared and he became brown and healthy-looking as they explored the countryside with the girls or took the train to Penarth, crunching over the pebbles to skim smaller ones into the sea. Sometimes they went as far as Barry Island, walking over the golden sands of Whitmore Bay to the edge of the water, listening as the hissing waves receded, to rise again and race up the beach in a lather of foam; breathing deeply of the sea air which, here on the shoreline, was tangy with the smell of seaweed that lay fat and glossy and sand-speckled in tangled masses.

Occasionally they took the tram to Victoria Park where the newly installed Billy the Seal, who had recently been brought to Cardiff by one of Neale and West's trawlers, was drawing the crowds. When at last the girls tired of the seal's antics they'd rush to see the chattering monkeys swing from perch to perch in their little house which was always surrounded by excited children.

Although Daniel always accompanied them and was equally attentive to Emma and the girls, their relationship hadn't really progressed. They were just good friends, and that was all. Emma felt keen disappointment when they parted casually at the gate.

'So long, girls,' Daniel would say. 'See you next week if not before.'

There'd be no tender lingering look between them and Emma would follow the girls into the house, her heart heavy.

When the ever shortening autumn days gave way to strong winds and squally showers she dreaded the approaching winter when she'd have to find excuses to go to Daniel's house, for the thought of not seeing him for weeks on end was unbearable. But when November came in, damp and foggy, and all thoughts of walks were abandoned, he called often on Saturday afternoons when he knew Sam would be at work, bringing cut-outs for the girls' scrap books and little culinary treats from his mother, who never tired of telling Emma how grateful she was that Daniel was now his normal cheerful self.

As Christmas approached, with the rich fruit cake and puddings stored away, and the girls clamouring to make colourful paper chains and put them up, Emma wished she could have a family party and invite all her aunts and uncles, and Ellie and David too if he would come. But it wasn't her house and she knew how Sam hated company even when it was people he knew.

It was Dorrie who brought up the subject one teatime at the beginning of December, saying, 'Couldn't Ellie come to tea, Emma? We've been to her house lots of times.'

The lots of times had been just twice but Emma let it go as Sam said, 'Who's Ellie? Is she a little friend of theirs?'

Emma had to hide a smile at the thought of the stout Ellie being anyone's little friend, but Dorrie was begging, 'Can she, Daddy?' and when Daisy added her plea, Emma explained about her cousin and how she'd loved playing with the girls.

'And Daisy and Dorothy get on well with her – that's nice.'

Emma was surprised and pleased that he'd roused himself to take part in the conversation but his next words belied any hope that he'd changed.

'I'm dreading Christmas,' he told Emma when the girls had gone to the parlour in search of a book. 'It was late in November last year that I lost Sarah, and I thought I'd go out of my mind.'

As he turned away she thought she heard him add, 'Sometimes I think I have,' and shivered, remembering the eerie night hours when she'd lain awake listening to him talking to someone who wasn't there.

Turning to her again, he said, 'I've been thinking, Emma, I can't face visitors myself but if it will please you and the girls, why don't you invite your cousin and her mother to tea on Boxing Day? I'd like to visit an old workmate of mine. He's a widower and lives alone. Perhaps you could pack me some slices of chicken and ham and a good slice of that cake you made. I'm sure he'd be very grateful.'

Perhaps Aunt Mattie will come too, Emma thought excitedly. Uncle Fred was sure to go out for a pint with his friends and David would have his own friends anyway.

Now Christmas couldn't come quick enough. As soon as she told them, the girls began to search their toy cupboard for things to keep Ellie amused.

'And there'll be all the things Father Christmas brings this year,' Dorrie said happily.

'He didn't bring us much last year,' Daisy reminded her, and when Dorrie replied, without finishing the sentence, 'But that was because Mama . . .' Emma made up her mind that this Christmas would be one they'd remember.

Preparations for the holiday were well ahead. Presents she'd bought for the girls were stacked in hat-boxes and put on top of the wardrobe well out of the reach of prying fingers. Colourful red and yellow paper chains were looped across the rooms from picture rail to picture rail, a bunch of mistletoe hung in the passage, and glossy, prickly-leaved holly endowed with plenty of red berries draped every picture in the house.

The girls were so excited waiting for their father to come home to see the decorations, but after saying gruffly, 'I see you've got them up then,' he took no further notice.

On Christmas Eve, with a big bowl of trifle waiting in the pantry, a piece of boiled ham cooling on the table, chocolates and sweets hoarded away and a plentiful supply of lemonade and herb and ginger beer standing on the flagstoned floor of the cupboard, Emma was waiting for the farmer who supplied them with eggs to deliver the fat chicken for which she'd already cleared a space in the mesh-covered safe in the yard. Remembering family gatherings from her childhood when her aunts had indulged in glasses of port and lemon, she decided to buy a bottle of port with some of her savings, and some dainty biscuits to hand around with the drinks after tea.

Sam had been very generous both with the housekeeping and money for the girls' presents, and at the side of their bed next morning were two beautiful dolls dressed in velvet coats and bonnets and a lot of small things to keep them amused. Sam was being more sociable than she'd ever seen him but Emma knew what an effort it was for him and sighed with relief when at last he took himself off to his room.

On Boxing Day he seemed to be really looking forward to visiting his old friend, taking a great interest as Emma prepared the delicacies he wanted and carefully put them in an airtight tin. He was ready to go out by the time the lunchtime dishes were cleared, and picking up the parcel, said, 'Bert's going to be pleased with these. Poor chap, he lost his wife two and a half years ago. It must be terribly lonely for him, having no children.'

'He'll be glad to see you,' Emma said. 'How long is it since you met?'

'I've only seen him twice since his wife's funeral,' Sam admitted. 'We were never close friends even when we worked together, but losing Sarah has made me realise what it's like for other people, and I remember how low he was at the time.'

As soon as Sam left, with the girls' help Emma put out little dishes of sweets and nuts, replenished the parlour fire, fussed with the cushions, then after combing her hair yet again stood looking out of the parlour window, anxious for her aunts and cousin to arrive.

The girls had put away their new dolls. Even they had realised how rough Ellie could be with things when she got excited. When they saw Aunt Mabel and their friend passing the window they all made a dash for the door.

Mabel had just asked, 'Isn't our Mattie here yet?' when there was another knock. Emma poured out three port and lemons and they settled down for a chat, but she'd no sooner put the glass to her lips than Mattie gasped, 'You've made these strong, cariad, but who's complaining?' They all laughed and went on laughing all through tea, with Ellie, enjoying for once being the centre of attention, mindful of her manners, eyes bright, plump cheeks wobbling with excitement as she squealed with joy.

After tea they played musical chairs with Aunt Mattie at the piano and Daisy and Dorothy giggling as they entered into a conspiracy to let Ellie win.

When Daniel came, saying he couldn't stay long, Ellie dragged him under the mistletoe and brought an unsuspecting

Emma into the passage to meet him, and to Emma's joy he took her into his arms and kissed her warmly, his lips clinging to hers, while Ellie, their only audience, proud of her achievement, clapped them enthusiastically.

Ellie isn't nearly as backward as everyone thinks, Emma told herself, grateful and happy for the helping hand. It had been a wonderful day and Daniel's kiss had made it perfect for it certainly hadn't seemed to be an obligatory one.

As the evening wore on she kept glancing at the clock, anxious that her visitors should be gone, or at least be doing something less boisterous than singing their hearts out at the piano when Sam returned.

When Sam set off on the long walk to his friend's house it was bitterly cold, with pavements and roof-tops rimed with frost under a leaden sky. He walked briskly to keep warm, his breath steaming on the wintry air. He was thinking of Bert and how they would commiserate with each other. Only two souls who had suffered the torments of bereavement could really understand.

Perhaps the poor chap would be too sunk in his own misery to bother with Christmas. He himself felt like that, but with Emma's help he'd had to provide the trappings even though he hadn't felt like celebrating, for he had the girls to consider.

As he raised the knocker of his friend's door he wondered for the first time if he'd been wise to come unannounced, but by the time he'd made up his mind there'd been no way of letting Bert know.

The woman who opened the door to him was plump and pretty and wearing a party hat.

Sam lifted his bowler and said he was sorry, he must have the wrong address.

'Who did you want?' she asked pleasantly.

'Bert Thomas,' he told her, but she was standing aside for him to enter the house.

'Bert is my husband,' she told him, then seeing his look of surprise, added, 'we've been married eighteen months.'

The kitchen door opened. There was laughter and chatter then Bert was coming towards Sam. He too was wearing a party hat, his face ruddy and smiling.

'Good Lord! It's Sam Evans,' he cried. 'Take off youer coat man, it's warm in here.'

But Sam didn't want to take it off. He meant to escape from all this conviviality as quickly as he could. He'd have been better off staying at home. At least there wouldn't have been so many there. He sat down and slipped the tin he was carrying underneath his chair. One glance at the dishes on the table with hardly a pin's point between them had more than convinced him his contribution wasn't needed.

'This is Gert, my wife,' Bert was saying. 'What brings you this way, Sam?'

The paper hat had slipped over one eye. Pushing it back with a laugh, he went on: 'These good people are all her relatives, too numerous to mention.'

There were chuckles at this and Sam saw now that they all wore brightly coloured paper hats.

The laughter and chatter had started up again. When he was settled with a glass of ale in his hand, someone began to play a mouth-organ and Gert got up. Clasping her hands in front of her and taking a deep breath that swelled her ample bosom, she began to sing 'Come Into The Garden, Maud' in a trembling high-pitched voice.

'Got married the summer before last we did,' Bert was

207

confiding in Sam's ear. 'No sense in both being lonely. Not much chance of that, though, with Gert's relations around!'

Sam was wondering how soon he could escape. The music, if you could call it that, was giving him a headache. But what excuse could he make? Then his foot touched the tin and in a sudden burst of inspiration he lifted it up, saying, 'I've got to deliver this by teatime. Just called in to see how you were on the way.'

'Oh, well, if you've made up youer mind . . .' Sam sensed the relief in his friend's voice. He said his goodbyes quickly, glad to get away from all these garrulous strangers. He didn't know Bert any more, perhaps he never had. His friend saw him to the door then Sam was alone in the darkening street. It wasn't yet four o'clock. He thought longingly of his comfortable bedroom at home, cosy in the firelight, the basket chair piled with cushions, books on a shelf at the side of the fire. If only he'd stayed home he could have escaped up there after greeting Emma's relatives for they wouldn't have wanted him to stay either.

He walked slowly at first, staring into the windows of shops closed for the holiday, wondering how he was going to pass the weary hours until Emma's relatives decided to go home.

A couple of hours later pangs of hunger made him open the tin he carried and take out a piece of cake. It tasted so delicious that he took out another. Emma was a wonderful cook.

Sam was about halfway home and unconsciously quickening his step when he saw the notice in the light shed by a street lamp. It was pasted outside a shabby hall and the words SPIRITUALIST MEETING in capital letters caught his interest. Tired and cold as he was, he felt a strange excitement stirring within him. If all else failed might not this be the way to bring

Sarah to him? Only last night he'd once again felt her presence in the room with him, though as yet she'd made no sign.

He'd reached Newport Road before he realised he hadn't looked to see when the meeting was to be held. Still he didn't really want other people involved, not yet, not until he was sure there was no other way. He'd feel uncomfortable parading his grief in front of strangers, but his need to communicate with Sarah was so great he knew he'd try anything to achieve it.

Lifting his watch from his pocket, Sam peered at it anxiously. Would Emma's visitors be gone by now? It would be eight o'clock by the time he got home.

To Emma's relief, for Sam could return any minute, Mattie finished the tune she was playing and closed the lid of the piano.

'I think it's time we were going, Mabel,' she told her sister who had also seen Emma watching the clock anxiously.

'I don't want to go yet,' Ellie wailed.

'Come on, love,' her mother coaxed. 'I'll just go and get your coat and you can put it on.'

'One more song, Auntie Mattie,' she cried. 'Only one more. Please!'

'It's quicker to give in to her when she's overtired,' Mabel told her sister.

'A short one then. How about "She's Only a Bird"?'

Aunt Mattie's plump fingers caressed the keys as she played the introduction. Ellie's flat voice soared tunelessly, managing to put everyone off key. As they started the second verse there was the sound of the front door opening. Before anyone could stop her Ellie streaked past them and into the passage with everyone following. The next moment, to their horror, she was planting kisses all over a very embarrassed-looking Sam's face.

Emma stood rooted to the ground with an equally immobile aunt on either side.

'Oh my God!' Mattie managed at last as Sam tried to wriggle free. When he finally pushed Ellie roughly aside she was red with rage and frustration. Dashing towards him once more, she swung her boot hard in the direction of his shin.

Chapter Twenty-Six

As Sam, face contorted with pain, limped his way upstairs, Emma followed. He turned to her, his voice bitter, to say, 'Just get rid of them, Emma, will you? That young woman's a fiend. She's not safe to be with. I don't want my daughters to see her again. Do you understand?'

After what had happened the moment he'd come through the door, Emma could hardly blame him, yet until now the girls and Ellie had seemed to be good for each other.

At the bottom of the stairs Ellie was threshing about in her mother's arms. Dorothy and Daisy, shocked by what she'd done to their daddy, were looking frightened and overtired. Her first priority must be to get them to bed, but how could she when even Aunt Mattie's commonsense couldn't bring order to the scene?

'He shouldn't have shoved her like that,' Mabel was saying over and over. 'My Ellie just wanted to be friendly, and what does he do? He pushes her away. It's only natural she's upset.'

'She kicked him Mabel, for God's sake. He'll be limping for days. She can't be allowed to go around kicking people just 'cos she's upset. Let's go now and give the poor man some peace.' Aunt Mattie had gathered their coats.

It was another ten minutes before they managed to get Ellie's coat on, her tears dried and her nose wiped, then, still wailing, dragged along by Aunt Mabel and Aunt Mattie who supported her either side, they made their way along the street, causing Emma further distress for in her mind's eye she could see the lace curtains twitching as neighbours wondered what on earth had been happening at Sam Evans' house to account for all that rumpus.

Just a short while before Emma had been looking forward to the time when her visitors left so that she could relive the moment when Daniel's lips had lingered so warmly on hers. She hadn't imagined the warmth of that kiss, she was sure of that. When the girls, still shaken at the turn of events, were at last settled down, she went downstairs. In the dimmed gas-light she stared up at the bunch of mistletoe that for a long moment had made her wildest dreams come true. Even the awful events of the last half-hour couldn't take that away, but she feared they could have long-term repercussions.

Should she go up to Sam? The poor man must be in a lot of pain. But when she tapped on his door he didn't even open it, but told her gruffly, 'You get on to bed. I'll see to my own meal when I come down.'

Emma washed the few glasses and cups and saucers that had been used since tea, and though it was only a quarter to nine made her way upstairs, calling out, 'Goodnight, Sam,' as she passed his door, so that he would know the coast was clear which was what he obviously wanted.

She snuffed out the candle and got between the chilly sheets, for in her rush she'd forgotten to bring the hot brick wrapped in flannel to put in her bed and spending so little time in her room except to sleep rarely bothered to light a fire.

A little while later she heard the clatter of dishes as he

prepared his supper. Poor Sam, cutting himself off from everyone as he did, there was no one to give sympathy when he most needed it. But he didn't want her company, he'd made that abundantly clear.

Sam sat in the firelight drinking his second cup of tea. For his supper he'd finished off the contents of the tin he'd brought back, together with two thick rounds of bread and butter. He still felt hungry, but was too tired to get up and cut another round from the loaf.

He'd had a miserable day, walking around for most of the time in the bitter cold. He wished now though that he'd stayed out a little longer and avoided Emma's relatives altogether. That woman – girl – whichever she was, should be locked up. He was frightened to think that he'd allowed his girls to play with her. Sam rolled up his trousers and touched his aching shin gingerly. He'd have a fine old bruise by tomorrow.

His thoughts went to Bert and the surprise of him marrying again so soon, and his eyes flew to Sarah's picture, assuring her that he would never marry anyone else. She had been his world and could never be replaced.

In a low voice he began to talk to her again but soon grew tired of the one-sided conversation. Perhaps one day in desperation he would go to one of those spiritualist meetings he'd seen advertised, but he'd give it a while longer. Tonight his leg was throbbing and his head was beginning to ache. Emma had lit the fire in his room before he'd returned. It would be cosy up there. Yawning widely, he got ready, locked the back door and, turning off the gas, limped upstairs.

On a bitterly cold morning just over a week later Emma was

taking down the Christmas decorations. Although it wasn't yet eleven o'clock it was so dark in the kitchen that she'd had to light the gas. Going over to the window and looking up at a sky heavy with the promise of snow, she thought worriedly, I hope it won't start before the girls get home from school.

The bunch of mistletoe that hung in the passage was the last thing to take down, and remembering the warmth of Daniel's kiss when they'd stood beneath it, Emma felt loath to remove it. He'd kissed her in the same way last night and just thinking of it brought a glow of pleasure as she brought a chair from the kitchen. She'd only just mounted it and was stretching fingers still tingling from the sharp holly leaves to reach the mistletoe when there was a knock at the front door.

'You shouldn't be doing that, Emma,' Daniel said when she'd let him in. 'I'll get it down in a minute, but meanwhile we might just as well make use of it, don't you think?'

Laughing as he pushed the chair out of the way, he took her in his arms. Holding her close he kissed her until they had to tear apart for breath. Then, his arms still about her, he said simply, 'I love you, Emma. I think I've loved you for a very long time.'

Emma whispered breathlessly, 'I love you too, Daniel.' I always have, she thought happily, from the moment we first met. She wanted to pinch herself to make sure it wasn't all a dream but the look in Daniel's eyes as he gazed down at her told her it was real and her heart leapt with joy. When his arms tightened about her and his lips met hers once more the feelings that she'd held in check for so long could be denied no longer and, with her heart hammering so loud she was sure Daniel could hear it, she kissed him as she'd longed to do many times in the past.

When at last they drew apart, Daniel looked at her in wonder, saying, 'Oh Emma! I can hardly believe it. I'm so happy you feel the same way.' Then, his arm still about her, he said simply, 'Will you marry me, Emma?'

It was the most romantic moment of Emma's life, satisfying her wildest dreams. What had changed Daniel over the months from a morose, unhappy man to the lover she'd so longed to have? But now he was looking down at her quizzically, waiting for the answer her heart was clamouring to give.

'I'd love to, Daniel,' she told him, smiling with joy.

'Shall we go tomorrow to choose the ring?' he asked, the kiss he gave her gentle this time. Looking serious, he confided: 'I told myself I'd never get engaged again after last time, but you're not like Cissie. I know you won't deceive me. Anyway, I had only myself to blame. We won't tell Mam until we've bought the ring, cariad, then we can surprise her.'

Then their arms tightened about each other again and this time it was the girls' knocking on the door when they returned from school that tore them apart. As Emma opened the door her heart singing with joy, an icy wind blew a flurry of snow indoors and she saw that the pavements were already peppered with snowflakes. Pulling his coat collar about his ears, Daniel stepped out into the street, saying, 'Close the door, Emma love, I'll see you later.' Returning to the room, Emma hugged to herself the knowledge that her dearest dream had come true.

They went shopping for the ring the following morning. In the jewellers, Emma chose a ring with diamond chippings set either side of an emerald but knowing she was only worrying about the expense Daniel picked up a lovely half-hoop of diamonds and slipped it on to her finger.

Outside, the promised snow had not settled as yet, and there was an icy wind tearing at everything, but despite the cold, Emma's heart was aglow and, looking up at the tall handsome young man by her side, she was overcome with love for him.

They went into a tea-room in the arcade to celebrate the occasion with iced cakes and a steaming cup of tea. Both knew it would be some time before they could marry but they were content.

When they reached Daniel's house there was still half-an-hour to go before the girls would be home from school. Alice Thompson was delighted with the ring, gathering Emma into her arms and kissing her before crying, 'Oh love! I couldn't be more pleased. We must drink to your engagement. Get the glasses from the sideboard, Daniel. I've only got parsnip wine, but it'll do.' And she was thanking God, though she should really be thanking Emma, she told herself, for the miraculous change in her son, from the morose, unhappy man when Cissie left him to this happy, smiling man today.

As they raised their glasses, Emma gazed lovingly down at the ring Daniel had put on her finger, anticipating the pleasure of showing it to Maud, Martha and her three aunts. She wouldn't be able to marry Daniel until the girls were older, of course, but there were plans to make and things to buy for her bottom drawer. Emma couldn't wait to start.

Sam often thought about the meetings he meant one day to attend but had no idea when they were to be held and shrank from asking anyone. Then in the spring, glancing through the small advertisements in the newspaper, he saw a notice that one was to be held the following Wednesday evening. Wednesday was his half-day; he'd have ample time to get ready and be at the hall by seven-fifteen.

Before Sarah died I'd have scoffed at anyone who thought they could get in touch with spirits, he told himself honestly, but the strong conviction he had that Sarah was near, and his deep need to be reassured had changed all that.

The evening meal was always earlier on his half-day, and when he'd told Emma he was going out she'd looked surprised and pleased, and had filled the jug on his wash-stand with hot water ready for him and left a clean towel by the bowl.

'It will do you good to get out, Sam,' she'd told him before taking the empty kettle downstairs.

She's a real treasure, he told himself. Wonderful with the girls and the housekeeping. He still found himself worrying about the propriety of their living under the same roof but there was no harm in it, they both knew their place. He'd never heard of any tittle-tattle, and now she was engaged to Daniel, the boy from the next street. Anyway everyone must know by now that he was as surely married to Sarah as when she was alive.

Sam had never attended a Spiritualist meeting, never met a medium; perhaps being a shy person by nature Sarah needed this kind of help. His hopes were high and he quickened his step as he neared the hall, nervous now at the thought of this new experience.

There were only about a dozen people as yet, but he sat down on a bench at the back and looked towards the dimly lit stage where a man – was he the chairman? – sat at a small table in one corner against the faded velvet drapes, while centre stage was a single chair and a larger table on which stood a carafe of water and a glass. People were whispering amongst themselves but when a stout pleasant-faced lady walked up the steps and on to the stage there was a burst of clapping. She wore a loose-fitting dress in a brown material, the wide-fitting sleeves falling back from her plump wrists as she raised her hands in greeting.

At first she just talked to the audience, assuring them that there was life after death, a passing into the spirit world. Sam listened intently, almost mesmerised as the soothing voice went on. Presently she paused, her head slightly to one side as though listening, and in a loud voice now she said, 'Someone is with me. I hear the name Harry. I sense this gentleman is sitting in the front row. Your father . . . Thomas, is it?' A man in the front row nodded agreement and she went on, 'Well, your father says you are thinking of changing your job and he urges you to do so for there'll be more opportunities for you in this new place. You haven't been well. It's too hot and steamy for you where you are now.' She paused and the man in front told her, 'I work in a laundry, it's affecting my chest.'

'Your father says this new job will change all that.'

The man was nodding at everything the medium said. Sam could see him clearly for there were very few people in between, but already Mrs Alice Buxton was looking in another direction, saying, 'They're crowding in now. I have a young girl who says her name's Tessa. She was twelve when she passed over last year. She's giving me her mother's name . . . Maryanne.'

A hand shot up in the middle of the hall, that of a woman with a hankie to her eyes, and the medium continued, 'Tessa wants you to know she's happy. She's with her nan and wishes you weren't so sad.'

A tall lady dressed in black rose and rushed towards the stage, crying: 'Tessa, oh Tessa love, tell me again that you're happy?'

'She says she's met Aunt Jinny, and that Jinny and her nan look after her.'

By this time Sam had realised with some disappointment

that even if Sarah did come through, a message only would be relayed to him. At first he was upset at the thought, but it would still be wonderful to make contact at all, to be told she was happy, to be assured of her love. When presently the medium said, 'I have a Sarah here,' his hand shot up quickly but she went on, 'She wants to speak to her husband Joseph whom she left so suddenly there was no time to say goodbye.'

Perhaps he was expecting too much on his very first visit, Sam comforted himself. Perhaps next time. He noticed a lady nearby smoothing a gentleman's tie lovingly between her fingers. That's what I'll do next week, he thought. I'll bring one of Sarah's scarves. Scented with lavender it would be from the little bags tied with ribbon that she'd kept in the drawer. Something of hers, something she'd worn and touched, something that had caressed her silky skin.

On the following Wednesday he got ready to go out and, laying his bowler on the bed, began to search for the blue silk scarf he remembered Sarah wearing. He'd searched three drawers and, looking at his watch, was beginning to panic, calling Daisy to help him.

'Why do you want Mama's scarf, Daddy?' she asked, lifting it from the bottom drawer and handing it to him.

'I wanted to see it again,' he said lamely.

Daisy gave him a curious look and went downstairs.

When he reached the dilapidated hall there were even fewer in the audience than last time. Presently the medium climbed the steps and took her seat at the table, and just as before she began to talk soothingly of the spirit world. Tonight they must have been longer arriving for she went on and on and people were becoming restive when she stopped in mid-sentence to declare, 'I'm getting the name Jessie. Is there a Sid in the hall?'

When a voice had acknowledged this she went on, 'She wants you to stop grieving and do something positive with your life. She says you were married twenty years ago tomorrow. You must be thankful for all the years you had together. She wants you to be happy and says to wait patiently for the day you'll be together again.'

The message was so apt it could have come from Sarah. Sam sat there expectantly until the meeting closed when disappointment engulfed him like a black cloud.

He was almost by the door and settling his bowler on his head when the medium, now dressed for outdoors, came up to him to say: 'I sense that you're losing heart, young man, but you must be patient. Some spirits are too shy for a public meeting. Perhaps it needs a special anniversary? But don't give up. It's still early days.'

Clutching at straws Sam thought of their wedding anniversary, 8 June, it would have been their tenth this year. He looked up to tell Mrs Buxton but she'd gone. Then he saw her, leaving the hall on the arm of a tall man with a beard.

Elated now with fresh hope, Sam made his way home. He saw now that Sarah who'd always been such a private person in life would never be able to parade her feelings in front of strangers. Even though he had been waiting so long for a sign the medium had said he must be patient, but patience had never been his strong point.

Chapter Twenty-Seven

It was 8 June and for days Sam had been behaving even more strangely than usual. This evening, just after he'd gone upstairs, Emma had heard him pulling drawers out one after another. Thinking maybe he couldn't find a shirt or something that she'd ironed and put away, she went up to ask, but before she'd knocked on his door which had been partly open she'd caught sight of several items of his dead wife's clothing laid out on the bed.

When he did finally come downstairs just after the girls had gone to bed, he kept looking at the clock. Presently, as though unable to contain his impatience, he asked, 'Have you much more to do, Emma?'

'I was going to iron the starched things.'

'Can't it wait till tomorrow?'

She knew that if she didn't iron them soon she'd have to damp them down again; besides tomorrow was the day for washing the bedroom oil-cloth and beating the rugs on the line, and there was shopping to be done and meals to prepare. But Sam was looking at her so impatiently that she said. 'I'll just wipe these dishes and put them away then I'll go up.'

His look of relief was hurtful. It seemed he couldn't wait to get rid of her once the girls were in bed. But she knew that it was his obsession with his dead wife that was the cause, and had long feared that Sam, although physically well, was a very sick man.

If it wasn't for the girls, she told herself, I'd have found another job ages ago.

It was real creepy listening to his voice night after night, a pleading, beseeching voice that went on and on. If only she could confide in someone. She'd thought of telling Aunt Mattie but she'd only try to persuade her to leave, and although he was their father, she couldn't abandon the girls to Sam.

When they were having a cup of tea together yesterday Maud had told her that someone had seen Sam going into one of those Spiritualist meetings. Was that where he went all dressed up? Anyway he hadn't come home any happier, but had seemed to be even more impatient than usual, like tonight, practically ordering her up to bed.

Just as it did every night, the talking began when she was upstairs. Emma's bedroom was directly above the kitchen and although she couldn't distinguish the words the tone was pleading.

Pulling the bedclothes over her head she tried to sleep, but it was a humid night and she had to throw them back again. It was too early for bed but what else could she have done?

Sometimes he raised his voice. Once she distinctly heard him cry out, 'Sarah! Oh, Sarah!'

Emma was on the edge of sleep, half dreaming, when she heard Sam yelling angrily, 'Sarah, why don't you speak to me? Today of all days I thought you would come.'

Emma jumped from the bed, her heart pounding, and raced downstairs, but the voice had become calmer again so she sat on the bottom stair, listening worriedly.

'Sarah, listen to me,' he was saying. 'Others make contact. I've been there, I've seen. Today on our wedding anniversary, I was sure you would come. I've been looking through your things, handling them, thinking it might bring us close. They smell of lavender as you always did. Oh God, woman! If you don't come to me soon, give me some sign, I'll see to it I come to you.' His words ended on a sob.

Then it became quiet, too quiet. Emma's nerves were at breaking point. What should she do? Sam wasn't sane at these moments. Supposing she came down in the morning to find him hanging from the banisters, swinging to and fro like poor Mr Davison in the next street? Getting up to go to the kitchen she realised she was only wearing her night-gown. She must be quick. There was a blue chenille dressing gown hanging on the back of Sam's bedroom door. She'd never understood why he didn't put it away but was grateful for it now.

Downstairs once more Emma tip-toed to the kitchen, her bare feet making no sound. At the half-open door she hesitated. Sam was sitting on the edge of the sofa staring at Sarah's picture, his hands pressed together as though in prayer, but if he was praying it must be to his dead wife.

Emma was more frightened than she could ever remember being but crept into the room and sat down near Sam, but with his back to her he didn't even sense she was there. Her heart in her mouth, she put a hand gently on Sam's shoulder and saw him turn with hope in his eyes, and stare down at the blue dressing gown. Next moment his arms were tight about her, and he was crying, 'Oh, Sarah! I knew you'd come.'

He bore a protesting Emma down to the sofa and, oblivious of her struggles, feeble against his own renewed strength, lifted the dressing gown. A moment later Emma's screams rang out as a searing pain tore through her, but there was no stopping Sam as he moved rhythmically, each thrust a new agony, sobbing: 'Sarah! Oh, Sarah!' over and over again.

When at last he lay still, breathing heavily, his arm still about her where she lay moaning and crying, he whispered, 'I didn't mean to hurt you, Sarah, my love. It's been so long.'

'I'm Emma,' she sobbed, then covered her face with her hands and began moaning again.

'Emma?' He shook his head disbelievingly. 'This is your gown, Sarah. I bought it for you when Dorothy was born.'

'I'm Emma.'

Taking her hands from her face, Sam drew her forward towards the firelight. He gasped, then in a shaken voice, cried, 'Oh God! What have I done?'

Feeling sick with disgust, sore and bruised, Emma tried to get up, to put some distance between herself and the man who had done this to her, but Sam pulled her down again to sit beside him, saying with a voice filled with regret, 'I wouldn't have had this happen for the world, Emma. I know now I must be mad. I've been praying for Sarah to come back and I believed she'd answered my prayer. That blue gown . . . it was hers. I'll make up any way I can. I'll . . . I'll marry you. It's the least I can do.'

'No!' she cried. 'No!' And pushed him away, filled with revulsion at the thought. It was Daniel she wanted to marry, Daniel to whom she was engaged. But would he still want her after this? Emma gave a sob of despair.

'But supposing you have a child? I'm so sorry, Emma. I must have been quite mad. I wanted Sarah so much, I wanted to believe. You must hate me, and I deserve that. Oh, God! What can I do?'

Ignoring his words, still sobbing, Emma got up and crept upstairs. Under the dim light on the landing she took off the dressing gown, intending to put it back on its peg, but as she folded it she saw blood stains and there were others on her nightie too. Sick with fright, she crept between the sheets and sobbed herself to sleep.

Chapter Twenty-Eight

Next morning Emma woke puffy-eyed to the awful realisation of what had happened. Her head ached and she wanted to bury it in her pillow and sob her heart out, but the girls must be got ready for school. Bruised in spirit as well as body she got up and, pouring cold water from the jug into the flowered bowl on the wash-stand, bathed her eyes and splashed her face, but it made little difference for her eyes were mere slits in the swollen redness and her heart was heavy with pain. How was she to face Daisy and Dorrie? What possible explanation could she give for the way she looked?

When she entered the kitchen Sam was already there, making himself a cup of tea. Obviously embarrassed, he said without looking at her, 'Don't forget what I said last night, Emma. If you need to we'll get married. I owe you that much.' Without waiting for her answer he went upstairs.

Blind anger gripped her as she realised that all Sam was worried about was if she became pregnant. Didn't he know that whether she had a baby or not he had ruined her life? It had come as a deep shock to her to realise that this was the way babies were conceived. The nightmare of last night would stay with her for ever. How was she going to tell Daniel? If only it could have been he on their wedding night who'd initiated her into married life. Daniel, she was sure, would be thoughtful and gentle. She loved him with all her heart and only with him would have wanted to express the deep love she felt.

'How soon can we be married?' he had asked. 'I know Mam will let us have two rooms until we can find a place of our own, and you two get on so well.'

But how could she leave the girls? They were still children, Daisy was nine now and Dorrie seven. Emma had thought she'd train Daisy to look after the house; she was already a good little cook, especially at making cakes or anything she liked. But there was a lot more to house-keeping than baking cakes. It was hard enough for a grown woman leave alone a child like Daisy. Scrubbing floors, beating mats, the endless washing and drying, mangling, ironing. Even when Daisy was twelve and could leave school it would be too much to expect of her, but at least by then Dorrie would be old enough to help.

Emma'd felt pity at the thought of Daisy's future, remembering her long-time ambition to work in a shop.

'You worked in a draper's once, didn't you, Emma?' she'd asked. 'That's what I'd like to do when I leave school. I'd like to work in the Baby Department.'

'Baby Linen they call it,' Emma had told her.

It was going to be hard to tell Daisy she was going to have to stay home to look after her father and Dorrie. It was a bleak future for a young girl, especially one as bright as Daisy.

Emma remembered thinking the three years she would have to wait for Daisy to leave school so that she and Daniel could get married was a very, very long time, but now, faced with the prospect of telling Daniel sometime before their marriage that through no fault of her own she was no longer a virgin, it didn't seem so long after all. What was it the priest asked of the congregation at the wedding service? Something like, 'If anyone knows any just cause why this couple should not be joined in Holy matrimony, speak now or forever hold your peace.'

Hot tears welled up again at the thought of maybe losing Daniel when she told him, and if she was going to have Sam's baby she was going to lose him even sooner, and be pitied or reviled according to their nature by everyone in the streets around. That Lena Brown would be smug with satisfaction, saying 'I told you so' to everyone she met.

Hearing the girls coming downstairs Emma dabbed at her eyes, wondering how she could account for her tears. The first thing Daisy said when she came down was, 'What's wrong, Emma? Has Daddy upset you again?'

She was nearer the truth than she knew but Emma told her, 'I'm a bit upset about something but I'll get over it, love.'

'Does it hurt here?' Dorrie asked, coming into the kitchen and putting her hand where she thought her heart was. 'Can't we kiss it better, Emma?'

''Fraid not, love.' She managed a smile for she and Daisy were always required to kiss Dorrie's hurts better, whether they were of the body or the heart.

When the girls had left for school she went to the calendar that hung on the back of the cupboard door to try and work out when she would know for certain if she was to have a child. It would be a fortnight at least. How was she to bear the uncertainty? And even worse, how was she to bear the awful scandal if the worst happened?

That morning, when Maud called over the garden wall, Emma didn't answer. The back door remained firmly shut and she hoped her friend might think she was out shopping for she couldn't face her well-meant scrutiny as yet.

229

I'll have to pull myself together, Emma told herself, so swallowed the lump in her throat and willed the tears to dry up. By the time the girls returned from school the puffiness around her eyes had begun to go down and she managed a wan smile when Dorrie said honestly, 'I was real worried about you being poorly, Emma, 'cause Mamma was poorly 'fore she went to Jesus.'

She put a comforting arm about the little girl and assured her she wasn't poorly any more.

For the very first time since she'd met him Emma avoided Daniel, knowing that in her present state he must guess that something was very wrong. Most evenings he called over after marking the work he'd set his pupils that day, so she went to bed at the same time as Daisy and Dorrie, leaving Sam to make whatever excuse he liked. But she knew she would have to face Daniel on Saturday for their little outings were by now a regular thing. By this time she hoped to be able to hide her feelings though her heart was in her mouth when on Saturday Dorrie told him, 'Emma's been poorly, Daniel. We was worried 'cos our mamma was poorly before she went to Heaven.'

'You should have let me know. I thought it was funny when I called twice and Sam said you were having an early night. He didn't tell me you weren't well.'

'I didn't tell him, Daniel, but I'm all right now.' But she wasn't, and fearing he'd sense it, did her best to laugh and join in the conversation as they flopped on to the grass at Victoria Park and began on their picnic. Today she was dreading the moment she usually longed for, when the girls went to explore and they were left alone.

Maud too had looked at her curiously the first time Emma had answered her call to have tea.

'I had a bad cold,' Emma told her, hating the lie. 'My eyes were all puffed up and my nose was red.' At least the latter part of her excuse had been true.

As the week passed and they were well into the next, far from avoiding her gaze Sam started looking at her anxiously for some sign that he was in the clear. Emma doubted that he felt as anxious as she did herself. When her period was late she was beside herself with worry, wondering if the worst happened was there any way she could creep away and lose herself in London or some other big city? She had some money saved but how could she possibly keep a job if she found one, with a baby on the way? Besides Daniel would look for her, probably even go to the police for help, and she'd be brought back in disgrace.

Sick with worry she tried to push her fear to the back of her mind, but it was always there. The housework had to go on as usual and when she took the girls to Clifton Street to help carry the groceries she forced herself to be cheerful for their sakes, knowing she could never seriously think of leaving them while they were so young, not even to avoid disgrace.

They had reached the top of Broadway and were turning into Clifton Street when a girl pushing a pram almost bumped into them, and Daisy cried, 'Hello, Flora. Is this your new baby sister?' And the girl, obviously a school friend, said, 'Yes, isn't she lovely? Mama's going to call her Violet. She says she's fast running out of names.'

Looking into the shabby pram, at the baby wrapped to its chin in a matted grey-looking shawl, Emma managed to say, 'She is lovely. How old is she?'

'Two months,' Daisy's friend told her importantly. 'She's goin' to be christened on Sunday.' Then with a quick 'Tara!' Flora pushed the pram away.

231

'We won't never have a sister or brother now Mama's gone,' Daisy said wistfully.

Emma prayed fervently that she was right for she had suddenly realised that if there was to be a little half-sister or brother for Daisy and Dorrie it would have to be hers.

It was with a deep sense of relief that a few days later she knew she wasn't pregnant. At least now she wouldn't be publicly disgraced, her child labelled a bastard, for she'd come to realise that whatever it might cost her she could never marry Sam. Apart from not loving him – all her love was Daniel's – she didn't even like or respect him any more. The way he'd selfishly pursued his own obsession in trying to contact his wife while having very little time for his two girls, despite the fact that after their mother's death they'd been equally bereft and sadly neglected, had sorely tried Emma's patience.

As the days passed Sam looked at her with eyes growing ever more anxious, and she knew full well that he didn't relish the thought of marrying her if it became necessary any more than she did him, but Emma ignored his worried look, deciding not to enlighten him but to let him suffer a little of what she'd suffered herself and would go on suffering. She felt almost heady with relief even though she knew the awful guilt she felt at not having told Daniel was only just beginning.

She thanked God that now she wouldn't have to confide in Aunt Mattie or her other relatives and see their looks of pity tinged with embarrassment, for her being one of the family the stigma would have affected their lives as well.

It was towards the end of June that, finding herself alone with Sam, she turned to leave the kitchen. Putting out a restraining hand, he cried, 'For God's sake, Emma, how much longer must I wait to be told? I take it you're going to have a child?'

'No,' she said, her tone of voice bitter. 'There's no baby, Sam, but that doesn't make it all right, does it? I take it your wife will forgive you if she knows up there? After all, you did think it was her. But what about Daniel? How do I tell him?'

'For Heaven's sake, Emma, you'll be mad if you tell him!' Sam said, and there was fear in his eyes. 'For both our sakes it's best no one knows. I've come to my senses now, Emma. Such a thing could never happen again.'

She hadn't heard him moving about downstairs for ages, but if she had and he'd sounded upset Emma knew she'd never have gone down to him, such was her bitterness. Whether she told Daniel or kept her secret for the time being and suffered pangs of guilt over her deceit, she stood a chance of losing him sooner or later, and she couldn't bear to think about that.

Chapter Twenty-Nine

Emma thought of little else but what Daniel would do or say if he knew her secret. His natural reaction would probably be to go for Sam, and she herself wanted him to suffer a little for he behaved towards her now just as though nothing had happened, but the thought of there being a fight or a loud battle of words between Daniel and Sam, with the whole street agog and probably guessing what it was all about, kept Emma silent but on edge.

When Aunt Mattie called to say, 'Why don't you go round to Mabel's and tell her, no matter what Sam did, you had no part in it?' Emma froze, her heart beating fast at the thought of what they might have heard. She repeated, a question in her voice, 'What Sam did?'

'Yes, you know, he's forbidden the girls to visit Ellie any more. Just let Mabel and Ellie know that it doesn't apply to you. Poor Mabel's having an awful time with her.'

'Of course I will,' Emma promised, sighing with relief and at the same time feeling guilty that she hadn't given her cousin a thought. Poor Ellie, she must think that Emma wasn't going to visit her again. She'd go tonight as soon as the girls were in bed.

'I'm going to visit my aunt and cousin,' she told Sam coldly when she came downstairs ready for outdoors.

'The mad one with the vicious temper?' He obviously hadn't forgotten that kick.

'But that was ages ago and Ellie can be a very loving person.' Emma felt she must stick up for her kin. 'It was just that she felt threatened when you pushed her away.'

'I'm the one who was threatened,' he told her. 'My leg was black and blue.'

'I know there's no excuse for what she did,' Emma said honestly, 'but in her mind Ellie's just a child.'

'And a spiteful, vicious one at that,' said Sam, having the last word as she went through the door.

'Am I glad to see you, Emma!' Aunt Mabel greeted her warmly. 'My Ellie loved playing with those little girls, then when you didn't come either she was inconsolable. She's sorry she was such a bad girl, aren't you, love?'

Ellie was sitting in the shabby armchair rocking one of her battered dolls. Throwing it down she rushed towards Emma, hugging her tightly and smothering her in kisses.

Aunt Mabel continued: 'Remember what I told you, Ellie. It's all right to kiss Emma and your Aunt Mattie, but never do it to strangers in case they don't like it.'

It was doubtful if Ellie even heard her mother. Looking pleadingly at Emma, she was saying, 'Won't you bring the girls to play with me no more, Emma?'

'They wanted to come,' Emma told her. 'It's their daddy who won't let them.'

Looking subdued, Ellie said, 'Aunt Mattie said I was a bad girl 'cos I kicked him.'

But being the child she was Ellie's mood changed quickly as she joined in the conversation, laughing excitedly when

Emma gave her a threepenny piece to spend at the sweet shop in the morning. Then she helped lay the tea-things and handed around the biscuits.

'You're looking peaky, Emma,' Aunt Mabel remarked when she could get a word in edgeways. 'Doing too much, I expect. Be a good job when you and that Daniel get married.'

'Can I be your bridesmaid, Emma?' her cousin pleaded. 'I could wear a pretty dress and have flowers in my hair.'

'We were watching a wedding last Saturday,' her mother explained. 'She's been trailing around in an old lace curtain ever since.'

'It won't be for years,' Emma told them, explaining about having to wait for Daisy to leave school so that she could look after the family.

'That man doesn't deserve your consideration, the way he hurt our Ellie,' Aunt Mabel protested angrily.

'It's the girls I'm thinking of,' Emma told her. 'They're too young to manage on their own.'

'Can I be a bridesmaid, Emma?' Ellie pleaded again.

'If you promise to be a good girl, but you'll have a long time to wait, Ellie love.'

Going home, Emma worried about the promise she'd made, knowing she should have waited to see what Daniel thought. She'd already promised Daisy and Dorrie that they could attend her and knew Daniel had two little cousins living in the valleys that his mother had set her heart on having as bridesmaids, but in view of Ellie's hopeful expression, how could she have said no?

She reached the house. Going through the passage towards the kitchen she could hear Sam's voice and wondered if he had visitors, but before she opened the door she realised that he was back at his old game, talking to Sarah, and this time he was pleading.

'. . . you know I wouldn't hurt you for the world, my love,' he was saying. 'Forgive me, Sarah, please! She wore your dressing gown. I really thought it was you at last, cariad. It was all a dreadful mistake, I've never really been unfaithful to you, but I can only live with what I've done if I know you forgive me.'

Not a word about the wrong he's done me! Emma thought bitterly. Knowing she couldn't face him without showing her disgust, she turned on her heel and made for her room.

On a stifling Saturday afternoon in July, Daniel arrived while Emma and the girls were still discussing where they should go.

'It's much too hot to just walk around,' Daisy grumbled, knowing that if they decided to go to the lake at Roath Park or the gardens in town she would have to put on her best clothes, and the thought of the high, lace-trimmed neck of her new dress and the narrow sleeves you couldn't roll up was unbearable on a day like today.

Emma and Dorrie agreed with her and Daniel said, 'Why don't we go to Penarth? There should be a cool breeze there from the sea.'

Their exhaustion forgotten the girls rushed upstairs with whoops of delight, coming down five minutes later, dressed in cool cotton dresses, to take over preparing sandwiches and cutting slices of cake while Emma went to get ready.

As they got off the train and walked slowly down towards the sea front the heat was almost unbearable but when they'd reached the pebbles they were met by a welcome breeze. Soon they were sitting on the pebbles, Daniel had taken off his jacket and boater and, after rolling up his sleeves, had unfastened his shirt at the neck. Emma too had removed her straw hat and unbuttoned her cuffs, while the girls, giggling with excitement, were getting ready to paddle in the sea.

When with squeals of delight they'd lifted their skirts and waded in Daniel took Emma's hand in his and gazing at her tenderly said, 'You look so lovely, Emma. I'm a very lucky man to have someone like you.' Then with a sigh he added, 'I wish we didn't have to wait so long.'

Would Daniel feel the same way if he knew her secret? Emma thought despondently. The girls would be happy for a while paddling in the sea; should she tell Daniel now while they were alone? If only she could unburden herself and be free of this awful guilt. But watching the girls as they ran in and out of the water, squealing at the hardness of the pebbles beneath their feet, turning to wave happily, she knew she couldn't cast a cloud on their day.

Daisy painfully picked her way over the pebbles to beg them to join her and Dorrie, so Daniel rolled up his trouser legs and she turned her back to pull off her stockings, feeling disappointment but also relief that the moment had passed.

'Daniel thinks there's going to be a war, Emma,' his mother told her a few days later. They were having a cup of tea in the kitchen and Emma was listening for a key in the door for Daniel would be home at any minute.

'Is it because of that Archduke who was killed?'

'I suppose so. He says the Germans are looking for an excuse.'

It was now nearing the end of July and Emma remembered Daniel showing her the piece in the paper about a month ago.

There'd been a picture of the Archduke Franz Ferdinand and his wife Sophia leaving the town hall in Sarajevo. They'd looked a handsome couple. A few minutes later, the caption had said, their carriage took a wrong turning and the heir to the Hapsburg throne and his wife were shot dead by a Serbian terrorist. Emma remembered feeling sad at the time but it had all happened so far away, how could it possibly be going to affect Great Britain?

A few minutes later Daniel came into the kitchen, a pile of books under his arm, and looking towards the table, said, 'Is there a cup of tea going? I'm as dry as a whistle.'

As she poured him a cup, Alice Thompson said, 'I've been telling Emma you think there's going to be a war.'

'You mustn't worry about it, either of you,' Daniel said, taking Emma's hand in his. 'I don't think it will affect us, not yet anyway. But there's been a further development after the assassination of the Archduke. It seems that Austria sent Serbia an almost impossible list of demands, and although they say they've complied with most of them, Austria has declared war. Mr Williamson, whose children I've been teaching today, gave me the *Daily News* to read. He says the whole of Europe's in turmoil. Anyway, enough about war. Why don't we take the girls to the park again after tea, Emma? It'll be cooler then.'

'I'll mind the girls if you like,' his mother offered. 'You never have any time on your own.'

For a moment Emma's heart lifted, until Daniel replied, 'Thanks, Mam, but I've got a better idea. Why don't you come with us.'

It was peaceful sitting in the shade watching the passers by. The nannies had long since taken their charges home. Couples with arms linked and eyes only for each other, strolled past. Sometimes a family dressed in their best walked sedately by, the younger children hand in hand under the watchful eyes of their parents. Daisy and Dorothy in their pretty muslin dresses and straw bonnets were on the far side of the flowerbeds talking to a friend. Daniel, his back against the bench, had closed his eyes while Emma and Alice chatted companionably. The peaceful scene seemed a very long way away from all the talk of war. Why should Britain get involved anyway? Emma thought. For once she hoped Daniel was wrong.

But within a few days things were moving fast. When Austria declared war on the Serbs, Russia began to mobilise its troops against Austria. Then on 1 August Germany declared war on Russia, and a few days later on France, at the same time invading Belgium and Luxembourg. Britain, honouring its pledge to Belgium, declared war on Germany. It was as though a touch-paper had been lit and, becoming rapidly out of control, set the whole of Europe on fire.

Chapter Thirty

The warm sunny days continued with everyone talking about the war that had been thrust on them so suddenly. Within a few days many thousands of men had volunteered for the forces and Emma knew a new fear. Would Daniel join up right away? But with a sigh of relief she thought, He has his mother to consider. He won't leave her. Not yet anyway.

Towards the end of August Sam came home to tell her he'd volunteered for the army and expected to be called within a few weeks.

'I put you as my next-of-kin,' he told her. 'After all, you'll be looking after the girls, they have no one else. I've made a will which I've left with my solicitor. I've left the house and some money to Daisy and Dorothy for when they grow up. Meanwhile I'm depending on you to look after things. You'll find I haven't been unappreciative of all you've done, and of course there'll be an allowance.'

'But supposing Daniel and I want to get married before you get back?' Emma asked in some dismay.

'Well, my going away needn't stop you. In fact, you could get married and live here. I doubt I'll get much leave. Having you look after the girls and the house has taken a great weight off my mind.'

He's got a nerve, Emma thought, but was relieved that he was going away. The way Sam talked it was almost as though he wasn't expecting to come back. Remembering the words she'd heard him say that awful night: 'If you don't come to me soon or give me some sign, I'll see to it I come to you,' Emma shivered.

When the flood of volunteers began to dry up, posters urging young men to join the forces appeared wherever there was space to stick them. Staring down from every available hoarding or wall, Lord Kitchener pointed a stern finger at any young man passing by. 'Join your country's army,' read the caption. 'God Save The King!' Another urged: 'Boys, come over here – you're wanted.' Yet another pictured six smiling young men in uniform and bore the message, 'Join the brave throng that goes marching along.' To young men keen to show their patriotism they'd prove irresistible.

Daniel seemed these days to have a great weight on his mind. He was all his mother had, but he too must have seen the posters and the newspapers were full of the war. So many young men had already left the street. Emma had seen them hugging mams and dads goodbye, a cardboard case with their few belongings at their side, but often they were accompanied to tram stop or railway station by the family, who'd return subdued and sad-eyed to wait impatiently for the first letter to arrive.

Emma watched Daniel. Knowing how he was suffering, she decided she couldn't add to it by telling him what lay so heavily on her conscience, even though Sam would soon be gone.

She hadn't known what to do about his assuming she was willing to take on full responsibility for the girls. He had already committed himself. If she refused, Daisy and Dorothy would be the ones to suffer. She and Daniel hadn't planned to marry for three years. Everyone seemed sure the war would be over by Christmas then Sam would be home again. Best leave things as they are, she thought.

The girls cried a little when their father went away. Emma took them to the station to see him off. The few times she'd been on a platform before had been for a day trip to the seaside and there'd been a holiday atmosphere about the busy bustling general station, with little boys in sailor suits, girls in cotton or muslin dresses and straw bonnets, most of them holding colourful tin buckets and lethal-looking spades, while waiting impatiently for the train to Barry Island.

Today there was a sense of deep sadness in the air, mams and dads clinging to young men who looked little more than boys. Bemused-looking children held on tightly to Daddy's hand. When, with a great roar, the train came in, belching steam everywhere, relatives clutched their loved ones in warm embraces. Sam had only the girls to wave him off forlornly as the whistle blew shrilly and he dashed for the train.

He'd told Emma how grateful he was for what she was doing and she could have felt sorry for him but for the shameful thing that had happened between them. She said goodbye stiffly, unable to show any regret at his going, and it was with relief that she took the girls' hands and threaded their way through the forlorn little groups down the steps and so out into the bustle of town.

In an effort to cheer them up, Emma took the children to a tea-shop where their sadness didn't last very long. As they each chose a bun oozing with cream from the plate of cakes on the table, they chatted happily, the parting forgotten. Sam had rarely played with them, had seldom been there when needed. What else could you expect? Emma thought. Each night now the girls would say a prayer for him; they'd look forward to his letters, be proud of the sepia photo of their father in uniform that would surely come, but they weren't heartbroken and she was glad.

Emma thought more than once about telling Daniel of Sam's offer if they wanted to get married, but the thought of what she had to confess kept her silent. Anyway, she thought, Sam has a nerve expecting Daniel to move in if we marry, and help out with the girls. Perhaps the war will soon be over, she thought, then things would get back to normal, but Emma knew that for her things would never be quite the same again.

It was the spring of 1915 when Daniel confided he was going to join up.

'I can't go on leaving it to everyone else, Emma,' he told her, taking her into his arms. 'It's troubled me for a very long time, not doing my bit, but everyone thought it would be over by Christmas. Mam understands how I feel though I know she doesn't want me to go. Cheer up, love. Perhaps it won't last much longer then we can all get on with our lives.'

Emma couldn't stop the tears rolling down her cheeks. He drew her to him and they clung desperately to each other. When at last they drew apart Daniel looked down at her tenderly, the longing still in his eyes, saying, 'We could have got married Emma and had rooms with Mam if you didn't have to look after the girls.'

There was a look of hope in Emma's eyes as she told him of Sam's offer, adding excitedly, 'We could live here, Daniel. There's nothing to stop us, especially now Sam's overseas.'

'But supposing the war finishes soon and he comes home? You'd still have to stay here, wouldn't you? You'd still have to look after the girls.'

Seeing the tears of disappointment as Emma fumbled for

her hanky, he added hopefully, 'But you could give in your notice, couldn't you, if Sam was home?'

'Daisy's not ten yet . . .' she began. But Daniel's arms came about her and he held her tight, his kisses growing more and more urgent. Presently he tore himself away from the embrace to say weakly, 'I think we'd better get married, Emma. The rest will have to take care of itself. Though I'll tell you now, love, I don't think I could live in the same house as Sam for very long.'

Even the twinge of conscience she felt couldn't spoil Emma's joy. She'd have to tell him soon, she thought. Oh! but not now. Nothing must ruin this moment.

Daniel's mother was delighted with their news. The rhubarb wine was brought out once more and the glasses raised in a toast, then Alice Thompson cried excitedly, 'There'll be no need for you to have a dress made, cariad. I still have mine! It's been packed away in tissue paper all these years and the fashion in wedding gowns hasn't altered that much since I was married at the beginning of 1890.' Then, clapping her hand to her mouth, she cried, 'Oh, but I haven't given you a chance to say what you want yourself.'

The dress was brought down and Emma gave a gasp of delight as it was draped over the back of a chair and she gently touched its silky folds.

'I was about your size then, Emma,' Alice laughed. 'Just look at me now.'

'You're just pleasantly plump,' Daniel told her fondly, and she laughed again, saying, 'You make me sound just like a Christmas chicken, son.'

Underneath her jollity was sadness that Daniel would soon be volunteering for the army, and Emma felt deeply about that too, but how could she marry him wearing this beautiful dress with its dainty, lace-trimmed bodice and sleeves? The moment she saw it she'd been filled with delight, only now she had no right to wear a white wedding dress, it would be living a lie, and on her wedding day too. Yet how was she to tell Daniel's mother she couldn't wear it without causing her to turn away in disgust?

'You do like it, Emma?' Alice asked, watching her as she smoothed her fingers gently over the skirt.

'It's really beautiful, you must have looked lovely in it,' Emma answered, resigning herself to wearing the dress, conscience or not.

The days flew. They went to see the vicar. The bans were being called. Daniel's mother had offered to keep the girls with her for a week after the wedding.

'There being a war on you won't be having a proper honeymoon,' she said. 'His dad took me to Rhyl for ours. It was the first time I'd ever been away from home. It'll give you a bit of a break, me having the girls.'

Emma kissed her gratefully. There'd only been one slight note of discord, and that was when Emma told them she'd promised Ellie she could be one of the bridesmaids.

'Oh, Emma!' Alice had protested. 'You know how unpredictable she can be. Remember what she did to Sam, and besides, Daisy and Dorothy are near enough the same age as my two nieces and they're so fair where my two have dark hair and eyes. They're going to look lovely, two in pink and two in blue, and four bridesmaids are more than enough.'

'I promised her ages ago,' Emma said determinedly. 'I can't let her down.'

Ellie had talked of little else since the marriage had first been discussed. Emma couldn't break that promise. She was having a pale mauve dress made for Ellie in a more adult style than the girls'. Her cousin was happy and excited, waiting for the wedding day to come. Emma couldn't go back on her word now.

Chapter Thirty-One

On a hot day early in June, as Maud gave a final pat to the long full skirt of the wedding dress, Emma stared into the mirrored door of the wardrobe, listening to the gasps of delight around her. The reflection that looked back at her showed no sign of the inner turmoil that had plagued her for so long. Her wide brown eyes were bright with happiness, the usually pale oval face pink with excitement. Emma's silky fair hair, loosened from its pins, cascaded in soft waves to below her waist, and the dress, the lovely dress that Daniel's mother had worn twenty-four years ago, fitted Emma's slim figure as though it had been made for her.

Now, as Maud and her Aunt Mattie adjusted the veil, setting the ring of orange blossom in place, there were murmurs of approval from those who'd crowded into the bedroom. Then Mabel said anxiously, 'I'd better go and see what Ellie's getting up to.'

When her other two aunts went downstairs to help with preparations for the wedding breakfast and Maud went with them, Emma was left alone with the woman who in less than an hour's time would be her mother-in-law.

Alice Thompson had tears in her eyes as she said, 'Oh, Emma, you look lovely. You *are* lovely too, you're all I could ever wish for for Daniel. Thank you, my dear.' And lifting the veil gently, she kissed Emma's cheek.

For a moment there was a sad expression in Emma's eyes, but over the weeks she had gradually come to terms with her problem.

If only I'd told Daniel after it happened it would have been just between us, she told herself. But then she'd been dreading the awful row that would have broken out between Daniel and Sam. As the wedding day approached, and with so many people involved, the bridesmaids' dresses made and the food and drink ordered, she'd thought it best to keep silent.

'There are times when it's best to let sleeping dogs lie,' her nan used to say. 'Best to say nothing if the truth is going to stir up a hornets' nest.' And that was surely what would have happened had she told.

The young bridesmaids were waiting in the middle bedroom, sitting quietly, two on either side of the double bed: Daisy and Dorothy lovely in their pale blue, Daniel's pretty dark-haired cousins in pink, each of them with flowers encircling their head. They made a lovely foursome.

Aunt Mabel must be keeping Ellie downstairs so's she won't get excited, Emma thought. She'd watched her cousin meeting the girls for the first time since the rumpus with some trepidation. They'd eyed Ellie cautiously at first but Aunt Mabel had laid down the law.

'No hugging or kissing today, mind, or you'll spoil your dress then Emma won't have you as a bridesmaid.'

So Ellie grinned sheepishly at them and soon they were all chatting as though nothing had happened.

The Thompsons' house was already overflowing when Clara and Martha arrived. Her aunts had told her ages ago to call them by their christian names, but old habits died hard and Emma still found herself calling them 'Aunt' most of the time.

The bridal car was expected any minute but Emma hugged her Aunt Clara warmly. She hadn't seen her for well over a year.

'Martha's downstairs,' Clara told her, wiping the tears from her eyes. 'You know Martha, she's got her apron on already.'

When the veil was arranged once more Mattie came to the door to say, 'Fred's waiting at the bottom of the stairs, Emma. He's really proud to be the one to give you away.'

Dear Mattie, Emma thought, she'd been so pleased for her, so helpful. They were a lovely couple, her and Fred; old Mrs Thomas had been the only fly in the ointment for them, and Mattie's dearest wish, their having a place of their own, seemed as far away from being realised as ever. But I can understand how Uncle Fred feels, Emma told herself. She is his mother after all. Although invited, the old lady hadn't come to the wedding but said she was going to attend the service at the Church, and she'd given them a lovely wedding present, a pair of pale blue china vases. She wasn't mean whatever her faults.

David was here though. At fourteen, he was almost as tall as his father. David had been apprenticed to the carpentry trade since he'd left school and had made a little stool for a wedding present. It was beautifully made with simple marquetry around the edge, and he'd obviously taken a lot of care.

The presents were laid out on the parlour table for everyone to see. When Emma had seen the stacks of towels and bedding, the sets of china, and the big canteen of cutlery that Clara and Lionel had sent, she'd wished with all her heart that she and Daniel had a place of their own to put them in even if it was only two rooms.

As she hugged Martha, putting her veil once more awry, her old friend told her, 'I've brought Esmeralda. I've finally given up all hopes of you coming home to us now. But I'm happy for you, love. I got Mattie to put the doll upstairs out of harm's way.'

A knock at the front door meant the bridal car had arrived at last and sent Mattie to Emma to fix the orange blossom in place yet again, then Uncle Fred proudly escorted her to the car.

In the church porch the bridesmaids awaited her with Ellie anxious to call Emma's attention to her new dress. They formed themselves into a little procession and walked sedately down the aisle.

Ellie was behaving impeccably, her head held high, a smug expression on her face. Emma breathed a sigh of relief as, the ceremony over, her cousin departed for home with the other bridesmaids. There was a little crowd, neighbours and most of the children from the surrounding streets, awaiting the bride's return. As soon as the beribboned car departed and bride and groom had gone indoors the neighbours moved slowly away, but the children waited excitedly hoping for a shower of coppers to be thrown. They weren't disappointed for Daniel had been saving them for weeks.

As he began to throw the money Ellie dashed past them in all her finery and before anyone could stop her was scrambling with the children in the road.

'Get up, Ellie!' Emma cried, horrified at what was going to happen to the bridesmaid's frock. But it was too late. As her triumphant cousin came towards them, clutching her coins and grinning with satisfaction, the frill at the hem of the now dirty and dishevelled dress, torn and hanging loosely, threatened to entangle Ellie's feet.

'Oh, Ellie!' Emma said again, but in a different tone of voice. Mabel, coming through the passage just then, held up her hands in horror and dragged the girl into the house, crying, 'Now look what you've done to your lovely dress, you naughty girl!'

Ellie's face crumpled as she let out a howl. Daniel's mother took in the situation and said soothingly, 'Never mind, love. Take it off and I'll wash and mend it soon as I can. It'll be good as new, you'll see.'

The wedding breakfast over, and Ellie and the other bridesmaids playing in the garden, Emma was able at last to have a long talk with Martha and her Aunt Clara. Soon, the washing up finished, they were joined by Mabel and Mattie.

After all these years Mabel still worked on a Saturday morning for Mrs Grey while their neighbour kept an eye on Ellie. As usual Mabel was full of tales of her employer's kindness and Emma reflected sadly that this seemed to be the only excitement in poor Mabel's life.

'Just given me a smart astrakhan coat, she has,' her aunt was saying. 'Lovely it is, but too small for Ellie. Wondering, I was, if it could be shortened and the pieces used to make it wider.'

'I think I know someone who could do that for you, Mabel,' Mattie told her. 'Learnt her trade she did before she was married. There's plenty of time anyway. Ellie won't be needing a warm coat like that for months.'

While they were still discussing the coat Martha said wistfully, 'We hoped you might have come to see us, Emma.'

'I couldn't very well leave the girls.'

'Oh, Emma, bring them with you,' Clara told her, 'and get Daniel to come too.'

Presently the talk amongst the guests inevitably turned to the war when old Mr Coles who lived next-door mentioned that he didn't think the Dardanelles campaign was going very well, and Daniel replied, 'The Allies had to take action after the Turks came into the war last November and attacked the Caucasus. The Russians weren't prepared for it and had to retreat.'

'Didn't an English and French naval squadron enter the Dardanelles and smash the Turkish defences in March?' Uncle Fred asked.

'Yes, but they failed in the end when they ran into floating mines in the Straits and lost three of their ships.'

'Enough about the war,' Alice Thompson said firmly, seeing the glum expressions around them.

'Now they're using poison gas in the trenches, it must be bloody hell out there,' their neighbour went on, and Emma remembered Daniel telling her that old Mr Coles was as deaf as a post.

When he didn't get any reply to this he continued: 'I read in the papers there'd been zeppelin raids on some of the towns in England.'

'Come to the kitchen with me and have a sandwich and a glass of beer,' Daniel's mother said diplomatically, shouting in his ear to make herself heard. 'Come on the rest of you, how about a sing-song round that piano? Will you play for them, Mattie? Let's try and forget the war for five minutes, shall we?'

As Mattie began to play and they sang, 'Oh, Genevieve, The days may come, the days may go . . .' the sweet sentiment suited everyone's mood, and with Ellie still playing with her friends there wasn't so much as a discordant note.

'Let's have "In The Gloaming",' Mattie suggested, turning

the pages of the song book until she found it.

They were half-way through 'Just A Song At Twilight' when Daniel joined them, whispering to Emma that it was time they were leaving.

'As soon as this song is finished,' she told him.

'"And the flickering shadows fall . . ."'

As the last tender words faded away Emma said goodbye to their guests and was hugged and kissed and wished well over and over again. But Dorothy, always nervous of being left with someone she didn't know very well, clung to her, crying, 'I don't want to stay here, Emma, I want to come home with you.'

'You can't, silly,' Daisy told her. 'Emma and Daniel are on their honeymoon.'

Knowing the girl had no idea at all what a honeymoon was, Emma smiled, saying soothingly, 'I'll be over tomorrow, love, and you've got Daisy with you.'

And Daniel's mother told the child, 'You can show me how to make those lovely cakes Emma brings over. We'll do some cooking in the morning, shall we?'

Knowing there was no shortage of cakes in the pantry, nor likely to be for quite a few days to come despite the fact that Emma and Daniel had been given a basket full of treats to take home, Emma thought gratefully, Alice has a special gift for smoothing troubled waters.

The summer day was nearly over, a bright orange sun sinking slowly, leaving the sky aglow as they strolled arm in arm, enjoying the cool breeze that had sprung up, both occupied with the same sobering thoughts. How long had they before Daniel's papers came? He'd volunteered only a few days before the wedding to make sure they had a week or two together at least. But there was something else on Emma's mind. Ought she to tell Daniel tonight? Looking at his happy face she was once more remembering her nan's advice.

'If the truth is going to stir up a hornet's nest, best let sleeping dogs lie.'

Well, what she had to say mightn't exactly stir up a hornet's nest but Daniel was bound at least to feel bitter and unhappy about it, and she wanted their wedding night to be perfect, something to cherish during the long parting to come.

Chapter Thirty-Two

Remembering her horror the night Sam had mistaken her for his wife Emma's heart beat fast with apprehension as, backs to each other, Daniel and she undressed. Still shivering at her memory, she pulled back the crisp starched sheet and got into bed.

As though sensing her fear Daniel's arms came about her in the now darkened room. Holding her close, he murmured, 'Don't be afraid, Emma love. I'll be gentle.'

And he was. With the long kiss that led up to their lovemaking her fears vanished and she began to respond to his growing passion, her arms tightening about him, her heart filled with love.

When suddenly Daniel flung himself away from her and lay staring at the wall Emma's heart lurched with fear and she asked in a small voice, 'Is something wrong, Daniel?'

'I'd have bet my life on your being a virgin.' His tone was bitter and each word stung her like a whiplash.

And so at last the sorry tale was told and she wished with all her heart that she'd been honest with him and told him before, but when Sam was still at home there would have been ructions and she'd been desperate the whole street shouldn't know.

'And here I am, sleeping in his bed, while I hate his guts!' Daniel said bitterly.

'It's my bed,' Emma told him. But it didn't really matter, the damage was done, nothing could alter that. Tears came to her eyes as she thought sadly, This is our wedding night. Within a few weeks Daniel will be gone.

Suddenly he jumped from the bed and began to pace the room, crying, 'The swine! The rotten swine! I swear if I meet him over there I won't wait for the enemy to get him.'

'Please, Daniel! He didn't know it was me.'

'Well, he'll know it's me all right when I meet up with him.'

Emma's sobs brought his arms about her as he said grudgingly, 'It wasn't your fault, but it really hurts that you didn't tell me.'

'I was afraid there'd be trouble between you and Sam. I didn't want everyone to know.'

'I'd have beaten the living daylights out of him,' Daniel insisted.

When Emma's sobs grew louder he took her into his arms and kissed her tear-stained face, murmuring, 'I can't promise to forget, love. And it isn't your fault so there's nothing to forgive. Only that you didn't tell me before. Come on, dry your eyes or they'll be wondering what I've been doing to you.'

'I don't want anyone else to know,' she pleaded.

'They won't. If I meet him over there it will be just between the two of us. It's been a terrible shock, Emma, and I'll always hate Sam for this. I never thought much of him anyway, the way he carried on. But we mustn't let this ruin our lives.'

Although his words were comforting she knew that he wouldn't be able to forgive, and prayed fervently he'd never meet up with Sam.

To all outward appearances they seemed to be a normal happily married couple. They went somewhere every day even if it was only into town. To dine in a restaurant was a rare treat for Emma, marred only by the look in Daniel's eyes when with any lull in the conversation he stared into space, and she remembered with foreboding the way he'd brooded over Cissie leaving him.

Emma was surprised to find herself glad when the following week the girls returned home. Daniel had gone back to his tutoring until his papers arrived, and in the evenings Daisy and Dorrie plied him with questions or begged him to play card games, leaving him no time to torture himself with his thoughts.

But at night, after they'd made love, Emma was aware of him lying stiffly by her side, staring at the ceiling. If only they could talk about it. But then she'd realise it wouldn't do any good. Action was the only thing that would satisfy Daniel, and with Sam away in France that was denied him.

Each morning Emma dreaded the arrival of the post, sighing with relief when the call-up papers didn't come. On the day they plopped onto the mat her spirits sank. If only things were right between them she'd have an easier mind, but often now Daniel's thoughts seemed to be elsewhere and she knew how his hatred of Sam was festering, clouding the pleasure they should have felt in each other's company.

In the bustle of getting ready to leave, of saying goodbye to friends and relatives, of seeing as much as possible of his mother, things had seemed almost normal between them. When the day of parting came, knowing how hard it was for Alice, Emma said impetuously, 'Come to the station with us, Mam.' But she felt relieved when her mother-in-law refused and Emma could look forward to those last precious moments alone with Daniel.

She managed to hold back the tears as they clung to each other until the sound of the guard's whistle tore them apart.

'Take care, Emma,' he told her, leaning from the carriage window to kiss her goodbye. 'I'll probably have leave in a few months.'

It was a crumb of comfort, but as the train gathered speed and she waved until it was out of sight tears streamed from her eyes and she was already regretting the things she hadn't said.

Dabbing her eyes, Emma hurried down the steps and out into the street. Reminders of the horror of war were all around her. Men with empty sleeves or trouser legs, sometimes both. Soldiers with pallid faces, and swathed in bandages, were being carried on stretchers or helped to waiting ambulances. Emma's heart was filled with pity for them and she longed to get home and put pen to paper and pour out her heart, but she wouldn't be able to post a letter until she received Daniel's first letter with his number and address.

Alice's eyes were red and swollen when Emma called on her on her way home. They cried together, but Emma knew that some of her own tears were for what might have been if only she'd never gone down to Sam that night.

Just over a week later they were having tea together when Alice said wistfully, 'You know, Emma, my dearest wish is that you'll have a child.'

It was Emma's dearest wish too but she knew that there was little chance of it happening for Daniel had explained that he was being 'careful'.

'If anything should happen to me,' he'd said, 'I wouldn't want a baby of mine brought up in Sam's house, especially when he returns home.'

Emma couldn't think of anything more wonderful than having Daniel's child, and if circumstances had been different she'd have begged him to let her have her way, but she'd hurt and upset him so much. Often in the days that followed his departure she wished she'd had the courage to put her own point of view, especially when she discovered that even her slim chance of her having a baby was no more.

She saw the disappointment too in Alice's eyes when she had to dash her hopes. His mother was taking Daniel's absence very hard though she tried not to show it. His letters to Emma were frequent and loving and she read them over and over again. It was what he didn't write about that worried her. Was he still brooding over what had happened with Sam? There was no way of knowing. The letter she longed for was the one saying he was coming home on leave, and as the summer days faded and the crisp tang of autumn filled the air she woke each morning to listen eagerly for the letter-box, and whenever the post was due during the day found herself unable to concentrate on even the smallest task.

Then one morning, early in October, Emma stood at the gate waiting for the girls to reach the corner and wave before going to school. She was just about to go into the house when she noticed a telegraph boy riding down the street and her heart missed a beat. Slowing down, he drew into the curb and handed her a telegram.

Emma's heart filled with dread at the sight of it and as the colour drained from her cheeks she held on to the iron spikes of the railings for support. Luckily Maud must have seen the boy from her window for suddenly she was there. Putting her arms about Emma she led her to the kitchen and, easing her down to the sofa, sat beside her, saying, 'Best open it, cariad. Maybe it isn't as bad as you think. You don't even know that Daniel's at the front.'

Emma's face was like alabaster. Fingers shaking, she fumbled with the telegram until, taking it from her gently, Maud slit the envelope and handed her the message. As Emma straightened it out the words leapt up at her: 'Regret to inform you Corporal Samuel Evans was killed in action, 4 October 1915. Lord Kitchener sends his sympathy.'

Relief was the first emotion Emma felt. Relief and a heartfelt thankfulness that it wasn't Daniel, but as Maud took the telegram from her she felt shame too for now the girls would be orphans, poor little things.

'What's going to happen to Daisy and Dorothy?' Maud wanted to know. 'Who did Sam put as next-of-kin?'

Suddenly the enormity of the situation came home to Emma as she admitted it was her. She would be responsible for them until they were old enough to live here on their own, many years from now. She and Daniel had only been married about four months. Even when the war was over and he came home the girls would still be her responsibility. It was rather different from waiting until Daisy was twelve and could leave school to look after her father and sister. Would it be one more nail in the coffin for their marriage, for Daniel would never forget that Sam was their father?

'How are you going to tell Daniel?' Maud was asking. 'Didn't he think you were looking after them just until Daisy left school? You were a fool, Emma, to let Sam name you as next-of-kin.'

Sam had done it so that she could collect the allowance, and to give himself peace of mind about the girls' welfare while he was away. It hadn't seemed important then; everybody had said the war would be over by Christmas and she'd intended to look after Daisy and Dorrie for another two years anyway. Now she shivered with apprehension. What was Daniel going to say?

But for now there were more pressing things to be considered. The girls must be told as soon as they got home. Emma decided nothing would be gained from fetching them home early. Knowing they would be back soon after twelve o'clock she laid the telegram on the table, wondering how best to break the awful news.

When they came into the kitchen she sat them down and took both their hands in hers, saying, 'You've got to be very brave, we've had a telegram.'

Two pairs of blue eyes watched her anxiously as she faltered and went on, 'It's your daddy . . . he's gone to be with Mammy now. He was killed fighting for his country.'

Then as the tears rolled down their cheeks she flung her arms about them and determined on one thing. Come what may she would never let them down.

Presently Daisy looked up to ask tearfully, 'Shall we wear black arm bands like Sarah Davies and Bertie James?'

'Yes, we'll have to make some,' Emma told them. 'We'll go to Clifton Street for the material this afternoon.'

'Won't we have to go back to school?' Dorrie asked hopefully.

'No.' Emma decided. 'You're both upset. I'll write a note for you to take tomorrow.'

'Daddy wanted to be with Mama, didn't he?' Daisy asked.

'Yes, he did. But he didn't want to leave you, I know that.'

'Did our Mama come to fetch him?' Dorrie's eyes were wide with fright.

'Of course she didn't. Your daddy was killed fighting for his country. You should both be very proud of him.'

'But we're orphans now, Emma,' Daisy said in a worried voice. 'What will happen to us when Daniel comes home from the war?'

'I'll never leave you,' Emma promised, hugging them again, remembering her own dread when her nan died and she'd feared being sent to the workhouse or an orphanage. Even now she could remember feeling sick and faint at the thought of ending up in either. 'I'll always be here for you,' she told them, and as two tearful little girls hugged her gratefully she was determined to keep her word.

Chapter Thirty-Three

That afternoon Emma took the girls shopping for black material to make arm bands, and, as she walked up the street, noticed that many blinds were already drawn, casualties becoming so frequent now that parlours seemed to be in almost perpetual gloom. Progress was slow as neighbours stopped them to offer their sympathy, and with each commiseration Dorrie burst into fresh tears.

Putting an arm about the child's shoulders, Emma cwtched her close, glad when they'd turned the corner into Broadway. Dorrie gave a final little sniff and dried her eyes. She could never abandon them to a children's home, Emma thought, as Dorrie slid her arm in hers, and remembered the turmoil of her own feelings on the day her nan had been buried when she'd waited anxiously to see if one of her aunts would take her in. Taking both the children's hands in hers, she squeezed them reassuringly.

There was a strong smell of unbleached calico and flannel as they went through the Manchester Department towards dress and coat materials, and when the right amount of black cloth had been measured against the brass rule set in the edge of the counter, and the assistant had sent the money and the bill pinging towards the cash-desk in the little wooden cup, Emma looked around her with interest. Before the war only young men had worked in the Manchester Department; carrying the heavy bales of cloth from fixture to counter and unblocking them when they made a sale was men's work, but with so many of them away fighting the department was now staffed by young boys and elderly men.

'Will I be able to work in a draper's now when I leave school?' Daisy asked hopefully.

'You've got another two years to go, better wait and see,' Emma told her, not wanting to commit herself just yet.

When they reached home and the chenille cloth had been lifted from the table she cut the material into wide strips, and the girls threaded their needles and began to sew, glancing every now and then towards their parents' photographs which flanked the clock on either side. Emma often wished she could remove Sam's for it was always catching her eye, reminding her of things she'd rather forget, but the children set such store by them, especially now.

When they'd finished the sewing they fetched an album from the parlour and turned the half-a-dozen pages of sepia photos all of their mam and dad and themselves. Emma had always thought it strange that there were none of anyone else in the family, no aunts or cousins, grandmas or grandpas. She'd been just a year older than Daisy when her nan had died and her aunts, uncles and cousins had always played an important part in her life.

Looking down at the album Emma saw a very different Sam, for here was a handsome smiling man, his dark eyes brimming with happiness as he posed with his family. There was one of Sarah holding a baby in a long embroidered gown. Daisy was quick to point out this was herself. In the next picture Dorrie was wearing the long gown while Daisy stood at her mother's side in a broderie anglaise dress tied at the waist with a wide sash. Both Sam and Sarah looked so proud as they posed with their family. For a moment, turning the pages of the album, Emma almost forgot her own hurt at his hands.

That night, when they knelt to say their prayers, Dorrie asked, 'Shall we still say "Please God, take care of Dada"?'

''Course we do,' Daisy told her. 'They're both in Heaven now so He'll take care of them.'

It had been an exhausting day, especially on the emotions, and Emma wasn't long behind the girls in getting to bed. She was just drifting into sleep when the screaming began, and dragging on her dressing gown, she rushed to the girls' room.

Just as she had when Emma had first come to the house, Dorrie sat bolt upright in bed, her eyes wide with fright as the piercing screams rent the air. She didn't seem to notice Daisy's arms about her or hear her sister's soothing voice. As Emma reached the bed and put out her arms, Dorrie tried to fend her off, crying, 'Go back in the corner, Mama. I won't come. I won't!'

Emma turned up the gas, illuminating the dark corners, saying, 'Look, Dorrie, love, there's no one there.'

'There was! There was! Over there.'

'That's your dressing gown hanging on the door.'

As she soothed the child, smoothing back the damp tendrils of hair, promising to bring them both hot milk and honey, Emma felt angry that Sam's ill-chosen words should cause Dorrie such distress. She'd thought the child was over these nightmares, but the shock of her father's death must have triggered them again. Dorrie was such a sensitive little soul.

'Look after her, Daisy, while I fetch the milk,' she said, watching them cwtch up together.

Next morning, wearing her new arm band, Daisy insisted on going to school, but an exhausted Dorrie lay tucked up on the sofa and Emma too had to stifle her yawns.

There were reminders of Sam everywhere. Emma decided to put them all away in case Daniel got leave and came home. His shaving mug and brush were on the shelf above the sink in the wash-house. A row of pipes in a rack by the fireside. They would never be needed now. She didn't like going into his room for it had been his very private domain and he'd spent so many hours there trying to contact Sarah, but the job had to be done. She wouldn't pry, just put his slippers and dressing gown in the wardrobe, hair-brushes in the drawer.

Unlatching the window, she lifted it to let in some air but with the few things tidied away she would be glad to close the door behind her. Emma was surprised to find she felt pity for what had become of the handsome young man in the photographs. It was the sad haunted man that she remembered and disliked.

She was about to leave the room when Sarah's blue dressing gown caught her eye, still hanging behind the door. Despite several washings faint blood-stains still remained, one more reminder of that dreadful night. Now Emma almost tore it from the door. Rolling it into a bundle, she went in search of some paper to wrap it in. It was something she'd wanted to do for a long time; she didn't want the girls asking questions. She would throw it away. Sam wasn't going to miss it now.

A few days later a letter came addressed to Emma, making arrangements for her to go to Sam's solicitor's office at eleven o'clock on the following Monday if it was convenient to her. After she'd showed it to Maud, her neighbour said, 'I don't think Sam putting you as next-of-kin is binding in any way,

Emma. They can't make you responsible for the girls. You want to be careful what you sign. Them solicitors can tie you up in knots if youer not careful.'

The following Monday at eleven o'clock sharp she was shown into Mr Davidson's office and seated in a comfortable leather armchair. The elderly solicitor, with his chubby pink cheeks and white side whiskers, soon put her at her ease.

'I'm very pleased to meet you, Mrs Thompson,' he said, taking her hand in his, then seated himself at his desk on which was a sheaf of papers and went on: 'Now that Mr Evans is sadly deceased we must endeavour to carry out his wishes. He was, I know, hoping that in the event of his death you would continue to look after his two daughters until they are old enough to manage on their own.'

In answer to his quick look of enquiry Emma nodded her head. What else could she do? But Mr Davidson was already saying, 'Your housekeeping allowance will of course continue and be revised from time to time. Would it be easier if it was paid into your bank account?'

'I haven't got a bank account,' Emma told him.

'Ah! But you soon will have,' he went on, smiling at her warmly. 'Mr Evans has left you the sum of £250 with his grateful thanks for all you've done for his girls. To the girls themselves he's left in trust the house and a sum of money they can't touch until they are eighteen. So you see, they have to have a guardian. You seem a little young for such a responsibility, but you've been looking after them very efficiently for quite a long time and now I understand you've recently become a married woman? How old are you, Mrs Thompson, if you don't mind my asking?'

'I'm twenty-one,' she told him, her mind still reeling from the large sum of money Sam had left her.

'The only alternative for the poor little souls would have been a children's home,' Mr Davidson was saying. 'Mr Evans was himself an orphan and brought up in such an establishment. He wouldn't have wanted that for his daughters. They have no near relatives. Their mother was the only child of elderly parents. Both mother and father are dead.'

Emma had been clinging to the hope that there might be relatives they could appeal to if Daniel was upset at having to take on the responsibility. Now her heart sank.

Alice wasn't likely to be pleased about the arrangements either though she'd been really sorry about Sam.

'They're bound to have someone belonging to them, even if they haven't kept in touch,' she'd said. 'You want to make enquiries, Emma.'

After shaking hands with the kindly solicitor, still in a daze at the news he'd imparted, she stepped out into the foggy November morning, her thoughts still on Alice as she made her way to the tram-stop. Alice longed so for a grandchild but Daniel had been away ever since they'd been married last June. Several times he'd been hoping to come home on furlough but it had been cancelled. The first time had been embarkation leave but instead his company had been urgently shipped to France. There'd been several other times when he'd been hopeful of coming home but that hope had come to nothing, although in Emma's opinion a furlough was long overdue. So she'd no means of telling if Daniel had changed his mind about having children while there was still a war on and he was on active service. She knew the fear that haunted him as it did all men serving their country in this awful war: Supposing I'm maimed for life or blinded? He'd never actually put it into words in his letters home, but she knew the fear was there, and with all the evidence on the streets as more and more crippled men came home in hospital blue, she knew his fears were justified.

Emma's heart was heavy at the thought but whatever happened she would always love and want him, she was very sure of that. But how was she to tell him about her new responsibilities? And would he make it an extra excuse for not wanting a family until there was peace? Emma had always been careful not to write anything that might worry him in her letters; everyone knew now of the dreadful conditions in the trenches. She mustn't add to his burden. He was bound to come home soon, she would tell him then.

As she turned into Broadway she became aware of a lot of shouting, faint at first but growing louder as she walked towards home, then she could see a small crowd gathered around a woman who was holding a peace banner aloft and standing on a stool or something. The crowd was obviously hostile, shaking their fists and hurling abuse. She heard one man cry: 'We've had a gutsful of youer sort, missus. My sons are all fighting for this country. Why don't you do something for the war effort instead of yelling youer 'ead off 'ere? There's sailors risking their lives bringing food for the likes of you, you pacifist bitch!'

'It's a cryin' shame, innit?' another agreed.

The crowd was growing restive, grumbling amongst themselves. Someone threw an egg and Emma thought, Best not to get involved. She was about to move on, wondering How they could afford to waste an egg with food growing shorter by the day? A tall man moved his head to say something to the man beside him and suddenly Emma had a clear view of the protester, egg dripping from her chin, stoically carrying on with her speech though it was a waste of time with the uproar all around her. Then Emma gave a little gasp and cried out, 'Miss Vera!'

Vera waved her free hand in Emma's direction, just as though surrounded by guests at a garden party instead of an ugly-mooded crowd. Emma then noticed the egg-stained sash Vera wore over her shoulder and could make out the words 'PEACE MOVEMENT'.

As Vera prepared to step down a woman rushed forward, trying to force her back onto the box, crying, 'You don't get away that easy, you traitor! My 'usband's lost a leg and my brother died from the gas.'

And another cried, 'My son died at sea, bringing food for the likes of you!'

I've got to do something, Emma thought. This crowd's getting ugly. Wriggling her way to Vera's side, she cried loudly, 'There's a copper the other side of the street!' And as all heads turned, she caught Vera's hand. Lifting their skirts, they ran like the wind until a stitch in her side made Emma stop breathlessly and look behind to see their pursuers retreating, tired of the fray.

'Thank you, Emma! Thank you,' Vera was saying gratefully as she wiped the egg away with a fine lawn handkerchief, but already Emma was beginning to regret getting involved as she remembered the trouble Vera had got her into once before. But now, seeing the stain spreading down the front of Vera's coat, she felt compelled to say, 'Come home with me, Miss Vera, and tidy up. It's only the next corner.'

'I always felt awful about your losing your job through me,' Vera admitted as they walked down the street.

'That's water under the bridge now,' Emma told her. 'I'm looking after two little girls now. Did you know I was married to Daniel?'

'Huw's tutor? Yes, I did. Is he still teaching?'

'He's in France, at the front,' Emma said, smiling ruefully as Vera said, 'Trust me to put my foot in it!'

By now Emma was opening the door and leading Vera through to the kitchen, thankful she'd polished and dusted last evening, leaving the place neat and tidy when she'd left this morning.

Vera stepped down into the kitchen and looked about her obviously surprised as her gaze went from highly polished leather sofa to the dresser with its matching willow-pattern china, the shining brasses on the mantel-piece, soft beige rugs on the black and red diamond tiles, and she said, 'You've got a lovely home, Emma.'

'I'm only keeping house,' Emma told her. 'Looking after the girls I told you about. Their father's dead. He was killed recently in France.'

'Oh! I'm so sorry. They're very lucky to have you, poor little souls. It's such a waste this awful war. I lost Arthur, we were engaged to be married,' Vera's eyes were filled with sadness and Emma put out a hand to grip hers sympathetically as Vera went on. 'It was last November, he'd only been in France a month. He was such a wonderful person, Emma, and he sympathised with our cause.'

Seeing Vera was near to tears, Emma asked quickly, 'What is this movement you're in now?'

'Well, as you probably know, the suffragettes have ceased to campaign until the end of hostilities. A number of our members have got jobs helping the war effort. I myself work in a soup kitchen in the docks area, but first I joined the Manchester Peace Movement and now I've come home to put into practice all that I've learnt there. You'd think people didn't want peace the way they carry on at our meetings.'

'It's because they've lost so much,' Emma said sadly. 'Husbands, brothers, sons. They've got to believe in the cause.'

'With such terrible things happening you'd think they'd be sick of the war,' Vera answered, shaking her head in puzzlement. 'In this year alone Germany has launched U-boat attacks against our shipping, and even against America with the sinking of the *Lusitania* and all the lives that were lost. America's not even in the war. There have been German air-raids against Yarmouth and King's Lynn, and now they're using that awful gas against our soldiers. Did you read about Nurse Cavell being shot in Brussels last month, Emma? With all the atrocities, you'd think people would be clamouring for peace.'

Remembering the headline in the *Daily Mail* about the middle of October, 'ENGLISHWOMAN EXECUTED', Emma nodded her head, saying sadly, 'They are, Miss Vera, believe me they are, but they'll only think the peace honourable if we win this awful war.'

'Poppycock!' she said briskly. 'And what's this "Miss Vera"? You're not working as nurse-maid in our house now, and I wasn't too keen on the title then. It's against my creed. We're friends now, you and I. It would be nice to keep in touch. But perhaps we shouldn't? Not while I'm with the Peace Movement. You've had enough trouble because of me.'

The kettle was boiling at last and Emma made the tea and was getting them a simple meal of cheese, bread and butter and pickles when Vera said, 'Just a cup of tea, Emma. I'm . . . I'm not hungry.'

Emma knew the confrontation had upset her more than she'd admit. But now she went on, 'I must fly as soon as I've had the tea. I've got a meeting this afternoon. I've found myself rooms in Partridge Road, Emma. It wasn't fair to Mother, my being at home. Father and I are usually at loggerheads.'

It had been nice talking to Vera, Emma reflected as she watched her going up the street, but it seemed unlikely her Peace Movement would succeed. People, even those who grumbled, liked to think they were patriotic, and those who'd lost loved ones were more likely to want revenge than a cease to hostilities. She hoped Vera wouldn't meet up with the hostile crowd on her way home. Her coat had been sponged and she'd removed the banner and her very recognisable hat, wearing instead a plain brown felt of Emma's.

As Emma closed the door on the damp, chilly day she felt sorry for Vera losing her sweetheart and in a war she didn't even believe in, a war she had the courage to campaign against.

Chapter Thirty-Four

Vera walked back along Broadway, crossing over to the other side of the road as she neared the street where she'd been given such a rough time. She smiled as she thought ruefully, My argument for a peace settlement almost caused a battle on its own! It was the story of her life, campaigning for unpopular causes.

Glancing down the narrow street from which Emma had rescued her, she wondered what had happened to her stool. It was only roughly made from unvarnished wood. One of the women's brothers had volunteered to make them by the dozen, which was just as well seeing how often they had to be abandoned. Then she saw it outside a house about a quarter of the way down the street. As she watched, despite the chilly dampness of the day, an old lady wearing a shawl and a man's cloth cap came to sit on it, puffing away at an old clay pipe.

Vera chuckled, thinking, I'm glad someone got something out of it. It was doubtful she'd ever get all the egg stain from her coat. That and the hat had been an expensive outfit, for Mrs Pankhurst had always encouraged her followers to dress like the ladies most of them were, asking, they didn't want anyone to think they were cranks, did they?

Vera missed the comradeship of the suffragettes, the frequent meetings at headquarters: informal gatherings, drinking tea and exchanging news and ideas. Those who'd joined the war effort in some capacity would have found the same companionship. But it was a thankless task working with the Peace Movement, standing alone on street corners trying to convince a hostile crowd. She herself was patriotic, or rather had been, but it was the horrors of war being heaped on those who were serving their country, the futile carnage often over a few feet of land, that made her stand alone arguing for a peace settlement before thousands more were sent to the slaughter.

'You don't mind the shame you are bringing on your mother, your brothers and sisters with your antics, do you, Vera?' her father had yelled. But she'd done nothing to be ashamed of. She'd stuck to her principles which was more than could be said of some.

By this time she had reached the house where she'd recently come to live, remembering with a heavy heart as she opened the door of her apartment that the fire had to be laid and lit and that there was a mound of washing to be done.

If only she could wave a magic wand or something and make Gwladys appear. Cheerful and chatty, Gwladys had always seemed to know instinctively whenever the fire needed replenishing. And Flo. She'd only ever seen the wispy-haired, red-faced little washer-woman from her bedroom window, coming or going from the house in Queen Street, and as she'd wrapped herself in fluffy towels after a bath, slipped on perfectly laundered underwear, or taken a spotless lace-trimmed hankie from the drawer, she hadn't appreciated all the hard work that had gone into the task. But she did now when she had to do things for herself, and not nearly as well.

Looking around the shabby room she couldn't help but compare it with the one she'd just left. Here, last night's ashes cluttered the grate. The table, chairs and a huge sideboard were of heavy, dark oak and showed the wear and tear of many previous tenants. She had tried to polish them but this only showed up the scars.

Thankful she had a meeting to go to that afternoon, Vera cleared the grate and laid the fire ready for the evening ahead, when, as on other nights, she'd drag the overstuffed armchair under the gas light and read until it was time for bed. Often Vera would dwell longingly on the comforts she'd enjoyed at her parents' house but she never felt sorry for herself for long. Her thoughts would return to this awful war and the suffering of the soldiers in the trenches. Compared to that, this room seemed like paradise.

Vera's thoughts now went to Emma who had helped her out of a tricky situation today. She was as lovely as ever with her gentle brown eyes and pale oval face. She mustn't take advantage of her this time, much as she would have liked to keep in touch. Emma was a married woman now and with the responsibility of looking after those two little girls. Perhaps if Arthur hadn't been killed at Ypres she herself would have settled down, but she doubted it for Arthur himself had been a socialist, sympathising with the suffragettes' cause. He'd been hoping to be elected to Parliament when the war was over. What a waste of talent. What a waste of love.

A few days before Christmas Emma answered a knock on the door to find Daniel standing there. Beside herself with joy, the soapsuds still clinging to her hands and arms, she flung her arms about him and their lips met.

'Why didn't you tell me?' she cried as soon as she'd managed to get her breath.

'There wasn't time, love. It isn't serious but I've got a blighty.' And he held his left arm out stiffly.

Emma's hand flew to her mouth but, shutting the door behind him, Daniel chuckled reassuringly, putting his good arm about her. By this time they were in the kitchen and as he held hands blue with cold towards the blazing fire Emma made a pot of tea, thankful that she'd been saving tinned stuff and whatever would keep in the hope that one day Daniel would come home. And here he was, looking thinner and paler than when she'd last seen him, and she'd noticed already that when the blue eyes weren't looking at her they held a haunted look.

'Any chance of a bath, Emma?'

'I'll get it ready while you drink your tea,' she told him, cutting a large wedge from the fruit cake that would normally have been kept for Christmas Day. 'The girls are out shopping with Maud, buying their Christmas presents, and if I know Dorrie when she's choosing something, they won't be back for ages.'

The washing water was growing cool on the bench in the wash-house but it didn't matter, nothing mattered except that Daniel was home.

The slipper bath was brought from its peg on the white-washed wall of the yard but Daniel insisted that despite his arm he should draw the buckets of hot water from the boiler at the side of the range. While he undressed Emma hung soft white towels over the brass rail of the guard and brought shirt, vest, pants and socks that had been waiting for this very day.

As she went to leave the room he put his arm round her waist, saying laughingly, 'Don't go, Emma love, I need you to scrub my back.'

She took the soapy flannel in her hands but before she could apply it Daniel's arms came about her again and they kissed, swaying together, until a knock on the front door made Emma clutch at a towel desperately, trying to dry her apron. Then, her face flushed, she patted her hair into place, pushing the pins tighter into her low bun, and went to open the door.

Alice stood there, a smile on her lips, her eyes bright, crying, 'What's happened, Emma? Where is he? Is he all right? Mrs Davies says she saw Daniel in Broadway. Oh, I can't wait to see him. Where is he?'

'He's having a bath, Mam. He was coming over afterwards. I was in the middle of the wash . . .' She pulled her wet apron away from her self-consciously, adding, 'I wouldn't have started if I'd known he was coming.'

It was chilly in the parlour waiting for Daniel to finish but coal was short; she couldn't afford to light a fire in a room that was seldom used. Emma brought two shawls from the closet under the stairs. Clutching hers about her, she explained about his injury as they listened eagerly for a sign that he had finished his ablutions. Then, his face pink now from the warmth of the fire and the hot water, Daniel put his head around the door to see who'd arrived. Next moment cwtching his mam to him with his good arm and kissing her cheek, he murmured, 'You don't know how grand it is to be home.'

More tea was made and they sat talking in the warmth of the kitchen until the girls burst into the house, their arms full of purchases, dropping them the moment they saw Daniel to fling their arms about him. Little Dorrie declared, 'It's going to be a real Christmas now.'

'How would you girls like to come and stay with me until Christmas Eve?' Alice asked. 'You could wrap your presents, and I was going to make mince-pies tomorrow. I could do with some help when I make some toffee this afternoon too.' She didn't need to say any more, the girls were already running upstairs to get their things, and Emma said gratefully, 'Thanks, Mam.'

Alice answered, 'You'll have little enough time together, cariad, but perhaps you could come over to tea?'

The washing water was stone cold when Emma finally got back to it, but with Daniel insisting on turning the handle of the heavy mangle with his right hand, soon it was finished and the rest of the work could wait, for even the smallest task was interrupted while their lips met. As their kisses grew more urgent Daniel took her hand and hurried her upstairs to the bedroom, and still daylight though it was, it seemed the most natural thing in the world.

They were dressing afterwards when he said with a chuckle, 'If the girls hadn't gone with Mam we couldn't have done that, Emma. It will be lovely when we can find a place of our own.'

'I can't leave them now, Daniel, not until they're grown up.'

'But you said in about two years . . .'

'I know, but Sam won't be coming back now. They'll be too young to leave on their own.'

'They must have someone?' Daniel's tone was resentful.

'There's something I should have told you right away, only I haven't had much chance,' Emma said nervously. 'Let's go down to the kitchen, it's cold up here.'

'Well. What is it?'

They'd reached the bottom of the stairs now but Emma didn't answer until the kitchen door had closed behind them. Then, licking dry lips, she said, 'It's about Sam's will.'

'How does that concern us?'

'Well, it seems he expected me to look after the girls until they're old enough to live here on their own.'

'I know he's dead but he can damn well expect!' Daniel cried angrily. 'Look, Emma, we're not long married. I was prepared to give up a couple of years. They're nice children and I'm fond of them, but there's a limit.'

'Sam left me some money, Daniel.'

'He did what?'

'He left me money with his grateful thanks for looking after the girls.'

'You mean he made darned sure you'd look after them? It was a bribe.'

'No,' she cried, anger in her voice too. 'It isn't a bribe.'

'Oh, Emma! Can't you see? He knew you couldn't refuse. I was hoping when this blasted war was over, we'd one day find a place of our own.'

'But we can, Daniel, as soon as the girls are old enough. He left me more than enough to buy a house. He left me two hundred and fifty pounds.'

'Do you think I'd touch a halfpenny of his money after what he did to you? God! you don't know me very well, Emma . . . Aw! Come on, I didn't mean to make you cry. Even though he's dead, Sam's still managing to upset our lives.'

Pulling her towards him, Daniel lifted her on to his knee. Cradling her with his good arm, he said in a gentler voice, 'We'll have to put all this behind us. I suppose we must look after the girls, but I won't touch any of the money, Emma, you can give it all to them.'

'Sam left them the house and quite a bit besides, they won't need it. Look, Daniel, I'll leave it in the bank for a rainy day. We'll have earned it, and the poor little souls need us. They've had enough upheaval in their lives.'

'Not many people are saddled with two grown girls as soon as they're married,' he said with a sigh. 'A good job I didn't give in to you about us having a baby of our own. You're going to have enough to do.'

'Please, Daniel! Give us a chance. I want your baby so much, and I know your mother would love . . .'

Daniel laughed, putting his arm about her again.

'Well, if you must know, Emma, I forgot all about taking care just now.'

Their lips met again, the tiff for the moment forgotten, but Emma was under no illusion. She knew that because of Daniel's pride the row over the money would raise its ugly head whenever the subject was brought up.

Chapter Thirty-Five

Despite the war and the shortages it had brought, it was a wonderful Christmas. Having Daniel at home had made it special. Christmas morning, while it was still dark, Emma could hear the girls moving about, their voices high with excitement. Dawn was just putting pale fingers across the sky when there was a knock on the bedroom door, and when she sleepily bade them, 'Come in!' Daisy and Dorrie rushed into the room, crying, 'Guess what we've bought you and Daniel, Emma?'

Getting out of bed and pulling her dressing gown about her, she said resignedly, 'I'd better draw the black-out curtains, then I can light the gas.'

By this time Daniel was awake and fumbling with the wrapping on the parcel the girls had given him, and Daisy was helping Emma with hers, her face bright with anticipation. When the tissue paper fell back to reveal a small, highly polished wooden box that was lined with red plush compartments Emma reflected wryly that, apart from her wedding and engagement rings and the locket she always wore, she had little to put into a jewel box, but it was quite an expensive gift for the girls to have bought and must have taken a lot of pocket money.

'It's beautiful!' she cried, hugging them both. 'But you shouldn't have spent . . .'

'Mr Davies put it away for us, Emma. It was in his window. We've been paying on it for months,' Daisy broke in to explain proudly.

By this time Daniel was trying on a grey woollen muffler, saying with a grin, 'Just what I wanted. Thank you, girls. How do I look?'

'You don't wear it with a night-shirt, silly,' Dorrie said with a chuckle. 'It's to keep you warm when the war's over. I wish you could stay home with us now, Daniel.'

Emma could see he was deeply touched at the child's remark. Daisy and Dorothy were already on their way back to their room, and Emma, now wide awake, said with a sigh, 'I suppose I'd better get up, there won't be any peace until I do. I'll bring you a cup of tea.'

But Daniel was already out of bed, pulling on his trousers, saying, 'You get back in for five minutes while I go down and light the fire.'

Emma found herself constantly trying to push to the back of her mind the thought that in a few weeks' time he would be going back to the war. But something else was worrying her besides the parting to come. Last night and the night before their sleep had been disturbed by his nightmares. On both occasions he'd woken with an anguished cry and she'd found him wildly threshing about, his body drenched with sweat as she put her arms about him.

Having lit the candle that first night Emma turned to find Daniel staring wildly at the shadows on the wall cast by the flaring flame. His fingers grabbing at the bedclothes, eyes wide with fear, he aimed a non-existent gun at the wall. Jumping from the bed, Emma had lit the gas and blown out the candle, then she'd held him close, rocking him gently to and fro as one would a frightened child, smoothing back the damp hair, kissing him tenderly, knowing only too well that out there in the trenches his nightmares became reality. By now most people had heard first-hand accounts of what the men were enduring in the foul, rat-infested trenches, and here he was reliving it in his dreams.

Sometimes during the day too he would sit staring before him, his face wearing a sad expression and, wishing with all her heart that she could take away his pain, Emma made up her mind that this must be a Christmas to remember.

Alice was coming for Christmas Day. Emma had been lucky enough to get a fat chicken from the farm that still delivered the milk. The girls had made everyone a paper hat, and with the best glasses filled with the rhubarb wine Alice had brought over, the table looked festive.

Thankful to be out of uniform for a while Daniel wore his own clothes. Emma noticed with concern how loosely they hung on him. While she carved the golden chicken, Alice and Daisy served up the roast potatoes, stuffing and cabbage. The pudding simmered on the hob while they talked and laughed, almost as though there wasn't the word war on everyone's mind.

The fire was lit in the parlour even though it would mean their being short of coal later on, and after tea Alice played the piano while they all sang carols until it was time for supper.

Emma found herself wondering what Vera was doing today, hoping she'd made it up with her father and gone home. She didn't want to think of her alone in those cheerless rooms in Partridge Road. It wouldn't have been wise to get involved with Vera again, not while she was on her hobby horse. Besides, she's sure to have friends in the movement, Emma comforted herself.

* * *

The day before he was due to go back Daniel put on his wedding suit to go to town with Emma and look around the shops. It hung loosely on him, but she said nothing, for he was so obviously enjoying wearing his own clothes. If only this awful war would end, she could look after him and feed him up. Still, she was lucky, wasn't she? Emma told herself. Daniel was here with her at this moment; so many women were already mourning husbands or sons.

It was a bitterly cold day, the sky grey and leaden, and to the girls' delight Daniel wore the muffler they'd given him for Christmas.

On the way back they got off the tram at the Royal Oak, anxious to be home by the fire. Approaching the next corner they saw a little crowd angrily shouting at a woman who was trying to get them to listen to her point of view, while a man at her side held aloft a Peace Movement banner.

Not Vera again, Emma thought as they drew nearer, then a middle-aged man rushed forward and set about pulling her from the step on which she was standing.

Suddenly Daniel moved into the affray, crying, 'Leave the woman alone, that's no way to treat a lady!'

'Lady?' The man's tone was derisive. 'A conchie she is, like you by the looks of it. Both my sons are at the front.'

'And mine,' came a chorus of voices, and all eyes turned to Daniel as the woman walked hurriedly away with the man carrying the banner. It wasn't Vera after all but Emma saw that Daniel was white to the lips as he took her arm and they went on their way.

'Why didn't you tell them?' she asked, worried that he was upset.

'I don't care what people like that think,' he answered.

This time tomorrow he'll be gone, Emma thought sadly. It didn't bear thinking about. She gripped his arm tighter as she said, 'I'm coming to the station with you in the morning Daniel.'

'I told you I'd rather you didn't, love. It will be easier to say goodbye at home.'

'It will give us another half-hour together,' she said simply, and as he looked down into her eyes shining with love for him, he said bitterly, 'Oh, God! When will this bloody war end?'

No one predicted that any more and it seemed ludicrous now that anyone had thought it would be over in a few months. With more and more countries getting involved, how could it end soon?

The next morning they left the house with enough time to spare for Daniel to have half-an-hour with his mother. Almost at once Emma found an excuse to go back home for something so that they could spend the time alone. Poor Alice. Daniel was all she had, and she would miss him as much as Emma was going to. It was a strong bond between them, the love they shared, and a comfort to them both.

On the tram they sat alone at the far end and held hands, gripping each other's tightly as though they never meant to let go.

At the station there were stretchers on the pavement waiting to be lifted into ambulances drawn up outside. Trying not to see the white faces and blood-stained bandages, Emma turned her head so that Daniel wouldn't notice the tears she hastily brushed away.

When they reached the platform they had to squeeze their way through until they found a space. Emma clung to Daniel's arm, her eyes never leaving his face. Then the rumble of an approaching train made them cling together desperately until the shrill whistle heralding departure tore them apart. Carriage doors were banging, men hanging from the windows to kiss children being held towards them. It was a poignant scene. A small boy still in petticoats was screaming, holding his arms out towards his dad.

Emma stood on tip-toe beside the compartment Daniel had got into but could barely see him over the heads of those crowding the window. With a loud hiss of steam the train began to move and suddenly Daniel was at the window, waving, and she waved back until, rounding the bend, the train was soon out of sight.

Her heart heavy, Emma slowly followed the crowd down the steps. Eyes were being furtively dabbed, some were openly crying, and suddenly her own eyes were misted and there was a painful lump in her throat. She longed to be home to give way to her tears.

'That's my youngster.' The soldier standing close to Daniel, swaying to the rhythm of the train, had fumbled to undo his top pocket and was now holding out a dog-eared sepia photo. Taking it, Daniel stared down at a curly-haired little boy, recognising him as the one who'd cried after his dad.

'You got any kids?'

'No,' Daniel told him. 'We got married last summer, spent only a few weeks together since then.'

'Youer in with a chance this time then.' The boy, for he was little more, gave Daniel a cheeky grin.

He'd been thinking that himself just before the soldier had spoken. He hadn't meant it to happen, but that first time not long after he'd got home had been so spontaneous. He hadn't been as careful as he should have at other times either, and

Emma wanted a child so much, had he any right to deny her? Thinking of her his heart swelled with love. In less than a year's time would he be going round pulling out a photo to show to strangers? Saying, his voice vibrant with pride, 'That's my baby.'

Would he still be here in a year's time? Daniel thought sombrely. He was on his way back to the hell he'd thankfully left only a few weeks ago and that was why he hadn't wanted Emma to have a child, not yet, not until he could be home to provide for them and look after them. But Emma wouldn't be short, thanks to Sam, he thought bitterly. It was the only thing that had marred his leave for, dead or not, he just couldn't forgive Sam for what he'd done to Emma. And then to leave her money! That Emma had earned it, that they would both earn it by taking responsibility for the girls, there was no denying.

'But I want none of it!' he cried bitterly.

'What's that you say, mate?'

Not realising he'd spoken his thoughts aloud, Daniel gave a surprised look at the man beside him.

This time tomorrow he should be back at the front and now had no illusions about what he was heading for. Any thoughts of glory had disappeared long ago.

If he closed his eyes he could still see young Roberts, his leg blown off at the thigh, screaming in agony for his mam, the rattle of machine and rifle fire almost drowning his cries.

By the end of the attack the trenches had been littered with corpses and men gasping for breath, dying in the mud. The scene was etched deeply on his memory, filling his mind at all hours of the day or night. Those at home didn't seem to realise. Despite the shortages and other deprivations they had to put up with, had they any idea what was going on out there?

But Emma knew. He'd seen it in the pity in her eyes after he'd had the nightmare on that first night. He wanted a son, of course he did, but not to go through what he'd endured.

This was supposed to be the war to end all wars. What a shambles! When would they ever learn?

February came in bitterly cold, the sky looking heavy with snow. By the time that Daniel's letters began to arrive once more Emma was allowing herself to hope that she was pregnant, and as the weeks went by the hope grew strong, until in her heart she was certain. Alice grew very excited when Emma told her, insisting she see the doctor to make sure everything was all right, and thankfully, apart from needing an iron tonic, everything was.

That very same evening Alice went to Clifton Street to buy some fluffy white wool to start on the layette. Very soon Emma began sewing little garments as they sat talking and making plans for the future when the war was over.

'I've still got the christening gown that Daniel wore,' Alice told her daughter-in-law, leading the way upstairs to the chest in the front bedroom where the best linen was stored, layered in lavender sachets with tissue paper in between.

As Alice shook out the lovely baby gown with its dainty eyelet embroidery and tiny pin-tucks around the skirt the scent of lavender pervaded the room.

'My mother made this for Daniel, and the only light she had to work by was an oil-lamp,' Alice said proudly. 'It's been put away ever since his christening. It would be lovely for his baby to wear it too.'

'It's beautiful,' Emma told her. 'Wouldn't it be wonderful if the war was over and Daniel home by the time the baby's born?'

But with the fighting on so many fronts it didn't really seem likely. Still, who knew what might happen? It was a long time until the end of September.

Like most of the other children throughout Britain, the girls had thrown themselves wholeheartedly into the war effort, and Emma was glad when at last with the lighter evenings they could go to the Church Hall on their own or with friends. Here they rolled bandages, painstakingly knitted comforters for the forces, and helped to make up parcels for the men overseas. In their free time they went around the houses collecting silver paper and rags from neighbours and friends.

'We're helping Daniel and all the others who are fighting, aren't we, Emma?' Dorrie would say proudly. They were so serious about it. As soon as she gave them their pocket money they'd be off to the Post Office to put some of it into war savings.

By now both girls were a great help around the house. While Dorrie dusted or polished the brasses and cleaned the cutlery, Daisy would scrub floors and cope with the ironing, and she was already a wonderful little cook. But she was still adamant that, as soon as she was able to leave school, which at the earliest would be the end of the year, she wanted to be apprenticed to the drapery trade. All through the years she'd never changed her mind about that.

There was no keeping the wonderful news from the girls, Emma was too happy about it to hide her joy, and after a few overheard remarks when she'd been talking to Maud, Daisy asked excitedly, 'Are you going to have a baby?'

When Emma nodded she cried, 'It'll be a little brother or sister for me and Dorrie, won't it? We'll be able to mind it for you and take it out in the pram.'

Emma looked at the girl tenderly, knowing that as yet Daisy had no idea how babies were conceived or born, only that you had to have a husband before God sent you one. Emma smiled at the thought of all those immaculate conceptions. Despite her age at the time she'd been ignorant herself until that awful night with Sam. And, although she was now a married woman and expecting a child of her own, she wasn't at all sure how it was to be born. She'd been meaning to ask Alice but somehow the words wouldn't come. Before they could form on her lips her face would be red with embarrassment and the opportunity would pass.

Looking now into Daisy's delighted face she knew that one day the task of enlightening the child would fall to her, and how was she to manage that when she found the subject so hard to talk about?

'Can I tell Dorrie, Emma?' Daisy was poised for flight.

'Why not? But it will be a long time before it's born.'

Daisy was already halfway up the stairs, anxious to impart the wonderful news.

Chapter Thirty-Six

Despite the morning sickness and various other discomforts, Emma was enjoying her pregnancy. The thought that Daniel's child was growing within her was a constant source of wonder, as was Alice's explanation of how it would be born.

Daniel's joy when she'd written and told him was all she could desire. Any lingering doubts about him wanting this baby were quickly dispelled.

'I wish I could be with you, love,' he wrote. 'I know Mam will take good care of you. Oh, Emma! It's even harder to be parted now. I can't wait to come home for good to my family.'

But they both knew that, short of another blighty, there was little chance of his coming home, and she thanked God that the injury that had resulted in his furlough would heal completely with time.

The aunts rallied round as they always had, each in her own way. Practical Mattie insisted, 'No more queuing for coal.' In vain Emma explained that it was Daisy who did the queuing. David, now a strapping lad of fifteen, was sent with an old pram as soon as he finished work on a Saturday. David was apprenticed to a carpenter and Emma knew her aunt's biggest dread was that the war would last long enough for him to join up. David took after Uncle Fred, easy-going and friendly, and with his mother's strong sense of duty always insisted on chopping wood for Emma when he came back with the coal, whistling cheerfully as he worked.

When Mattie told Mabel about the expected baby she was equally pleased, coming around at once with Ellie, who, giving Emma a sloppy kiss, asked eagerly, 'Where's the baby then?'

'Oh, Ellie! I told you, not yet,' Mabel said impatiently, raising her head and clicking her tongue.

'Where is it then? Still in the nurse's bag?'

'It's in here, love,' her mother told her with a laugh, laying her hand gently on the small mound of Emma's tummy.

But Ellie giggled, saying, 'Don't be daft. The nurse will bring it in her leather bag like she did Mrs Minton's. I love little babies, Emma. Can I mind it for you?'

The thought of entrusting her precious babe to Ellie horrified her but September was months away so she smiled at her cousin and said nothing.

As Emma watched them going up the street, her plump, kindly aunt and stout, ungainly cousin, she felt a sudden misgiving. Supposing her child was born like that? How would she bear it? Yet Aunt Mabel never complained. Ellie needed almost as much care now as she had as a child. And Mattie had said her bouts of temper were getting worse. It was herself who should be offering help to Mabel, not the other way round.

The worry grew in her all day. And when Mattie came around that evening to show her a little jacket she was crocheting, Emma confided her fears.

'Oh, Emma love, you've nothing to worry about,' she assured her niece. 'Poor Mabel was very unlucky. Ellie would have been normal, but in labour Mabel was for days and then the baby was starved of oxygen at the birth.'

As soon as Clara was told the good news she wrote to Emma saying that she and Lionel would be coming to see her on Sunday evening. Emma knew Clara had mentioned evening because with food growing scarcer all the time, she was afraid that coming to tea would put a strain on their resources.

She hadn't seen Clara, Lionel or Martha for ages. The girls went everywhere with her, and for the same reason, shortage of ordinary commodities, she hadn't liked to descend on them.

Emma would never forget how kind everyone had been to her when she'd lived in Duke Street, and she still remembered her time there with affection, except for that incident that had made her feel compelled to leave.

Daisy was excited at the thought of meeting the owner of a drapery emporium. She made dainty little cakes out of very little for them to have with a cup of tea. Long before the shining black Austin motor car, a rare sight in these streets, drew up outside, Emma and the girls were watching for them from the parlour window and Daisy had opened the door before they could even get out of the car, which in a matter of minutes drew all the small boys of the street like a magnet. As they came to gape and touch, Emma said, 'Someone had better watch the motor, hadn't they?'

'We'll look after it, won't we, Daisy?' Dorrie offered.

As they pulled the door behind them Emma saw the look of disappointment in Daisy's eyes and knew she'd been hoping for a chance to speak to Lionel about her longing to work in a drapery shop. But she meant to ask him herself even though Daisy wouldn't be able to leave school until they broke up for Christmas.

So presently, when there was a lull in the conversation, Emma asked, 'Would there be a chance of Daisy's coming to you as an apprentice, do you think? She doesn't leave school until December.'

'I'd be delighted to have her, Emma. She seems to be a bright, intelligent child,' he answered. 'The staff situation is topsy-turvy at the moment, particularly in the Manchester Department. Old men and young boys we've got to manage with now, Emma. I won't put women there, they're not made for carrying heavy stuff like bales of cloth, and it's nearly as bad elsewhere. Lots of the girls have left to go into munitions or on the trams or to work on the land.'

'Daisy would like to work on Baby Linen.'

'I can't promise that, I'm afraid, not yet anyway. I'll have a word with her before I go, Emma, and I'll keep her wishes in mind.'

When the tea-things were laid Emma went out to give a neighbour's boy some coppers to look after the car, smiling as she watched him strutting up and down. Woe betide any boy who took more than a peek!

As soon as they came into the kitchen Lionel produced two shining half-crowns, pressing one into each girl's palm and chuckling as he said, 'I expect you can find a use for those?'

'Thank you! Thank you!' they cried. Dorrie reached up and kissed his cheek but Daisy made do with a grateful smile.

When Daisy followed Lionel into the parlour Emma thought of the day she herself had started work, remembering her pride in the new black dress with its lace collar and cuffs, and being introduced to Miss Coles who managed the haberdashery counter where she was the new apprentice. She could picture Miss Coles now with her almost black eyes and fresh complexion. She'd been strict but fair.

The time she'd spent in Duke Street had been the happiest

of her life until she'd met Daniel. Uncle Lionel was still a very handsome man and as kind as he'd always been. Then she remembered his kissing her that night he'd drunk too much at the New Year's party. It was that kiss that had caused her to flee the shop because it had upset Aunt Clara so. But it had been completely innocent though she knew he'd always had a soft spot for her, and in return loved her generous, kindly uncle.

They were coming out of the parlour and, as she stepped down into the kitchen, Daisy's eyes were shining. Lionel was saying, 'I'll pick you and the girls up one day this week, Emma, show young Daisy what she's letting herself in for. Though it'll have to be Miss Evans, mind, when she comes to work for us.'

'Martha wanted to know when you were coming to see her, Emma. It's been such a long time,' Clara was saying. 'It's a long way for you, I know, and with petrol rationed Lionel can't often use his car, only for business.'

'Yes, well, Friday I have to go to the warehouse. I could pick you up on the way back. About four o'clock, if that's all right with you and the girls? Have a bit of tea with us. I'll bring you home between eight and nine.'

When they'd gone Daisy could hardly contain her joy even though Friday was still a long way off, and Emma wondered how on earth she was going to wait until Christmas. But perhaps on Friday when she saw the long hours the shop assistants worked, she might change her mind.

Friday came at last and the girls were allowed out of school early. They were all excited about going to Duke Street, Daisy for obvious reasons, Dorrie about her first ride in a motor-car, Emma at seeing Martha – for her wedding day had been the last time they'd met.

As soon as they saw the car coming up the street Emma

301

locked the door behind them and they were soon settled on the deeply buttoned leather seats, warm from the heat of the late-spring day. While Lionel cranked the engine the girls sat bolt upright, looking out anxiously, hoping their friends would be home in time to see them.

When they got out Daisy gazed admiringly at the deep windows and the wooden dummies on which were displayed the new length dresses, daringly only to the calf, a fashion brought in to save precious material.

Martha was at the top of the stairs, waiting to enfold Emma in her arms, saying: 'I'm so happy for you, love.'

Then they were ushered into the apartment and everyone was talking at once. As soon as tea was over Clara and Lionel had to leave, she to the cash-desk, he to walk around the departments and sign the bills, promising as he went out to come back for Daisy when things quietened down.

Daisy and Dorrie asked permission to go out on to the landing to watch all the bustle going on below. When, after a long chat with Martha, Emma joined them and glanced down at the busy scene, there were two elderly women seated on bentwood chairs at the Haberdashery counter and a young assistant bringing out more and more blocks of lace for their inspection, unpinning and loosening a little of the lace for them to see. Although the counter was now almost covered with lace the women were shaking their heads. The one in the enormous hat adorned with feathers was saying something as they rose to leave, and the assistant was smiling with a politeness Emma was sure she didn't feel.

As they made for the exit an elderly man in a rusty black suit hurried to open it, bowing to them as they went through to the street. Nothing's changed, Emma thought, remembering the day the same thing had happened to her. It could well have been the very same customers. The assistant was lucky that Uncle Lionel was nowhere in sight, he would have wanted to know why she hadn't made a sale.

'What do you think of it, Daisy? Do you still want to work here?'

But looking into the girl's shining eyes, she didn't need to wait for an answer.

At that moment Lionel passed the foot of the stairs.

'I'll come for you in about ten minutes to show you round,' he promised.

'Where is the Baby Linen Department?' Daisy asked, leaning over the banister.

'You can't see it from here,' Emma told her. 'Don't make up your mind, love. You may have to work somewhere else.'

When Daisy had gone to look around the shop, Clara popped her head around the door to say, 'I've left my assistant in the cash-desk. I just wanted to tell you, love, that Lionel and I want to give you the layette. If it's a bit early yet perhaps you could choose it nearer the time?'

'Oh, Clara!' Emma was hugging her aunt. They were always so generous, but would she need a full layette with all the things that were already being knitted, crocheted or sewn for this baby?

When Martha brought out a little jacket that she was making in a lacy design, Emma hugged her too, the memories crowding her mind. Martha hadn't changed very much over the years, but Aunt Clara looked older, flecks of silver threading her dark hair and her face much thinner than it had been. Uncle Lionel was even more handsome than she'd remembered, his hair and moustache as glossy as ever.

'Twopence for your thoughts, Emma?' Martha was giving her an amused look.

'I was just thinking so little has changed in all these years.'

But it had of course. They were all older now, more tolerant of each other. And the shop had changed too, if not in appearance. The heavy oak counters, the glass display cases, the bentwood chairs seemed to be timeless. But she'd noticed that the women behind the counters now were mostly either very young or old enough to be retired. But her uncle had told her a lot of the women had left to do men's jobs in the factories: munitions, trams, driving the ambulances, anywhere they could take over.

Lionel had told her Miss Coles had left to look after her mother, and that Tom and Artie were fighting in France. She remembered those evenings when Artie had taken her to the music hall with Tom and Elsie, and when she enquired about her former friend, whom she remembered having such a pretty pink and white complexion, she was told that Elsie was working away on munitions, and that the last time she'd come home she'd been as yellow as a guinea!

Chapter Thirty-Seven

It was a hot still day towards the end of August that cried out to be spent by the sea or under shady trees, but Emma, cumbersome now in the eighth month of her pregnancy, felt too exhausted to do either.

The girls had gone to the tide-fields taking a picnic of cheese sandwiches, some cake, and a bottle of herb beer. Emma had envied them their youthful energy as Daisy and Dorrie rushed around getting ready and then ran up the street to a neighbour who'd invited them to come with her and her daughter, an only child.

Emma had waved until they were out of sight then, closing the door, she'd gone to the parlour and taking Daniel's letter from the mantelpiece settled down in the armchair nearest the window to read it once more. She'd been so worried until it had arrived yesterday, the first word in over three weeks, and Alice had been thankful to know that a letter had arrived at last.

Emma spread the pages on her lap and began to read but she already knew the words of love and longing by heart. Where was Daniel now? Was he up to his knees in mud in some awful trench? Although Daniel never complained, returning soldiers left them no illusions about conditions over there. Emma hurriedly switched her thoughts to the future, a future in which

305

Daniel came home each evening to his wife and baby son or daughter, a future where Alice came often to cwtch her grandchild and Emma's relatives came to tea.

Taking last night's *Echo* from the magazine rack, Emma folded it and began to fan herself as she lay back against the cushions and closed her eyes, and was just dozing off when there was a sharp knock on the front door.

Going through to open it she wondered if the girls had forgotten anything, but they had been gone some time. It's probably Alice or Maud, she thought, ready to greet whichever it was with a smile.

When she saw the telegraph boy in his belted tunic and peaked cap Emma went cold with dread. Taking the envelope from him with trembling fingers she managed to make it to the stairs, her heart pounding, unable to open the telegram in case it confirmed her terrible fears. How often she'd dreaded this moment as she'd watched a telegraph boy ride down the street, her heart beating fast until he'd passed the door. Then hope stirred in her, perhaps after all it wasn't? Emma tore at the envelope and the cruel words seemed to leap up at her:

REGRET TO INFORM . . . CORPORAL DANIEL

THOMPSON . . . KILLED IN ACTION

A sickness was rising in her, a grey mist growing darker until it enveloped her and Emma's head fell forward.

'Emma, you left the door open.' Alice stood in the doorway, her mouth open in surprise, then taking in the scene, she rushed to the stairs and as she gently lifted Emma's head the girl gave a low moan and opened her eyes. It was then Alice saw the telegram still in her hand. Filled with foreboding, she took it, giving an anguished cry as the words sank in she let it flutter to the floor. Then her arms came about Emma and they clung together their tears mingling until Alice said in an anxious voice, 'I must get the doctor for you, Emma. That was a bad faint. This baby is all we have of Daniel now.'

'Leave it until the girls get back, Mam.' Emma's lips trembled as she was led towards the kitchen and tears flooded her eyes once more.

Alice's throat worked convulsively as she tried to stem her own tears and Emma cried, 'Oh, Mam! I'm sorry I didn't think . . .'

'The baby, Emma. We must keep you calm. I'll ask Maud, she'll know who to send.' Alice was already making for the door.

When a very upset Maud came in she'd already sent a neighbour's boy for Doctor Armitage. Making a pot of tea, she poured two hot sweet cups and insisted they drink some, but Emma sat staring before her, tears rolling down her cheeks. Maud was thankful when almost at once there was a knock on the door and Doctor Armitage followed her into the kitchen, explaining that he'd been making a call in the street when the boy had given him the message.

After examining Emma he told them in a relieved voice that all seemed to be well.

'I know just how you feel, my dear, and I know it's going to be hard, but you must take care of yourself for the child's sake,' he said. 'When it's born, this baby will be a great comfort to you and your mother-in-law.'

Taking a bottle from his bag, he poured a small amount of liquid into the glass Maud handed him and urged Emma to drink it up. Then turning to Alice who was also a patient of his, he said, 'I think you'd better have something as well, Mrs Thompson.'

Alice shook her head and, nodding towards Emma, said, 'Better keep my wits about me I had, Doctor.'

He turned next to Maud.

'Could you send that youngster to my surgery about one o'clock? I'll have made up a bottle for her by then.'

Leaving the kitchen door open, Maud saw the doctor to the door and Emma and Alice heard him say, 'A bad business, especially at such a time. This dreadful war has something to answer for.'

And Maud replied, 'I expect you see a lot of sad cases, Doctor.'

By the time she came back to the kitchen Emma was lying on the couch, her eyes closed.

'It looks as though it's working already, Alice,' she said. 'You should have had something yourself, God love you.'

Alice shook her head.

'Emma's got the baby to consider,' she told her. 'She'll have to face up to it when she wakes up, though, poor little soul.'

Maud was making for the door now, saying, 'I'd better see if I can find young Albie, ask him to go to the surgery about one o'clock.'

As she closed the door, Alice shivered. Despite the warm tea she felt cold right through, her heart heavy with grief. A letter had come from Daniel only that morning and, as usual, it had been full of his plans for when the war was over. She'd come around to show it to Emma whom she knew had had one the day before. It would be behind Daniel's picture on the front room mantelpiece. Emma had told her a long time ago that she'd put his picture in the parlour so that she could go in there and look at it in peace whenever she wanted to.

Alice went to the parlour now and lifted the likeness down.

Taking it to the window, she pulled the blind aside. As she looked into her son's eyes, tears filled her own so that she saw only a blur. As they poured down her cheeks she put the picture back, propping the letter against it once more, but her hands were shaking so it kept falling down.

Sitting in the deep armchair by the empty grate, she rested her head in her hands and let the tears fall, memories flooding her mind so that they fell even faster. Poor Emma will wake to her grief, she realised. At the thought of her daughter-in-law, Alice dried her eyes and went back to the kitchen, but Emma still slept, her fact white and taut.

'Thank God there's to be a baby.' Alice hadn't meant to speak the words aloud. She watched Emma stir restlessly then open her eyes. Saw the awful realisation of what had happened dawn in them. Then they were clinging together, and Emma was saying in a small, sad voice, 'I always loved Daniel, Mam, since the first day I met him.'

Soon the girls came home, excitedly talking about the sights they'd seen on the foreshore. Maud went to them as soon as she heard them pulling the string behind the door, shushing them, explaining about the telegram, watching the happy expressions wiped off their faces as Daisy said sadly: 'Just like Dada. Poor Emma, what will she do?'

'The poor little baby won't have a father,' Dorrie said. 'I don't think I'll lend the war any more of my pocket money. I wish it would stop.'

As the weeks went by Emma would often shut herself in the parlour, taking Daniel's picture in her hands and hugging it to her breast. She understood Sam a little better now, had sympathy with the longing he'd had to get in touch with his Sarah. She would never go as far as that but she often talked

309

to Daniel as she held his picture close.

She was glad now that she'd put it in here where she could come quietly to gaze at it and think. Alice knew nothing of her son's dislike of Sam or the reason for it, but the real reason Emma hadn't put Daniel's picture with Sam's in the kitchen was because she'd felt they'd make uneasy bedfellows.

Emma and Alice were longing for the baby to be born, and Alice, Maud and Mattie fussed over the expectant mother, bringing little treats to tempt her appetite.

'Think of the child,' one or the other would say, as though she didn't already think of it all the time. And she did eat and she did take exercise, however low she felt, for if anything happened to her and the child survived then Alice would have to bring it up as her nan had done Emma, and every child needed its own mother, someone young who would play with it and try to make up for its not having a dad. Her nan had been old and the aunts had said it was too much for her. Emma had never forgotten that.

Clara came in the car, thoughtful as ever, bringing mourning outfits for Emma to choose from, for as she said, 'You certainly won't feel like going to the shops and you can do without the expense.'

'I was just going to wear a black arm band,' Emma told her. 'There won't be a funeral, not even a grave to tend.'

Clara drew her close. Swallowing the lump that came to her throat, she said, voice vibrant with emotion, 'Oh, my dear!'

The days of waiting seemed endless in Emma's grief. August gave way to September, the warm days passing slowly, and as time went on she grew impatient for the child.

Just before dawn on the last day of September she woke from a troubled sleep to become aware of a pain in her back which grew worse as she watched the dawn breaking and the sun come up.

Fully dressed by this time she roused Daisy and sent her for Alice who was with them almost at once. All through the long day the pains had grown stronger. The midwife had come but had been called away to another case, saying cheerfully, 'It'll be some time yet, 'fore it makes an appearance, Mrs Thompson. Be back in about half-an-hour I will.'

And she had been, and several times since, telling Emma, 'You never can tell with first babies.'

Now as another contraction started she gripped the midwife's hand, hearing Alice's worried voice, saying, 'I still think we should send for Doctor Armitage.' And the midwife's reassuring words, 'Don't worry, everything's normal. It'll be here any minute now.'

Then Emma was engulfed in pain and as it receded and she was urged to push, felt the child slipping from her body, and heard the midwife saying triumphantly, 'You've got a lovely boy, Mrs Thompson.' And Alice's voice, shaky with relief, crying, 'Thank God!'

Exhausted as she was, Emma waited impatiently for the newly washed babe, wrapped tightly in a shawl, to be put into her arms. As she looked down at the small puckered face and the sheen of gold hair she thought he was the most beautiful child she'd ever seen. Alice gazed adoringly down on him, and as they smiled at each other she asked, 'Will you call him Daniel like you said if it was a boy?'

'Danny,' she said. 'We'll call him Danny. Will someone tell the girls that Danny has arrived?'

Chapter Thirty-Eight

For Emma preparations for the coming Christmas were bittersweet. It was wonderful having a baby in the house, but memories of last year when Daniel had come home so unexpectedly tugged at her heart.

At almost three months Danny was plump and dimpled, and with his wide blue eyes and the promise of fair curls, according to his doting grandmother he grew more like his daddy every day. At the slightest encouragement Alice would bring out the photograph album and point to a picture of her son at about the same age, and although the sepia photo couldn't compare in colouring to Danny's rosy cheeks and deep blue eyes, Emma knew that Alice was right.

She went through all the motions of preparing for Christmas, helping Dorrie with the decorations, saving some of the precious eggs, margarine and sugar for cake and puddings, and ordering the chicken as usual. But her heart wasn't in it. The war was dragging on and on with more and more wounded on the streets, many on crutches standing on street corners in all weathers, selling matches and boot laces to supplement their meagre pensions. Despite the look of hopelessness in their eyes Emma envied them. They were alive, they would go home to their wives and families at the end of the day. But it was a crying shame, she thought. They'd given their country so much and were now on the scrap heap, unable to do the jobs they'd left to go to war.

The day after Daisy finished school in December she started work at the shop in Duke Street.

'Took to it like a duck to water,' Martha told Emma when just before Christmas she brought their presents.

Danny was being cuddled in her arms. She tickled him gently under the chin and was rewarded with a smile.

'Lionel was wondering if it wouldn't be better for her to live in after Christmas,' Martha went on. 'With the lamps dimmed, the streets are so dark, and nobody's allowed to show even a chink of light.'

'I've been worried myself,' Emma told her, 'especially on the late nights. She missed a tram last Friday, but you know Daisy. She's not afraid of the dark or anything else.'

'What do you think of Lionel's suggestion then?'

'Dorrie would miss her, they've never been parted.'

'Well, she could come home for Sunday. Daisy's all for it though she did say she would miss little Danny.'

Remembering the welcome she herself had received Emma could well understand Daisy wanting to live in over the shop, what with Martha spoiling her and Clara and Lionel taking such an interest.

'It would be wonderful having someone young about the place again,' Martha was saying. 'Reminds me of the day Clara brought you home Emma. You were such a lovely little girl.'

'It was good of Lionel to find her a place on the Baby Linen counter. She was so excited because he let her dress the models to put in the window.'

'Well, he says she's got quite a flair for arranging things on stands. He's been watching her at work on the counter.'

It was arranged that Daisy would live in as soon as she went back after Christmas. Soon it was Christmas Eve and the house looked festive with last year's decorations. A plump chicken sat on a large oval plate on the marble shelf of the larder for there hadn't been room for it in the mesh-fronted safe hanging in the yard. Mince pies were cooling on a rack in the kitchen, and a fruit cake and pudding waited in the pantry.

Everything is the same as last year, Emma thought, only Daniel won't be coming home. Not this year or ever again. Tears would come to her eyes when she thought like this which was nearly all the time. Then she'd look at Danny and thank God she had him, and kiss and cwtch him to her until the hot tears threatened to drop on his curly head.

Alice was to spend Christmas Day with them, and they did their best, both of them, to make it a happy Christmas for Daisy and Dorrie. In the evening Mattie and Fred came with David for a sing-song around the piano. Mattie had just put her fingers to the keys when there was a knock at the door and, as Emma opened it, Mabel and Ellie stepped in.

'Ellie wouldn't give me any peace. Wanted to see the baby she did,' her aunt explained. 'I told her he'd be in bed by now but Ellie got her hat and coat, you know how stubborn she can be.'

'Danny's asleep, Ellie,' Emma told her, but her cousin was already making for the stairs. Quickly catching her up, Emma knew Ellie's protests at being forced to go downstairs would wake him anyway, so quietly she opened the bedroom door, and, putting her fingers to her lips to show Ellie she mustn't talk, a gesture her cousin was quick to copy, they went over to the cradle where Danny slept, golden lashes curling on his rosy cheeks, one tiny hand resting on the pillow.

Ellie bent forward and was about to pick him up when Emma quickly restrained her saying, 'You can play with Esmeralda if you like, Ellie.' She saw the small eyes in her cousin's big round face light up.

Lifting the doll from its cushions in the basket-chair with one hand, and gripping Ellie's tightly with the other, Emma drew her down the stairs.

When the parlour door was once more shut tight and Ellie settled in the armchair, crooning to the doll, they began to sing. It wasn't very musical for Ellie's lullaby as she rocked the doll struck a discordant note, but they laughed at themselves, and Aunt Mabel looked so happy with a glass of wine in her hand and a generous wedge of cake on a plate by her side, and Ellie looked happy too, her tongue between her teeth as she painstakingly took the doll's boots and socks off and then tried to put them on again. Emma felt the old compassion for Aunt Mabel's lot and half wished she'd invited them both to dinner and tea, but commonsense told her that with all the shortages, and taking into consideration Ellie's enormous appetite, she couldn't have coped.

Although she had only worked for a week Daisy entertained them with stories about the shop. When at last everyone was ready to leave Fred saw Alice safely home, then he and Mattie took Mabel and Ellie under their wing. The air was crisp and cold and silent when Emma stood by the front door watching them go up the street. She hugged her arms round her for warmth as she waited for them to reach the dim lamp and turn to wave to her.

The girls had gone to bed so she went back to the parlour, and taking Daniel's picture in her hands, sat down in the armchair by the dying fire.

316

'Oh, Daniel!' she whispered, pressing the cool glass of the picture against her cheek, her heart swelling with longing for him. Would it ever fade, this deep need to be with him, the pain of losing him? It was a different longing than she'd felt when he was at the front, for then there'd been the future to plan for and the hope of his soon coming home. Now Alice's company was a great solace as they shared their sorrow and their memories, and little Danny was a wonderful comfort to them both.

'I do hope you can see your son, Daniel,' she whispered as she put the picture back in its place. Young Danny was her future now. He was her hope.

Chapter Thirty-Nine

'Bless 'im! Shame 'e can't 'ave some icing on 'is birthday cake,' Maud said, glancing at the table spread with a white damask cloth on which was laid a plate of chicken and ham paste sandwiches, one of thinly cut bread and butter, two dishes of wobbly red jelly in the shape of rabbits and one of blancmange. In the centre stood a well-risen sponge cake that had cost Emma most of the week's ration of sugar, fat and eggs.

'Danny's only just two, Maud,' she told her friend. 'There'll be plenty of time for iced birthday cakes when this awful war is over.'

Maud looked at the tall, slim young woman she'd grown to know and love. The big brown eyes still held a look of deep sadness in their depths, the heart-shaped face was thinner and even paler than it used to be, but somehow this made Emma even lovelier. Now she was saying, 'Alice was telling me only the other day that at a wedding breakfast she went to there was a cardboard cover on the wedding cake. It was meant to look like icing and was decorated on top with wedding bells and a little china bride and groom. When they took the cover off to cut the cake there wasn't even any marzipan.'

'Never known things as tight as they are now,' Maud

grumbled. 'Fed up with this blasted war everyone is. Four years it's been on mind.'

Emma was concentrating on keeping little Danny still while she pinned on the collar of the new sailor suit Clara and Lionel had given him, together with a growling teddy bear. As she looked down lovingly at his wide blue eyes and fair curling hair the likeness to Daniel pulled at her heartstrings. But her son's second birthday must be a joyous occasion, she told herself, smiling tenderly down at him.

The last two years had not been easy. At first, she'd gone on crying herself to sleep every night, but now Danny's needs kept her busy and his sunny nature lightened her heart. With Alice, she'd been able to share her grief at losing Daniel and the heartfelt joy of having his baby. Her aunts and kindly Maud saw to it she was never lonely, and it was now mostly in the small hours that her heart cried out for Daniel. Emma could never foresee a time when it wouldn't be so.

Four of Danny's little friends were coming to tea. She'd had to restrict it to four now that sugar, butter, bread – the National Loaf was a dirty brown colour and not very palatable – and eggs were rationed, and things that weren't were in such short supply you could queue for hours for them.

'Birfday cards, Mama,' Danny was demanding, pointing to the mantelpiece where propped against the ornaments were the glowing colours of the greetings cards with their curly gold birthday messages, but Emma wanted her aunts to see the display before they got crumpled by sticky small fingers.

Alice had brought her card over early that morning together with her grandson's birthday present: a clockwork horse and carriage complete with driver and whip. When it had been wound up and set down on the oil-cloth Danny had shouted in delight as it set off on a collision course towards the fender, where it turned over, wheels still whirring madly, the horses' hooves beating the air.

With all the practice they'd had knitting comforters for the soldiers, the girls had made him a smart cap and muffler set, and from Mabel and Ellie there were sweets and a painting book. Only Mattie and Fred's present still hadn't arrived and Emma knew that any minute now her aunt would be coming through the door with the bright red-painted wooden engine that Fred had been working on for months. He'd made it large enough for Danny to sit on and push along with his feet, and Emma knew that once Danny saw it he wouldn't want to play with anything else.

She was glad he'd have new things to keep him occupied for Danny was growing restless at being kept indoors so much. Alice minded him gladly while Emma did the shopping for both of them were worried about the awful Spanish 'flu that was sweeping the country and most of the world. That morning when she'd gone to Clifton Street Emma had held a large hankie to her mouth and nose, and such was the widespread fear of the epidemic that had taken so many lives already, many were wearing masks.

What with the war dragging on and on, food shortages, all places of entertainment closed and shuttered because of the risk of infection, there was an air of gloom everywhere, especially for those like herself whose loved ones would never come back.

Thank God for Danny, she thought, gazing at him fondly. He was such a comfort to her, and to Alice too.

When he'd been a baby in arms that first winter she'd carried him Welsh fashion in the fine flannel shawl Alice had given her, the baby safe and warm cwtched close to her heart, melting some of the gnawing pain that had been with her constantly since her loss.

A knock on the door brought Emma to her feet but Alice had rushed to open it and brought two small boys into the kitchen, looking frightened and overawed at being parted from their mams, and Emma found herself watching them carefully, making sure that neither of them was sickening for the dreaded 'flu.

The party was soon underway and when Mattie arrived with the train it was a great success as the children fought over whose turn it was next. Emma was proud of the way Danny let them all have a go.

The last of the children had been picked up and Emma was just about to sit down for a well-earned rest when Dorrie went to answer the door. Emma heard her give a cry of delight.

'It's Daisy!' she called out, and next moment they were both in the kitchen. Emma could see by Daisy's expression that something was very wrong, even before she said, 'It's your Aunt Clara, Emma. She's ill, very ill. The doctor says it's Spanish 'flu. Miss Sloman, who worked with her in the cash-desk, died of it a few days ago. She's been asking for you but Uncle Lionel doesn't think you should come. Martha and your uncle wear coats and masks when they go into her room.'

'But how are they managing? Is Martha doing the nursing?' Emma asked worriedly.

'Yes, poor Martha's worn out. My bed's been moved to a room on the other side of the landing and I'm not allowed anywhere except the kitchen.'

'If she's that ill, I must see her,' Emma told her, fear of catching the infection vying with love for the aunt who'd done so much for her.

'I'll see to Danny,' Alice told her. 'I'd better fetch my night things in case you don't get back tonight. I won't be more than ten minutes. It's best Danny stays here where everything's familiar to him.'

The remark made Emma smile for Danny spent so much time at his nan's house it must be almost as familiar as his own.

When Alice arrived bringing her night clothes, just in case, Danny climbed straight on to her lap. Emma hugged and kissed him, saying, 'Be a good boy for Nana, Danny.'

But when he saw that she was wearing her hat and coat he began struggling to be free of Alice's arms, and Emma put down her holdall with a sigh to hug him once more and tell him, 'Mama shouldn't be very long. Nana will tell you a story, won't you, Nan?'

As Alice nodded and lifted Danny back on to her lap, Emma and Daisy shut the door behind them before he could protest.

An old school friend of Daisy's called to her as soon as they got on the tram, and telling Emma she wouldn't be long, Daisy joined her on the slatted seat. Looking out of the window at Newport Road, the dark silhouette of the trees stark against the pale early-evening sky, Emma's heart was heavy for Spanish 'flu was a serious illness and very infectious too. But soon her thoughts were back with Danny, and the further the tram took her away from him the more worried she became. In all his young life they'd never been parted for more than an hour and she'd always been there to tuck him into bed.

By the time they got off the tram the sky had darkened to a gun metal grey with dark clouds promising rain. Not wanting to bring Martha downstairs to answer the side door they went in through the shop, the window blinds drawn and the lights dim. In five minutes the assistants would be shrouding the displays and adding up the bill-books, so while Daisy gave Emma her hat and coat and hurried to her counter, Emma went upstairs, her heart heavy with foreboding.

As soon as the door opened to her knock she was in Martha's arms, then her friend was saying, 'Clara's been rambling. She seems more herself now, but she's very ill Emma. Mattie was here not an hour since but it's you she's been asking for. Have a cup of tea first then put on this mask and coat before you go in. I've hung sheets steeped in disinfectant about the door.'

Emma had been wondering what the sickly-sweet smell was that pervaded the apartment.

'How's young Danny?' Martha was asking. 'Lionel didn't think we should send for you but you'll be all right if you take precautions. He's been marvellous with the staff, told anyone who feels ill to stay away on full pay, and he's bought up a stock of those Formamint tablets for them. You could suck one of them, Emma, before you go in.'

So at last, dressed in a white coat and wearing a linen mask, she went in to the sick room where Lionel had placed a chair for her well away from the patient. Emma's eyes looked towards the bed where her aunt appeared to be sleeping and she was shocked at the thin, drawn face that looked grey in the low gaslight. When Clara opened her eyes they seemed sunken into her skull. When her lips moved but no sound came, Emma instinctively drew her chair a little nearer and Clara made an effort to speak again. Her voice a hoarse whisper, she said, 'Emma . . . my dear . . .' There was a long pause before, with great effort, she went on. 'I want you – to look after Lionel – Emma. Make him happy again.'

Clara's eyes closed wearily, her breathing laboured. With a

great effort she opened her eyes again and, looking straight at Emma, said, 'You have – my blessing, cariad.'

When her breathing became even more laboured, Emma dashed from the room to fetch Martha, her puzzled thoughts in a whirl. Why should her aunt ask her to look after Lionel? Martha had been taking care of them both for a very long time. But what was she thinking of? Aunt Clara would get better. She'd soon be well enough to look after Lionel herself.

Waiting anxiously for Martha to come back to the kitchen, she wondered what little Danny would be doing now? The kitchen clock said eight o'clock so he'd be tucked up in bed, his new teddy probably discarded for the old battered one he loved so much, the one that had once been Daniel's. But would he be asleep, she worried, or would he be restlessly awaiting her return?

When she heard Martha's footsteps along the corridor she looked up anxiously. The expression on Martha's face was grave as she said, 'Well, she seems to be sleeping now but her breathing's bad. Even in her sleep she seems to be struggling for breath. Can you stay for the night, Emma?' Martha asked hopefully. 'I know Lionel won't want you going for the tram on your own now it's dark. He can't leave Clara and neither can I.'

'Of course,' Emma told her, swallowing her disappointment, yet relieved that the decision had been taken from her.

That night Emma slept fitfully, her thoughts torn between worrying about Clara and the trauma of being parted from her little son. When she'd met Lionel after the shop had closed she'd been shocked at his haggard face and the look of fear in his eyes. It was obvious that Clara meant everything to him just as Daniel had to her. But her thoughts soon went back to Danny. They'd never been parted for a single night before, he must be wondering why his mama didn't come. She pictured the puzzled blue eyes watching the door and promised herself that she'd go home tomorrow if it was only for a few hours.

Soothed by the thought, Emma fell into an uneasy sleep from which she was disturbed by the sound of footsteps hurrying along the landing and voices whispering. Dragging on her dressing gown, she opened the door, her heart beating fast with fear as she saw Martha, candle held aloft, coming towards her.

'Clara's taken a turn for the worse,' Martha whispered when she drew near. 'Struggling for breath she is. Doctor's been sent for. It'll be young Doctor Hughes now. His father's taken ill himself through all the work.'

They were anxious minutes for Martha and Emma as they waited for the doctor to arrive and then to come out of the sick room. When Lionel joined them, having brought the doctor back with him, he paced the room, his hands clasped tightly behind his back, face pale and taut.

When presently young Doctor Hughes tapped on the kitchen door Lionel rushed to open it. Lowering himself wearily on to one of the kitchen chairs, the doctor said, 'I'm afraid it's what I feared. She has a secondary infection. Pneumonia has set in. It's always a danger at this stage of influenza. I'll be back in less than an hour. I've got two more urgent calls to make.'

As soon as he'd seen the doctor to the door Lionel went back to the sick-room and Emma's heart went out to him. He was still there when the doctor came again. When he'd gone Lionel paced the room again, all the usual warm colour drained from his face. There would be no more sleep that night. Emma dressed quickly, knowing she wouldn't be going home to Danny right now.

Clara died a few hours later with Lionel at her side. The

blackout blinds remained drawn, the shop shut. Martha cried as she bustled about and Lionel shut himself in the parlour and didn't come out until the undertaker arrived later that morning. With nothing to do, Daisy was sent home and Emma was torn between the sorrow she felt at her aunt's death and a deepening worry at being parted from little Danny for so long.

Chapter Forty

The day after the funeral, the household in Duke Street was thrown into a state of panic by a letter Martha received in the afternoon post. A neighbour who lived next-door to her sister Megan in the Rhondda village where Martha had been brought up, wrote to tell her that Megan was ill and could Martha come home?

'She says it's my sister's heart. Oh, Emma, what can I do? I should go right away but who'll see to Lionel? He hardly knows what day it is just now and you're going home this afternoon.'

Emma's heart sank. She'd only been home a few days, had spent the whole of yesterday helping with the funeral, and had come to Duke Street this morning to see if there was anything else she could do. Remembering the cool reception Danny had given her after she'd been away for several days, she didn't want to be parted from him again. Instead of dashing into her arms for a welcome hug he'd stayed on Alice's lap, and when she'd tried to hand him over to Emma he'd clung to her all the tighter. They'd just been getting back to normal when she'd had to leave him for a whole day for the funeral but she said now, 'I could come out in the daytime Martha. See to the cooking and cleaning?'

'But how about young Danny?' Then answering her own

question, Martha said, 'Bring him with you, Emma. Bring Dorrie as well.'

Emma was worried about the girl having all that way to go to school but Alice promptly solved the problem, saying, 'I'll be glad of her company here, Emma. I shall miss Danny though. How long do you think you'll be away?'

'I hope it won't be for too long. It will depend on how Martha finds her sister.'

'Lionel and Danny will be good for each other,' Mattie said when she met her in Broadway as she and Danny were on their way to get the tram. 'Here, let me carry that holdall, I'm going your way anyway.'

'Thanks, Mattie.' Emma relinquished the bag gratefully and lifted Danny into her arms.

'For goodness' sakes, make him walk!' Mattie cried. 'Too many petticoats around spoiling him, that's the trouble. Making a rod for your own back, you are, girl!'

Used to Mattie's outspokenness Emma put Danny down, knowing in her heart that her aunt was right. There was always one of them dashing to fulfil Danny's every wish. She was every bit as bad as Alice and Dorrie. Emma decided to change the subject.

'Fred hasn't heard anything yet?' she asked, knowing that Mattie was worried now that men of fifty-one were being drafted.

'No, and I sincerely hope he won't. I know that's selfish especially after Daniel . . .' Her voice trailed away.

'It's bound to finish soon, Mattie,' Emma said soothingly.

There was an air of despondency everywhere. Another winter looming and still the war dragged on. So many young men dead or maimed, and now this epidemic of Spanish 'flu that was sweeping the country and claiming so many lives. And just to add to the misery, coal and gas now rationed with all the other essentials.

They'd reached the tram stop. Kissing Mattie goodbye, Danny climbed eagerly on to the step, and was halfway up the spiral staircase before Emma caught him up and carried him, protesting, down to the lower deck to pay her penny fare.

Staring out of the window she was thinking of Mattie's words. It was difficult for her not to spoil Danny when he was all she had. If only Daniel was coming home at the end of this awful war. Martha had said bringing him with her would cheer Lionel no end. Poor Lionel, he'd looked so sad since Clara went, and when the shop was closed he spent hours alone in his room.

Danny had never been to the shop. Now as he stepped inside and saw the display stands and the busy counters where little wooden cups kept whizzing to and fro over his head, he stopped to watch open-mouthed. Martha was ready to leave and a cab had been ordered to take her and her luggage to the station.

Danny watched from the parlour window as the cab drew away from the curb, his face pink with excitement, turning to ask her, 'Where they go, Mama?'

'To the station, love, where the big trains come in. I'll take you there one day when there's time.'

But it won't be for a while yet, she told herself, remembering the Spanish 'flu and the danger of being in crowded places. There was so much to show Danny when she was able. All the places she'd explored with Martha when she'd first come to live in Duke Street. They'd been magic afternoons, the sun dappling the waters of the canal at Mill Lane as they'd rested against the wall watching the barges go by. When it was cold or raining or both they'd stroll through the high domed arcades with their ornate glass roofs, and gaze into the shop windows until it was time for Martha to take her to the tea-shop halfway down where they'd refresh themselves with delicious sarsaparilla or a pot of tea. The market stalls around The Hayes had always fascinated Emma. Lamps swaying in the wind, a bright oasis in the pre-war darkness; the raucous cries of the stall-holders as she'd clutched Martha's arm wondering what she was going to buy next.

These days with a war on the streets looked seedy and rundown: the street lamps painted so they showed only a glimmer of light, blinds drawn over window displays from dusk to daylight, not a chink of light anywhere. Then there were the pitiful casualties of war on nearly every corner and, particularly when it was wet, inside the arcades. Men who shook as though with the ague. Men with trouser legs pinned up or the tray containing their wares suspended on a string from their necks because they no longer had two hands to hold it with. Showing Danny these haunts could wait till better and safer times, she decided.

She heard Lionel's footsteps in the passage and as he came into the room his face lit up when he saw Danny peeping shyly at him from behind the heavy brocade curtains. Looking at Emma, he said, 'Where's Danny? Didn't you bring him with you?' And Danny jumped into the room, crying happily, 'Here I am!'

From that moment the ice was broken and Danny followed Lionel like a small shadow whenever he could, and Lionel, despite his grief, did his best to entertain the boy. Sometimes though Lionel would shut himself away with his grief, apologising afterwards, saying, 'I wasn't fit company to be with, Emma. I get these black moments since Clara died and I don't want the boy to see me like that.'

Whenever he took a break from the shop, and especially on a Sunday, the two were inseparable, and if the weather was good Lionel would take Danny for walks into the nearby countryside and they always seemed to come back with Danny riding piggyback.

Lionel was so thoughtful towards everyone, so anxious not to burden them with his grief. Emma couldn't help remembering how Sam's obsession with his wife's death had clouded the girls' lives and her own. She herself must have been difficult to be with during those first months after Daniel's death, but she'd had Alice to share her grief and she'd tried not to upset Daisy and Dorrie for they'd known so much sadness in their lives already.

Three weeks passed and still Martha hadn't returned. They'd had several letters from her but the last one told them that as her sister had had a heart attack, she shouldn't now be left on her own. Emma was worried about being away from home so long, leaving Alice to look after Dorrie.

'If you're worried, Emma, you must go home,' Lionel told her. 'We shall muddle along. But I know I'm going to miss you, and this young shaver.' He rumpled Danny's curls, then as the boy beamed up at him said, 'How'd you like to come down to the shop with me, Danny? It's time you were introduced to some of the assistants, young man.'

Danny's hand in his, they went downstairs. Leaning over the banister, Emma watched until they reached the first counter and the assistant smiled down at the boy as she took his proffered hand. Then on to the next with Lionel striding in front, hands clasped behind his back, and Danny doing the same though

Emma never remembered him walking with his hands clasped behind his back before. It brought a smile to her face until she thought, Danny's going to miss this when we go home. But when would that be?

To Dorrie's disappointment the school leaving age had just been raised to fourteen for at Lionel's invitation she'd been planning to follow Daisy and work in the shop when she too would live in. Emma knew when that happened her own role of looking after the girls would be finished. But who was to take care of Lionel and Daisy with Martha gone? Already she knew in her heart that she didn't want to go home. Danny was happy, and Lionel, instead of shutting himself in his room, spent his free time with the boy. And, Emma told herself, if she did stay and Dorrie came too she'd be doing the job Sam had entrusted her with, looking after his girls.

Alice was the only problem and Emma felt bad about leaving her on her own for she must be lonely and missing Danny. But what else could Emma do?

Alice had tried to make light of it when Emma explained the situation in an apologetic little voice, adding, 'You know you'll be welcome there anytime, and I'll bring Danny to see you whenever I can.'

Alice's lips were quivering but she'd managed a smile as she said, 'With Martha gone there's nothing else you can do, cariad.'

Leaving Danny with his nan she'd gone to the house to make sure everything was all right. It might be shut up for a very long time. Emma called Maud over the garden wall to let her know what was happening.

'I'll drop in to see you whenever I'm at Alice's,' she promised, wishing there was more time to spend with her old friend. Then, when she got back to Alice's, she stayed longer than she'd meant, not having the heart to take Danny away so soon.

'Nana must come to us for Christmas, mustn't she, Danny?' Emma said as they were getting ready to leave. Lionel wouldn't mind and she couldn't bear the thought of Daniel's mother being all on her own.

With Lionel recently bereaved she'd been wondering what they should do about Christmas, but with two young girls and Danny looking forward to it she'd have to make preparations. It was November already.

A few days later the church bells began to peal out and went on and on. When people realised the war was over they rushed joyously into the streets.

Looking down from the parlour window Emma was amazed at how quickly the crowd gathered, singing, dancing, waving Union Jacks. Lionel had gone to close the shop and send a stockroom boy for a paper. Today of all days his hadn't been delivered. When he brought it in Emma saw the headlines in large black letters:

THE WAR IS OVER
(Official)
Armistice Signed At Five O'clock Today
Hostilities Cease On All Fronts
Six Hours Later

'Would you like to go out and join them, Emma?' asked Lionel, opening the window wide.

The noise was deafening. Someone was playing a concertina, accompanying the crowd singing 'Tipperary'. Others were waving Union Jacks, shouting their joy. When she didn't answer and he saw the tears in her eyes, Lionel cried, 'Oh, Emma! I'm sorry. I'm a blundering old fool. I never thought about your losing Daniel in the war.'

Tears, fuelled by the tumult of emotion that swept over her, rolled down her cheeks. She was glad the war was over, very glad, but its ending had brought home to her anew the fact that Daniel would never be coming back.

Lionel shut the window and put a comforting arm about her shoulders, and taking the hankie from his breast pocket gently dried her tears. But now they'd started she couldn't stop them. Lionel was always so understanding, he was a dear, kind man. Presently she gave a final little sniff and managed a watery smile.

'Feeling better now?'

Emma nodded, telling him, 'Losing Clara so recently, you must feel awful. I'm sorry.'

'Yes, I miss her every moment, Emma. But it's different for you. Daniel would have been coming home if . . .'

The tears sprang afresh to her eyes but she managed to hold them back. Seeing them he said, 'Oh, Emma! I'm such an insensitive fool.'

'You're not, Lionel. That's the one thing you're not.'

He went across to the window again, opened it and called her to his side. There were more people than ever now, jostling each other good-naturedly, blowing whistles, waving flags. It was like a carnival with everyone milling around. One group began singing 'Pack Up Your Troubles', only to be drowned out when another started on 'Keep The Home Fires Burning'.

'I must get Danny,' Emma said. 'Today is history. He mustn't miss it. And I am glad it's over, Lionel. Truly glad.'

'Wrap yourselves up, I'm coming with you. Half my staff

are out there so let's join them. Come on, young shaver.'

Lionel swung a bewildered Danny on to his shoulders then they started down the stairs and through the side door to join the excited crowd.

Chapter Forty-One

'Lionel wants you to come to us for Christmas, Mam.'

'You must have asked him, Emma?' Alice looked pleased but her voice sounded uncertain.

'I didn't, really! He knows how you must be missing Danny. Lionel's always thinking of other people even though he's still breaking his heart over Clara.'

'Poor man,' Alice muttered sympathetically. 'We know what it's like to lose someone, don't we, cariad? Well, if you're sure about it, I'd love to come. Tell him I'm very grateful. I'll bring a few things to help out.'

It was no use telling Alice not to bother. Emma knew she'd insist on bringing her welcome. It was what most people who visited did these days and was much appreciated. This year in particular it would take all Emma's ingenuity to make the table look festive, but for the girls' sakes as well as Danny's she must put on a show.

On Christmas Eve, with a bright fire in the parlour, last year's trimmings up and the many cards displayed, it looked warm and seasonable, and when Alice arrived she exclaimed in delight at the large pleasant room and was very soon seated in a comfy armchair drawn up to the fire with a small table by her side on which were a cup of tea and a plate of biscuits. But before she'd even had time to lift the cup, Danny was on her knee, eager to tell her all about his exciting new life.

Despite his concern that everyone should have a good time, Emma watched Lionel anxiously, knowing his thoughts were of last year when Clara had been alive and well, especially when once or twice, pleading work still to do, he went off to his room to be alone for a while. Although his eyes were sad he smiled at everyone when he came back and began to ply them with sweets and nuts and offer Emma and Alice more wine even though everything was already on display and it was easy to help themselves.

'Putting on a brave face he is, Emma,' Alice whispered when next he left the room. 'Lionel's such a nice man, isn't he?'

When before dawn on Christmas morning Danny discovered the large rocking horse with the long silky mane by the side of his bed, his yell of delight woke up most of the household.

Dinner was a triumph considering the stringent times, and Emma, watching Alice's for once bright eyes and flushed cheeks, worried again about the lonely years ahead for Daniel's mam, realising that since she and Danny, and both Daisy and Dorrie, had come to live in Duke Street, Alice must be very lonely indeed.

When Christmas was over and the shop open again Emma soon began to realise that Lionel really did have something on his mind. When both Clara and her equally qualified helper had died within one week, Lionel, engrossed as he was in his grief, had put two inexperienced young assistants into the cash-desk with only the briefest of instructions as to their job, and being in a state of shock and sorrow had failed to keep his eye on them as he should have done.

'The books are in an awful mess,' he confided to Emma. 'I

don't for a moment think either of them is dishonest, it's just incompetence. My own fault for leaving them to their own devices.'

'What are you going to do about it?'

'I was wondering if you could spend a couple of hours of an evening, Emma, helping me to sort it all out? Like I said before, we could get someone in to help with the house.'

'But I haven't had any experience of the cash-desk either,' Emma told him. Nevertheless, arithmetic had always been her best subject in school even though she'd left at twelve years old to work in the shop.

With Lionel's help Emma enjoyed these sessions in the evenings with the books spread out on the parlour table, rubbing out, adding in, altering the inaccurate totals, and when finally they'd got things up to date, Lionel said ruefully, 'We'll have another lot to sort out next week. I'll have to put someone else in instead of Miss Williams, she's hopeless at columns of figures but was well liked behind the counter. Miss Thomas is getting on quite well since I took the trouble to explain it all again.'

As he spoke Lionel was looking straight at Emma. Gently stroking his silky moustache he said, 'I was wondering, how would you like to take charge of the cash-desk?'

'Me? A cashier? Anyway, who would look after Danny and you and the girls? Unless of course you've heard that Martha's coming back?'

'By what she wrote in her last letter, Emma, Martha has no intention of coming back. She seems to have her hands full where she is. But I was wondering . . . do you suppose your mother-in-law would like Martha's job looking after us all? She'd see plenty of young Danny then. And I'm sure you'd soon learn, Emma. Miss Thomas seems to be getting the hang of things now so you wouldn't have to be there all of the time, especially when things are slack.'

Emma was staring at Lionel open-mouthed. Not only was he offering her a job as cashier, he was offering Alice work as well. But supposing, like Miss Williams, she wasn't any good in the cash-desk? Yet in her heart she knew it was only training she lacked. Lionel wouldn't be a hard task master, she'd probably be able to see quite a lot of young Danny, and she had been worried about saving for the day when the girls were old enough to live alone in the house their father had left them, when her allowance for looking after them would stop. If she was working in the shop when that happened, and Alice was living here too, no one could point a finger if she stayed on in Duke Street. Besides Emma had known for a very long time that she never wanted to leave here again.

Lionel was looking at her anxiously, waiting for her answer, wondering if he was going too fast.

'If Alice will come and look after things, I'm willing to have a try,' Emma told him at last. 'I think she'll just love the chance of being here with Danny.'

Since they'd all left to live over the shop Alice had more than enough of her own company. There were always the neighbours of course and a chat over the garden wall or shared pot of tea. But as she sat in the wooden armchair by the fire watching the glowing coals shift in the grate, the nights seemed very long. She'd never been much of a reader, preferring to keep her fingers busy with needle and thread, but sewing only gave her more time to think. From the time he was a little boy Daniel had always loved books, but then he took after his dad.

It had been lovely at Christmas to feel part of a family again, and being able to share little Danny's Christmas had been the best thing of all.

When Emma arrived to tell her about Mr Emmanuel's proposal Alice didn't hesitate to accept, except to wonder aloud about all the travelling it would entail.

'I think he means for you to live in, Mam,' Emma told her, wondering if this would be a stumbling block.

Alice thought a moment before saying, 'I could, I suppose. The house was bought and paid for many years ago. But I wouldn't ever give it up, Emma. It's best to have a place of your own to come back to. It would suit me fine now though to be with you and Danny and see the little fellow growing up.'

Glancing around her, she added, 'Daniel's father brought me here the day we were wed. Real proud I was that we had a house of our own and didn't have to go into rooms.'

Lionel went to fetch Alice the following Monday and as soon as she'd had a cup of tea and settled in Emma went to the cash-desk to start her new job and was soon getting on fine with the plump, sloe-eyed Miss Thomas who was now proving herself reliable and efficient despite the bad start. From the ornate glass windows of the cash-desk which was entered by a flight of a dozen wooden steps they had a good view over the whole shop, a view that, like a kaleidoscope, changed almost every minute of the day.

There was Lionel in his neat black trousers and smart tailed coat patrolling the counters, dashing off whenever a member of staff called, 'Sign, please!' And behind every counter the assistants in their plain black dresses with white lace collars, heads bent over the merchandise or arms upstretched as they arranged the displays. Then there were the mainly elderly men

343

of the Manchester Department lifting bale after bale of heavy cloth, hoping vainly no doubt that Madam would approve of the last one they'd staggered to the counter with. Then there were the customers, mostly fashionably dressed women though the elder ladies seemed still to favour garments with a dust fringe sweeping the floor, while younger ones wore the shorter length skirts.

Few women in shawls entered the portals of Emmanuel's Emporium. The larger drapery stores in town were as much a place for showing off the latest fashion as they were for purchasing it.

Emma was remembering the first time she'd set foot in this shop, the very smell of it had excited her, but she'd felt shy and out of place in the new clothes Aunt Clara had bought her until she'd entered the room upstairs and been drawn straight into Martha's motherly arms.

Emma soon found that on a Friday and a Saturday in particular neither she nor Bessie Thomas had much time to look down on the shop. The busy little wooden cups would come whizzing towards them to be quickly dealt with and sent on their way. But there were many quieter times during the week when she could slip upstairs to see Danny, and with Alice looking after them all and happy to do so, Emma could relax and feel content.

Sometimes though she wondered how Martha was getting on. Was she happy like she said in her letters or was she grieving for the place that had been home to her for so long?

Chapter Forty-Two

On the day Martha left Duke Street and boarded the train that would take her to Glas Fynydd, worry over her sister's illness was mixed with regret at having to leave Lionel at such a time. Martha knew that she herself was going to miss Clara every hour of the day, but poor Lionel had lost his wife and companion, and just when he needed Martha there to keep things running smoothly she had to go home to the valleys to look after Megan. Worry over her sister increased as the engine drew to a grinding halt yet again. If only the old train would go faster! she thought anxiously.

By now the urban scenery had given way to fields and hedges and so to a backdrop of bleak mountains with an occasional pit wheel standing stark against the winter sky, and huge slag heaps scarring the grassy slopes.

As the train drew into a small halt the carriage was invaded by women in shawls with baskets on their arms and she was roused from her reverie by friendly lilting voices. When someone cried, 'Martha!' she turned and saw a neighbour she'd known since she was a child and her face broke into a welcoming smile.

'Come to look after Megan, 'ave you, gul?'

Martha nodded and asked in an anxious voice, 'How is she, Carrie? I should have been told before.'

'A lot better. Still under the doctor she is, mind. Dai's been good as gold, seeing she takes it easy. Had a bit of bad news yourself, 'aven't you, gul? That friend of youers dying so sudden.'

Martha agreed, adding, 'That's why I haven't been to see them this month, but I wrote to ouer Megan and she didn't say anything about being ill in her letter.'

'Come on sudden it did like. Complained of pains in 'er chest, then she collapsed.'

As the train ground to a noisy halt Martha reached for her holdall. Now everything was familiar, both the station and the street outside, for Martha had been born and brought up in this village in the cottage where her sister lived. She hadn't expected anyone to meet her for Dai would probably still be down the pit. Martha was glad of Carrie's company as they trudged up the steep hill. Presently her old friend said breathlessly, 'Out of puff I am, gul. These 'ills will be the death of me.'

Martha laughed, saying, 'Well, you've had enough practice, Carrie, living here all youer life.'

Now Martha slowed her steps to accommodate the older woman who had been their mam's best friend and would now be in her mid-seventies at least, but the brown eyes were still bright and alert and the thin cheeks flushed with colour as she bent forward to struggle up the steep hill.

'Ever think of coming back 'ere for good?' she asked Martha, stopping again to get her breath. 'Been to Cardiff a few times myself I 'ave. Too salty for me, them shops in town. Then if you do buy something you got to cart it all the way back.'

They walked in a companionable silence until they'd almost reached the top of the road, the houses now seeming to concertina into each other on the steep gradient. When they stopped to part ways, Carrie said, 'Saw that Bella Williams I

346

did now jest. Done up to the nines she was, the snooty bugger, and to think 'er mam 'ad to borrow our cooking pots to put on the fire every time they 'ad a 'ot meal!'

Martha watched with affection as she opened her gate and went into the house, then she continued up the straggling dirt path to where a row of colliers' cottages clung to the mountainside. Lifting the latch of the second door in the row she stepped down into the flag-stoned passage and called softly, 'Megan, I'm here.'

'In here, cariad,' a voice came back, and opening the door to the kitchen Martha saw her sister resting on the couch.

'There's lovely to see you,' were Megan's first words. Martha sat down on a wooden chair, putting her arms about her younger sister and telling her, 'You should have sent for me before, Megan. How have you been managing?'

'Well, you know the neighbours around here. I haven't been allowed to lift a finger, and Dai's been very good. But you've had troubles of youer own, Martha. Who's looking after Clara's husband now?'

While Martha explained about Emma helping out, she was drawing the iron kettle deep into the hot coals of the range and laying the table for tea.

'I haven't got to keep to my bed all the time now, but Doctor Harris says I've got to try and rest because I tire so easily,' Megan told her.

'There won't be any need for you to do a thing,' Martha answered, to which Megan protested, 'I don't want to be an invalid all my life.'

But looking at the purple shadows beneath the brown eyes and the pallor of her cheeks Martha knew that her sister was very far from well.

Glancing around the kitchen as she drank her tea, she felt a wave of nostalgia for that long ago childhood when she and Megan had shared a bed in the tiny room upstairs. In her mind's eye she could see them now on their way to the school in the village, wearing long dark dresses covered by stiffly starched pinafores, hair drawn neatly back into fat plaits. Summer Sundays had been the best, though, when dressed in their best clothes they hurried to Ebenezer chapel to sing their hearts out in the choir. But there'd been bad times too that even a thrifty mother and sober father couldn't shield them from, times when Dada was too ill with the coal dust on his lungs to work, times when his coughing would rouse them from their sleep. Then, for the first time, they'd had to join those picking the slag-heap, and, shame of shames, stay home from school until Dada could find something to tap their leaking boots with.

Finding some meat in the pantry and onions and potatoes in a bag on the floor, Martha soon had a savoury stew simmering on the hob. When Dai came in, being a collier's daughter she was familiar with the procedure. While he rolled up the rag rug and brought the tin bath from the yard to put in front of the fire, Martha put on a cap and sacking apron she found behind the wash-house door. Hanging his pit clothes over the line, she beat the coal-dust from them, then hung them in the wash-house until Dai's next shift.

A short while later he emerged to empty the bath, pink-faced now except for the blue marks which years of working with the coal had left on his skin. He was dressed in a pair of cord trousers with a waistcoat over his collarless flannel shirt. The kitchen was full of the savoury smell of lamb stew and dumplings, and after a few spoonfuls he said, 'By God, Martha, you haven't lost youer touch.'

As the days passed Martha was surprised to find she was enjoying her new life. Besides she was needed here. Doctor Harris had said Megan must take things easy, a thing no collier's wife could ever afford to do. Someone must climb the steep hill with the shopping, turn the handle of the heavy mangle in the yard, scrub the flagstones. As she steadily grew stronger Megan was allowed to do dusting and some of the cooking, especially the bread and cakes at which she was a dab hand.

The old familiar ways soon came back to Martha. It was almost as though she'd never left. Meeting old friends, walking the mountain paths well wrapped up against the cold, drinking in the pure fresh air.

Emma had written to tell her not to worry, that she would look after things until Martha returned, easing her mind about that. But soon she had to admit to herself that, with Clara gone, she didn't really want to return to Duke Street even when she was able. Lionel and Emma got on well together, always had. But would Clara's last wishes ever be to pass? When her aunt had asked her to look after Lionel, Emma hadn't understood but had taken it literally, and just as well, for Martha knew that Daniel still filled Emma's heart.

When, after a while, Lionel wrote to tell her to take as long as she needed to look after her sister, but ended the letter by asking if she thought she'd ever be free to come home, Martha knew that here in Glas Fynydd was home and that never again could she leave the only real family she had. So she wrote to tell him she wouldn't be coming back, discovering to her joy with Emma's next letter that she'd done Alice a very good turn, enabling her now to be with the little grandson she loved so much.

Chapter Forty-Three

From her high stool in the cash-desk Emma looked down on the busy scene below, her eyes darting from one aisle to another until she saw Lionel bending over a bill book while the assistant, wooden cup in hand, waited for him to sign. As he turned to smile at the customer and no doubt utter some pleasantry, Emma sighed, not understanding her own sudden flood of feeling or why she found herself searching for him whenever there was a minute to spare.

Over the last two years life had settled into a pleasant routine. While she worked in the cash-desk Alice looked after everything in the apartment. Luckily she was an excellent cook which was as well, for Martha had always kept a good table. Alice herself was happy and content just being with her family, but Danny sought Lionel's company whenever he could, following him around like a small shadow.

At nearly four years old he would soon be starting school. Emma had no worries on this score for since they'd come to live in Duke Street he'd steadily grown in confidence and now pestered them daily to take him. With his fair curls cut short and his new tweed knickerbocker suit, Danny looked every inch a schoolboy.

Now Emma's eyes went to the Baby Linen where Dorrie

had earlier in the year at last been apprenticed. Having to spend an extra two years in school had been a bitter pill for her to swallow but the law was the law and no amount of fuming on her part could alter it.

Now on this early September day in 1920 the store was bright with autumn sunshine filtering through the plate glass windows, reflected in the many mirrors and highly polished counters and fixtures. Customers were still in their summer gowns with the new low waistline, the shorter length skirt showing silk stockings and dainty shoes, not a buttoned boot in sight today, and Emma was reminded of Lionel's prediction that there would be a fashion revolution which it seemed to her had already begun.

As they had increasingly over the last two years, Emma's eyes sought Lionel once more. All his old confidence and charm had returned, and although he often spoke of Clara and took flowers to her grave every Sunday morning, the melancholy expression had completely disappeared and he was his old talkative friendly self once more.

As she watched him walking slowly around the counters, hands behind his back, eyes alert, Emma wondered what Alice would say if she knew the commotion Lionel was causing in her daughter-in-law's heart.

I still love Daniel, Emma protested to herself. How could she have fallen in love with someone else when Daniel was her world? But she knew too the pleasure and comfort she derived from watching Lionel, a pleasure that had increased steadily over the years. She could no longer deny her feelings but there was pain too in the realisation, for she was sure that Lionel's heart was as much Clara's now as it had ever been.

She hadn't seen him approach the cash-desk. Now, as the door opened and he came in, Emma bent her head over the books in sudden confusion, thankful when a couple of wooden cups came rushing towards her and she could keep mind and hands busy. When she'd despatched the second Lionel said, 'It's a lovely day, Emma. I think I'll leave Barnes in charge for an hour this afternoon while I take Danny to the park. That's if it's all right with you?'

'Of course you can. He'll love it.'

Danny was ready long before Lionel had finished his lunch, fetching his hat and coat and staring longingly from the window, then when they were leaving chatting to Lionel all the way downstairs. Wishing she could go with them, Emma rejoined Bessie in the cash-desk.

'Gone then are they, cariad? You should have gone too. Manage fine I can if you want to catch them up,' Bessie told her.

Her heart leaping at the thought, Emma shook her head and became very busy pronging bills on to the hook, her cheeks warm with colour.

That evening after Danny was in bed and Lionel had gone to a business meeting, Emma looked up from her knitting to find Alice watching her with a tender expression. As their eyes met Alice put down her sewing to say, 'You love him, don't you, cariad? Lionel, I mean.'

Covered with confusion, a hot denial rose to Emma's lips, but finding she couldn't utter it, she said simply, 'I love Daniel, Alice, I always will.'

'I know that, cariad, but youer young still. Don't make the same mistake I did, Emma. My husband, he was a Daniel too, died when our son was very young. I too thought I couldn't possibly love anyone else. How could I when I'd loved my husband so much? So I built my life around young Daniel. But as you get older it can get very lonely, Emma. If it wasn't for you and little Danny I wouldn't have anyone now. And you wouldn't have to worry about upsetting the boy, he worships Lionel.'

'Lionel loves Clara. Always has.'

'I think he's afraid to speak to you, Emma. Afraid he'll frighten you away.'

Emma stared at her in surprise. Alice could know nothing of the reason for her leaving Duke Street all those years ago. Emma had long since realised she need never have left, that it happened only because Lionel, on his own at that New Year's Eve party, had been happily bemused with drink.

There was the sound of footsteps on the stairs. Lionel's meeting must be over early. Alice rose to put the kettle on the heart of the fire and Emma to lay the table for supper.

'How did the meeting go?' Emma bent her head over the cutlery drawer as she asked, hoping to hide the blush that had come to her cheeks at the thought of what she and Alice had been discussing.

'There's some talk of them knocking down the other side of Duke Street, widening the road; giving us a clear view of the Castle,' Lionel told them, a worried frown on his face. 'It's bound to interrupt trade, but if they do go ahead with it, it's going to be years before anything comes of it.'

With the three of them discussing the merits and demerits of such a scheme over supper and long afterwards, it wasn't until Emma had turned off the gas-light and got into bed that her thoughts went once more to Alice's words. Daniel's mother was such a generous soul in every way, and to think she'd been worried in case Alice guessed how she felt about Lionel! Emma could no longer deny her thoughts even to herself. Did he feel anything for her or was his kindness and gentleness towards her simply family affection? If so she must be more careful about hiding her feelings. She hadn't managed to hide them from Alice after all.

Chapter Forty-Four

It was the morning Danny was to start school and Emma was more nervous than he was. While her son waited impatiently for her to take him she wished she could put it off for a little longer, until the weather got better perhaps or at least until after Christmas, but the arrangements had been made and, watching Danny's eager face, she wouldn't have had the heart to disappoint him.

A sudden squall of rain lashing the windows and cascading down the panes sent her searching the cupboard for galoshes and umbrella, but while she was still looking Lionel popped his head around the door to say, 'I'm just going to fetch the motor, Emma. Can't have young Danny getting soaked on his very first day.'

When they drew up outside the school Lionel got out too and they went together up the steps and through the door marked 'Infants', joining the throng of children being divested of very wet hats and coats while dripping umbrellas made miniature lakes on the floor. Emma felt a sudden surge of gratitude at Lionel's thoughtfulness in getting Danny there warm and dry for his first day at school.

As they followed the other children and stood uncertainly in the corridor a lady came out of a classroom and, having asked

Danny's name, took him by the hand, telling them she was his teacher and they could pick him up again at twelve o'clock. Resisting the urge to kiss her son goodbye, Emma waved as he went off with the tall middle-aged woman but Danny didn't give a backward glance until they were at the door. Then, with an answering wave, he was gone from sight.

It was the longest morning Emma had ever spent. She tortured herself with thoughts that wouldn't go away. Was he hungry? She'd packed some biscuits for his mid-morning break, had he still got them when he went into class? Would he be too hot in the thicker jersey she'd made him put on? Would he be homesick? Emma told herself in vain that her worries were ridiculous, he'd only be gone for three hours. Soon the school bell would be going for the lunchtime break and the rain was coming down as hard as ever.

At a quarter to twelve Lionel came into the cash-desk pulling on his coat and saying, 'It's still pouring down. No sense in getting wet. I'll fetch him, Emma, unless you want to come along?'

Business was slack on a Monday morning so for the second time that day she got into the motor and they headed for the school. Danny was putting on his coat in the lobby, laughing as he talked to another boy of about his own age.

'This is Jimmy,' Danny introduced the boy proudly. 'He's my friend.'

The ginger-haired boy gave them an engagingly gappy smile before running towards someone waiting at the door.

On the way home Lionel and Emma were amused at the number of times Danny mentioned Jimmy's name. It was Jimmy this and Jimmy that and Jimmy says. Smiling indulgently at him they reached Duke Street and Emma prayed the rain would ease before he had to return, otherwise it was going to play havoc with Lionel's working day.

She was alone with Danny in the dining room when he asked wistfully, 'I haven't got a Dada now, have I, Mam? Only the one in the picture that I kiss goodnight?'

'Daniel's your father, Danny, you know that.'

'Jimmy thought Uncle Lionel was my dad because he brought me to school. He says he must be if we all live in the same house.'

'Ssh, Danny!'

Emma had just noticed Lionel standing in the doorway. Cheeks scarlet with embarrassment, she turned towards the fire, her back to him as he said, 'No, I'm not your father, Danny, I only wish I was. You tell your friend Jimmy that you're very proud of your dad. Gave his life for his country he did. Daniel was a very brave young man.'

Taking the boy by the hand he opened the door saying, 'Tell your nanna we'll be about five minutes. And stay with her Danny. I want to talk to your mam.'

When the door was firmly closed Lionel came over and took Emma's hands in his. Drawing her down to the sofa he said in a low voice, 'I haven't dared to say this before, Emma, for fear you'd pack your bags and leave, but now I feel I've lost you already the way you always turn away, and anyway after what I was told today there seems little point in telling you how much I love you.'

As she opened her mouth to reply, her heart surging with hope, Lionel put a finger gently on the lips to silence her and went on, 'I think I've known for a very long time. It's Daniel isn't it? No one can ever take his place?'

With a deep sigh of relief, she said, 'I love you too, Lionel.

I thought the same about you and Clara.'

'You love me?' His voice was full of wonder yet he made no move to take her in his arms and she saw his eyes were filled with pain as he said. 'It seems we can never marry, Emma. I only found out today that a man can't marry his niece, even though we're only related by marriage. It's a ridiculous situation.'

The tears spilling over, Emma said in a choked voice, 'It was hard enough when I believed you didn't love me Lionel. But now . . .'

His arms came about her and he held her close, his chin resting gently on her hair, and choked with emotion he said, 'I'm so afraid you'll go away and leave me, Emma. You brought me happiness I thought I'd never know again, and it's what Clara wanted I'm sure of that. Young Danny is like a son to me and he would be my son if only we could marry.'

'Perhaps whoever told you is wrong, perhaps after all we can . . .'

But Lionel was shaking his head. 'Not unless they change the law,' he told her sadly, 'they did just that in 1907, made it possible in some cases to marry a relative of a deceased spouse, but it didn't include our situation.'

When there was a knock on the door Emma smoothed down her hair trying to compose her racing thoughts, her mind in turmoil, but her son had eyes only for Lionel, as he asked, ''case Jimmy wants to know, will you ever be my dadda?'

'I can't promise that old son,' Lionel told him, 'but I'll be the next best thing, an uncle who'll look after you like a dad.'

Danny was already at the door when he turned to say, 'I forgot to tell you nanna says the stew is ready.'

Emma went to the dining room with a heavy heart. Such a

short while ago she'd been unhappy because she'd thought Lionel didn't return her love but then there was always hope that one day he might. Now a black cloud seemed to envelop the future and there appeared to be no way out. Perhaps she should leave here, go away as she had once before, but how could she now Alice had come to keep house just to be near her grandson? Anyway where would she go? The house Sam had left his daughters had been let on a short lease until they were old enough to live there on their own. How could she and Lionel go on living in the same house knowing their love for each other could come to nothing? And Alice knew how she felt, she must tell her it could never be. 'The boy needs a father,' Alice had said. 'He hangs on Lionel's every word.'

Danny had no memories of his father, not of his own anyway, for Daniel had died before he was born. Every night with an uncharacteristically serious expression he kissed the sepia photograph of a young man in khaki uniform. A young man who'd volunteered to fight for his country and had lost his life before he could see the son who bore his name. Emma was sometimes afraid that with only a photograph to show him it was going to be difficult to make his father real to the boy.

Chapter Forty-Five

Emma stood at one of the long Georgian windows in the fashion department looking out over the wide new road to where the walls and mellow stones of Cardiff Castle were bathed in sunshine. The shops on the other side of Duke Street had been demolished about five years ago, and the dust and debris had long since been cleared away.

It was a lovely spring day in 1928 and Emma was already anticipating the pleasures of the afternoon ahead when, with the store closed for half-day, she intended first to gaze down on the rippling waters of the Taff from the parapet of the bridge on the other side of the castle grounds, watching as it meandered between green banks as far as the eye could see, before taking a walk in the shady gardens. Perhaps Lionel will come with me, she thought, her expression softening. Her love for Lionel grew deeper with each frustrating year. Despite a few more silver hairs, and a sad expression, when she caught him unawares, he was still a handsome man. Not being able to marry had been a bitter blow to both of them but they still cherished the hope that one day the law would change. It hadn't been easy living in the same apartment but neither of them could bear the thought of being parted.

Danny, now nearly twelve, had won a scholarship to Cardiff

High School and it was Lionel who'd bought the uniform and books and made it possible for him to go.

'Emma!'

Torn from her reverie Emma could hardly believe her eyes when she saw Vera and her mother laden with parcels and smiling warmly.

'Mrs Bishop, Miss Vera,' Emma cried in surprise and delight, 'how lovely to see you.'

'We were so sorry to hear about Daniel,' Mrs Bishop murmured sympathetically. 'I was told that you had a little son, Emma. He must be a great comfort to you.'

'Not so little,' Emma told her with a smile. 'He's twelve years old and tall for his age. He's at the High School now,' she added proudly.

'We'll have to hurry, dear,' Mrs Bishop reminded her daughter, 'the cab will return for us in less than half an hour.' Turning to Emma she said, 'Vera is getting married next month, my dear. We've been busy buying some things for her trousseau.'

'I'm so pleased for you, Miss Vera,' Emma told her. 'I hope you'll be very happy.'

'I've told you before, Emma, no more Miss Vera. You don't work for us now.'

'Vera is marrying a missionary. They won't be leaving for a while but when they do they'll be settling in Africa. I can't get used to the idea. We're going to miss her terribly.'

'Oh, I'm so pleased for you. I hope you'll be very happy,' Emma cried again, and looking into Vera's shining eyes, she thought, she is happy too. She must love him very much, and it seemed that as a missionary Vera had at last found a cause that even her parents couldn't object to. Mindful of the time Mrs Bishop and Vera went off to the lingerie counter and Emma to her desk, her thoughts in a whirl.

As she neared the cash-desk Emma was ashamed of the pang of envy she'd felt when Mrs Bishop had told her of the coming wedding. 'But I'm really glad that things are going well for Miss Vera at last,' she told herself, remembering with sadness that Vera too had lost a sweetheart during the war.

Were those few brief weeks she'd spent with Daniel as his wife all she'd ever know of real happiness? Emma asked herself. Then she thought of Danny and of Lionel's love and devotion and she blinked the gathering tears away and pushed open the door telling herself, 'You've a lot to be thankful for, Emma Thompson.'

It was quiet in the cash-desk for this last half an hour before they closed. Emma allowed her eyes to roam over the counters enjoying the patchwork of colour made by the displays. So much had changed since the war, particularly in the lingerie department. The old steel-reinforced stays and bodices now replaced by hip girdles in delicately patterned cotton twill with adjustable suspenders and hook-and-eye fastenings. There were lace-trimmed satin brassieres, designed more to flatten the figure than enhance, embroidered crepe-de-chine petticoats with wide lace trim on the hem and the wide legs of the matching knickers. To be fashionable every woman was supposed to have a figure like a drain-pipe with not a curve in sight, but nature being what it was few women managed to attain this perfection or even wanted to.

In the middle aisle of the store, Millinery and Accessories made a fine splash of colour; the hat stands containing dainty straws and felt cloches in many lovely shades, matching scarves tied into bows with flyaway ends, gloves in finest kid and cotton lace, handbags in the softest of leathers, all to tone with the elegant shoes on a stand at the side with ankle straps and high heels, one, two, or three bar, or lace-ups, all a far cry from the buttoned boots Emma had worn until the end of the war.

Daisy's voice breaking into her thoughts brought Emma round to face the door.

'Did you say you had a message for Maud? We'll be going home in about ten minutes.'

'Oh! I meant to write her a little note. I haven't seen her for ages, Daisy, I want to ask her to come to tea.'

'I'll cash up while you write the note,' Bessie told her, and as she drew the paper towards her and took up the pen Emma thought how lucky she was to have an assistant like Bessie Thomas, reliable and conscientious she'd also proved to be a very good friend.

Daisy and Dorrie had gone to live in their house just after Daisy's eighteenth birthday and with Maud's help they were getting on very well. It was Maud who on winter days put a match to the fire so that the kitchen would be warm on their return, and it was Maud who would put a hot-pot in the oven or keep her eye on a pot roast. Knowing Maud was next door, Emma hadn't been worried when the girls had left Duke Street to live on their own.

Emma folded the note and handing it to Daisy joined Bessie in counting the cash. The shop blinds were already drawn and the staff were hurrying out through the side door to begin their well-earned half day.

Chapter Forty-Six

'Oh Emma! I've been watching you from the doorway and you look so sad,' Lionel said, closing the door and coming into the room.

She'd been thinking of all the wasted years when she and Lionel could have been married if only they'd been allowed. It was now 1931. Later this year Emma would be thirty-seven, and Lionel was almost fifty-two, but he was a man who bore his years well, the few silver hairs only made him look more distinguished, whereas when she'd discovered a single grey hair one morning in her own fair hair she'd been horrified.

'Emma! Would you still want to marry me if you could? I'm an old man now though, and I don't know that I've the right to ask you.'

She saw his eyes were twinkling before he drew her close and kissed her as they hadn't dared since they'd known that marriage was impossible, and suddenly her heart began to beat fast with hope.

Lionel had released her and had taken her hands in his, his face flushed and happy as he said, 'Our waiting is over love. They've passed a new law.'

'Oh! Oh!' Emma flung herself into his arms again and they clung together until she had to draw breath to ask,

'When Lionel? When was it passed?'

'Yesterday, the thirty-first of July. Oh Emma! We can make our plans now, get married as soon as possible.'

There were so many things to be done, Emma told herself excitedly, so much to arrange, yet all she wanted just now was to stay here in Lionel's arms, knowing they had every right to be close, and enjoying the knowledge that their dearest wish was about to come true. But Alice must be told, and both her aunts. She'd tell Mattie and Mabel this afternoon. They had known of her and Lionel's deep disappointment all those years ago. Now the law had made it possible at last their marriage would come as no surprise.

Mattie, outspoken as ever, had said at the time, when Emma had told her she'd never marry again unless it was to Lionel, 'Never's a very long time, girl, and there's no guarantee they'll change the law. You should grab happiness if you get the chance.' But Emma had made it known that she was prepared to wait for Lionel until the end of her days.

Remembering this, Emma felt suddenly defensive as she knocked on Mattie's door, but she needn't have worried, her aunt was delighted with her news, saying, 'Oh! I'm so glad, cariad. Sit down while I make us a cup of tea. Pity I haven't got something a bit stronger to toast your happiness. Your uncle Fred will be delighted too. Always saying, he is, what a pity it is for you both.'

Emma had caught her in the middle of cleaning the windows. Freshly laundered lace curtains were draped over the head of the couch waiting to be hung. 'David and Ceinwen and the children are coming for a few days tomorrow,' Mattie told her. 'Bit of a crush it is all of them sleeping in the back bedroom still it's worth it to see them. Betty will soon be six and Bobby's nearly three.' Mattie took the latest photographs of her grandchildren down from the mantelpiece. Emma looked down at the chubby pair both with David's fair colouring and curly hair. 'I saw these last time, Mattie, they are lovely children, you could take young Bobby for David when he was that age, couldn't you?'

'Looks as if they'll stay in the valleys with her mother. Got a decent job he has in the town and you've got to go where the work is.'

When she arrived at Aunt Mabel's small house, Mabel was delighted too. 'Only those without a man can know how lonely it can be, cariad. If it wasn't for my Ellie . . .' and she gazed fondly at her stout daughter huddled in the same tatty armchair that Emma had tried to sponge clean when she'd lived here as a child all those years ago.

Hearing the word 'marriage', Ellie sat up, her eyes for once bright with interest, for it was still to her a word that meant dressing up in a frilly dress and having nice things to eat. She remembered being a bridesmaid once, Ellie's eyes slewed towards the picture on the mantelpiece, and there she was in a pretty dress standing next to the bride and groom. She'd never forgotten that day, not with the picture always there to remind her.

Ellie got up and shambling across to the mantelpiece, took the picture down and brought it to Emma, saying rather than asking, 'Ellie will be your bridesmaid again.'

Filled with consternation, Emma wondered how she could explain that it wasn't to be that sort of wedding. She would have a new outfit, something she could wear afterwards but there would be no bridesmaids; they both wanted it to be a quiet affair. But Ellie was begging for an answer. What would

Lionel say if he had this unlikely bridesmaid thrust upon him?

Emma stood up and took both of Ellie's plump hands in hers. 'I won't be wearing a long white dress this time, Ellie, just an ordinary costume,' she told her. 'But you'll be very welcome to come.'

'A pink dress with frills,' Ellie insisted, pointing to the photograph.

'You can't wear a dress with frills, love, not at your age,' Mabel told her. 'But don't worry, Mama will find you something nice to wear.'

Knowing Mabel's fondness for dressing Ellie in the odd assortment of garments her employer gave her Emma's heart sank.

She took her worry home to Lionel but he refused to be upset at the thought. He did however make a suggestion, 'Why don't we have Ellie here to choose? We could get Miss Ellis to put out several outfits in her size, ones you approve of. Then Ellie can choose the one she likes. We can't disappoint the poor child.'

That the poor child in question was sixteen stone and two years older than Emma herself seemed irrelevant. Ellie was still a child and would be to the end of her days, but Emma knew that if crossed her cousin could be much more trouble than any youngster.

When the wedding day drew near Ellie came to choose her outfit. Miss Ellis had been carefully briefed to put anything remotely frilly away. As the choosing was after hours this had been easy to accomplish.

At first Ellie shook her head at everything she was shown. Nothing if not single-minded, a pink frilly dress was what Ellie wanted and nothing else would do. Then, when they'd finally persuaded her to try things on, the suits that had been put out proved impossible, for if the jackets were a reasonable fit the skirts wouldn't fasten around Ellie's waist.

Emma drew Miss Ellis aside to ask, 'Is there a dress and coat that would be suitable? I think perhaps that would be best.'

And so a blue dress was found with a frilly lace collar, and a lovely coat the very same shade of blue and in the latest style, a coat with no waistline and fastened by a single mother-of-pearl button on the hip. Ellie was delighted with the pretty dress and clapped her hands with joy. Then she was taken across to Millinery where a hat was chosen with a small brim. Here again the more ornate models had been put out of sight. And so to the shoe stands for a pair of elegant bar shoes. Fashions had changed so rapidly since the war that many departments had to be renamed, the Mantle Department, for one, for there hadn't been a mantle in stock for many a long year, instead at the entrance to the department a wrought iron and gilt archway proclaimed 'Ladies' Fashions'. The last ten years had been a time of constant change, and nowhere more so than in the drapery trade.

When it was time to persuade Ellie into the cubicle once more to get into her old clothes Emma anticipated there'd be a fuss, but when Mabel told her, 'There's iced cakes with cherries on top waiting for us in the kitchen,' Ellie couldn't get out of the new outfit quick enough.

Emma breathed a sigh of relief. Ellie was happy, so Mabel was happy, and due to Lionel's common sense a small crisis had been averted.

The wedding day dawned warm and sunny, and much to Emma's delight Martha arrived while they were still at breakfast. Martha still made the occasional visit but they fell into each other's arms both of them remembering old times, then after a cup of tea and buttered toast Martha insisted on donning her apron, and together with Alice soon brought order out of chaos.

Danny taking a rare day off from school looked handsome in his new grey suit. At nearly fifteen he was tall and broad shouldered, and looked very smart.

When Daisy and Dorrie arrived the first thing they did was to put the curling tongs into the glowing coals of the kitchen range to crimp their hair until Alice and Martha smelt it singeing.

After a great deal of thought, Lionel had decided not to close the store for it wouldn't have been a quiet wedding they both wanted if many of the staff turned up at the church. Instead they were to come upstairs in little groups to partake of cake and wine.

The apartment was buzzing with excitement by the time Lionel's friend George arrived to do the honours as best man. Uncle Fred came soon afterwards for he was to give Emma away for the second time. A lump came to Emma's throat at the thought of the last time she'd walked down the aisle on Fred's arm. In her mind's eye she saw Daniel smiling lovingly down at her as she'd reached his side. But Daniel had gone and Clara too. Lionel and Emma loved each other and it was their future together that mattered now; theirs and Danny's too.

Presents covered the table in the sitting room and spilled over to the cabinet in the corner. Old Mr Barnes had presented them with a lovely cut-glass fruit bowl and server on behalf of the staff. The dear old man had been so shaky as he held the heavy bowl they'd all been relieved when at last it was safely in Lionel's hands. Mr Barnes's pink face had beamed with pleasure as he gave his little speech, but Emma knew that very soon Lionel would be making a presentation to him on the day he at last chose to retire. But now the wedding cars were arriving at the front door and soon Emma, lovely in a dove grey costume and shell pink crepe-de-chine blouse, her bobbed hair curling about the brim of a smart cloche hat, was walking down the aisle on Fred's arm. Ellie, very conscious of her new clothes, had insisted on walking behind them, and, with her mother's warnings still ringing in her ears, she behaved perfectly, her head held high and her steps slowed to keep pace with Emma and Fred.

As Emma reached Lionel's side, he turned and with a loving smile whispered, 'You look so beautiful.' She slipped her hand in his and squeezed it gently.

After the ceremony was over and they'd signed the register they all grouped on the steps of the church for photographs to be taken. Then, making sure that a delighted Ellie caught the bouquet, Emma and Lionel were showered with rice and good wishes as they hurried to the waiting car.

More Enchanting Fiction from Headline

HOME IS WHERE THE HEART IS

A Heartwarming Liverpool Saga

Joan Jonker

When fun-loving, eighteen-stone Eileen Gillmoss announces that she's expecting a baby, her husband Bill thinks it's another of her jokes. After all, it's twelve years since Edna, their youngest, was born. But when it sinks in that a baby really is on the way, Bill is over the moon and decides the family should move out of their two-up-two-down terraced house in Liverpool to one with more spacious accommodation.

Eileen digs her heels in at first, reluctant to leave the house she loves and friends and neighbours so dear. But a scare in the early stages of her pregnancy strengthens Bill's resolve to provide a more comfortable home for his wife and he finds the answer when a house becomes available in the road where their best friends Mary and Harry Sedgemoor live. Before Eileen knows what's hit her, she's installed in a smart home in a tree-lined road, with posh new neighbours.

Then tragedy strikes and Eileen must come to terms with a loss far greater than leaving her beloved neighbourhood. She tries to put on a brave face, but she can't fool the people who love her, who miss the smile on that round, chubby face and the laughter ringing through her house. They vow to make amends and fate steps in to lend a helping hand.

Packed with sympathetic characters and a wealth of emotions, Joan Jonker's Liverpool sagas, including *When One Door Closes* and *Man Of The House* (also available from Headline), bring to life a close-knit Liverpudlian community in a bygone age.

FICTION / SAGA 0 7472 4861 3

More Enchanting Fiction from Headline

The Farrans of Fellmonger Street

FROM THE BESTSELLING KING OF COCKNEY SAGAS

HARRY BOWLING

When widowed Ida Farran runs off with a bus inspector in 1949, she leaves her five children to fend for themselves. Preoccupied with the day-to-day task of earning enough money to keep the family together, eighteen-year-old Rose battles bravely on, thankful for the mysterious benefactor who pays the rent on their flat in Imperial Buildings on Fellmonger Street, a little backwater off the Tower Bridge Road.

Life isn't easy but between them Rose and her younger brother Don just about manage to make ends meet – though the welfare would soon put the three young ones into foster homes if they believed Rose couldn't cope. Recently, however, Don has become rather too friendly with the Morgan boys. Everyone knows the small-time Bermondsey villains are a bad lot and Rose is desperately worried Don might end up in trouble. But even this concern pales into insignificance when Rose finds herself pregnant. Now it'll need a miracle to keep the Farrans of Fellmonger Street together.

FICTION / SAGA 0 7472 4795 1

A selection of bestsellers from Headline

LAND OF YOUR POSSESSION	Wendy Robertson	£5.99 ☐
TRADERS	Andrew MacAllen	£5.99 ☐
SEASONS OF HER LIFE	Fern Michaels	£5.99 ☐
CHILD OF SHADOWS	Elizabeth Walker	£5.99 ☐
A RAGE TO LIVE	Roberta Latow	£5.99 ☐
GOING TOO FAR	Catherine Alliott	£5.99 ☐
HANNAH OF HOPE STREET	Dee Williams	£4.99 ☐
THE WILLOW GIRLS	Pamela Evans	£5.99 ☐
MORE THAN RICHES	Josephine Cox	£5.99 ☐
FOR MY DAUGHTERS	Barbara Delinsky	£4.99 ☐
BLISS	Claudia Crawford	£5.99 ☐
PLEASANT VICES	Laura Daniels	£5.99 ☐
QUEENIE	Harry Cole	£5.99 ☐

All Headline books are available at your local bookshop or newsagent, or can be ordered direct from the publisher. Just tick the titles you want and fill in the form below. Prices and availability subject to change without notice.

Headline Book Publishing, Cash Sales Department, Bookpoint, 39 Milton Park, Abingdon, OXON, OX14 4TD, UK. If you have a credit card you may order by telephone – 01235 400400.

Please enclose a cheque or postal order made payable to Bookpoint Ltd to the value of the cover price and allow the following for postage and packing:

UK & BFPO: £1.00 for the first book, 50p for the second book and 30p for each additional book ordered up to a maximum charge of £3.00.

OVERSEAS & EIRE: £2.00 for the first book, £1.00 for the second book and 50p for each additional book.

Name ....

Address ....

....

....

If you would prefer to pay by credit card, please complete:
Please debit my Visa/Access/Diner's Card/American Express (delete as applicable) card no:

Signature .... Expiry Date ....